Brown-Eyed Earl

The Earls Trip Novels

Earls Trip
Manic Pixie Dream Earl
Brown-Eyed Earl

Brown-Eyed Earl

JENNY HOLIDAY

KENSINGTON PUBLISHING CORP.

kensingtonbooks.com

Content warnings: discussions of miscarriage, pregnancy sabotage, toxic parents, spousal abuse, death of family members, elderly parent with dementia, forced marriage.

KENSINGTON BOOKS are published by

Kensington Publishing Corp.
900 Third Avenue
New York, NY 10022

ISBN: 978-1-4967-6017-3 (ebook)
ISBN: 978-1-4967-6016-6

First Kensington Trade Paperback Printing: November 2026

10 9 8 7 6 5 4 3 2 1

Printed in the United States of America

The authorized representative in the EU for product safety and compliance
is eucomply OU, Parnu mnt 139b-14, Apt 123
Tallinn, Berlin 11317, hello@eucompliancepartner.com

As the man once said, the harder you work, the luckier you get.

—Ted Lasso

She had been forced into prudence in her youth, she learned romance as she grew older: the natural sequel of an unnatural beginning.

—Jane Austen, *Persuasion*

1

Let There Be Light

September 8, 1823
Earls Trip, day 1

"The Earl of Harcourt for you, my lord."

Simon Courteney, the Earl of Marsden, put down his book, startled. He had merely intended to pass the time until Archie was due to collect him, but he felt as if he'd lived a lifetime in the quarter hour he'd been reading.

Novels: Who knew?

He shoved the book into his satchel, though he wasn't sure why. He would be caught out, as he had been last year. He wouldn't mind. He might even try to entice the boys to read this one. Perhaps it was time to incorporate a book club into Earls Trip.

"Good morning," he said, standing as his friend, Archibald Fielding-Burton, the Earl of Harcourt, entered the library. "My apologies for having made you come inside. I intended to meet you out front as per usual." Simon liked to think of himself as the sort of person who was at the ready when it was time to go. The sort of person who was prepared and therefore never surprised. He disliked surprises.

"It's quite all right." Archie looked around. "What is different here?" He squinted. "Perhaps nothing. I haven't been inside your house for . . . nigh on a year? Can that be correct?"

It was. Simon rarely invited people over. He himself didn't like being home, so why would he subject his friends to the place? He felt, though he knew he was being illogical, that it was better not to mix Archie and Effie with the ghosts of Number Seven Park Lane. He didn't want the dead to taint the living. Well, he didn't want the *living* to taint the living, but happily, there was no danger of that today. Mother was at Galecroft.

"I have taken down the family portraits that formerly hung in here," he said in answer to Archie's question.

"Ah, yes. Who was in here? Not your generation, I don't think?"

"No. The library was home to my late-seventeenth- and early-eighteenth-century forebears." He smirked. "Shall I recite their names for you?" He'd been made to memorize them as a boy. The former residents of this room were John, the third earl, and his wife, Agnes, pictured separately and in various configurations with their children, the eldest of whom was also John and who would go on to become the fourth earl at the age of twenty-four. John begat James begat another James. And so on and so forth.

"Oh, goodness, no," Archie said cheerily. "No recitations on my account."

"I decided to lighten up the place, given that I spend so much time here. I have censorious ancestors staring me down in the rest of the house. A man's library should be his sanctuary." And it was. The library was the only room in the house that felt like his. "The walls have been repapered, too." He'd chosen a cream damask that stopped just short of being yellow. "You may recall that the walls used to be papered in a rather aggressive, dare I say lurid, violet floral. Which was fine, as far as these things go—I don't care overmuch what is on my walls—but the spots where the paintings had been were dark and the rest was quite faded. It called to mind a pugilist with his front teeth knocked out." He hadn't been able to countenance the pattern made by the unfaded spots. It had, somehow, been considerably less symmetrical than his perception of such when the paintings had been up.

"It looks grand," Archie said. "Are you ready to go?"

"I am." Simon had never been more ready for an Earls Trip, in fact, even though he had also never been more trepidatious about an Earls Trip.

"That's all you have?" Archie inquired outside as a footman hefted a valise into the coach. "No trunk of books? No trove of papers? No weight of the world?"

That last question gave Simon pause, but he merely said, "I have adopted a new packing philosophy."

"Have you indeed?" Archie looked as if he were trying not to laugh.

"I haven't brought any books. Well, I've brought novels, but no real books."

Archie did laugh then. "Are novels not real books? Clementine would scold you for saying as much."

So would Miss Brown.

"You know what I mean." Simon climbed into the coach and settled himself against the squabs. "My reading this fortnight is to be refreshing. Absorbing in a way my usual material is not."

Although he *was* treating his reading of late as a forensic enterprise. He considered the latest bookmark. He had thought of nothing else since he'd found it last night. What did it mean?

"I am not planning on doing any work at all over the next fortnight," he declared, perhaps to convince himself as much as Archie.

"Who are you and what have you done with Simon?" Archie teased. "You can't fool me: You are a lookalike impostor with a fondness for novels and an eye for interior decor."

"Oh, I am still myself. I have made this decision, but I guarantee I shall fret about it. I shall feel the loss of my books and papers as a visceral thing, akin to going about in society hatless and coatless." Simon could tell from Archie's quizzically amused expression that for him, the notion of appearing sans coat and hat was not quite the scandal it would be for Simon. "I tell myself, though, with a certain degree of sternness, that Parliament has just adjourned. Surely I can take a holiday. Well, we always take a holiday this time of year. You understand what I mean. A true holiday."

At least for the first week. Simon suspected the second week wasn't going to be very . . . relaxing.

Archie's quizzical expression turned fond, and it occurred to Simon that perhaps he ought to hang portraits of his *friends* in the library. They called themselves a found family, and in his experience, found families were loads better than the real thing.

"A winning strategy," Archie said. "Your Parliamentary concerns will still be there in a fortnight. You may actually find them easier to wrangle for having had the holiday."

"That's what . . ."

Miss Brown said.

"I've been telling you as much for years," Archie said. "A wonder you've finally listened."

"My lord!" Simon's housekeeper came running down the stairs just as the coach was pulling away. "You've forgotten your lemons!"

Oh no. Simon closed his eyes. How had he forgotten the lemons? And why had Mrs. Tavish not put them in a proper sack? When he opened his eyes again—he had learned the hard way that hiding from the truth achieved nothing—Mrs. Tavish was brandishing two dozen lemons in a string satchel, the plump yellow fruits rolling around almost lewdly for anyone to see.

"Yes, you've quite forgotten your lemons," Archie remarked, not bothering to disguise his amusement as the bag was pressed into Simon's possession. "Shall I inquire as to why you aren't packing a pile of work this year but you *are* packing lemons?" Archie rapped on the ceiling of the coach, and they finally rumbled off.

"I wonder if we should bother making a wager about Effie this year." Simon hoped the glaringly obvious change of subject would be tolerated.

It was. Archie said, "'Tis uncharted territory. On the one hand, he shan't be in the garden composing a poem, or beset by unexpected suitors, or drowning in waistcoats he tried on and discarded before attending a ball the previous evening. So he's less likely to have completely forgotten the trip."

"On the other hand," Simon supplied, "even without all the trappings, he remains Effie."

"Indeed."

"Still," Simon said, "we ought to lay a wager for tradition's sake. I say it will take us thirty minutes to extract him."

"All right. I will counter with ten. Even if he's not ready whatsoever, how long can it take to make himself so, given his current situation?"

"You may have a point, but as I said, he is still himself."

This year, they were collecting Effie from his rooms on Grub Street rather than from his fine house on Hanover Square. Having upended his life to become a printer and poet, these days he had a much smaller home and a much smaller wardrobe, and nobody from polite society, excepting Simon and Archie, called on him.

They shook on the wager, and soon they were pulling up in front of the unassuming soot-covered building in which Effie, technically the Earl of Stonely, lived.

"Oh, look, he's not outside waiting for us," Simon said with a smirk. Simon and Archie always needled each other about the Effie wager. It was part of how Simon knew their annual holiday had truly begun. "We'd better go up."

"Good morning," Effie said as he opened the door for them. Unfortunately for Simon, he was wearing a coat and hat. "Give me two minutes."

"Yes, but only two," Archie said.

"You're not even going to invite us in?" Simon asked. "What if we want to greet *your wife*?" He emphasized the two syllables as part of an ongoing jest. Effie and his wife, the magazine editor Julianna, had been married only eight months, and Effie had spent the earliest days and weeks of their marriage seizing every opportunity to utter the phrase *my wife* and its variations such as *my lady*, *my bride*, and even, once, until Julianna swatted his arm and told him to stop being so melodramatic, *my helpmeet*.

"I know what you're doing, Simon," Effie said. "You've made your usual wager, and you're trying to make me dally. But how can I deny you the opportunity to greet *my wife*?"

He swung open the door and called, "Jules!"

She came from the far room, wiping inky hands on an apron. "Good morning to you, my lords."

"How goes the magazine business?" Simon asked, and because they didn't stand on ceremony with Julianna, though she sometimes still did with them—witness the my-lord–ing—added, "Have you any tea? Or perhaps something stronger?"

"We've port in the coach," Archie said.

"Yes," Simon said, "but a cup of tea here first would be the perfect aperitif."

"Is this all your luggage?" Archie bent to pick up a small trunk just inside the doorway.

"It is, and I am fully packed," Effie said. "You shall simply have to concede, Simon. I am a new man."

Effie aimed one of his fond smiles at them, and Simon could feel his own lips curling upward. Effie *was* a changed man in some ways. His external circumstances had been altered dramatically. He'd effectively if not legally given up his earldom, shaking off the scandal that had ensued and leaving estate matters to his half brother in favor of making it in business with his wife. They published a magazine called *A Lady's Life,* chapbooks of Effie's poetry, and undertook printing jobs for others on the press they owned. The contraption was named Cordelia, and Simon sometimes thought Effie loved it as much as any child.

In other ways, though, in the ways that mattered, Effie was the same as he'd always been. The walls of his home were hung with paintings, the press was churning out magazines, and he was living a life full of love.

"All right," Simon said, feigning annoyance as he threw up his hands. "Let us go."

"Goodbye, my love," Effie said, turning to Julianna and pressing both hands to his heart. "I shall count the days."

"There you go again with the mawkishness," Julianna said with exasperated fondness, shooting Simon a conspiratorial eye roll. "I shall see you all in a week's time."

"Yes!" Effie sounded cheered, as if this were news to him, though the change in plans for this year's Earls Trip—namely, the addition of the ladies for its second half—had been discussed ad nauseam.

In the coach on the way out of town, Effie read aloud a sonnet he had recently finished. Archie delivered a monologue about having changed the planned orientation of the new plunge pool at his hunting box so bathers would have a vista of a nearby brook.

Simon sat back and let the voices of his friends wash over him. Every year, he embarked upon Earls Trip with a divided mind. He knew he needed these trips. A dose of his friends, and of quiet—even if his friends were very talkative, these trips conferred an elemental calm on his soul—always helped him recover from the preceding session of Parliament. But at the same time, some part of him resisted the trip.

He never wanted to leave his work behind. He struggled to disengage his mind. Work was important to Simon, and he made no apologies for that. This last session had achieved mixed success. Yes, he and his allies had passed a gaols act, but they were no closer to compelling the inspections required to actually effect meaningful change. He was anxious about what could reasonably be counted on next year.

It wasn't only work. He worried about the London house in his absence. He was always happier when he and Mother were in different locales—he in London and she at Galecroft was generally how it went these days—but he didn't like leaving the house empty of family. What if the servants forgot to latch the door at night?

He was fretting about Galecroft, too. A storm at the estate a few weeks ago had taken the roofs off two cottages, so in addition to the unexpected expense of replacing them ahead of schedule, he had two tenant families living in quarters that were too cramped.

And of course there was that other . . . matter.

His head was full of concerns.

But this year, he was trying something new.

He was simply going to, through sheer force of will, leave those concerns behind.

At least for the first week.

He pulled out his novel and, after a few pages, discovered one of Miss Brown's markers.

A thrill fluttered through his chest. He sometimes thought he enjoyed finding these markers in the novels Miss Brown lent him as much as he enjoyed the novels themselves.

But perhaps not this one, which was a small piece of paper on which she'd written the words "I cannot think well of a man who sports with any woman's feelings; and there may often be a great deal more suffered than a stander-by can judge of."

The words were a lance to his chest.

He told himself not to be so vainglorious. Why on earth would he presume to think Miss Brown was thinking of *him* when she jotted down those words?

She was probably thinking of . . . the other fellow.

Anyway, from what she'd told him about her notes, this could be quite old. Years old.

The notion did not calm him.

Simon told himself the swirling in his stomach was due to the lurching of the coach, which had cleared the cobblestones of town in favor of rutted dirt roads.

Some people said novels were the devil's work. He was not one of those people, but it was certainly the case that novel reading could be . . . destabilizing.

He set the book aside and cleared his throat, drawing the attention of the others. "Isn't it about time for the rules?"

"I suppose it is," Archie said, handing out glasses and sloshing a few fingers of ruby-red port in each of them. "This is the part where I would traditionally say, 'Gentlemen. Welcome to Earls Trip 1823.' But can we call it Earls Trip anymore?"

"Certainly we can," Simon said.

"Half of it anyway," Effie said. "Week one is Earls Trip, and week two is, what did Clementine and Olive call it, Earls-Plus-Girls Trip?"

"They did indeed. In fact, they've been talking of nothing else for the past few weeks." Archie rolled his eyes, but affection for his wife and her sister was evident in his eyes. "But you are correct, Simon, just because this year is different doesn't mean we bin the rules."

"I should think not," Effie said. "When a man upends his life utterly, he needs *some* tradition to hold on to."

"I would suggest," Simon said, "that the rules are more important than ever, given that ladies will be in attendance." He wagged a finger at Archie. "You can't be waving a gun around with ladies present. With your *mother* present."

Archie's mother, who was afflicted with a disease of the mind, was the chief inspiration for this year's altered tradition. Archie hated to leave her, even in the capable hands of his wife and of Miss Brown, her longtime companion. Simon himself had suggested the new arrangement, noting that although Archie insisted he was fine to take the usual fortnight away, it was easy for them to change things round. The dowager aside, Archie and Effie were married men now. Things weren't the same as in their bachelor days, so Simon had suggested they adapt.

As if Simon had ever been adaptable.

He *was*, though, when it came to his friends. Or at least he could learn to be.

The thing was, he had made this suggestion ages ago. Not that long after last year's Earls Trip, in fact. Well before the . . . upheaval of the last month.

Before his . . . acquaintance with Miss Brown had deepened.

"I shan't be waving a gun around," Archie said, "but I do feel the need to remind you that we are bound for a property that has historically been a hunting box. It is therefore well-provisioned with guns. So the question you ought to be asking isn't whether I've *brought* a gun—it's whether the armory is safely locked." He sniffed, but his eyes danced. "Which it is."

"You know he hasn't fired a gun since he almost shot me on Earls Trip 1818," Effie said to Simon, and Simon had to smile at the cheerfulness with which Effie recalled his near demise. "And we all know that the rules are, at this point, merely notional."

"Notional, perhaps, but important traditions nevertheless," Simon said.

"You are, of course, correct," Effie said. "And as I previously noted, I have a newfound devotion to the idea of tradition."

Simon made a make-haste gesture. "Let us get on with it, then."

"All right." Archie lifted his glass and the others followed suit. "Gentlemen. Welcome to Earls Trip 1823. Allow me to remind you of the rules. Number one: Every time Marsden says the word 'Parliament,' he must down a dram of whisky."

"Which I shan't be doing, as I haven't brought any work," Simon said.

"I thank you not to interrupt," Archie said with feigned annoyance.

"Number two: Stonely, formerly Featherfinch, is strictly prohibited from writing poems, unless they are naughty ones. And should you be harboring any concerns that I fancy myself above the law, we come round to number three: Harcourt is not permitted to shoot anything. And finally," Archie continued with a flourish, "the most important rule of Earls Trip . . ."

They spoke in unison. "What happens on Earls Trip stays on Earls Trip."

"Is that true anymore, though?" Simon asked.

"No, indeed," Effie said. "The happenings of the last two Earls Trips spilled so far over into regular life that both you and I are married, Archie."

"And welcoming the resultant gate-crashers this year," Simon added.

"Hush," Archie said. "We *just* agreed the rules are traditional, if notional."

"Goodness!" Effie exclaimed. "We are going to be quite outnumbered." He began counting on his fingers. *My wife* will be joining me. Archie has a veritable harem joining him: Clementine, Olive, his mother." He stopped and eyed Simon. "I am sorry that Earls-Plus-Girls has left you . . . girl-less, Simon."

"You forgot Miss Brown," Simon said, though of course Miss Brown, while a member of Archie's household, did not *belong* to anyone, least of all Simon.

"I did, didn't I?"

"You did." Though Simon couldn't fathom how anyone could ever forget Miss Brown.

2

A Shocking Proposal

Four weeks earlier
August 11, 1823
Twenty-eight days before Earls Trip

Diantha Brown was in the music room when her life fell to pieces, scattering as surely as the playing cards she dropped when Mrs. Saunders swept in and announced that she had a caller and that his name was Mr. Hill.

"A caller?" A weak echo was all Diantha could manage as she tried and failed to stand, her legs having ceased to function properly.

A spark of hope: Perhaps her ears were similarly afflicted. Perhaps she had misheard. "I beg your pardon. What did you say the caller's name was?"

The housekeeper frowned at the cards strewn across the gleaming parquet. Diantha followed her gaze and made eye contact with the king of hearts.

Diantha had always thought irony an overrated literary device.

"Mr. Hill," Mrs. Saunders said.

Diantha had not misheard.

Everyone always thought she didn't have any family, but that wasn't true.

Well, it was partly true. She had no family by blood, but she did have one relation by marriage.

Get up, she ordered herself.

"I've put him in the small parlor." Mrs. Saunders paused. "He seemed . . ."

He seemed as if he didn't belong in the large drawing room in which Mrs. Saunders typically installed guests. Mrs. Saunders, who was very good at her job, had chosen correctly. If Diantha had to speak to Mr. Hill, it was better done in a small, out-of-the-way room at the back of the house.

Get up.

"Is Mr. Hill alone?" she inquired, though she wasn't sure whom she was imagining might have accompanied him. It certainly wasn't going to be Amalthea.

"He is." Mrs. Saunders glanced at the dowager, who was happy this morning, absorbed in her painting. "I'll sit with her ladyship while you receive him."

Get up.

Diantha got up.

She always did.

Enoch Hill looked exactly the same as when Diantha last saw him, seven years ago at her sister's wake. It was an accomplishment, in a way, considering his fondness for the drink and for stuffing his face with the cheese and butter he always said did not agree with him.

Diantha's own countenance was vastly changed from the nineteen-year-old she had been when he'd shipped her here. But she supposed the gulf between nineteen and twenty-eight was far greater than that between forty-four and fifty-three.

"Mr. Hill." She bobbed a stuttering curtsy—her legs were still not entirely obeying her will. "What a surprise."

"My wife died."

"Oh." That set her back on her heels. "I'm so sorry." Diantha had never met Enoch's second wife, but she knew her to have been young.

"She died in childbirth." He paused. "As did the child." Another pause. "A boy."

"Oh, Mr. Hill." Diantha had no love for this man, but she wouldn't wish such a tragedy on anyone. "Did you and your late wife have other children?" They'd been married six and a half years, Enoch having remarried so soon after Thea's death it would have raised eyebrows had they been moving in polite society, so it seemed possible, even likely, there were other children.

"No. We'd been trying since our wedding night, and she never quickened until this time. It seems my curse is to wed barren, or near-barren, women. Four years with Amalthea and nearly seven with Anne, and each marriage yielded only one ill-fated pregnancy."

Something in Diantha bristled to hear him refer to Thea as barren, though she could not argue with the fact that marriage had not produced children for her sister and Enoch.

And given that Enoch's second marriage had taken six and a half years to do so, she was tempted to ask if perhaps the impediment was his.

She checked herself. That had been an unnecessarily cruel impulse. Enoch had wanted a son so badly. Diantha remembered many things about Enoch. Most she wished she could forget, but one happy remembrance was the day Thea told Diantha she was with child. *Perhaps it will be a fresh start, Di,* Thea had said. Diantha had been skeptical, but she'd kept her reservations to herself. They'd worked together to prepare Enoch's favorite meal and, when he'd come home from the pub that night, surprised him with the news. He had smiled so widely that Diantha realized he was missing one of his front teeth. She had lived in his household for a year by that point and hadn't known.

Diantha was always having to remind herself to be kind. She wished it were a quality that came naturally, but, alas, she had to work as hard at it today as when she was young. Happily, unlike the old days, she didn't live under the same roof as someone who was constantly poking the bear that hibernated inside her.

Having successfully tamped down that flare of anger, sorrow rushed in to fill the void. She missed her sister so terribly, even after all these years. She couldn't help but wonder if Amalthea would still be around if it weren't for Enoch. It was a nonsensical thought, of course. Enoch hadn't given Thea scarlet fever; it had come from a neighbor's child. But if Thea hadn't been married to Enoch, she wouldn't have had that particular neighbor. If Thea had been full of ire and bile like Diantha, instead of empathy and the milk of human kindness, she wouldn't have found it necessary to visit that sick child and her family.

Diantha shook her head to chase away the memories. There was no point in relitigating the past. Especially not when the present was so concerning.

Although perhaps she was being overly wary. Perhaps Enoch had found some keepsake of Thea's as he was clearing out his second wife's things and had thought to deliver it to Diantha, though that would have been uncharacteristically thoughtful of him.

"I'm very sorry to hear of your misfortune, Mr. Hill." She pasted on a small smile she hoped wasn't too welcoming. "To what do I owe the pleasure of this visit?"

"I'm here to discuss the future."

"I see." She paused. "I can't think what advice you could want from me on the matter." Although perhaps she sold herself short. Thea always used to say that Mr. Hill was so cruel to Diantha because he resented her intelligence.

"What advice *I* should want from *you*?" He laughed, but there was no mirth in it. "I can't think of such, either, girl, because such a scenario does not exist. I'm not here for advice, not to dispense it nor to receive it." He eyed her for an uncomfortably long time, as if he were considering how to deliver bad news, but she knew that couldn't be the correct interpretation, for Mr. Hill relished delivering bad news. Bullies always did.

"I've decided to take you as my wife."

She gasped, which she hated to do in front of him. But she was suddenly winded, as if he'd punched her in the gut. He *had*, metaphorically.

Breathe. Think. Ironically, it was by paying attention to the ever-present ache in her shoulders that she was able to come back to herself.

Mr. Hill wasn't her guardian anymore. She had long since attained her majority. He had no control over her.

It merely felt as though he did because he once had, over both sisters.

Thea and Diantha used to take long walks, just to get out of the house, which had been gloomy when Mr. Hill was away and borderline intolerable when he was resident. They'd always taken the same route—to the park and around a small lake therein. One day, Thea had suggested they vary their routine. She'd wanted to look in a shop window she'd heard contained a pretty display of ribbons. Looking was all the sisters could do in those days, but neither of them had lost their appreciation for fine things even as their family's fortunes had fallen, so Diantha had readily agreed.

But when it had come time to make the turn that would take them onto the high street, Diantha had gone the opposite direction, toward the park. Thea hadn't said anything, and it had taken Diantha half a block to notice she was sisterless. The two of them had laughed and laughed. Diantha suspected she remembered that afternoon so vividly because of all the laughing. It had been as if they were starving and laughter an unexpected banquet.

Thea had said, "Your body's memory of our customary route was stronger than your will to vary it."

This felt like that. Diantha had never been able to defy Mr. Hill.

But she was older now. She made her own living, meager as it was. Here, today, her will could override her habitual obedience when it came to this man.

Here, today, her will *would*.

"While I am quite flattered by your thoughtful proposal, Mr. Hill, I am afraid I must decline."

It was a miracle her easy tone did not betray the frantic beating of her heart, for once the words were out, fear started to take hold in earnest. She pushed it down.

"You must *decline*?"

She would have expected the question to be asked sneeringly, but he was back to barely concealed amusement, as if he were an ogre taking delight in being about to squash a mere human. Once again, she reminded herself that she was safe. She was independent.

"Yes, though again, I do thank you for your consideration." She hated to thank him for anything, but experience had taught her that placating bullies was often necessary—the "lose the battle to win the war" adage applied here. "I am not inclined to leave my position in this household."

"You would rather continue paid employment than marry and have children."

"I would rather continue paid employment than marry and have children," she affirmed, as if reciting his words back to him might make her message stick.

When Diantha had come to take up her role as companion to the then newly widowed Lady Harcourt, she'd yet to attain the age of majority, but no one had had to twist her arm to persuade her to accept the position. As was the case for ladies' companions from time immemorial, she'd had no choice. She'd known that. Well, she'd had a choice. She could have married. Thea had.

Diantha hadn't intended to repeat her sister's mistake back then, and she certainly didn't now. She was no longer a minor. She could choose her own fate—within the narrow lane she occupied.

"I'm offering you the chance to have your own family," Mr. Hill said. "To be the mistress of your own household."

She could see how, on paper, and from the point of view of a man, those things would seem important, though it irritated her that he spoke as if he hadn't heard what she'd *just said.*

"What will you do when the dowager is gone?" he asked.

It was a good question. From anyone else, she would have

deemed it a fair one. It was something she tried not to think about. Diantha's wages were adequate but not terribly generous, since they came with room and board. As a result, she had a little nest egg accumulated. Not enough to keep her comfortable for the rest of her days, but by her calculations, with six more years' worth of wages, she could get there. In her more optimistic moments, she imagined the dowager lasting that many more years. Her mind was in decline, but she was strong in body. Hale. Diantha therefore had time enough to grow the nest egg, to make it big enough for her purposes. She hoped.

Diantha was well aware that a hope was not a plan, but what choice did she have?

Still, she didn't want to get into it with him, so she settled for a vague answer. "You needn't worry about me, Mr. Hill."

"I don't *worry* about you, my girl."

Diantha bristled at the phrase *my girl* coming from this man's lips.

"I never worried about you. You were always the smart one, if a little high in the instep. Therefore, I assume it has not escaped your attention that I haven't made a *proposal*, to use your term. I am not here to *ask* you to marry me." He paused for an uncomfortably long moment. "I am here to *tell*."

Oh, this was bad.

No. She ordered herself to reframe the situation. This was unfortunate, but, again, she had the legal, if not societal, advantage.

She huffed a fortifying breath and bore up to the task at hand. "Mr. Hill, I don't wish to be rude, but I have long since attained the age of majority. It was within your power to send me here, but it is not within your power to remove me. Therefore, I must—"

"My only criterion is that my third wife be respectable. Chaste. What better candidate than a gel such as yourself who has never married?"

He was speaking over her, something that made her discomfort with the confrontational nature of this interaction edge toward anger. Again, she made an effort to swallow her spleen.

"I did consider that perhaps a widow who already had children might be advisable. That way I would be assured that—"

"Mr. Hill." If he could speak over her, she could speak over him. "Allow me to remind you again that I—"

"I shall require two children, at minimum."

Oh, for Heaven's sake. The very thought was revolting.

"Since Thea eventually did get with child, I can safely assume you will, too. And you are younger still than she was that time."

Diantha wanted to cast up her accounts.

"We shall, of course, have to allow a suitable period of mourning for my wife to elapse. Six months, say."

He was maddening. In general, but also, six months? To mourn a wife of so many years? What a pig.

Of course, that was exactly how long he'd waited between wives number one and two.

"That should give you enough time to get your affairs in order here," he went on. "I did consider the question of whether to give Lord Harcourt your notice now but determined that such haste isn't wise. What if he wants to replace you sooner than later? Where would you go then?"

"I . . . can't imagine."

Certainly not to the retirement cottage of her dreams, to the life where she was in charge of her own money and her own fate. She needed several more years for that. Still, she wasn't going anywhere with Enoch Hill, ever.

"I could put you up, of course, but where? It cannot be with me. That would not be proper."

That would not be proper? *That* was where this man drew the line?

Enough. She had to stop this. "Enoch, forgive me." She hated the shape of his Christian name in her mouth, but it might help him hear her. "You've taken me by surprise, so perhaps I haven't made myself clear: I won't marry you."

That stopped his stream of nonsense. He leered at her, taking his time and letting his gaze fall to her feet and travel back up. She was wearing an unremarkable day dress, but something about his regard made her feel tawdry. She stood straighter and lifted her chin, both actions contrary to what she felt like doing, which was curling up in a ball out of his sight.

"As I said, it isn't a discussion," he said.

"There we are in agreement. You haven't the power to compel me, therefore no discussion is necessary."

"Don't I?" His ruddy face twisted into something resembling a smile, and she felt again as if she might be ill.

She was about to reiterate that no, he hadn't that power—she was aware that Mr. Hill wasn't the sharpest needle in the sewing kit, but honestly—when he pulled out a piece of paper. Cream linen. The kind stocked here and at Mollybrook. The kind Diantha used to write her letters on, back when she had people to write to. Back when she had a *person* to write to. A sister.

He began reading, holding the paper in front of him as if reading a royal proclamation. "'I hesitate to share this story, which was told to me in confidence, but after some soul searching, I determined its teller wouldn't mind, given the circumstances.'"

Oh. Oh no. Diantha's mouth flooded with the tang of metal. She knew those words. She knew this letter.

"When did you find that letter? *Where* did you find it?" She had instructed Thea to burn it. Diantha didn't care for the way her questions came out, soft and breathy, but they had to be asked.

She was surprised when he answered readily. "I found it in your sister's things after she died. She saved all your letters."

That he hadn't discovered the letter until Thea was already gone was some comfort. Diantha had no doubt Thea would not have survived the discovery of the sisters' correspondence. In addition to the contents of the letter Mr. Hill held, some very unflattering things had been said about him in others.

She wondered that Mr. Hill had kept the letters for so long. Had he foreseen a future in which they might provide him a useful bit of leverage? She wouldn't have thought him capable of such strategic forward thinking.

He returned to his oddly formal recitation, and Diantha knew what was coming: the tale of a dalliance Lady Harcourt undertook in the summer of 1808, a story the lady had recounted to Diantha. A story the lady would *not* have recounted to Diantha had she been in full possession of her faculties.

Why had Diantha decided to tell her sister? What right had she to do so?

It had been sheer force of habit. The sisters had told each other everything, in person and, after Diantha came to work for Lady Harcourt, via letters. A thought wasn't a thought until it was verbalized, or written, to Thea.

She missed that so very much.

But also, Thea had been enjoying somewhat of a flirtation with the butcher, and Diantha had wanted to illustrate that morality wasn't always black and white.

She had been trying to suggest that her sister find happiness where she could.

She was fairly certain she had said nothing overtly about the butcher in her letters to Thea. That must be the case, for had Mr. Hill believed the sisters had plotted to cuckold him, he would not be here on a mission of matrimony but of murder. She supposed that was some cold consolation.

Mr. Hill continued reading: "'She said that, paradoxically, the summer in question, and her activities therein, served to *strengthen* her marriage. The freedom and joy she experienced had a kind of rejuvenating effect. It allowed her to return renewed, better prepared to bear the circumstances of her life.'"

Diantha had thought she was being circumspect by not naming Lady Harcourt, but why had she thought that a sufficient precaution? She'd known Thea would recognize her unnamed lady narrator, so why shouldn't Mr. Hill? He wasn't the sharpest needle, yes, but he had always been very finely tuned to gossip, gossip so often being a source for leverage and therefore gain.

"'She wasn't saying that outcome—a refreshed marriage—justified her actions, merely that her actions had that unexpected benefit. She was remarkably philosophical about the supposed sin. She—and her son—had spent years victim to her husband's tyrannical impulses.'"

Yes. Just as Thea had been victim to this man's tyrannical impulses.

And the butcher had been such a jovial man.

Mr. Hill continued. "'She felt her suffering inoculated her, morally speaking, and mused about whether the unkindness she had done her husband *was* actually an unkindness, given that he didn't know about it.'"

"Mr. Hill. I don't need to hear any more. I—"

He ignored her. Continued speaking as if she weren't even present, as if he *were* issuing a royal proclamation.

She reminded herself that she was not his subject.

Yet.

"'But I am telling you this backward,'" he read. "'I have yet to tell you about the summer in question. I very likely don't need to spell it all out. You can imagine that she had a perfectly lovely summer. Her husband was in Town. She was at the seaside. The man in question was a painter also visiting the shore. She showed me a miniature of her that he painted. I, of course, didn't know her back then, but I believe there *was* a quality of freedom, of liberation, depicted in her countenance that went beyond the mere fact of her relative youth.'"

"Mr. Hill, that is quite enough."

"I'm not sure it is."

A knock on the door had him falling blessedly silent.

It was Mrs. Saunders with tea. Diantha didn't know whether to be glad for the interruption or dismayed that the arrival of refreshment would seem an invitation for Mr. Hill to settle in and stay awhile.

As the housekeeper set down the tray, Diantha tried to calm herself: her heart, her breath, her very being.

Mrs. Saunders was taking her time leaving—a person didn't become an effective housekeeper without being at least a little nosy—so what choice did Diantha have but to ask, "Do you still take your tea with three sugars and a generous splash of milk, Mr. Hill?"

Mrs. Saunders finally left as Diantha poured. Mr. Hill took several leisurely slurps before saying, "Thea was always talking about how clever you were. I assume you grasp the meaning of my recitation of your letter."

"I'm not sure I do," Diantha said, though of course that wasn't true. His meaning was blackmail, but she wanted him to spell it out. Perhaps she held out some faint hope that hearing his own vile plans aloud might inspire shame.

"You will marry me, or I will make the contents of this letter public."

There it was, and with no shame whatsoever. "No one is named in that letter," she tried, knowing the point was weak.

"You are named. You signed it. You, Miss Diantha Brown, companion to the Dowager Countess of Harcourt—whose husband was very much alive in the summer of 1808."

Dread, heavy and acid, was spreading through Diantha's gut.

She wanted to ask again why he had set his sights on her. But perhaps it wasn't so mysterious. Perhaps he couldn't get anyone else. Barbury was a very small place. It was possible that, two wives in, everyone knew him for the blackguard he was. Blackmail may be all he had, a sort of macabre reverse dowry.

"You are a single, respectable woman. I am in want of a wife." He downed his tea in several more slurps, clattered his empty cup into its saucer, and stood. "I shall return in six months' time, at which point you will accompany me to Barbury for the reading of the banns, or I shall ruin the reputation of your beloved Lady Harcourt—and all the rest of them."

Mr. Hill wasn't gone thirty seconds before Mrs. Saunders appeared under pretext of collecting the tea things, though typically she would have dispatched a maid for such a job.

"Who was that?" she inquired with a studied casualness.

"That," Diantha said, "was my only living relation."

She braced herself for an expression of shock, and it came, though Mrs. Saunders was nothing if not in control of the outward display of sentiment. Instead of a gasp, she exhaled slightly more vehemently than usual, almost as if she were whistling—though Mrs. Saunders would never do anything so vulgar as whistle.

Being a lady's companion was a curious thing. It required one to have no relations of means, but also to come from a respectable family.

Diantha wasn't dim. She understood that respectability and means were not the same thing. She understood—intimately, viscerally—the concept of genteel poverty. It was just that it had always struck her as a maddening paradox. She had secured her position as companion to the Countess of Harcourt by virtue of Diantha's mother, the daughter of a baronet, having been a childhood friend of the lady. Barbury, where Diantha had grown up, wasn't too far from Mollybrook, the Harcourt country estate.

"That was my only living relation *by marriage*," Diantha clarified. "Mr. Hill was my late sister's husband. He was for a time my guardian."

"How nice. I hope he is well."

I hope he is well meant *What did he want?*

Diantha considered her options. She could take the housekeeper into her confidence. Mrs. Saunders was clever, and, Diantha suspected, a veritable font of secrets, as effective housekeepers tended to be. Perhaps she would be able to think of a way out of this dilemma.

But no. She would keep her own counsel for now. Six months was a long time. Surely she could discover a remedy. At the very least, she ought to undertake a financial inventory. Perhaps she could accelerate her plans to retire. Or lower her standards. She had lived in poverty before, and she supposed she could do it again if it came to it, though her entire modus operandi since she left her sister's house had been to amass enough money so that she never had to return to a life of deprivation. Some people said money couldn't buy happiness, but those people had never been poor. Anyway, it wasn't happiness, precisely, that Diantha had been saving for. It was independence. True independence. A life that no one could take from her, gamble away, or otherwise threaten.

"His lordship would like to see you," Mrs. Saunders said. "He asks will you come to him in his office when it is quite convenient?"

Diantha blinked, a little taken aback. It was not unusual for Lord Harcourt to summon her. They were allied in caring for his mother. She couldn't help but fear, though, that this particular summons, coming at this particular time, did not bode well.

Had he found out, somehow, about her spectacular lapse in judgment? Had he encountered Mr. Hill on the latter's way out? Perhaps Mr. Hill had reconsidered his stance on letting things be for six months.

For the first time in all this, shame flooded in. She thought she had taken care with the wording of that letter. She hadn't named names.

It hadn't been enough.

Of *course* it hadn't. She should have foreseen this outcome. Or if not this specific result, she should at least have taken heed of what a bad actor Mr. Hill was. How could she have committed those words to paper and posted said paper to his house? She would have liked to attribute her actions to the carelessness of youth, but Diantha had never been careless. She'd never had that luxury.

Well, if Lord Harcourt knew about her transgression, there was nothing for it but to bear the consequences. She deserved them.

"Miss Brown." Lord Harcourt stood upon her entrance. The two of them had a curious relationship. In many ways, they were in the trenches together, had been for years. They collaborated in soothing the dowager in her worst moments, when she was deep in the grip of her troubled mind and physically lashing out. They savored the small victories when she enjoyed moments of lucidity or displayed flashes of her still-present sense of humor. They possessed a shared understanding, one that can only be conferred by experience, of the burden of caretaking. It went beyond fellow feeling: Lord Harcourt often solicited Miss Brown's opinion on his mother's decline, or consulted her about what the doctors said.

All this meant that they had, in some ways, grown close.

Yet there remained an air of formality about the way Lord Harcourt treated Diantha. He stood when she entered a room. He never used her Christian name. This was another paradox of life as a companion. She was deeply embedded in the family. She *knew* them. She knew their secrets—in the case of the dowager, she knew a very big one. Yet she was not one of them. They paid her wages. She slept in a modest room adjacent to Lady Harcourt's.

She was among them but not of them.

Lord Harcourt was a decent man, though. That was what mattered. He had given Diantha a good life, better than anything she had imagined after her father's fall from fortune and her sister's disastrous marriage. She knew him to be a devoted son and a loving—nay, besotted—husband.

It was astonishing, really, to think how Lord Harcourt could coexist with Mr. Hill in the same category called *Men*.

Lord Harcourt's friends, too. Diantha had followed the Parliamentary session of 1820, in which Queen Caroline was tried for adultery. She had been utterly astonished when Lord Harcourt's bosom friend Lord Marsden had stood and given a speech in favor of the rights of ladies to divorce their husbands on grounds of adultery.

How could one man attempt to force a woman into an unwanted marriage, while another stood up and publicly championed their rights as related to the institution?

She thought of the lemon drops Lord Marsden had given her last time he called on the family. She tried to ration them, dear as they were. But she had a sweet tooth and was fond of the tart sugariness of lemon in particular. Lemon drops reminded her of childhood, of happier, more prosperous days.

She would allow herself one later, when she was done with Lord Harcourt. It would soothe her. Perhaps its tartness would even galvanize her sufficiently that she might think of a way out of her predicament—assuming she survived this meeting with her employer.

She dropped an abbreviated curtsy, bracing herself for what could well be her second disastrous meeting of the day. If it was, at least this one wouldn't be an ambush. It would be the administration of justice.

"Miss Brown." Lord Harcourt came around from behind his desk and led her to a pair of chairs near the fire. "I wanted to discuss this year's Earls Trip."

She had been spared. For today at least. She sat gratefully. This was a discussion she was more than prepared to have. "Yes, I've been meaning to suggest that your mother and I repair to Mollybrook in advance of your departure. She will fare better there while you are gone."

Diantha considered that last sentence. *She will fare better there while you are gone.* Earlier in her employment, two or three years ago even, she would not have phrased it thusly. She would have said *She may fare better there while you are gone*, the equivocation of the word *may* standing in for the more definite *will.* Diantha would have been hesitant to so openly offer an opinion, to share it almost as if it were fact. Which it was. The dowager *would* fare better at the family's country estate in her son's absence. They were only in Town at the moment for a consultation with her doctors, something that was happening with increasing frequency but without, in Diantha's estimation, very much to show for it.

"Mm," Lord Harcourt said, and Diantha did not take his easy agreement for granted. He respected her opinion. It was gratifying. It told her that, as tedious as her work sometimes was, it was meaningful.

She didn't want to give it up. She didn't want to give *them* up. Her throat thickened. Tears amassed.

"Isn't it ironic that while I am in her company, Mother doesn't recognize me?" Lord Harcourt mused. "Yet when I am away from her, to hear you tell it, she grows upset?"

Diantha swallowed, forced back the threatening tears, and ordered herself to remain composed. "I am not sure it's so ironic, because I don't know that it's the case that she doesn't recognize you."

"Come now, Miss Brown. You are too intelligent to be dispensing false flattery."

"It isn't false flattery. Of course, most of the time, your mother doesn't know your name or that you are her son. Your shared past is, by and large, gone. But your physical presence calms her. So mustn't it follow that some part of her knows you? That, not to be too mystical about it, her heart knows you?"

Was she mistaken, or was the earl about to tear up? Weepiness: It must be catching today.

She rushed to continue, to spare him the scrutiny. "Which isn't to say you shouldn't take your trip. We have had this discussion before. Time away is essential to the caretaking endeavor. We shall get along just fine without you. The new countess soothes your mother, too. Not in the same way you do," she hastened to add, both because it was true and because she understood that it was important to Lord Harcourt that his mother needed him uniquely. Which she did.

"What else soothes my mother?"

"I beg your pardon?"

"What else soothes my mother. Music, yes?"

"Oh, yes. Songs from her youth, particularly."

"What else?"

"The gardens at Mollybrook."

"Yes, yes. What else?"

Diantha found this line of questioning curious. Lord Harcourt was intimately involved in his mother's care. Not in the corporeal way Diantha and some of the servants were—he left the dressing and bathing of the dowager to them—but he knew her habits and quirks and was familiar with the rhythms of her days.

He must have his reasons for this Socratic style of questioning, and she was happy to indulge him. "Water soothes your mother. Being immersed in it." The servants drew a nightly bath for Lady Harcourt, which Diantha would have found extravagant even in her plentiful youth.

"Aha!" Lord Harcourt raised a finger to the sky as if Diantha were a student who'd hit on the answer to a thorny question. Except he didn't look like a teacher, he looked like a little boy about to tear into a bag of sweets. "Miss Brown, I have recently completed the construction of a plunge pool at Gurglewood."

"Gurglewood?" she echoed.

"Gurglewood." He paused. "The name of my hunting box."

Ah, yes, she knew he had such a property; she just hadn't known it to be thus named.

As if he could see inside her mind, he said, "I'm trying out names for it. What do you think of Gurglewood?"

"It's . . ."

"The property isn't too terribly far east of Mollybrook. We decided to stay closer to home for this year's Earls Trip. It's quite pretty. There is a brook that runs strong and clear, and a small thatch of woods."

"Ah. Hence the name. Gurglewood."

"Yes. Too literal?"

She wouldn't presume to verbalize her agreement, though she suspected Lord Harcourt would only smile if she did.

"Well, it is superior to River's Embrace, which was Lord Stonely's suggestion." He snorted. "While the brook is lovely, it is hardly a river, and I should think being 'embraced' by a river would be an unpleasant, perhaps even fatal, occurrence."

"Yes, River's Embrace is perhaps a tad *too* poetical." Lord Harcourt's friend Lord Stonely was a poet who tended toward the dramatic. Though Diantha had read and enjoyed many of his poems, she preferred novels. And when it came to reading Lord Harcourt's friends' writing, she was more inclined toward Lord Marsden's speeches, which were often printed in the papers.

"I shall continue to ponder the matter," Lord Harcourt said. "The matter of a name arose because while the property has historically been a rustic, masculine retreat, I've undertaken a renovation, the centerpiece of which is a pool for taking the waters. You may or may not be aware that natural springs exist in the area."

"I am familiar with Royal Turnbridge Wells, which I believe must be nearby?"

"Precisely. Have you taken the waters there? 'Tis the same water that flows under . . . Gurglewood."

"No, no. I am merely aware of the existence of it as a spa town. I grew up in a village called Barbury, which isn't far."

"Right. I forget that you haven't always been with us, Miss Brown. But of course you came via the friendship of our mothers, which was aided, I am sure, by geographic proximity."

"Yes," she said carefully. She had never been sure how much Lord Harcourt knew about her family's tragic history. She suspected that Lady Harcourt, then of sound mind and recently widowed, had insisted on Diantha as her companion, and that Lord Harcourt, newly the duke, had simply written the necessary letters—and arranged the necessary bank drafts.

"People say the waters in the region have healing properties," he said. "All manner of curative claims are made. I don't know about that, but immersion should lift the spirits regardless, do you not think?"

Oh, Lord Harcourt. He had built a pool for the mother who no longer knew him as a son.

"Perhaps we can visit with your mother at some point? Is that what you are suggesting? If so, I think it a fine idea." Perhaps Diantha would be able to take the waters, too. She didn't think of herself as overly sentimental, but there was something about the image he had conjured of a pool next to a brook. She would like to try it at night, under the stars. Though she supposed the darkness would mean one wouldn't be able to see the brook. Still, one of the things she missed from her life in Barbury, perhaps the only thing—other than her sister, of course—was the freedom to be outside at night. There was something about a cool night draped with winking stars that, speaking of soothing, had a pleasantly tranquilizing effect.

And who knew? Perhaps the waters did have curative properties and would temper her bilious nature.

"That is precisely what I'm suggesting," Lord Harcourt said. "Next month, the second week of Earls Trip."

"I beg your pardon?"

"The three of us gents shall go as usual for the first week, and the second we will be joined by my wife and her sister, by Stonely's wife, and by you and Mother."

For the second time today, Diantha found herself without words.

While she appreciated Lord Harcourt's devotion, she was not inclined to interfere with his holiday. Caring for an ill parent was not for the faint of heart, and she truly believed that his annual trips with his friends were essential for his well-being.

"We really can manage without you, my lord. Though the idea is very generous."

"It wasn't my idea; it was Marsden's. Earls Trip has to change with the times, he claims. Two of us are married. We're all older. We've different responsibilities than we had when the tradition started, and rather than chuck it all out, we've decided on . . . what word did Marsden use? 'Transfiguration.'" He chuckled. "The transfiguration of Earls Trip."

Transfiguration. Lord Harcourt probably thought Lord Marsden meant the word in its colloquial sense, the idea of changing the appearance of something. And possibly that *was* how he'd meant it. But Lord Marsden had been to seminary. He often used religious metaphors in ways Diantha wasn't always entirely sure *were* metaphors. It was one of the many mysterious yet compelling aspects of his character.

"It is all settled." Lord Harcourt brushed his hands together, and gone was her partner in caretaking, her fellow soldier. Her employer had returned. Which was fine. It was good to remember, especially today, her role in this household.

Dismissed, Diantha sneaked to her room for a brief respite. She took the long way, up the servants' staircase in the back. She wasn't required to use that staircase, but it would save her from passing the music room in which Mrs. Saunders sat with Lady Harcourt. She did not want Mrs. Saunders to know she was taking a break. There was no express rule against it, but Diantha was companion to Lady Harcourt, and the only thing that supplanted that was being summoned for an audience with Lord Harcourt or directed elsewhere by him.

She sat on her bed with a thud, taxed by the weight of all that had transpired in the past hour. If Diantha had ever lamented the dullness of her life, she was cured of such folly. The unfortunately named Gurglewood sounded lovely. It would be a true holiday, if a working one. One of the unrelenting bits of sadness in Diantha's life was that she never got to go anywhere, to do anything. She felt shallow admitting that she cared about such things, but her world had become so small. To go somewhere, even if it was only to one of the family's houses, was a thrill.

Or it would have been, had it not been for the devastation of Mr. Hill's visit.

She needed to remain calm. She needed to *think*. Six months. Mr. Hill had said he would return in six months. Surely she could come up with a solution by then.

Diantha retrieved the tin of lemon drops from her bedside table. Gurglewood. River's Embrace. She wondered if Lord Marsden, the third of the Earls Trip trio, had made a suggestion as to a name for the property. Everyone thought Lord Marsden staid and overly serious, but Diantha thought it possible he was misunderstood. She'd recently been lending him novels when he called on the family, and on more than one occasion he'd returned a volume to her with a surprisingly astute, dare she even say fervent, observation. Even his speeches in the House of Lords, though reportedly delivered with equanimity and sobriety, were, if she parsed them closely enough, sprinkled with glimmers of passion.

She popped a lemon drop into her mouth, and the tart shock it delivered was nothing next to the idea that crashed into her head.

You are a single, respectable woman, Mr. Hill had said.

She couldn't do anything about the former—not that she wanted to anyway—but perhaps she could affect the latter.

It was a dramatic solution.

But she had a dramatic problem.

Last time Lord Marsden called on the family, she asked him how he kept so calm in the sometimes boisterous environment of Lords. "People are saying the most outrageous things, and you are so placid," she had observed.

His answer: "I approach Parliamentary matters with logic and moderation. I endeavor to approach *all* matters with such qualities deployed. It is rather difficult to shock me, Miss Brown, dare I say even impossible."

Hmm.

The girl who used to live inside Diantha would have taken that dare.

3

An Even More Shocking Proposal

Simon was in the library in his shirtsleeves when Mrs. Tavish knocked.

"My apologies for bothering you at this hour, my lord, but Miss Brown is here. She says she must see you urgently."

"Miss Brown?" Simon opened his mouth. Closed it. Opened it again and made an unsuccessful attempt at verbalization.

Mrs. Tavish must have taken pity on him, for she said, "Miss Brown of Lord Harcourt's household," as if Simon did not know.

"Show her in." He paused. "Though perhaps I ought to receive her in a sitting room?"

The question had been rhetorical and not in earnest, but one of the things Simon appreciated about Mrs. Tavish was that she generally couldn't, or didn't care to, make the distinction.

"I should think here is suitable. I can't imagine Miss Brown is here on a social call at this time of evening." Mrs. Tavish didn't sniff. She didn't need to.

"Very well."

And there she was, clad in a long-sleeved black dress with tiny mother-of-pearl buttons that ran all the way up to her chin.

He rose and performed an abbreviated bow. "Miss Brown. Shall I call for tea?" He should have thought to do so before Mrs.

Tavish retreated. He was making a mull of this. He was just so discombobulated by her presence.

"No, thank you. I am here on a matter of business."

"In that case, please take a seat." He led her to a pair of wing chairs that faced the fireplace, which wasn't lit, as it was unseasonably warm, even for August. "Is everything all right with Harcourt? The countess? The dowager countess?" He couldn't think why Miss Brown would be the one to deliver bad news about Archie's household, but he also couldn't think why else she would be at his house at nine o'clock on a Monday evening on a "matter of business."

She did look rather businesslike. Simon did not know textiles, but the black dress seemed a thick, robust fabric. It wasn't her usual fashion. Most of her day dresses—as far as he could tell, she had five—were made of fabrics that looked softer, less weighty. And they were either light in color or printed with a pattern. There was one in particular, cream with small blue flowers, that was quite striking.

"My lord, I realize it is highly unusual for me to call on you in such a manner, but I was hoping to prevail upon you to assist me in a matter of some urgency."

"Unusual, but not unwelcome. How may I help?"

She regarded him for a long time. Simon had known that Miss Brown had blue eyes. He'd always thought them noteworthy in that they were quite a dark shade. He might even have called them navy, and how often does a person see navy eyes? Now, though, he could see that while he had not been mistaken per se, his adjective—navy—had been insufficient. There were flecks of dark gray there, too, and the ring around the outer edge of the iris was such a dark blue, he might even call it black. Or perhaps not black, but—

"I would like you to ruin me."

It was a good thing Simon was sitting, for he was certain his legs had stopped working. They felt like blancmange. He couldn't have heard her correctly. Had she not just said she was here on a *matter of business*? "I beg your pardon?"

She huffed a small sigh, as if she were his governess and finding him not up to snuff. He ought to be offended, he supposed. This was his house, and she was saying the most outrageous things; she could hardly fault him for his bewilderment.

"I suppose I shall have to provide some context."

"Please do," he managed, congratulating himself on the mild—on the surface of things—delivery he achieved.

"I must ask that you hold what I'm about to tell you in the strictest confidence."

"All right." Though perhaps he oughtn't be so easy with his agreement. What if she confessed a crime?

No, not Miss Brown.

But where had that confidence come from? Simon thought he knew Miss Brown, but did he truly? He conversed with her when he called on Archie's household. She lent him novels.

Could criminals not converse and read novels?

No. Simon's acquaintance with Miss Brown might have been, on the surface of things, superficial, but he *did* know her. He couldn't quite explain how, but he did.

"You can tell no one what I am about to reveal." She leaned in, lowered her voice, and whispered, with as much fervor as any actress, "*Not even Lord Harcourt.*"

It was possible to apply many adjectives to Miss Brown. She was intelligent, well-read, kind, and pretty. And, if he trusted his gut, not criminally inclined. He sometimes wondered if she was also impatient, perhaps even quick to anger, for sometimes, only very occasionally, he thought he saw a flare of something forbidding in her otherwise accommodating demeanor. Even so, he had never thought to call her melodramatic. He would have laughed if he wasn't so befuddled.

"You must *promise*," she said, "and I know you are a man of your word."

"You do? How?" The question was beside the point, but he needed to know the answer.

"I have followed your Parliamentary career. Your votes, your speeches, the causes you champion. They speak to your good character."

"Miss Brown, you'll forgive me for saying that I don't think most people would rate parliamentarians as moral paragons."

"Surely it depends on the parliamentarian. Everyone heard you give that speech during the trial of Queen Caroline, in which you argued for the rights of ladies to divorce their husbands on the grounds of adultery."

He shook his head. "What has that to do with anything?"

"I have, in the years since, considered you a champion of women. I admit I have read that speech nigh on a dozen times. I became rather fixated on it for a while, if you must know."

Simon shook his head. He was at sea.

"And you were initially bound for the Church, were you not? Certainly a vicar is a moral paragon."

"I do not think you have met many vicars."

"My lord. You are morally upstanding. A man of good character. I *know* this."

Perhaps he oughtn't to be arguing. If he knew Miss Brown without having spent a terrible lot of time with her, perhaps she likewise knew him. Regardless, her insistence was flattering.

"We digress," she said. "I am in need of help, is the point. Help in the form of ruination, and I can only tell you why if you promise to keep my counsel. I trust that you will do so, if you say you will."

What could he do but agree, if not on moral grounds—one ought to help ladies when presented with the opportunity to do so—then because he might die of curiosity if he didn't get to learn why the on-the-shelf companion to Archie's elderly mother believed herself in need of help in the form of ruination.

He placed a hand over his heart. "All right."

She mirrored his gesture, placing her hand over her heart,

and if he didn't know better, he would have said she performed a spell to align their heartbeats—she *was* wearing that severe black dress—but of course that was ridiculous. The pang in his chest was merely a reminder that he had yet to eat dinner—he'd been working too intently to eat this evening and had rebuffed the tray Mrs. Tavish had attempted to deliver.

"I find myself facing the prospect of an unwelcome marriage," Miss Brown said, "and I would like to avoid that fate."

"An unwelcome marriage?"

Who, in the name of all that was holy, had proposed marriage to Miss Brown? While Simon was fairly certain he was holding himself together outwardly, his legs still felt odd. He jiggled one to see if it would work. It didn't seem promising.

"Yes, one might even call it a forced marriage."

"A forced marriage?"

Simon was aware that he was going to have to do more than parrot Miss Brown's words, but the blancmange problem was apparently spreading to his brain.

"Yes, and I've been over and over my options. I fear the only thing that will make the . . . gentleman in question withdraw his suit is the prospect of his intended being damaged goods."

"You cannot simply refuse him?" Simon asked.

"He is . . . very persuasive. And very determined."

Oh, dear Heavens. Simon tried the other leg. Nothing. "And you want me to . . ."

"To ruin me. Yes."

Simon took a beat. And several more beats. "How would this . . . ruination occur?" Hypothetically. For he could not seriously entertain the idea. He could barely even speak the word aloud.

"The usual way. We are found in a compromising position at a party. The party bit will prove challenging. I don't go to many. I don't go to *any*. But Lady Harcourt still receives the occasional invitation, and I am hopeful that with enough lead time, I can manipulate the household such that we will attend a party sometime in the next few months. Or, if it isn't too much to ask, perhaps *you* could host a party."

If it wasn't too much to ask? She was conceding that asking him to host a party might be overstepping, but asking him to ruin her at said party was a reasonable request? The world had turned upside down.

"Regardless, there shall be a party. And then we can arrange to be closeted together in a room." She paused. "And of course arrange to be caught out, too; discovery is the essential bit."

Simon's stomach lurched at the notion of being "closeted together" in a room with Miss Brown. Conducting themselves in such a fashion that society would shame them. Being discovered.

The scenario made him sweat. It was a terrible idea.

Yet also . . . not terrible?

No. *Terrible.*

He placed a palm on the arm of his chair to steady himself, belatedly realizing that he was already sitting down and not in need of steadying. It merely felt that way.

"You needn't actually ruin me!" Miss Brown cried suddenly. "Oh, my goodness, I have made a hash of this. I am seized with panic."

Seized with panic? Miss Brown had, heretofore, been the picture of matter-of-factness. If she was panicking, she was hiding it well.

Unlike him, he feared, judging by her worried expression. He had thought, mere moments ago, that he was keeping calm outwardly. He feared that was no longer the case.

She leaned in as if imparting a secret. Reflexively, he angled himself to meet her, as if they were in a noisy, crowded drawing room and not utterly alone in his library.

Simon had never before been utterly alone with Miss Brown.

He leaned back again.

"We merely need to create the appearance of ruination," she said.

"The appearance of ruination." The parroting continued.

"Yes. Should someone come across us appearing to be in a compromising position, that would be sufficient to brand me as unmarriageable. There needn't be any *actual compromising*."

Was that . . . disappointing?

No, of course not.

"All right, so something happens, something that does not involve any actual compromising but merely the appearance of such. Then what? Sketch the post-discovery scene for me."

"What is there to sketch? We will be discovered." She raised a thumb. "You will refuse to marry me." A forefinger joined the thumb in the visual list she was making. "I will be ruined." Finger three. "And that"—she brushed both palms together as if ridding herself of an unwelcome bit of dust—"will be that."

"Yes, except for *my* reputation."

"What do you mean? It is the lady's reputation that is the social currency here, is it not?"

"Yes, but only a rake of the worst sort would refuse to come up to snuff in such a situation."

"And you do not want to be thought of as such?"

"Can you blame me?"

"Of course not, but you overlook the fact that you are rich. A peer. You'll easily shake off the stink. Men always do."

"The stink?" Good God.

"Yes. My reputation will be ruined forever. Yours will be rehabilitated by the next Season, particularly if you make it known that you are turning your mind to marriage." She paused. "If that was what you were worried about."

Simon had always thought he might marry one day, back when he was imagining himself living a quiet life as a country vicar. Since inheriting, he'd known he couldn't consider taking a wife until his mother died. He would never subject anyone, much less someone he esteemed enough to marry, to the cruelties of the Dowager Countess of Marsden.

Still, there was no reason Miss Brown should know that. It was perfectly reasonable for her to assume that he, an eligible peer of the realm pushing thirty years of age, would be turning his mind to the succession.

He cleared his throat. "I am disinclined to marriage at this point in my life."

Miss Brown seemed overly delighted by his stance. "So you are not concerned over your fate in the marriage mart—which, as a handsome, intelligent aristocrat, of course you needn't be. So that's one problem you shan't have to worry about, should your reputation be briefly dinged."

She thought he was handsome?

"Are you a member of a club that will expel you? Have you friends who will turn on you? A job to lose? Will you suffer materially?"

She thought he was *handsome*?

He didn't answer—he wasn't capable of speaking just now—so she answered for him.

"No, no, no, and no. What you're up against, if I may be so bold, is a little social discomfort. It will be temporary, and superficial."

He had to stop this. Perhaps she was deluded enough to think he was handsome. But that wasn't all he was. "You are forgetting, I think, that I am an honorable man." He refrained from adding *You just said so yourself.*

"I am not forgetting. That is why I am here, asking you to help me."

"Even if I cared not a whit for what others would think of my actions, *I* care. *God* cares."

She opened her mouth. Said nothing. Closed it.

"You want me to pretend to ruin you and then refuse to marry you. You, who are companion to my dearest friend's mother. Even if I *could* 'shake off the stink,' as you say, you can't possibly imagine that Archie would ever speak to me again. So the answer to one of those questions you just rattled off is *yes*. Do I have friends who will turn on me? Yes. Because they are also men of honor."

Miss Brown remained silent.

"And what of you?" he asked. "Suppose you achieve your desired goal: ruination. Then what? You're cast out of society. You have no family, I believe?"

She found her voice. "I shall secure a position as a governess. Somewhere else."

"Somewhere else?" He was back to echoing her words. It couldn't be helped. She was saying the daftest things.

"Not London. Not Kent."

Kent was where Archie's country estate was, and where Miss Brown and Archie's mother spent most of their time.

"Where, then?"

"I was thinking perhaps Scotland."

"You are going to secure a position as a governess in *Scotland*?" He raised his eyebrows.

"I am well educated," she said, a hint of affront in her tone. "I may not use that education a great deal, but I do have it. And I will thank you to stop repeating everything I say in the form of an incredulous question."

He smiled. She was being uncharacteristically illogical, but her wit was as sharp as ever.

"I'm not questioning your credentials. I'm merely finding it difficult to imagine a family of good reputation engaging the services of a ruined woman as a governess."

"What about a family of . . . less good reputation? Do not they need governesses, too?"

She must have interpreted his expression correctly—he was trying to stop asking the incredulous questions she'd called him out for, but he could not help what his face betrayed—for she said, "Well, I shall find a way forward. If I may speak freely. . . ?"

He made a go-ahead gesture but couldn't resist adding, "Are you not already speaking freely?"

"I come from poverty, and if need be, I can accustom myself to it again."

"Miss Brown, I am unsure how we have come so far down this conversational path. May we backtrack and you tell me a little more about this forced marriage business?" He wanted to get back to the bit where she was courting ruination in order to avoid an unwelcome union. "Who has proposed to you, and what power has he to compel your answer?"

She looked at him for a long time, with an intensity that ought to have made him uncomfortable but somehow did not. "I have made a mistake."

"What do you mean?"

"My errors have been both substantive and philosophical."

"Miss Brown, forgive me, but *what* are you talking about?"

"I hadn't thought through what your appearing to ruin me would mean for your friendship with Lord Harcourt, for your self-regard, or for your faith. For these errors in judgment, I apologize. I can say only that my distress has overtaken my common sense. I am sorry to have taken up so much of your time."

She started to get up.

He had no idea what came over him, but he reached out a hand and caught her forearm. It was covered in that heavy black fabric. He couldn't help but spare a moment to consider that if she'd been wearing one of her usual dresses, he would now be touching her skin.

Simon hadn't a great deal of carnal experience, and none of it was recent, but the most shocking thing about touching women, to his mind, was how *soft* their skin was.

Something stirred in his guts.

"The error you just spoke of—of not taking into account my friendship with Archie or my concern over my own moral code—that was your so-called substantive error?"

"Yes," she said evenly, gazing at him mildly, as if his hand wasn't still resting on her arm, as if he hadn't taken the extraordinary—and extraordinarily rude—step in order to prevent her from leaving.

"And what," he said, endeavoring to match her mild tone, "was your error of philosophy?"

She didn't hesitate to answer. "Presuming that someone like you could understand what it is like to be alone in the world. Alone in a household full of people. Alone, period."

He knew now what was stirring in his gut.

Anger.

He removed his hand from her arm. "Miss Brown, allow me to show you around my house."

4

Fashion Tips for Ambushes

A *house tour*? What a strange thing for Lord Harcourt to offer. In general, but also after all that had passed between them.

Diantha had no idea what to say. What to do. She had indeed made a mistake coming here, a grave one, and she wanted nothing more than to flee. Well, that wasn't true. Her greatest desire at the moment was the ability to unravel the weave of time. To go back several hours to when she'd hatched this inane plan, and . . . unhatch it.

Honestly, she was as embarrassed to have Lord Marsden think her unintelligent as she was that he should think her impolite, or even brazen. Of course an honorable man like Lord Marsden wouldn't want to risk his own reputation.

She needed a less honorable honorable man. She smiled despite herself.

But . . . perhaps that was *exactly* what she needed.

She resolved to consider the matter later. For now, she still had to contend with Lord Marsden. He had taken his hand off her arm, but he was standing at the door, his expression expectant, bordering on impatient.

Because she had no idea what to say, she fell back on the comportment training of her girlhood. "A house tour would be lovely."

The library was in the back of the house. She followed him out to the foyer, the centerpiece of which was an enormous mahogany staircase. She tilted her head up to admire the high ceiling with its elaborate cornices. There was a large medallion in the center, set into which was a painting. It depicted a pair of angels, each one holding . . . Were those *rifles*? How odd.

"Ahem."

She transferred her attention from the house to the householder. He was poised at the bottom of the staircase, clearly waiting for her. She would have thought a house tour might start with one of the rooms off the foyer—she could see through one door to an opulently upholstered settee—if not the impressive, if peculiar, foyer itself. But this was his house tour.

He mounted the stairs, and she followed. "This is my father," he said, stopping abruptly at an enormous painting of a severe looking man dressed in black. He climbed a few more steps. "And this is my brother, James." James was fairer than Lord Marsden and wearing a wide smile. Another two steps. "And this is my other brother, Michael." Michael was smiling, too, and holding a fishing rod.

"They look like twins," Diantha remarked.

"They were twins."

"Oh, I didn't know."

"My lord? May I help with anything?"

The housekeeper, peering up at them from the foyer.

"No," Lord Marsden said tersely. And then, more gently, "Thank you. Miss Brown will be leaving shortly. I'll see her out myself."

The housekeeper nodded, bobbed a curtsy, and retreated, but not before darting her gaze to Diantha. Oh, dear. Diantha truly hadn't thought this through. Perhaps she did not need to arrange for ruination; perhaps it would happen anyway, depending on how loyal Lord Marsden's staff were. She considered the rifle-wielding angels. Perhaps Lord Marsden was, secretly, an eccentric. Perhaps his servants were accustomed to behavior others might deem improper.

She could only hope.

"The twins." Lord Marsden gave a sharp rap on the frame of a portrait depicting the brothers astride matched horses. "They did everything together, including dying."

She waited for him to say more. She'd known Lord Marsden inherited his title when his brothers died in a fire—everyone did; it had been the talk of the ton. They'd gone together to look at some horses in Yorkshire, and the inn they'd been staying in burned down. She thought perhaps Lord Marsden would fill in some details, given that he was the one who brought up their deaths.

He did not. He merely continued his ascent, gesturing at paintings as he went. "This is them together when they were about ten. And here is my mother with them when they were twenty." In the latter, a woman who looked like a feminine version of Lord Marsden's brothers sat on a settee as her sons stood behind her. Each young man rested a hand on one of her shoulders, and she looked content, almost smugly so.

"I know your brothers died tragically," Diantha offered. "I am sor—"

"And here is my grandfather, the thirteenth earl."

For Lord Marsden to interrupt her was unprecedented. He was ordinarily so attentive and polite. When they spoke about books, which they'd been doing recently since he had taken to visiting Lady Harcourt with some frequency, he always seemed genuinely interested in what Diantha had to say.

He kept pointing at paintings as he climbed, his speech and his gait alike becoming more insistent. The thudding of his boots on the stairs grew louder. "My grandfather again, with his wife, my grandmother, and their children—my father and his brother and two sisters. And here's the twelfth earl. He waved an arm. "And so on. I can name them all—I was drilled in family history as a boy—but you would find that unbearably dull."

"I'm sure I wouldn't."

He had reached the top of the stairs. He turned and looked down at her—she was still half a dozen steps behind him. He was a tall man to begin with, but from this angle and in such close proximity to the portraits, he appeared almost like a painting come to life. A very forbidding painting. He wore dark brown breeches. His hair was also brown, and cropped unfashionably short. Though it was too dim to make out his eyes, she knew them to be brown as well. The only break in all the brown was his white shirt. She had never seen him without a coat before.

He didn't have the easy countenance of his brothers. Still, there was something . . . compelling in his sternness, his unstinting regard.

"Don't lie, Miss Brown. It doesn't suit you."

She was astounded that he would say such a thing, and she was only half successful at swallowing the resultant gasp. But she had been much bolder than he, just minutes ago, with her proposition. Perhaps it was an evening for audacity, for revelation.

He was on the move again, speaking to her but not looking at her as he walked. "I am, at my core, profoundly uninterested in adhering to social mores I consider nonsensical, and so many of them are. I recognize the obligation to do so in company, but I don't see the need to in my own home. In fact, that's one of the consolations of my situation."

So perhaps he *was* responsible for the strange painting on the ceiling in the foyer.

But also: "the consolations of his situation"? What did that mean?

She opened her mouth to protest that she wasn't lying about finding his recitation of the family lineage dull, but of course that would be another lie, and she had the feeling he would sniff that one out, too. It wasn't that she was bored by this narrated tour of the family portraits, more that she wondered what the point was. Was there going to be an examination later?

She followed him silently down a long corridor. A man on a mission, he was taking great big strides, his boots still thudding with each step. He disappeared through a wooden door with a brass handle, and she had to hurry to cover the last few steps.

She'd assumed he was taking her to a sitting room, or a quasi-public area of the house, but this was a bedchamber, a lady's bedchamber that opened onto a lavishly furnished sitting room.

"These are my mother's rooms."

"Oh, I don't think—"

"She's in the country."

"Still, I—"

He pointed to another painting, a large one in an elaborate gilt frame that hung on one side of a looming canopied bed. "My brothers, again."

She was beginning to understand. It had not escaped her notice that Lord Marsden didn't have a portrait on the stairs; nor had he appeared in any of the family groupings. And here, in his mother's inner sanctum, he was also not represented.

Before she could think what to say, he flung open the doors of a wardrobe, exposing his mother's clothing.

"My lord, I really must protest. This is—"

One side of the wardrobe was lined with drawers. He pulled one open and beckoned her closer.

She hesitated. She wasn't sure why. She wasn't scared of him. Just that there was a severeness about him, an intensity of purpose that, again, wasn't upsetting per se, but it had her on notice. She had never seen him like this. Which, she reminded herself, was a ridiculous thing to think. She'd come to his home, uninvited, and made an outrageous proposal. How could she be surprised that he would react passionately?

She went to stand next to him, and though they weren't touching—she took care to make sure of that—she was acutely aware of his arm a few inches from hers. Not only was he not wearing a coat, his sleeves were rolled up. Which, again, she could hardly remark upon given that she'd appeared unannounced at an impolite hour. Diantha was certain she had never before considered the anatomy of the male forearm. It—or Lord Marsden's, anyway—was lean and graceful, shot through with prominent veins glowing faintly blue against his skin, which was itself dusted with a fine smattering of hair.

The blue cast of his veins should have brought to mind cold, but she almost fancied she could feel heat radiating from his skin. She'd felt the same earlier, when he'd laid a hand on her sleeve.

Impossible—then and now. Even if he were doing the radiating she was imagining, which he *wasn't*, she was wearing the dress she'd worn to Thea's funeral, and to her mother's before that. It was long-sleeved and made of sturdy bombazine. It had seemed more appropriate to the occasion, which she'd been thinking of as a business call but was in fact more of an ambush.

What did a lady wear to an ambush? She feared she had made a misstep but reminded herself that if she had, her dress was a minor one in the pantheon of the evening's miscalculations.

She turned her attention to the drawer. They were looking at a collection of jewelry. None of it appeared terribly precious—those pieces were probably under lock and key somewhere. This seemed more like the everyday jewelry a peeress would wear. She saw a strand of pearls, some earbobs she expected were paste, though well-made. And a locket, which Lord Marsden had picked up and handed to her.

"Open it."

Diantha knew what she would find. And, yes, pasted inside the locket were small likenesses of Lord Marsden's brothers, one on each side.

"I suppose a mother likes to memorialize her deceased children," she said. And while it was certainly true that any mother would mourn her lost children, the absences in these pictures, in this house, were notable.

She handed him the locket. "How much older were your brothers?"

"Eight years." He dropped the locket back into the drawer with a carelessness she had never seem him display. "And mind you, they were kind enough to me, but we weren't close. How could we be, with that large an age gap? They were busy living their lives, and I was an accident."

"Oh, come now."

"'Tis true. My mother used to jest that she got the heir and the spare over with in one fell swoop and I was the surprise 'spare spare.' She did use the word 'surprise,' and nothing like 'unwanted,' but one could hear the subtext."

Oh, dear. She wanted to say she couldn't imagine anyone being that unkind, but she didn't have to imagine, did she? The world was full of unkind people.

Thinking of Mr. Hill reminded her of her larger mission.

She had clearly failed. Now all she could hope was to extricate herself with a minimum of damage and start working on the idea of a less honorable honorable man. Or perhaps just a less honorable man, period.

"Were we at my country house, Galecroft," Lord Marsden said, "I could show you a memorial to my brothers. Their graves are there, of course, but there are also trees planted in their honor, and a section of the gardens Mother had ripped out and replanted solely with white hydrangeas. And, of course, there are more portraits at Galecroft. Another locket. The one she wears there contains locks of their hair. That"—he slapped the drawer containing the locket rather forcefully—"was merely her 'city locket.' It goes better with the gowns she wears here. Allegedly." He slammed the door of the wardrobe, and soon they were on the move, back down the stairs.

She had no earthly idea what to say. She'd wondered, a moment ago, if Lord Marsden was a closet eccentric. Perhaps he was a misanthrope. The notion was upsetting. She had clearly made a grave error, with her wild proposal, but it would pain her to learn that the earnest Simon Courteney, Earl of Marsden, champion of so many causes, including, it would seem, the rights of ladies, was secretly a cynic.

He came to a halt back in the foyer. Instinctively, she looked up again, almost feeling she'd imagined the rifle-wielding angels. But no, there they were.

"Ah, yes. How could I forget?" One could not mistake the bitterness in his tone. "Another likeness of my brothers. You will, I trust, be familiar with the usual renderings of angels. They may be holding spears, or bows and arrows?"

"Indeed. Or harps." She paused, trying to think of gentler depictions of the Heavenly host. "Or flowers."

"My brothers were avid hunters, so my mother had them immortalized thusly."

How odd. But also how sad. Diantha might not know this version of Lord Marsden, she might have grossly misjudged him, but she understood what he was trying to tell her. She was inclined to face it head-on, to name it.

She looked him in the eye and said, "Earlier, when I said you didn't know what it was like to feel alone, I was wrong. This is the message your tour is meant to impart."

Something in his countenance relaxed a tad, and he gave a curt nod. "I will fetch your coat from the library."

She'd been going to say more, to apologize for the assumption, for coming here at all, but it seemed she was being dismissed.

He was back a few seconds later, helping her into her coat, and as he handed over her bonnet, he fingered the ribbon on it. It was a pretty ribbon, one of her favorites, but of course, he didn't know that. Perhaps it reminded him of someone.

"How are you getting home?" He corrected himself. "How are you getting back to Berkeley Square?"

She appreciated the revision, for it signaled that he understood that Lord Harcourt's home wasn't her home.

Diantha had no home.

"I am walking."

"No, you are not." He sounded very irritated.

"It is not far."

"Be that as it may, I cannot allow it."

"You cannot *allow* it?" She took umbrage. "With due respect, Lord Marsden, I am not a sheltered girl."

He gazed at her for a long time, his face so composed, so impassive, that she wondered if she had imagined the entire interlude wherein he marched her around his house and into his mother's bedchamber and shouted at paintings. He looked now very like the Lord Marsden she knew, the one she had expected to encounter, the calm one who said it was impossible to shock him.

"Very well, then. Good night, Miss Brown."

She was shocked—by his easy agreement, by the way he performed a stiff bow and let her walk out of his house.

Outside, she gulped the cool night air, taking some consolation that although her errand had been an utter failure, at least she was outside. She and Thea used to sit in the garden at night and try to see the stars. She tilted her head back. There wasn't much to see, city and cloud conspiring against her.

She was halfway home when she realized Lord Marsden was following her. Sensing a presence, she glanced over her shoulder, catching him ducking into a shop doorway. She was fairly certain he saw her seeing him, but he said nothing, so neither did she.

She spent the rest of the walk making a mental inventory of gentlemen with whom she was acquainted who were less honorable than Lord Marsden. She didn't know many gentlemen, so it was a very short list, but on it was just the man she needed.

5

The Gentlemen's Cave

September 8, 1823
Earls Trip, day 1

As they drew closer to their destination, Archie perked up. Not that he had previously been un-perked, merely that Simon observed him jiggling with increasing intensity. Archie was, generally, a jiggler. He had trouble calming his nerves, and his hands. But this was something apart from that. It was more of a happy jiggling.

Listen to him: *a happy jiggling.* He sounded like Effie.

Simon knew the feeling, though, the happy-jiggling feeling. He was jiggling internally. There was nothing like an Earls Trip. The journey had helped him shake off that vague feeling of resistance that always accompanied the onset of their holidays.

As they turned up the drive, Effie caught Simon's eye, glanced at Archie's hands, which hovered over his lap as he pressed his fingertips together in rapid succession, and met Simon's gaze again. They shared a bemused smile, Archie oblivious as he leaned his entire torso out the window.

"Here we are!" Archie sounded like he had when they were schoolboys anticipating something wonderful, and he hopped out of the coach before it fully stopped.

"I marvel that we've never been here before, Archie," Effie said a few moments later as he and Simon alit. They stood and took in the redbrick house, modest compared to Mollybrook, but still handsome, shaded by graceful oaks.

"I hated coming here as a boy." Archie eyed the house with curiosity, as if seeing it for the first time. "Father and I came on annual hunting trips, and from the moment I arrived, I began counting down the days—hours—until we were meant to leave."

That accorded with the stories Simon and Effie had heard over the years.

"And yet . . ." Archie tilted his head as he continued to contemplate the house.

"You wanted his approval," Effie said. Effie understood the often complex relationships between men and their fathers.

Simon was the odd man out here, for his bothersome parent was his mother. He hardly remembered his father. Not that he'd been so terribly young when the old earl died. Just that he and his sire had so rarely been in the same place at the same time. Simon had been shipped off to school as soon as he'd been old enough, and in the summers at Galecroft, he'd made himself scarce, running off to amuse himself in the chapel with books and drawing paper. His chief memory of Father was sitting at the table at Christmas or Easter or some such occasion that necessitated the entire family be in company, and listening to him talk. Or listening to Father and James and Michael talk. The adage about children being seen and not heard applied to Simon. Not that anyone told him that directly. More that he had been, initially, too young to meaningfully take part in the discussions, and by the time he was, the dye had been cast. No one needed to hear from the spare spare.

"Indeed," Archie said. "I used to look forward to those trips with my father, at least in the early years. It always felt like a chance to clear the slate, so to speak."

"Did it work?" Simon asked, though he was almost certain he knew the answer.

"No."

"It never does," Simon said, and it was only when the other two swung around with matching looks of mild alarm that he realized how bitter his tone had been. He tempered it. "I merely meant that people don't change."

"Don't they?" Effie asked. "Perhaps not usually, but is it not possible? Did *I* not change?"

"No," Simon said firmly. "You arranged the circumstances of your life such that your true self, which had previously been sublimated, could come to the fore."

"Goodness, Simon! I adore you for saying that. That was equal parts poetical and logical."

"It is also true," Archie said. "Though you were not so sublimated that *we* didn't know your true self."

"Yes, but you were the only ones who did," Effie said earnestly.

Archie clapped a hand on Effie's back and said, in a jocular tone that signaled an end to the sentimental portion of the afternoon, "Come around back, and I'll show you the pool."

"Shall we carry our things inside first?" Simon asked, looking around. A groom had met the coach and was, together with Archie's driver, leading the horses off. But no servant from inside had met them.

"I've given almost everyone a week off," Archie said. "Except for the housekeeper, the cook, one maid, and one groom. Remember our year at Quintrell Castle?"

"Yes, indeed," Simon said. "I think I still have the lump on my head from when a chunk of plaster fell from the ceiling and nearly took me out." He eyed Effie, who'd been responsible for planning—or not planning—that year's holiday.

"Yes," said Effie, cheerfully absorbing the implied criticism, "but I think what Archie is getting at is that it was great fun to be on our own that year."

"Yes, we discovered the joys of our evening meal being served all at once, in its entirety, instead of in a series of removes," Archie said.

"You can eat the pudding first if you like," Effie said. "Or exclusively."

"And such an approach comes with a pleasant lack of hovering servants," Archie said. "The ladies will arrive in a week, and the staff will have much more work than they've had in years, given that I'm almost never here, so I also thought an unexpected week's holiday might have a bolstering effect."

"So we are on our own," Simon said. It was a comforting thought, when so much of the past month had been . . . not comforting. The image of Miss Brown, in her severe black dress, was as fresh and at the forefront of his memory as ever. He shook off his unease. "And presumably, the house won't be literally falling to pieces, so our solitude won't come with a side of grievous bodily harm."

"We can gather our things later," Archie said. "I want to show you the pool first."

They followed Archie around to the back of the house. The garden was newborn, as evidenced by its extreme greenness and uniformity. At its edge, right before the manicured turf gave way to rougher grass, was a pool. One reached it via a gravel path. They followed Archie down it. From here, one could see—and hear—a brook in the distance, emerging from the woods that bordered the house.

"Oh, Archie, you've really done it," Effie said.

"It isn't much, and I've yet to have any flowers or trees planted—I thought to consult with Olive and Clem on that—but I am rather pleased with myself."

Effie squatted at the edge of the pool, which was lined with slabs of limestone. He took off his gloves and dipped a hand in. "Oh my, that is chilly!"

"Well, it's groundwater. It's not like at Bath where the water is warm. Which is why . . ." He pointed to another path radiating out from the pool. "I've had that firepit constructed. We may warm ourselves here after immersion."

"Perhaps also before," Simon suggested. "It might provide a kind of inoculation against the shock of the cold water."

"Oh, and we can cook meat over the flames!" Effie said excitedly, but then he looked at Archie guiltily. "Or, we can cook vegetables over the flames."

"I am looking mightily forward to some roast lamb," Archie said. "In making the arrangements for most of the servants to take a holiday, I did particularly request a leg of lamb for night one."

Effie and Simon shared an amused gaze over Archie's head. Archie had said the same thing last year but, once presented with the meat he'd professed to want, he hadn't been able to eat any of it—his animal-loving wife, who herself eschewed the eating of meat, had influenced him even in her absence. Effie gave a little nod that seemed to Simon to say, *We'll believe that when we see it.*

"Though I don't think a leg of lamb can be cooked over an open fire," Archie said. "At least not by us."

"Shall we try out the pool?" Simon suggested.

"Yes, but first let me show you around inside, and we can decide on sleeping arrangements."

Archie led them down another gravel path, a longer one, that eventually terminated at a small outbuilding. "This is new. A dormitory of sorts. I thought we could lodge here when the ladies arrive so they may have the run of the main house. The question is, would we prefer to sleep here this week, too, or to start in the main house and move here for week two?"

"Archie," Effie said, "I don't mean to be indelicate, but where will you and your lovely wife. . . ?" He cleared his throat.

"Are you asking because you truly want to know or because you're wondering where you and your lovely wife can . . ." Archie cleared his throat in the same manner Effie had.

"Oh, for Heaven's sake," Simon said. "You lot are besotted. How embarrassing for you."

"Well," Archie said, "the ladies shall have their own bedchambers in the main house."

Simon wondered if that included Miss Brown, or if she was staying with Archie's mother. Not that it mattered in the least.

"Hmm." Effie wrinkled his nose as if the notion of visiting his wife in her bedchamber in the house did not appeal.

"There is also an old shack of sorts in which my father used to keep his hunting rifles," Archie said. "But I've taken your advice to heart and had them all locked in the root cellar. So if you've a mind to tryst in a falling-down armory, have at it."

Effie seemed cheered. "And where would one find this falling-down armory?"

"Behind this structure. There isn't a path. You shall have to hack your way through the underbrush."

"How thrilling."

Archie led them through the front door of the outbuilding, which opened onto a small sitting area with a settee oriented toward a fireplace, a sideboard that appeared well-stocked with libations and glassware, a small dining table, and a side table stocked with a chessboard and several decks of cards. The whole place was rather dim, there being very few windows.

"'Tis a sort of gentlemen's cave!" Effie exclaimed.

An archway in the middle of the large space divided the living area from the sleeping area, the latter of which was furnished with three beds. They were tucked closely together with only a few feet between them. Small nightstands stood between them.

"It is like being back at school," Simon observed, and though he was not, generally speaking, nostalgic for their school days, he did think back fondly on some of the nights they passed whispering in the dark.

"It is like being back at school, except without the Nigel Nettlefells of the world," Archie said, naming a particularly odious classmate of theirs. "Of course, in the main house, we can each have our own bedchambers. So it's entirely up to you two."

"Let's stay here in the gentlemen's cave!" Effie said. "Hold up. What's in there?" He led the way to the small room in question. "Is this a water closet?"

"It is," Archie said.

"Well, aren't you just the most modern?"

"I figured since I was building new, I might as well install the latest conveniences."

"How does it work?" Simon, who had always been interested in architecture and associated fields, asked.

"There's a cistern on the roof that collects rainwater. In theory. I don't think it's rained very much. When you open the valve, gravity pushes the water down. I would demonstrate, but one doesn't want to waste water."

"Well, that settles it," Effie said. "We shall stay here." Seeming then to think better of himself, he added, "If you agree, Simon. Perhaps you'd rather have your own space. Be free of us."

In truth, Simon could think of nothing he'd rather do than bunk in with the boys, just as they used to. "Let us stay here." He rolled his eyes, but he was grinning. "A decision I shall surely come to regret after a week's time."

Two hours later, they'd dined—Archie had, as predicted, not eaten the lamb—stripped, and were gathered around the edge of the pool.

Effie dipped a toe in. "Oh, my Heavens, that is cold!"

"Yes," Archie said. "This may be the fatal flaw in my grand plan."

Simon tested the water. "It's not that bad. The key is not to overthink it. Just get in."

Simon, demonstrating, had to swallow the yelp that rose though his chest—the water was bloody freezing—in favor of remarking, calmly, "Oh, capital. You've got built-in benches."

"Yes." Archie tapped the edge of the pool. "Out of this same stone."

Simon settled himself and tilted his head back. It wasn't fully dark yet; the sky still retained a hint of navy. The first stars were winking out.

Simon's attention was drawn back to earth by Effie, who, though he was slender and graceful on land, entered the pool as if he were an elephant, slashing and making quite the racket. "This *is* that bad, Simon!"

"Hush," Simon said. "Breathe."

Effie rolled his eyes.

"No one is forcing your hand here, Ef."

"Oh, I know. I'm just being difficult."

Archie joined them, letting loose a low whistle at the cold.

"You get used to it," Simon said.

It was true, with the cold water but also more generally. A person could get used to less than ideal circumstances.

"Gurglewood is a terrible name for this place, Arch," Effie said, and Simon reminded himself that these were, in fact, ideal circumstances. The water was cold, but he was with his mates. A fire awaited them. Earls Trip had begun.

6

The Dowager Countess of Marsden

August 13, 1823
Twenty-six days before Earls Trip

When Simon called on his brother James's widow the morning after Miss Brown's extraordinary visit, he was afraid he wasn't fully right in the head.

"Simon!" Frances swept into the drawing room in which he'd been installed, her cheeks pink and her smile wide. "To what do I owe the pleasure?"

Good question. He had no idea why he was here. Just that he'd awakened this morning, after a profoundly unrestful night, feeling a pull to visit James's widow.

"I haven't seen you for ages," she said as she offered her cheek for him to kiss.

He heard censure in her tone, though probably there was none. Frances wasn't the kind of person who communicated through subtle signals and undercurrents of sentiment. He was accustomed to being communicated to thusly, especially by women, but that didn't mean everyone was guilty of it.

He had to check himself: That wasn't true anymore, was it? He didn't communicate a great deal with women generally, but these days, most of the women in his life were generous of spirit, easy with their conversation and, he liked to think, their friendship. He was thinking, of course, of the wives of his friends: Clementine and Julianna.

He was thinking of Miss Brown.

Miss Brown, whom he had treated terribly last night, marching her around the house and shouting at her.

By the sober light of morning, his behavior seemed incomprehensible. It was as if some other man had taken over.

In his defense, perhaps that was because another lady seemed to have taken over Miss Brown. The Miss Brown he knew would never have come to him—to anyone—asking him to ruin her. He took some comfort in their mutual incomprehensibility.

"I am sorry I haven't called in so long," he said to Frances.

She pulled him to sit next to her on a settee. "*I* am sorry I haven't called on *you* in so long."

He smiled. This was exactly what he meant about generosity of spirit. Frances had been kind to him from the first day they met. Simon had been a mere boy, but her kindness hadn't been false. It had been accompanied by genuine interest in him as a person, something his younger self had found novel and compelling.

"I've been terribly busy," Frances added, wagging her eyebrows in a fashion that suggested he was meant to ask why.

"What has you so occupied, if I may know?"

"I shan't tell you." He was about to demur when she added, "I shall *show* you." She rang a bell, and a footman appeared. "Could you have Wallace join us, please?"

Simon sat up straighter. He hadn't expected they'd be joined by anyone else. He didn't *want* to be joined by anyone else. Even though he didn't know why he was here.

And who was this gentleman Frances was calling by his Christian name?

"My lady." The footman opened the door and seemed to be holding it for an invisible guest.

Oh! Wallace was a cocker spaniel. There wasn't much that made Simon laugh out loud, but the appearance of Wallace did.

"Simon," Frances said with exaggerated solemnity, "I'll thank you to temper your amusement and meet Wallace."

"He's very handsome."

Wallace had black ears and a white face and big brown eyes.

"In fact, he rather matches your own countenance."

Frances also had dark hair and pale skin and big brown eyes.

"Are you calling me handsome?"

Oh, dear. Implying that a lady was handsome instead of pretty or fetching or what have you was probably a mistake. Simon winced. He wasn't good at people.

But it didn't matter, for Frances understood him. "Wallace is indeed very handsome, as am I. Unlike me, though, Wallace is very young. Four months to be exact, and he is a terrible handful. He is why I haven't called. I've been up at all hours with him."

Simon refrained from pointing out that a servant could train Wallace. That wasn't how Frances lived her life. When you were hers, you were hers. His brother had been very lucky. Until he hadn't.

"I have to say," he remarked as Frances picked up Wallace and settled him on her lap, "I never took you for a dog person."

James had kept hunting dogs, and Simon had never seen Frances pay them any mind, much less dote on them to such an extent that she cleared her social calendar.

"I'm not. Or I wasn't. But the dreadful neighbors had a litter, and Wallace was the runt. And, well, now I'm a dog person."

"Were they set to put him down?"

"Not strictly based on his size. Which would have been one thing, but apparently Wallace is small of stature *and* of intellect."

Simon laughed. Again.

"Well, not 'apparently,'" Frances went on. "Wallace is undeniably quite stupid."

She lifted him so he was at face level and cooed, "Handsome, but a bit dim, isn't that right? I have a type, don't I?" She laughed as she returned Wallace to her lap.

"Oh, don't look so scandalized," she said to Simon. "Your

brother had many wonderful qualities. He was generous and fun and, you have to admit, extremely lovely. But you got the brains in the family, and you know it."

Simon wasn't sure how to respond, but her words made him smile. Frances had always been cheeky. His mother had called it brazenness, but Simon had always found Frances's forthright wit refreshing.

"So, yes, the neighbors were planning to put Wallace down." She shuddered. Frances had a tendency to present herself as world-weary, but in truth, she had a soft heart.

"I'd forgotten how terrible the neighbors here are," Simon said.

When Frances first married James, she had regaled them with appalling tales of her parents' dramatic and entitled neighbors.

"I hoped they had mellowed in my time away," Frances said. "But instead, I think they've become meaner and louder."

"You could have stayed at Galecroft, you know." He had told her that no small number of times, but it bore repeating.

"And fight your mother over the dower house? I think not."

He resisted pointing out that Mother had not moved to the dower house. She would never do that.

"We both know there will only ever be one Dowager Countess of Marsden." Frances's eyes twinkled. "Even if there are two."

In terms of titles, things were indeed messy. When Father died, James, as the older of the twins by two minutes, inherited and became the Earl of Marsden. Frances therefore became the Countess of Marsden, promoting Mother to the rank of Dowager Countess of Marsden—though Mother hadn't seen it as a promotion, a fact she'd made abundantly clear to everyone. And now that James was dead, Frances was *also* the Dowager Countess of Marsden, though there were subtle differences in the way the two women, were they ever to appear in company together, would be referred to and addressed.

But, legalities and social conventions aside, Simon knew exactly what Frances meant when she said there couldn't be two dowagers.

"Poor Simon, you're awash in widows. You'd better never

marry," Frances teased, "or there shall be one Countess of Marsden and two Dowager Countesses of Marsden, and we shall all expire of bewilderment." She must have seen something in his countenance he had thought hidden, for she suddenly looked alarmed. "You know I am in jest, do you not? Nothing would make me happier than for you to marry—to marry for love, I mean."

He cleared his throat. "There's that cottage near the lake at Galecroft—quite apart from the dower house. I told you I'd've been happy to fix it up." He wasn't sure why he was hammering away at this matter she considered settled. Just that traditionally, the widow of a peer stayed on as a member of the household. He felt a duty of kinship. But it went beyond that: He liked Frances. He missed her. "Or for that matter, you could've elected to stay in the house here in Town. You still could." He hesitated over saying more. To do so made him feel unpleasantly vulnerable. He decided to risk it. "I should enjoy your company."

"Ah, Simon, and I should enjoy yours, but, if I may speak forthrightly: dear Heavens, no." She spoke with another twinkle in her eye, but Simon understood that she meant what she said.

"Mother isn't in Town that often," he said weakly. It was true, even if it was an insufficient argument.

Her expression turned earnest, serious. "With my beloved James gone, why would I endure your mother in any dose?"

He understood. The reason he was in residence at the London house so often was precisely to avoid his mother, who spent most of her time at Galecroft.

And that, essentially, was why he was here, was it not? He could pretend not to know, but he was here to question Frances about what it was like to be his mother's daughter by marriage.

"I was willing to endure her for James," she went on. "Without him, I'm not. Even for the pleasure of your company, my dear Simon. It is as simple as that, and as cruel."

"It's not cruel to want to *avoid* cruelty. It's sensible."

Which was exactly what he was doing, with his disinclination toward matrimony while Mother was still around. Right?

He ought to just ask his questions. A natural opening was available now in that they were already talking about the challenges presented by Mother.

"Frances, would you tell me what your relationship with Mother was like?"

"It wasn't good."

"So I've gathered. And I understand. But I should like to know the details of its . . . not-goodness."

She narrowed her eyes at him. "Why?"

"Call it a need for fellow feeling."

"Well, then, I shan't mince words."

He had to smile. "*Have* you been?"

"I have indeed." She set Wallace on the floor by her feet. "Your mother was an absolute harridan." She smiled, a bit sadly. "Would you like me to elaborate?"

He was a bit taken aback, though he shouldn't have been. "Please do."

"Your brother and I hoped to have children, but we were not so blessed."

That was, alas, not a surprise. Simon had wondered—silently, to himself—why his brother and Frances hadn't, in their several years of marriage, had children. His mother had wondered, too, *un*silently.

"Your mother poked at the topic constantly. It's difficult to explain exactly what it was like, to be in her sights. She would often give me gifts for our nonexistent child, for example. A christening gown she had embroidered for 'if it is ever needed.'"

Simon could hear the tone in which the words would have been delivered—a performative sort of martyred resignation. One couldn't find fault with the words themselves, but the delivery gave them an entirely different meaning.

"Yet at the same time, I often got the sense that she *didn't* want James to get an heir."

"How do you mean?" Simon said, though he thought he understood.

"She resented me, I think, for the time James spent with me."

Yes, Simon knew this feeling. Still, he felt compelled to issue a protest. "You were his *wife*."

"Yes, but I think she fancied herself the most important woman in his life. In Michael's, too. I shudder to think what life would have been like had Michael married as well. By way of example, whenever I tried to do something for James, bringing him a cup of tea, say, she would, were we out of sight of anyone else, take it from me rather forcibly and do it herself. I can't imagine what it would have been like had she been acting that way twice over."

"I am sorry," Simon said. Her tale reinforced his own resolve to leave marriage for the future—the post-Mother future.

"And she always knew, somehow, when my menses were late." Frances regarded him. "Am I causing you embarrassment?"

"No," he said, though she was. What was a little embarrassment in exchange for the truth?

"I assume because the maids told the housekeeper and the housekeeper told her." Frances's voice cracked, and she cleared her throat before continuing. "But it matters not. The point is, she always seemed to know. She would make small comments, indicating that she and I were in on a shared secret."

Simon had observed Frances to have a quick wit and a sparkling personality. She was quick to laugh and always seemed to be at ease in the world in the same way Michael and James had been—and that Simon himself was not. But here, her voice had gone uncharacteristically flat.

"You see, I got with child twice over the years." She closed her eyes and wrung her hands. "I lost them both."

"Oh, Frances," Simon began, his heart breaking, but she held up a hand, and he understood that she wanted to continue her tale. He well knew how expressions of genuine sympathy could stop one in one's tracks. It was probably the reason some part of him resisted embarking on Earls Trip each year—it could be almost painful to be with people who understood one's situation and empathized.

"Your mother gave me a certain type of tea when I was expecting," Frances continued. "She would tell me with a wink that it was good for a lady in my condition. I used to think it a gesture of *kindness*." Bitterness had crept into her tone. "I thought it her way of making an overture of friendship, or at least of peace. I have observed, in my life, that people like your mother who are full of bile, who are jealous and ungenerous with their time and regard, are usually that way because someone made them so. Most people aren't born villainous. I still believe that, though your mother certainly tested the bounds of that belief.

"So I—foolishly, recklessly, it turned out—accepted the apparent olive branch. I drank the tea. Which tasted terrible, I might add.

"The last time I drank the tea—the second time I was with child—was a week before James and Michael died. I made an offhand remark to Julie, a new lady's maid who'd come to Galecroft—you remember when Becky retired?"

Simon nodded. Becky had been a servant of forty years and was—he hoped—enjoying her retirement.

"I told Julie, in an attempt to take her into my confidence, the way one does with a servant with whom one is going to become intimately acquainted whether one likes it or no, that your mother was bringing me tea, and that it tasted awful. Which meant I told her about the pregnancies. I was trying to ingratiate myself, I suppose. She seemed alarmed. She asked me if it had been belladonna tea. It couldn't be, I replied. Your mother was terrible, but she can't have been *that* terrible." She paused, seeming to gather herself. "The new maid asked me to describe the tea's taste, and the next day, brought me a cup and asked me to try it, to confirm it was the same type your mother had been giving me." She paused, her lips pursed. "I did."

Oh no. *No.* Simon didn't know what belladonna was, but he didn't have to, to know what was coming next. He wanted to cover his face with his hands, but it was important to give Frances his full attention.

"Belladonna is an herb that spurs the premature expulsion of a pregnancy. Midwives give it to ladies who find themselves in a bind."

"*Frances,*" Simon said, unembarrassed by the anguish in his voice, by the tears he was suddenly doing a poor job holding back.

"Yes." She bent down and picked up Wallace and returned him to her lap, threading her fingers through his fur.

Simon wondered if he'd gotten everything about Frances wrong. Perhaps she wasn't fun and breezy, so much as she was covering up great anguish. Perhaps Wallace wasn't so much a sudden charity case as he was something to do with her ever-wringing hands.

"So," she said, "you can see why, although I miss you and I rather dislike living here with my parents, I cannot move back into your household."

"I understand."

"When James and Michael died, my first thought was that your mother would never get over it. Not that *I* would never get over it, though I felt myself plunged into the pits of grief. Just that she would become impossible."

"To say I'm sorry feels entirely inadequate."

"Be sorry for what I went through, but don't be sorry for what she did."

"What's the difference?"

"The difference is that you are a fine man, empathetic and kind. You are not responsible for the behavior of your mother. You are not responsible for anyone besides yourself."

If only that were true. Simon was responsible for so very many people. In some ways, as a member of the House of Lords, he was responsible for everyone in England. In a more concrete sense, he was responsible for the staff at his houses and his tenants at Galecroft. In an even more concrete sense, as the head of his family, he was responsible for certain individuals, namely, his mother.

The image of a woman in a black dress asking him for help intruded on his list.

"Besides," Frances went on, "I don't want to be a widow the rest of my life." She gave a small chuckle, a bitter one, but it was nevertheless good to hear. "Of course, I shall always be a widow. But I don't want it to be *all* that I am. Living in your household as the dowager countess—the second dowager countess—would remind me at every turn of my status. We women have it quite difficult, you know. We are wives, thus defined as appendages to our husbands. But then once they are gone and we are widows, we somehow remain appendages. Have you heard tell of soldiers returned from the wars with legs amputated who say they can still feel the pain of the missing limb?"

"I have."

"It's rather macabre, but I see myself as the reverse. The limb without the body. Here"—she gestured around the room—"I may at least be a daughter. Still an appendage, I suppose, but of a different sort."

What she had said devastated Simon, though he could not argue with her logic. "You could marry again," he suggested quietly. He would be happy to see it occur. He would attend and strew flowers at her and her chosen groom.

"Yes. Even in the depths of my initial grief, an awareness dwelled. I was still young, or young enough. I suppose I harbored a secret hope that I might marry again someday, and have children. Perhaps that was silly. Now that so many years have passed, it seems so."

"I don't think it's silly, and it hasn't been that many years." Something caught in Simon's throat. Frances would make a wonderful mother.

"Well, there would have been no chance had I'd remained at Galecroft. Can you imagine how your mother would have reacted if she'd seen me entertaining suitors—after a suitable period of mourning, of course."

"No, indeed." He smiled, but only because Frances was smiling. She had recovered her signature good humor. He didn't know, anymore, though, if it was genuine or if it was a front, if it papered over other, less amiable sentiments. "The thing I can't work out is that Mother was so devoted to James, to the idea of him as the heir. To Michael, too, but mostly to James. It should follow that she would *want* him to have a son. It should follow that she would be supportive of his marriage. Kind to his wife—the mother of the next heir. Or, failing that, at least anticipating the arrival of said heir."

"You would think so." Frances shrugged. "I suppose that's partly why I never gave any thought to the tea. Even if it wasn't an olive branch, it never occurred to me that she wouldn't be looking forward to a grandchild. A child who would have been, after all, half of her beloved James."

"It could still happen, Frances," Simon said quietly. "You could still have a family."

"Oh, no, I am too old for that now. I would have been quite an old mother even back then. I recognize that initial impulse, after James's death, as a kind of hysteria. But I have enjoyed a kind of freedom these past years, even living here with my parents, that I wouldn't have had if I'd remained in your household." She grinned, a big wide one signaling the end of the wrenching portion of their conversation. "Although, one never knows. Perhaps I am about to meet a charming widower with lovely children who won't resent me at all." She threw her head back and laughed, and Simon's heart swelled with affection for her, but also with sadness for all that had befallen her. And with anger for the actions of his mother.

It was a great deal for one heart to contain.

"Are you quite all right?" She'd stopped laughing and was regarding him with concern. "I have overstepped. I am sorry."

"You haven't overstepped whatsoever. Or if you have, I'm sorry you didn't do it sooner."

Her brow furrowed.

He clarified. "I'm sorry it took my brothers' deaths and the despicable actions of my mother for us to have this conversation."

"I am, too. I can see so much of James in you, even as you are simultaneously your own person."

"What was he like?"

"You're asking me to tell you what your own brother was like?"

"Yes. He and Michael were so much older than I. We rarely spent time together. And Mother was so . . ."

"Obsessed with them?"

He chuckled. "Of course, I loved him. I loved both of them. But in the way a younger brother looks up to older brothers. I don't know that I truly *knew* either of them." He paused, wondering whether to say more, but what was this visit turning out to be but an opportunity to voice what had remained unsaid for far too long? "That was why I was so fond of you when we first met. You paid me so much kind attention. You may not remember, but I had an interest in architecture, and I had sketched a plan for a tenants' cottage that I thought would be more comfortable, and efficient, than those we had at Galecroft. You did a smashing job feigning interest in it."

She regarded him for a long time. "It was not feigned. You were a remarkable young man. You still are."

"Not so young anymore," he said, attempting to mimic her blithe affect but, he feared, failing.

She didn't speak for a long moment, but when she did, her face had softened so utterly that she looked years younger. "Your brother could make me laugh like no one else. He wasn't a scholar, but he had a . . . silly heart. I know that sounds ridiculous. He was . . ." Her attention was drawn by Wallace, who was attempting to wiggle his way out of her lap. "James was like a retriever, loyal and sweet and silly. My suitors prior to him had been much more serious-minded. One of them fancied himself a poet." She rolled her eyes to demonstrate what she'd thought of her former swain's literary ambitions. "Let us just say that he did not have the talent that your friend Lord Stonely does." Frances set the still wriggling Arthur on the floor and patted his head. "James used to apologize to me about your mother. About the way she treated me. And he used to lament that she wasn't doing right by you."

"He did?" Simon had always assumed his brothers took the maternal attention they commanded as their due.

"Oh, yes. He was forever fretting that she and your father weren't taking enough of an interest in your education. He was worried you weren't genuinely interested in the Church."

"I was . . ." What? "I was not *not* interested in the Church," he said weakly.

Thankfully, she said no more on the topic. "Simon, may I ask—of course you don't have to answer—why this line of questioning all these years later?"

No. Well, yes, she could ask. But he could not answer. Not in any specific way. But perhaps he could tell her a not-lie. "I have been thinking, in a broad, generalized way, about marriage. About the succession, given that I'm the only one left. About what it might be like to bring a wife into the household."

"Oh, no, you can't do that."

"Right."

"It's your mother or your wife. Both can't survive."

He nodded curtly. "I thought as much. Thank you for . . . illuminating things for me so thoroughly." He was, suddenly, exhausted. He didn't know how to extricate himself.

Well, no, given all that had happened this evening, all that had been said, why was he standing on ceremony? He rose. "I am sorry to leave so abruptly, but I am, truth be told, a bit overcome."

"Of course." She stood and came around to embrace him. He wanted to hold on for longer than was seemly.

He forced himself to let her go. "I understand why you stay away, but you know you are always welcome in my home—both of them."

"I like it better when you come here."

"Well, then, I shall endeavor to do so more often."

She graced him with a smile, a great big one. "Please do."

7

The Other Dowager Countess of Marsden

August 14, 1823
Twenty-five days before Earls Trip

"Simon, darling." The Dowager Countess of Marsden—the first one—swept into the library as if she owned the place.

She did not own the place, the fact of which Archie and Effie frequently reminded Simon.

Simon took a breath. He had not expected to see his mother today. It had only been a day since his audience with Frances, and his heart was still battered by all that had been revealed. He had hardly slept or eaten. He'd known he was going to have to say something to his mother, *do* something about her. He couldn't hear what he'd heard, absorb what he'd absorbed—into his very bones, it felt like—and remain disengaged.

Still, he hadn't thought he would have to do so just yet.

Simon's mother appeared to float as she approached his desk; she paused—hovered—for a moment before lowering herself into a chair in a single, smooth movement.

When he was a boy, Simon had thought her apparent floating charming. It had made her seem larger than life. Larger than his life, anyway, which wasn't saying much. Of course, it was only her penchant for overlong dresses, and not any kind of supernatural bent, that was responsible for his childish illusion. It was important to remember that.

"I thought we might go over next month's invitations," she said, setting a stack of paper on the desk.

"I didn't expect you so soon." He'd known his mother was planning a stint in Town, but last she'd written it was to inform him to expect her the week after next. At which point, he had only a week to weather until Earls Trip—and he had been considering spending that week at Galecroft, even though it would mean a terrible lot of travel hither and thon.

Not that the particulars of when she showed up should matter. What was he going to be ready to say, or do, in two weeks' time that he wasn't ready to say, or do, today? *I didn't expect you so soon* was an excuse, and a weak one at that. He might not be ready or able to solve all the problems of the House of Marsden, but he could at least not lie to himself.

She plucked the top invitation off the pile. "We have been invited to the Amesbury ball, and I've already sent our acceptance. I didn't see any way to decline."

"I believe the way to decline is simply to write a note to that effect. You're terribly sorry to miss it, you are overdue for a catch-up, perhaps you can get together next time you are in Town, et cetera, et cetera."

He had spoken sharply. Both his words and his tone were unprecedented, and she had taken note. He could tell by the ever so slight raising of her eyebrows. She had them under control within seconds, but he, so attuned to the minute shifts in mood of this woman, had noted their brief rise.

"The Amesbury ball is one of the major events of the autumn," she said. "Historically not very well attended, as most people have already scattered with the end of the Season, but it had quite the buzz about it last year, and it will be a good way to test the waters."

"Test the waters?"

"You're nearly thirty, Simon. We've both got to face the fact that you must marry."

"I *beg* your pardon?" Where the *hell* that that come from?

"How will that ever happen," she went on, ignoring his query, "if you never *go* anywhere?"

For a brief moment, Simon wondered if his mother was, in fact, a witch. She had never, not once, brought up the idea of his marrying. She hadn't said a word about the succession. He had always assumed it was because of her . . . not to put too fine a point on it, but her fixation on his brothers. And, after his heart-wrenching conversation with Frances, he wondered if she cared about the next generation at all.

Had she somehow heard his conversation with Frances? Did she know what had prompted him to seek out his brother's widow? Could she see inside his heart?

Dear God. He needed to get a hold of himself.

"We've both got to face the fact, you say," he said, trying to buy some time to get his thoughts in order. He'd always had the idea that many unmarried men of his station found themselves the object of motherly meddling. Goodness, there was that opening line of *Pride and Prejudice*: "It is a truth universally acknowledged that a single man in possession of a good fortune must be in want of a wife." Vastly amusing in the context of a novel but perhaps less so in real life.

"Yes," she said, gazing at him evenly as if daring him to defy her.

"I cannot attend the Amesbury ball. I shall be on my annual trip with Harcourt and Stonely," he said, as if geographic absence were the only reason he wouldn't be attending.

She looked put out. "Well, I shall be attending a musicale this evening, hosted by Miss Olive Morgan, your Harcourt's sister by marriage. Some kind of experimental orchestra." She wrinkled her nose. "But the music is no matter. Miss Morgan is very popular among young ladies. There will be scads of them there." She paused, tilted her head. "We might even consider Miss Morgan herself. She is odd, to be sure, but her pedigree is good."

Oh, dear God in Heaven. He took a breath. "I have already sent my regrets to Miss Morgan for the musicale." He'd considered going, purely to show his support for Olive, who was increasingly acting as hostess in her father's household. She was developing a penchant for events Mother deemed experimental—odd musical performances, salons where people recited poetry Simon did not understand. In the end, Simon's antisocial nature and disinclination toward the unusual fare Olive showcased—he was a beginner when it came to ordinary novels, after all—had prevailed.

"Well, I have not sent *my* regrets," his mother said. "I shall attend, if you would be so good as to escort me."

If you would be so good as to escort me meant, in this context, that it was a given that he would. Simon had no idea what to do, in the bigger scheme of things, but he did know one thing: If he gave in here, it would mean he was ceding to her campaign to "test the waters" when it came to the marriage mart.

"I cannot attend," he said, attempting to use his "Parliament voice." The boys were always telling him he was very impressive when speechifying—had that been part of how Miss Brown had been misled as to what kind of man he was?—and he had of late been attempting to use that same tone, or timbre, in regular life. "I am otherwise engaged."

"What are you doing that is more important than—"

"I must take my leave, in fact. I am overdue. Good day, Mother."

What Simon had to do that was more important than attending Olive's musicale was to call upon Archie and his mother. They were in Town, and he did try to call when that was the case.

It was possible, however, that Archie himself would not be at home. He might in fact be at Olive's musicale. Archie's wife, Clementine, who was Olive's sister, was *not* in Town, but Archie, while probably disinclined toward spending an evening listening to an experimental orchestra, was exceedingly fond of his sister by marriage.

As Simon turned onto Berkeley Square—he had decided to walk to Archie's house in order to shake off the encounter with his mother—he considered what, if anything, he might say to Miss Brown. The passage of another day since her extraordinary visit had him even more chagrined. Having reflected on the matter a bit more—well, a great deal more; it was very nearly all he'd been thinking about—he had come to the conclusion that while he regretted the manner in which he'd delivered his message, he did not regret the content of said message. Miss Brown had misunderstood him on two counts. First, in thinking that he could participate in her wild ruination scheme, and, second, in assuming he was the type of person who wouldn't understand what it was like to be alone in the world. But misunderstanding was not a crime. It was an error, and one that should have been corrected more gently.

It was a lovely day, the blue sky just beginning to give way to dusk. Archie was very likely to be at home in the garden with his mother and Miss Brown. Nay, it was almost certain. Archie, a devoted outdoorsman, would not want to be closed up inside on such an afternoon.

Simon was greeted warmly by Mrs. Saunders. "I'm sorry to tell you that his lordship is not at home."

"Oh," Simon said, having apparently been convinced enough by his own lie to be mildly surprised by this news.

She gestured for his hat. "He is attending Miss Morgan's musicale."

"Right. That was tonight, wasn't it?" His face heated as a lie to himself became a lie out in the world. "I admit I am not the ideal audience for musicales. I sent my regrets."

"Lady Harcourt will be delighted to see you, though."

Yes, but would Miss Brown be delighted to see him? Almost certainly not.

"How is the countess of late?" he asked.

"Largely unchanged from when you last saw her." Mrs. Saunders led the way out to the back garden where the lady in question—and her companion—were sitting at a table under a small but stately beech tree. He studied them for a moment before his presence was announced. If he didn't know better, he'd have thought they were mother and daughter, the way they sat together yet did not converse, each woman absorbed in her own pursuit, Miss Brown penning a letter and the dowager painting at an easel. There was an air of quiet amiability about them, of familiarity, as if they had passed many a summer afternoon in this fashion.

"My lady, Miss Brown," Mrs. Saunders said, and Simon regretted that his presence was going to upend the serene scene.

Indeed, Miss Brown fumbled her quill and quickly slipped the letter she'd been writing into an envelope and the envelope into a book.

The women turned, and as Mrs. Saunders finished announcing him and took her leave, Simon almost had to laugh at the identical looks of bewilderment on their faces.

The dowager was bewildered because she was trying to place him. He was accustomed to that.

"Marsden, you say?"

"My lady," he said, going to stand before her and bowing. "Yes, though you may remember me more readily as Archie's school friend Simon. And my brother James—or my father before him—as the Earl of Marsden."

The lady made a vague noise of agreement, but Simon knew from experience that she didn't remember him. The points of reference he'd given—his family, and, more tragically, her own son—were out of her reach today, as they had been most days recently.

Miss Brown's bewilderment, however, was less easily parsed. She hadn't expected him, and now that he was here, she probably he no idea what to expect *from* him.

He wanted to tell her that he had come in peace.

"Have you met my friend, Miss Brown?" the dowager asked. It was a good day, then, relatively speaking, if she knew Miss Brown. To hear Archie tell it, she had of late often mistaken Miss Brown for her own mother.

"I have indeed."

"She is very pretty, don't you agree?"

"I do," Simon said, praying that the burning sensation in his ears and cheeks was not accompanied by a telltale redness. They had navigated exchanges like this before, the dowager's affliction having relaxed her sense of propriety. If she'd asked this question two days ago, Simon would have agreed easily—for it was a true statement—unafflicted by burning skin, and they would have moved on.

Also, Archie would have been here.

"I am sorry you missed his lordship," Miss Brown said, moving the conversation—thankfully—on to less fraught topics. She spoke stiffly, though, as if she were in an uncomfortable social situation, which he supposed she was.

Simon, willing himself to affect an air of affability he did not feel, said, "My main objective was to visit the countess." He smiled at the lady, who looked happy enough. "And my secondary objective was to return this to you, Miss Brown." He set *Pride and Prejudice* on the table, hoping she would understand that what he truly meant was that he wanted to set things right between them.

"I am sorry that I forgot to give this to you last time I saw you." He paused, wondering if he should say more. Why not? It wasn't as if the dowager was going to pick up on his hidden meaning. He repeated his apology with a few words omitted. "I am sorry about the last time I saw you."

He spoke softly, but she heard him. He could tell by the way she tilted her head, as if she were contemplating a puzzle. It was a pose he recognized: She struck it when she was thinking intently.

She did not, however, say anything; no absolution was dispensed. He wished she would speak. He refrained from squirming under her regard, but it was a close thing.

"Did you read that book?" the dowager asked, and if there were undercurrents of . . . something swirling beneath the surface of his conversation with Miss Brown, the dowager's bright, cheery tone confirmed that she had indeed been oblivious to them.

Simon cleared his throat. "I did. I thoroughly enjoyed it. I am curious which of Miss Austen's books Miss Brown might recommend next."

"*Mansfield Park*, I should think," Miss Brown said, and he was startled by her voice, though he had wanted nothing more a moment ago than to hear it.

"I wonder," Simon said impulsively, taking the book back and flipping through the pages until he found what he was looking for, "if you meant to leave this inside, Miss Brown."

It was one of her markers.

A person may be proud without being vain.

Simon had found several of these markers, bits of paper with quotes from the novel in question scrawled on them, in past volumes lent to him by Miss Brown. He had always found them fascinating but had let them be. He had no idea why he was bringing this one to her attention.

"Oh," Miss Brown said, reaching for the scrap.

Simon found himself reluctant to give it up, but to refuse to return it would make him seem unreasonable. Petulant. He was trying to repair her opinion of him, not see it further eroded.

"'Tis a habit of mine," Miss Brown said, "copying out a particularly striking excerpt. I use whatever scraps of paper are on hand, but then, as you see, I tend to forget my scribblings and am always finding them later when I reread books."

"How do you decide which bits to copy down?"

"There's no rigorous method. Just whatever strikes my fancy."

"What struck your fancy about this one?"

She didn't answer for so long, he assumed she wasn't going to, that they were back to silence. He still didn't have the acquittal he was after.

"Did you ever forget something but you didn't *really* forget?" she asked suddenly.

Yes.

"What I mean," she added, though he was not in need of clarification, "is, do you ever hold one fact, or belief, in your mind even as you simultaneously understand the opposite to be true? Do you ever have a thought, and its opposite, at the same time?"

Why else was he here to call on Archie even though he had known Archie wouldn't be at home? "Yes, Miss Brown, I do."

She seemed buoyed by his understanding. "I loved to read as a girl, and had access to a great many books. My family underwent a fall from fortune . . ."

Was he mistaken or was she eyeing him closely, monitoring him for any reaction to her recounting of this fall? He kept his countenance unchanged.

"For a number of years after that fall," she went on, "I had only a handful of books at my disposal. I learned to value them highly, and I read them many times over. I used to enjoy finding those markers my younger self had left. I would try to remember why I'd copied down that particular passage, what it had meant to my old self, puzzling out if it was a message from her to me."

The idea of sending notes to one's future self was so simultaneously lovely and devastating that it took Simon's breath away, and he was not prone to histrionics.

"A fall from fortune, you say?" the dowager asked, and Simon wished she weren't here.

He didn't want to talk about that. He wanted to know more about those notes from the past.

"Yes, unfortunately." Diantha turned to Lady Harcourt. "If you hadn't taken me on as your companion, I would be quite destitute." She spoke matter-of-factly, with no shame whatsoever, which Simon found both remarkable and admirable. "You knew my mother, back when you and she were both girls, and though you never said as much, I think you offered me this position when you learned about the death of my sister, with whom I lived until I came here."

"Oh, did your sister die? What happened?"

"She contracted scarlet fever."

"And your parents are gone?"

"Yes. I am alone in the world." She glanced at Simon and

held his gaze for a beat before returning her attention to the old woman, and was he mistaken or had there been a flash of warmth in her expression?

Perhaps he had been forgiven.

"What did you mean, earlier," Simon asked, "when you asked if I had ever forgotten something but not really forgotten? If I had ever held a thought, and its opposite, at the same time?"

"Oh, only that I used to say that I would 'forget' my little notes, but in retrospect, I can see that I left those notes for myself to find. I wasn't truly forgetting."

Did it then follow that she had left this note for *him* to find?

No. He was overthinking the matter, overthinking being one of his greatest talents.

"Now I am fortunate enough to have access to quite the library," she went on. "The new countess is a lover of novels, and I visit bookshops and lending libraries. So I don't do as much rereading as I used to. But I suppose I have kept up my note habit."

Mrs. Saunders appeared with a fresh pot of tea. Miss Brown poured a cup for the dowager, who said, "Three sugars, please."

"Oh, you've quite the sweet tooth, it would seem," Miss Brown said warmly, as if she didn't already know how Lady Harcourt took her tea, as if she hadn't doctored hundreds, if not thousands, of cups to her specifications.

"I admit I do."

"I have never seen you take your tea with anything less than three sugars," Simon said fondly.

"Oh, have you seen me take tea? Have we met before?"

"Yes, I am Simon," he said. "Earl of Marsden, but Simon to you. I am a longstanding friend of your son, Archie."

"And have you met my mother?" the dowager said, gesturing to Miss Brown.

Oh, dear. When he arrived, Simon had noted that the dowager *wasn't* mistaking Miss Brown for her own mother, something she had been prone to doing of late. He was about to issue a correction, but Miss Brown shook her head ever so slightly and said,

"Lord Marsden, before you arrived, Lady Harcourt and I were reminiscing about how utterly she enchanted society with her singing voice in her youth."

"I am not so terribly old, now, Mother!" the dowager protested.

"Well, neither of us is getting any younger!" Miss Brown exclaimed, and the two of them shared a laugh.

Simon had always thought Miss Brown's eyes quite striking. He had never seen her laugh before, though, at least not up close. When she did, little wrinkles appeared at the corners of her eyes, and they somehow bracketed those startlingly dark-blue irises in a way that was . . . inexplicably pleasing.

"I will never catch up with you, though!" the dowager said gaily.

"That's true," Miss Brown said.

Simon marveled at what a deft touch Miss Brown had with Lady Harcourt. How, although she was, in a way, deceiving the older woman, she was also being very, very kind.

Two truths that should be opposed, held simultaneously.

Simon wondered if it was time to go. He had come in search of pardon, and perhaps that private, amused glance earlier had been such, or as close as he was like to get. It was just that he was worried about this business of a forced marriage—or the perception of one. Surely she could say no, and that would be the end of it?

"We were trying to remember the words to a song before you arrived," Miss Brown said.

"Yes," Lady Harcourt said, "and we only have some of them." She sang her next sentence out loud, in a high, clear soprano. "'Of all the girls that are so smart, there's none like pretty Sally.' That is all we can recall. Do you know the next line?"

"I do not, but it must rhyme with Sally, mustn't it?" He tried, "'I walked down from the hill to visit her in the valley'?"

"Oh, that's a good one!" Miss Brown exclaimed, and she seemed to mean it. "We've been trying to conjure a second line, but our attempts have been quite a bit more outlandish."

"Yes, we rhymed 'Sally' with 'magically,'" the dowager said wryly.

"Let's hear it," he said.

"'Of all the girls that are so smart, there's none like pretty Sally. For her to take my hand I'd have to be magically . . ." The dowager paused for effect and added, "'Inclined.'"

They all laughed.

"That last word doesn't belong." She turned to Miss Brown. "Sing him the other one."

"Oh, I couldn't. I have nowhere near the voice you do."

"Well, *that's* true."

Miss Brown and Simon shared an amused glance. He was reminded of a conversation he'd had with Archie recently, in which Archie had recounted some advice Miss Brown had given him regarding his mother. While it was understandable to mourn the woman they had lost, if one endeavored to be fully present with the woman she *was*, one might be surprised at how satisfying her company could be.

Simon joined the dowager in exhorting Miss Brown to sing, and when she relented, he was treated to a smoky alto rendition of Sally's fate: "'Of all the girls that are so smart, there's none like pretty Sally. But Sally does not like me, so she dresses very drably.'"

"Sally has my sympathies," Simon said earnestly, though he suspected his eyes were dancing. "Everyone is always accusing me of sartorial drabness."

The three of them laughed heartily, and soon each was trying to outdo the others with lyrics more outlandish than the last.

"I should take my leave," Simon said, setting his cup in his saucer as they ran out of rhymes. Before, when he'd been pondering a departure, he'd been reluctant to go. Now, he would be happy to take his leave on this high note.

"Must you go so soon?" Lady Harcourt said, and she looked genuinely saddened.

"My lady," Miss Brown said, "remember we are for the family hunting box in a month's time? You will see Lord Marsden there."

"Oh, yes!" She peered at Simon. "Are you dreading this trip, sir?"

"No, of course not. I am looking forward to it."

"You are saying that with words, but you are not saying that with your countenance."

He smiled. Lady Harcourt's observation skills had not been lost along with her recognition skills.

"I must admit, and I know this is illogical, that some part of me always resists going on holiday. I know I will enjoy it once I'm there. And perhaps 'enjoy' is too anemic a word. I find my annual holidays with Harcourt and Stonely profoundly restorative."

"But?" Lady Harcourt asked, again hearing what he wasn't saying.

"But I fret about Parliamentary matters. And household matters. But mostly Parliamentary matters."

"But all of those matters will still be there when you return, will they not?" Miss Brown asked.

"Yes, of course."

"And do you not think they may prove easier to manage after you've had a break from them?" she asked.

"I do think. I *know.* For that has historically proved the case. Nevertheless, I have a terrible time, in the moment, *believing* it. I said I was not being logical. I persist in bringing a great deal of reading material each year. I endeavor to think through the arguments I intend to advance in next year's session—that sort of thing."

"Well, this year you should only read novels. In fact, I shall fetch my copy of *Mansfield Park* now, if you will sit with her ladyship for a moment."

Miss Brown's letter was peeking out of the book she'd been reading.

He shouldn't.

He tried to distract himself with conversation. "I think you will enjoy the trip, my lady. I believe Archie has told you about the pool he's constructed there?"

Archie had told Simon he was talking about the trip a great deal, in hopes of familiarizing his mother, who didn't always travel well, with the concept.

"A pool, you say?"

Simon told her what he knew about the project, eyeing the letter the whole time.

He really shouldn't.

He did.

Dear Mrs. Baldwin,

I am Miss Brown, companion to Emma, Dowager Countess of Harcourt. You may remember me from the teas Lady Harcourt used to host. You have likely heard of Lady Harcourt's illness. It has caused her to lose touch with friends. She has of late been asking about you, and expressing a desire to see you. Might I invite you to call, perhaps the week of 8 September? And, if it isn't too much trouble, could you ask your son to accompany you? Her ladyship was always so fond of him and rem—

The letter ended with a blot of ink, probably the result of Simon's arrival having startled Miss Brown.

He wanted to laugh at himself, at his clumsy espionage. Here he had thought he would find . . . what? A clue to the identity of Miss Brown's unwelcome suitor? A window into her inner life?

Neither of which would have been any of his affair.

He replaced the letter in the book and continued talking to the dowager about Archie's renovations at the hunting box. Miss Brown arrived partway through his speech and, when he was finished, Lady Harcourt asked her, "Will you go into the pool with me?"

"Certainly I will."

"You are a good girl." So, apparently, Miss Brown was no longer playing the role of the dowager's mother.

She *was* a good girl, and not in the way Lady Harcourt meant it. She didn't mean ill, but calling Miss Brown a girl was a reflection of the differences not in their age so much as their status. Some part of the dowager must know that Miss Brown's role was to serve her. Miss Brown, though, *was* good. In the moral sense. In the way she so expertly and compassionately threaded the needle of easing the dowager but not lying to her. It was quite the skill.

"I have taken the liberty of adding a second book I thought you might enjoy," Miss Brown said, and Simon felt certain this meant he was forgiven for his indecorous behavior of two nights ago. "It is quite a departure from Miss Austen, though."

He wanted to tell her he would read anything she gave him but held his tongue.

She sat next to him and didn't let go of the books when Simon grasped them. She leaned toward him and said, "You said you forgot to return *Pride and Prejudice* last time you saw me. Can you refresh my memory as to when that was?"

He was being tested. He knew the answer—he had always been a good student.

"I suppose it must have been last time I called here." He affected a posture of thoughtfulness. "Perhaps a fortnight ago, when you first arrived in Town?"

"And you haven't seen me since then," Miss Brown said, and he didn't know if she was asking or telling.

"Just as you have not seen me since then," Simon said, and the books being held between them seemed to conduct a river of understanding. A joint commitment to pretending the other night had never happened was being struck. Though he wasn't sure how he was meant to forget her reported threat of being forced to marry.

As if she could see into his mind, she said, "The matter we discussed when we last saw each other has been resolved." She paused. "If you were curious."

"I am glad to hear it."

Miss Brown stared at him a beat longer, and with a firm, satisfied nod, let go of her side of the books. She turned to Lady Harcourt. "As for our planned bathing expedition, my lady, I must confess that my willingness to accompany you isn't all selflessness. I am curious as to whether the waters will help me, too."

"What do you need help with?" Simon blurted before he could think better of it. He was about to issue a retraction, for the question had been invasive and impolite, but she surprised him by answering easily.

"I get terrible aches in my shoulders."

"But you are so young."

"It has always been thus, at least since a bout of scarlet fever I had as a child."

"This is the same bout that killed your sister? But no, that can't be right . . ." Simon was doing the arithmetic in his head. Miss Brown had come to Archie's household as a young woman nearly a decade ago, whereas her sister had died more recently.

"Oh, my dear," the dowager asked, true sympathy in her expression, "did your sister die?"

"She did, my lady. Seven years ago."

"So there were two family bouts of scarlet fever," Simon said.

"Yes. I had it has a child, and my sister nursed me through it, remaining unaffected. I therefore believed she was somehow . . . insusceptible." Her voice had wavered toward the end of her last sentence, and she had to stop and clear her throat. "But no. She contracted it years later, and her case proved fatal."

"I am sorry," Simon said. "It seems cruel that fate would have spared her once only to take her from you later."

"Was it fate?"

"What else would it be?" he asked.

"God?"

"Oh."

"What do you mean, 'Oh'?"

"Only that this is a different discussion than I was anticipating."

She tilted her head and looked at him for a long time. She had been doing that rather a lot today, striking her thinking pose. Just when he thought he might wilt under her scrutiny, she said, "Do you ever think about how it is that some people are born into the soft hand of luxury, while others cannot aspire to a higher station than serving that first group?"

"I think about it every day."

"You *do*?"

"Yes," he said, and it came out rather tersely, though he hadn't intended that.

"I have offended."

"No. But . . ." He really should take his leave. He did not. "What do you think the gaols act last session was? What do you think my vote in the trial of Queen Caroline was? What is all my work if not an attempt to chip away at the essential social dilemma to which you refer?"

"*Can* it be chipped away at?"

"What is the alternative? Throwing up one's hands and giving up?"

He wasn't sure why he was arguing. He still sounded testy. He *was* testy, suddenly. He should have left after all the singing about Sally in the valley.

"No," she said. "I meant that perhaps one needs not to chip, but to—"

"If you're talking about a French–style revolt, you have lost me. Violence is not the answer."

"I wasn't talking about that!" She was sounding testy, too, as if she thought he was deliberately misunderstanding her. How could that be, though? All he had to go on was her words.

"Well, what were you talking about, then?" he asked, forcing himself to speak calmly.

"I don't know! Something between chipping and chopping!"

He had to smile at that. He had to agree with that. "What, in your estimation, is the difference between fate and God?"

Her eyebrows shot up. Fair. That had been quite the question.

She was spared from having to answer it, to his regret, by the dowager, who said, "I think I should like to go inside now."

Right. He was meant to be leaving, not initiating discussions about freewill and divine intervention. He stood. Bowed. "Give my regards to Archie, will you?"

Simon had visited this garden many times, but this was the first time he'd been here without Archie present. Lady Harcourt was a curious brand of chaperone. He and Miss Brown had not risked speaking openly about what had occurred between them—her clandestine visit to his house, her shocking proposal, his equally shocking behavior—with the dowager present. Yet they *had* been able to speak freely about some rather weighty topics.

And more important, they had been able to mend fences—he thought—in a way they most certainly would not have been able to with Archie present. Archie would have been made immediately suspicious.

"Of course we will convey your greetings, my lord," Miss Brown said. "As I said, he will be sorry he missed you."

Simon was feeling bold, buoyed by the afternoon of silly song and serious symposium, and by the knowledge that whatever threat Miss Brown had been facing was apparently gone, so he said, "*I* am not sorry to have missed *him*." He could not resist adding, "I saw Harcourt mere days ago, whereas I haven't seen *you* for a fortnight, Miss Brown."

He almost winked. But then he remembered that he was not the sort of man who winked.

8

The Joy of Baking

September 9, 1823
Earls Trip, day 2

The morning of their first full day at Gurglewood—Archie really needed to come up with a better name—Simon got up before the others and ventured into the main house to pay a visit to the kitchen.

He found it a hive of activity, though all the bustling came to a halt once his presence was noted. He picked out the cook right away, a short ginger-haired woman with flour on her arms muttering at what appeared to be a pie crust.

"My lord." The housekeeper, who was breakfasting with a maid at a table that stood between him and the cook, rose, flustered. "What is it you desire? You should have rung." She brushed her hands on her dress. "We shall make haste with breakfast."

"Please, sit." They had arranged to have breakfast served at eight, and it was only half seven. "I want for nothing except an audience with the cook."

The cook did not look pleased to see him. In his experience, cooks did not appreciate having their territory invaded by interlopers. One needed to mount a charm offensive. Charm wasn't something Simon was overendowed with, but he was willing to give it a go.

"It's the heat, isn't it?" he asked, nodding at her pastry. "It melts the butter in the dough."

She looked bewildered, which he supposed was an improvement over dour.

"It's hot outside, and even hotter in here. I believe you are attempting to laminate some dough, so working quickly is important, and here I am mucking things up."

She remained bewildered, but if he wasn't mistaken, some curiosity was creeping in. He pressed on.

"I have always had an interest in baking. The cook at Galecroft, my family's estate, was kind to me." He wondered how much to say. Well, why not go with the truth? In his experience, cooks appreciated directness, and brevity. "And I was a boy in need of kindness. She used to let me help make ginger biscuits, which were an especial favorite of mine." Baking had soothed Simon as a child. He ought to take it up again. Baking was predictable. Scientific, even. You followed the instructions, and you got a cake, say. If the cake fell, there was only one reason why: You forgot the leavening agent. If you tried to make a puff pastry in hot weather like this, which it seemed this woman was doing, you needed to start with very cold butter.

And not be interrupted by noblemen seeking the indulgence of whims.

"I've come with an offering. I don't know if it will be welcome or no, so feel free to rebuff me." He produced the bag of lemons from behind his back, and watched her eyes widen. "One of the ladies coming next week is particularly fond of lemons, and I wondered if I might prevail upon you to make a posset, or biscuits, or what have you. Anything lemony, really. You will know better than I."

She eyed the bag of fruit, and her resistance softened. "Where did you get this many lemons?"

"I would like to say I grew them. I have tried, in my orangery, but I've not had luck. I've three lemon trees but no lemons. I imported these."

"This is enough lemons to make many a confection. I make a very good orange cake with almonds. I believe the recipe could be adapted to feature lemons. I could start with that."

"That sounds delightful. But next week, yes, when the ladies arrive?" He set the bag on the workbench near her.

"You don't want to do a test? I haven't had much occasion to bake here in years. Not since his lordship and the late earl used to come on their visits, and they weren't asking for cakes."

Simon let loose the final volley of his charm offensive. "I trust you."

She smiled earnestly. "I have some oranges. I shall conduct a test run with them, and if successful, we can do a lemon version next week."

"Splendid. Please let me know what I can do to assist."

"It's better during the day," Effie said that afternoon as the three gentlemen gathered around the pool. He dipped a toe in. "Still excruciating, mind you, but better."

"The key is to think about something else," Archie said, staring at the sky.

"I think the key is to pretend that there is an innocent child, or animal, at the bottom of the pool in need of rescuing," Simon said.

"Goodness, Simon!" Effie exclaimed. "How uncharacteristically dramatic of you."

Simon shrugged and demonstrated, lowering himself into the pool in one smooth movement. He wasn't really thinking of a creature in need of rescue so much as he was concentrating on the bottom of the pool and pretending that at it lay the key to compelling inspections for the gaols act. But he couldn't say that without breaking the "no talking about Parliament" rule.

The others joined him, and there was a flurry of exceedingly unmanly shrieking, which devolved into a fit of laughter, the latter of which Simon couldn't help but join. It was so ridiculous to be here, but also so wonderful.

"I have to say, I can't quite imagine the ladies submerging themselves thusly," Simon said once they'd stilled and were submitting to the bone-chilling water.

"I think perhaps ladies have hardier constitutions than we appreciate," Effie said. "For example, they go through a terrible lot of pain in childbirth."

"How much pain do you think is involved in childbirth, exactly?" Archie asked, his shoulders hunched up around his ears, as if that were going to make him warmer.

"Oh quite a lot," Effie said. "Julianna told me her sister said . . . Hold up." He looked at Simon, and Simon knew instantly what he was thinking. "*Archie.* Is Clementine expecting?"

Archie's answer was a grin that appeared equal parts gleeful and terrified.

"Huzzah!" Effie shouted, and Simon found himself slightly overcome. Archie was going to make such a good father. And Clementine a mother. He met Archie's gaze as Effie continued carrying on. He pressed his hand to his heart and endeavored to communicate without words, the joy he felt for his friend. He hoped he was not communicating any of the sadness the announcement induced, over his brother and Frances's losses.

Archie must have gotten the correct message, for he nodded and mouthed, "Thank you."

"What are you going to name the child?" Effie asked. "Oh, will you let me name her?"

Archie pulled his gaze from Simon's, but not before shooting him a wink. "How do you know it's going to be a her?"

"Or him," Effie amended. "But I have a feeling it will be a girl."

"Well, either way, no, I shan't let you name my child."

"If it's a girl," Effie, undaunted, said, "you must continue in the fruit tradition."

"The fruit tradition?" Simon, genuinely perplexed, asked.

"Yes, you know. The Morgan sisters: Clementine and Olive." Effie turned to Archie, his eyes narrowed. "What about . . . Apple?"

"That seems entirely too modern," Simon said. Like something one of the members of the experimental string quartet Olive so loved would name a child.

"Yes, you're right," Effie said. "I have it! Plum!"

"You are not naming my child," Archie said, but he was laughing. "But . . . if you were, what if it's a boy?"

"Well, to start, please don't name him after yourself."

"I ought to be offended!"

"It isn't about your actual name. Though 'Archibald' *is* rather dreary, don't you think?" Before anyone could answer he said, "But 'Archie' is delightful, a bit regal, even, and so very you. Still, a man should not pass his name on to his son. He may mean well, but with the name, one passes expectations, and while it is perfectly reasonable to have certain expectations of one's children, they ought to be about character. A man oughtn't to expect his son to be a miniature version of himself."

Again, Simon was feeling rather sentimental. Many people, perhaps even the world at large, thought Effie a silly, lightweight sort of man. But he had real insight and wisdom.

He thought of Frances, calling James silly, and then explaining what James meant to her.

"A title is enough," Effie went on. "So if it's a boy, give him his own name." He tilted his head back and contemplated the sky, "Perhaps . . . Gilbert."

"Gilbert?" Archie wrinkled his nose.

"It is German for 'bright.'"

"You are not naming my child, though I do thank you for your enthusiasm. Both of you. By the by, I must swear you both to secrecy. It is early days. Clementine told me not to tell anybody."

"But by 'anybody,' she cannot have meant us," Effie said.

"I am sure she didn't," Simon said placatingly. "Yet, let us keep Archie's confidence."

"If it is a girl," Archie said, "we are thinking of naming her after my mother—Emma."

"How lovely," Simon said. "And speaking of your mother, how is she faring? Is she doing any visiting?" He was wondering how the reunion with her old friend, Mrs. Baldwin, had gone, though come to think of it, the proposed week for the visit was the current, so he could hardly expect a report.

"No visiting, alas," Archie said. "She isn't up to it."

Hmm. Simon wanted to press, but he hadn't told Archie he'd called that day. He assumed the housekeeper, or Miss Brown, or someone, had. But it hadn't been mentioned. And what would he say? *I snooped in Miss Brown's private things on a visit to your house that you may or may not know about, and I found a letter inviting one of your mother's friends to call?*

"She seems in good spirits, though," Archie said. "None of the more distressing episodes of recent years has been in evidence of late. I am optimistic about how she will fare here."

"Well," Simon said, putting away his curiosity. "Emma is a lovely name for a girl."

"You know what else is a lovely name for a girl?" Effie asked with a glint in his eye. "Plum."

Archie groaned. "I think not."

"It will grow on you."

"I guarantee it won't."

"It will! Plum! Feel how light and pleasing it is to say. Plum!"

This time, Archie dismissed the ludicrous name not with words but with water. Soon, the three of them were engaged in a splash fight, as if they were children.

When the battle frittered out, they were all panting.

Archie pushed back his wet hair. "At least that exertion provided a bit of a warming effect."

"Speak for yourself." Effie hoisted himself out of the pool. "I can endure this torture no longer. I cannot fathom how the air can be so warm and this water so cold." He looked down at himself. "This temperature does not present certain aspects of a man's anatomy in the most advantageous light."

Archie snorted, heaved himself out, and grabbed the shirt he'd left by the edge of the pool. "I started a fire, even though it's still light."

Simon followed their lead, dressing quickly and stooping to pick up his spectacles and the book he'd left by the side of the pool.

"Did you think you were going to read in the water, Simon?" Effie asked.

"I had a mind to. I wasn't expecting the proceedings to be so boisterous."

"Only you would be able to read in such an uncomfortable setting. It's as if you can divorce your body and your mind." Effie dragged one of the chairs that encircled the firepit closer to the flames. "Oh, that is *nice.* Almost makes the cold worth it."

"What are you reading these days?" Archie asked, adding another log to the fire.

Simon held the book up to show them.

"*Frankenstein*!" Effie exclaimed.

"Yes, it was just published in a second edition. The first edition was published anonymously, but this edition bears the name of its author—Mary Shelley."

"You seem to have developed a fixation on lady novelists," Archie said.

Simon had made a strategic error. Questioning about the book would lead to questioning about when and where he had acquired it, which of course had been on his unreported visit to Miss Brown. No, his visit to the *dowager.*

He should have said something about that visit. It was strange that he hadn't.

"I've read novels by two ladies," he said. "Miss Austen, and now Mrs. Shelley. I'm not sure that constitutes a fixation."

"Hmm," Archie said, and was he putting together that Miss Brown had lent Simon the book?

"So what if I am fond of lady novelists?" he said by way of distraction. "I think it is possible that ladies have a unique view on the foibles of society."

"Do you?" Effie asked. "Why?"

"I suppose because many of them are relegated to the edges of society, of power. They are the proverbial wallflowers, if you will. It affords them a vantage point from which to observe."

"I think you are correct," Effie said. "But from what I hear about *Frankenstein*, it can hardly be attributed to the observations of a wallflower."

"No, I suppose not," Simon had to admit.

"Perhaps I ought to take up novel reading," Archie said wryly. "It seems everyone around me is doing it."

"Novels are quite diverting, it turns out," Simon said. "Especially the more fantastical ones. They distract one from one's worries—utterly. Though I am not sure 'distract' is a strong enough word."

"What did you think novels did?" Effie asked with amusement.

"I don't know! I hadn't read one since school. And those I remember as rather a slog."

Effie turned to Archie. "I have to say, I didn't have 'Simon Discovers Novels' on my agenda for Earls Trip 1823."

Simon sighed. At least he had diverted them from the question of how he had acquired his copy of *Frankenstein*.

"Simon," Archie said. "Is something the matter? You told me you were taking a new approach to this year's trip, that you hadn't brought any work, et cetera. But, and you will forgive my bluntness, you seem rather withdrawn."

Simon sighed again.

"Out with it, then," Archie said.

"I paid a visit to my brother's widow a month or so ago, and she shared with me some news that . . . well, not to put too fine a point on it, but that has the potential to upend my life."

He went on to tell them everything he had learned from Frances, because that was what they did on Earls Trips, and it was such a tremendous relief. And perhaps he was being extra forthcoming in an attempt to make up for not telling Archie about the visit to Miss Brown.

The visit to the *dowager*, he corrected himself—again.

The boys listened with their usual mixture of attentiveness

leavened with just enough wry observation to keep things bearable. Simon finished with, "How can I carry on as I always have with Mother, ignoring each other as best as possible but essentially coexisting?"

"Well, if you want to do so, I suppose the way you do it is simply to . . . do it," Effie said.

"I cannot unknow what I now know, though."

"Then I suppose you shall have to reconsider the nature of your relationship," Archie said.

"I cannot recommend highly enough leaving one's entire family behind for a life of honest labor," Effie said, and though Simon knew he was in jest, he answered as if the suggestion had been made earnestly.

"We cannot all turn the operations of our estates over to beloved half brothers—the existence of whom, I hasten to add, suggests that one hasn't thrown over one's *entire* family."

"Yes, yes," Effie said. "Anyway, you are far too conscientious to do anything like that."

"Yet I cannot let my mother's deeds go . . . what is the word? Unpunished? That seems overharsh."

"At the very least, it seems she should know that you know," Effie said.

"And that you are angered," Archie said.

"It seems so simple when you say it like that," Simon said.

"I am confident you will do the right thing," Archie said, and Effie added, "You always do."

As per Archie's request, their evening meal was served all at once.

"I instructed the kitchen to keep things simple," Archie said as he joined Effie and Simon, already assembled, in the dining room as the maid set a roast goose on the table, joining a platter of glazed carrots and another of roasted potatoes. "I didn't think we needed more than a handful of dishes."

"The cook says to tell your lordships that this is the orange cake," the maid said as she brought out the final dish.

"*The* orange cake?" Effie wondered. "Is it famous?"

"Everything looks delicious, thank you," Simon said, dismissing the maid and reaching for the cake.

"Oh, starting with the famous orange cake, are we?" Effie teased.

Effie always ate the pudding first when they dined this way, but Simon generally hewed to a more traditional sequence.

Simon didn't bother answering. He cut himself a slice, took a bite, and sighed. It was wonderful. Moist and sweet, but the almonds gave it complexity that would otherwise be absent. This would be divine with lemons.

"I say, Simon, what have you done to your nose?" Archie asked as they tucked into the goose. Well, some of them did. Simon had carved and had served some to Effie and himself. He hadn't bothered offering Archie any. "I meant to ask you in the coach."

Simon made a show of chewing, buying himself time to come up with a story. He should have prepared one after incurring the wound the night before the trip. "A shaving injury," he said mildly.

"How did Mr. Janes let *that* happen?" Effie said, referring to Simon's long-suffering valet—Simon had never seen the point of a wardrobe that was anything more than practical.

"Yes, and how is a shaving injury on the bridge of your nose?" Archie asked.

"Did you want some goose, Archie?" Simon said in an overloud voice as he used the serving spoon to move some of the meat from the serving platter toward Archie's plate.

Archie recoiled, recovered himself, and said, almost primly, "No, thank you." He then turned to talking about how delicious—and filling—the carrots had been, and Simon's aim of changing the subject away from his wound was achieved.

When the maid came in later to clear the dishes, he said, "Will you please tell the cook— What is the cook's name?"

"Christine, my lord."

"And what is your name?"

"Polly."

"Polly, will you please tell Christine that the orange cake was wonderful?"

Before the boys could remark on the unusual degree of interest Simon was showing for cake, he said, "I was thinking, Archie, about the impending arrival of the ladies and the problem of how cold the pool is. Could you simply add hot water? Or would that dilute the alleged curative properties of the water? Or perhaps it would tax the servants unreasonably."

As a diversionary tactic, the question worked.

"I am not sure Clementine should immerse herself regardless," Archie said.

"Julianna will be undaunted by a little cold," Effie said of his wife. "As, I imagine, will Olive."

"Yes," Archie said. "But my mother."

"Who is the one you built the pool for," Effie said, though Archie had never said so explicitly.

"It is for all of us," Archie said. "It's not a bad idea, Simon. If we have two ladies willing to brave the cold, and one abstaining, we may as well see what Mother prefers. We can ask her when she gets here."

"You forget Miss Brown," Simon said with mildness he did not feel. They were always doing that.

"I do, don't I?" Archie said. That was exactly what he'd said when Effie had been counting the ladies accompanying them this year.

"You do," Simon said, perhaps a little too vehemently, for Archie was looking at him oddly.

"Well, we shall ask all the ladies for their thoughts when they arrive."

The time until that happened went both quickly and slowly. The boys passed the days in the usual way, rambling through the countryside, riding into a nearby town and poking around, drinking more than was advisable, talking while Simon and Effie ate meat and Archie pretended to. This trip had the novel addition of the pool, which they continued to enjoy. Well, Simon enjoyed it. The others were fixated on the unpleasantness of the temperature. But even they appreciated a session by the fire after a bracing dip.

The other novel bit this year was that Simon made friends with Christine.

Historically, there was a certain temporal rhythm to an Earls Trip. Simon was an early riser and Effie a night owl. Archie, who seemed not to need a great deal of sleep, generally spent time one-on-one with Simon in the morning and with Effie at night. Of course, that was only around the edges: The three of them spent the bulk of each day and evening together.

This year, Simon told Archie to sleep in. When, on the first morning, he'd attempted to rise with Simon, who had been trying to sneak out of the gentlemen's cave, as Effie persisted in calling it, Simon whispered, "You needn't be getting up with me, you know." When Archie tried to protest, he said, "I appreciate that you have, historically, but your wife will be here next week. As I said, traditions must evolve. And I can see you rubbing your eyes! Go back to bed. I shall be fine. In fact, I was looking forward to a little solitude this morning, if I am being perfectly honest."

It was somewhat of a lie, and it had worked. It had allowed him to spend the mornings baking with Christine.

"I much prefer cooking," she said the morning the ladies were due to arrive. They were debating the merits of cooking versus baking. "Less fussy. More instinctual."

"I haven't the instinct, I suppose," Simon said. "I find baking immensely satisfying. If you can read, you can bake. One merely needs to follow the directions. And isn't it something of a miracle that a list of simple ingredients—eggs, sugar, flour, butter—can yield something so delicious?"

"The rub here, though, is we don't have a recipe for lemon pound cake."

"Yes, but isn't the point of a pound cake that it contains a pound of everything?"

"Certainly not a pound of lemon, though."

"Ah. I see."

Christine was planning on serving the lemon-almond cake—the successor to the orange version from last week—at their evening meal one night soon, but Simon had brought so many lemons that she'd suggested whipping up a lemon pound cake to serve the ladies when they arrived.

"We shall have to rely on your cooking instinct as to how much juice to add," Simon said.

"Not just, or primarily, juice," Christine said, producing a rasp. "'Tis the grated flesh that will impart the most flavor, without upsetting the proportions of the ingredients."

"I would've had no idea," Simon said, genuinely fascinated as she began rubbing the fruit against the rasp.

After demonstrating, she handed Simon the tool. He wasn't as fast or as accurate as she was, but she was a patient teacher, instructing him not to go so deep as to grate the bitter pith. It reminded him of childhood afternoons spent in the kitchen at Galecroft. Simon generally looked back on his youth at home—as opposed to school, where he had Archie and Effie—with antipathy. It was a sort of reverse nostalgia. But his sessions with Christine were reminding him that there had been some happy times, too.

He missed Galecroft, sometimes.

"What is happening in here?"

Simon looked up to find Archie regarding them with a bemused expression. Simon and Christine no doubt made for a puzzling picture, a cook and a peer of the realm, both wearing aprons, hunched together over a workbench.

"I have discovered a renewed interest in baking, and Christine here tolerates my presence."

He flattered himself that now, a week into their stay, she did more than merely tolerate him. Initially, she'd remained suspicious, but he'd cracked her, with his honest enthusiasm and genuine desire to learn.

"You have a renewed interest in baking?" Archie echoed.

"Yes." Simon gazed mildly at Archie, daring him to say more.

"Meaning you at some point in the past also had an interest in baking?"

"Yes."

Archie shook his head. "Well, I was only popping in to remind the kitchen that my wife does not eat meat. And to say that . . ." Archie looked uncomfortable. Simon knew why.

"It's all right, you can trust Christine. And she likes a good challenge." He turned to the cook. "The countess does not eat meat, but she is in a . . . state where proper nourishment is important."

"She is in a state where she can't keep much of anything down, if I'm being perfectly honest," Archie said.

Christine smiled, which made Simon chuckle. He'd been days into his acquaintance with Christine before he got a smile.

"Do not worry, my lord. I understand perfectly, and I know just what to feed her."

"See?" Simon said.

"Yes, well, thank you. What are you making?"

"Lemon pound cake," Simon said, as if making lemon pound cake was a perfectly usual thing for him to be doing at seven in the morning while on holiday.

"Well, I'll leave you to it."

Simon said to Christine, "Don't you just hate when people interrupt your work?"

Archie posted a groom to watch for the arrival of the ladies that afternoon, and the boys passed the time playing cards. When the groom sent word that the coach—Archie had sent it back to fetch the ladies—had appeared at the end of the drive, they went outside to meet it. Archie was doing a marginally better job than Effie of concealing his excitement over the arrival of his wife—whereas he was pacing in front of the house, Effie was positively vibrating. Simon knew Archie's tells, though, and he observed that his friend was both excited and anxious. It made sense, given Clementine's condition.

Effie's wife, Julianna, was the first out of the coach, taking her husband's hand and rolling her eyes affectionately as he launched into a speech about a regional magazine he'd purchased on one of their trips into town.

Julianna was followed by Archie's wife, Clementine, and her sister, Olive Morgan. Archie helped them down one at a time, and embraced each in turn. Clementine had been at Archie's country estate while he'd been in London with his mother, and Olive lived with her father, so the three of them hadn't seen one another for a while. Olive was talking animatedly, and Archie was nodding as if he were listening, but he was quite openly staring at Clementine's belly, which did not look any different from usual. Though Simon, not having spent any time looking at Clementine's belly, had to admit that he was not an authority on the matter.

"Mother," Archie called as his mother poked her head out of the coach window. "Hold up, I shall assist." He began extricating himself from the ladies, but Simon waved him off and went to help the dowager.

Something was happening in the coach. The dowager had retreated inside. Simon peered in, and there she was. Miss Brown. She appeared uncharacteristically disheveled, no doubt from the journey. She was not wearing a hat. Her dark hair was arranged in a chignon of sorts, but several locks had come loose from their moorings. It made for . . . quite the picture. He cleared his throat.

She shot him a beleaguered smile. "Her ladyship has had a long journey. I think I ought to get out first, then we can both help her down."

"Of course."

Simon leaned into the coach, reaching across the space. Miss Brown shuffled toward him. When her hand made contact with his, he realized with a start that she wasn't wearing gloves.

"I'm not wearing gloves," she said, and if he had been less overcome by the sensation of her bare skin against his, he would have laughed at how perfectly, and how promptly, she echoed his exact thought.

This was what he had wanted, that night, when he'd placed his hand on her forearm. He had wanted to touch skin, not fabric. And here it was, that skin, and it was an utter shock.

He revisited her statement in his mind. *I'm not wearing gloves.* Had there been a note of apology, of sheepishness, there?

"Think nothing of it, Miss Brown. We do not stand on ceremony on Earls Trip."

She graced him with a smile such as he had never seen from her before, not even when he last took his leave from her. He'd thought that smile wide, genuine, had felt lucky to be in receipt of it. But *this* smile. It transformed her very being. She looked a decade younger than her years. Had she been a happy girl once, before the family fall from grace she had referenced?

She was wearing a fichu of white linen tucked into the bodice of her dress, a seafoam green one he recognized. Bending awkwardly to shuffle across the coach had dislodged it. He didn't think she realized. As she hovered at the door, she was hunched forward to avoid hitting her head. The posture, and the fichu failing at its job, put the deep V made by her breasts pressing against each other on display.

Dear Heavens. Simon began to sweat.

He ought to look away.

He couldn't look away.

His vision was becoming blurry. Was he . . . about to *swoon*?

Look at her smile, he told himself. That was a more valuable, because rarer, sight.

It took some effort, but he wrenched his gaze from her bosom to her face. Thankfully, she seemed not to have noticed his impolite ogling, for she was surveying the scene behind him, the couples and friends reuniting, the house, the graceful trees.

"Oh!" she said quietly, "I am so happy to be here." She was speaking generally, he knew, but given her low tone, he could almost fancy she was speaking just to him. She did meet his gaze then, and her smile changed. Though it remained wide and bright, it shifted to allow in a hint of self-deprecation, of guile. "Of course, I am so happy to be anywhere!"

She laughed, so he laughed, too, and took the liberty of reaching for her waist and swinging her down from the coach. And if he let his hands linger slightly longer than was strictly necessary once she was on her feet, it was not remarked upon.

They worked together to help Lady Harcourt down, and once they were all assembled, Archie threw wide his arms, grinned, and said, "Welcome to Gurglewood, ladies."

9

Ambidexterity Is an Underrated Quality in a Gentleman

September 15, 1823
Earls Trip, day 8

Diantha's head was spinning. It had been so long since she'd been anywhere, and this place, Gurglewood—the name was not growing on her whatsoever—was such a dramatic departure from her daily life.

A tour of the grounds had been followed by a tour of the house. She and Lady Harcourt were shown to adjoining rooms. They had traveled with many of the dowager's household items, including a counterpane she was inordinately fond of, and Diantha noted that Lord Harcourt had papered the walls in a floral pattern similar to that in his mother's rooms at Mollybrook. The suite was as familiar as they could make it.

After getting them both unpacked and settled, it was time for the evening meal. Diantha dined with the family at home, and that often included a visiting Miss Olive Morgan. But somehow, the addition of the others made the evening much livelier. It was Lord Stonely, she supposed. He was so theatrical. And his wife was so intelligent, so witty. Diantha found herself slightly awed by the assemblage.

No, she was lying to herself. It was not "the assemblage," but the presence of Lord Marsden that had her discombobulated. She wasn't sure why. She had met him many times before, including alone at his home when he'd been in his shirtsleeves.

But at dinner, she was exquisitely aware of him, seated at her right. He was left-handed, it turned out, so their arms bumped a few times.

"I'm terribly sorry, Miss Brown," he said on the second such occasion. "I'm usually better about compensating."

"You needn't adjust your stance on my account," she protested. She didn't want him to; that was the horrible truth. Something had happened since their last meeting, or perhaps because of it. Something had shifted between them. Part of it had to do with the fact that he was clearly going to keep her secret. She had to assume that if he'd been going to tell Lord Harcourt about her immodest proposal, he would have done so already. That he was keeping her counsel put them in a kind of secret alliance.

But it was more than that. She was newly aware of him as a person. Well, that was a daft thing to think. Of course he was a person and had always been. She was newly aware of him as a *corporeal* person. As a man. She almost fancied she could feel the heat radiating off his hand, which given his left-handedness, and the relatively small size of the dining table, was mere inches from her own.

"A left-handed person in a right-handed world learns to adjust," he said. "It is no trouble." He shifted away, and she experienced a momentary stab of regret that Lord Marsden wasn't going to be the agent of her ruination.

But, she reminded herself, it wasn't going to be a true ruination. It would merely be the *appearance* of ruination. She had been quite clear with Mr. Baldwin in that regard last week when he and his mother came to call. They'd strolled to the back of the garden to give the older ladies some privacy, and she had made her immodest proposal—she was becoming practiced at immodest proposals. He had, as she'd predicted, jumped at the chance to turn an easy profit. She had chosen well. Diantha knew gamblers, and she remembered his mother's stories about him, from back when Mrs. Baldwin and Lady Harcourt were close and socialized frequently.

But the enthusiasm he had displayed for the mechanics of the proposed sequence of events, beyond what she offered to pay him for it, had inspired her to make sure he understood the meaning of the phrase "the appearance of."

So there was absolutely no point in wishing Lord Marsden were going to be the one to do it. It was all settled, and it was cleaner this way. With Mr. Baldwin at the helm, Lord Marsden's friendship with Lord Harcourt would not be imperiled. His reputation would remain untarnished.

Everything was unfolding as it ought to be.

She just wished he hadn't moved his hand away from hers.

"You should have seen them try to beat the left-handedness out of him at school," Lord Harcourt said.

"How awful!" the younger Lady Harcourt exclaimed.

She had a kind heart—too kind for her own good, sometimes, Diantha thought.

"Yes," Lord Marsden said. "The headmaster thought it the mark of the devil."

"No!" the countess cried.

"Can you really be so shocked, Sister?" asked Miss Morgan, the younger of the Morgan sisters, and, to Diantha's mind, the more practical one. Diantha had gotten to know Miss Morgan a little since Lord Harcourt married his countess. She quite liked her and felt that had circumstances been different, they might have been friends.

"Certain types of men see the mark of evil everywhere, do they not?" Miss Morgan asked.

"I suppose so," the countess said.

"I would venture to say that a certain sort of man even goes looking for such 'marks,'" Miss Morgan mused. "Many men, I find, are unduly motivated by the perception of grievance. They search for it everywhere, and they inevitably find it." She turned to Diantha. "Don't you agree, Miss Brown?"

"I wouldn't know" was all Diantha could manage. It was just as well, as she could add nothing to the conversation. As a general rule, Diantha tried to listen more than she spoke. It wasn't that anyone had ever told her to make herself unobtrusive, just that she needed to remain employed and as such strove to be attentive but not overly assertive in social settings. When she did speak, she kept her voice calm, mild. Sometimes, such circumspection proved difficult. Here, that was not the case. To hear ladies openly discussing the shortcomings of gentlemen as a class—in the presence of several specific gentlemen—was shocking enough that she found herself at a loss for words.

"I concur," said Lady Stonely. She was a magazine editor, yet she was a woman of few words, at least in company, so when she did speak, she tended to command attention. "Women are often chided for being too sentimental, but I find it is gentleman who have a natural tendency toward upset."

"Indeed," Miss Morgan said, spearing a parsnip as she added gaily, "Present company entirely excepted, of course."

Diantha still could not believe the ladies were speaking like this.

"Eventually," Lord Stonely said, ignoring all the talk about gentlemen and their temperaments, "Marsden learned how to do everything right-handed."

"Truly?" Diantha exclaimed, and rather loudly, too—apparently she had forgotten her stance against overenthusiastic interjection. She had never heard of a person able to use both hands with equal facility. "Can you *write* with both hands?"

"Indeed, I can," Lord Marsden said. "But left is much more comfortable, so with my school years behind me, I am reverted to my heathen ways." He waved his knife around with his left hand, and everyone laughed.

"Can you do *everything* with both hands?" Diantha was still set back on her heels a bit, though she wasn't sure why. This wasn't, in the scheme of things, that dramatic a revelation.

"I'm not sure what else there is: writing, dining."

"Shaving?" Lord Stonely asked, and the three gentlemen snickered in what appeared to be a private amusement.

Lord Harcourt said, "There is all manner of pastime, too: archery, cricket, polo, what have you."

"You will recall that in school, the last time I undertook such pursuits—because I was compelled to—I was equally bad with each hand." A murmur of laughter ran through the assemblage, and Lord Marsden turned to Miss Brown. "So I suppose the answer to your question is yes, I am equally adept, or equally incompetent, with both hands."

As dinner wound down, Diantha would have thought the ladies would withdraw, but it seemed that, just as Lord Marsden had said, the group did not stand on ceremony on Earls Trip. As plans were made for gentlemen and ladies alike to decamp to the drawing room, she said, "I think it best that Lady Harcourt and I say our good nights." Diantha had been keeping an eye on the dowager, who was seated between Diantha and her son. She had, heretofore, seemed happy enough. She had followed the conversation, and even joined in when it landed on the topic of what flowers and trees Lord Harcourt ought to plant on the newly refurbished Gurglewood grounds. Still, the lady often became agitated in the evenings, and Diantha thought it better to withdraw. "It has been a long day full of unfamiliar events and settings," she added.

This was the awkward part, when she departed with the dowager as though she were a servant. But there was nothing for it, and she smiled as everyone wished her good night. When she made eye contact with Lord Marsden, he opened his mouth as if he were going to say something, but then he shut it abruptly.

The dowager was in fact tired from the long day, and with the help of a maid called Polly, Diantha got her tucked in with a minimum of trouble. She retreated to her adjoining room and left the door open.

"Would you like me to sit with her, miss?" Polly asked. "Then you can rejoin the others?"

Yes. She would like that more than anything. But that wasn't why she was here. "You are kind to offer, and I thank you for doing so, but no."

After Polly retreated, Diantha realized with dismay that she'd left her book downstairs. She and Lady Harcourt had passed some quiet time that afternoon in the drawing room. She stood at the door and cocked her ear. She could hear everyone down there, talking and laughing.

Lord Marsden had said he knew what it was to be alone. Far be it from her to discount anyone's lived experience, but she would wager he didn't know what *this* was like. Sitting alone outside the party. Close enough to hear but as far away as ever.

She shook her head. What was she *doing*? Mounting a competition over who was lonelier? She went and sat by the window.

She ought to get used to it. In five months' time, she would be more alone than she'd ever been.

But also busier, and perhaps that would be some consolation. She had pledged to pay Mr. Baldwin an amount that would deplete her savings by half. She was, as she had told Lord Marsden, no stranger to poverty. And it wasn't as if she would be plunged into such a state immediately. She would have enough money left to rent a room somewhere for a while. But she would have to figure out a way to support herself, and if it wasn't going to be as a companion or a governess—she took Lord Marsden's point on the matter—which were the only occupations open to a lady in her position, she would need to get creative, like her mother had. Take in piecework, perhaps.

She was going to have to abandon her silly cottage fantasy, that much was certain.

There was a tap on her door.

It was Lord Harcourt, peeking his head around. "I thought to say good night to Mother." He held out a hand to forestall Diantha from rising from her chair. "Don't get up."

She beckoned him in and pointed toward the door to his mother's adjoining room.

"Is all well?" he whispered as he passed by.

"Yes, my lord. I think you may find her already asleep. She was very drowsy just now."

He disappeared for a minute, and when he came back, he said, "She is indeed asleep. I confess I find myself relieved at how smoothly the day appears to have gone. You were correct in your observation that her routines have been entirely upended. But I see that you managed to pack so many of her favorite, familiar things. Thank you."

"And I see you papered her bedchamber so that it would remind her of home."

Lord Harcourt did not like to be complimented. She could see him preparing to deflect, so she took the opportunity to say, "Lord Harcourt, I left my book downstairs. Would you mind terribly waiting while I go fetch it?"

"Of course not. Please take your time."

The chattering grew louder as she approached the drawing room. She hoped not to make a scene and was relieved to see that everyone was engrossed in a card game. With any luck, she could slip in and out unnoticed.

She glanced toward the armchair tucked into another corner where she thought she might find her book, and discovered she'd been wrong. Everyone was engrossed in a card game, minus one gentleman.

"Pardon me, my lord," she whispered as she approached, and Lord Marsden looked up, an expression of bewilderment giving way to a smile.

"Miss Brown! Will you be able to join us, after all?"

He was rising. She waved to indicate that such formalities were not required. "I am merely here to retrieve my book." She pointed to where it was resting on a side table on the far side of his chair.

He held up the book he was reading. She recognized the copy of *Frankenstein* she'd lent him. "I am so engrossed that I am compelled to hide here in the corner instead of playing with the others." He picked up her book. "I was speculating on whose book this was. I had it narrowed down to one of the ladies, and I wondered if it was yours."

"How did you know it belonged to a lady?"

He read the title aloud. "*The Sketch Book of Geoffrey Crayon, Gent.*" That doesn't give away much, but there is a brilliant purple ribbon marking the page. I suppose it could have been Stonely's, but he tends to read poetry on these trips, and the ribbon felt to me as if it belonged to a lady."

"I have an inordinate fondness for ribbons," Diantha said. And that purple velvet one was a beauty.

"Ribbons?"

"Yes, ribbons." She smiled. He sounded as if he'd never heard of such a thing. "You know, of the sort you might find on ladies' bonnets, for example."

"You do have a hat adorned by a very striking ribbon. It is the color of the sun as it begins to set on a hazy day." He took off a pair of spectacles as he spoke. She hadn't realized he wore them. But then, she hadn't before had occasion to observe him reading. They suited his face.

"I admit to being more flattered than I ought that you noticed," she said, ordering herself to attend to the conversation. He really did have the loveliest eyes, though, under those glasses. They were the most extraordinary shade of brown, rich and warm, leaning almost toward rust.

"I suppose I noticed because most ribbons you see are blue, or white, or green. Or any color, really, but the . . . usual versions of those colors." He paused. "I am not making sense."

"I know exactly what you mean."

His eyes were brown but not mere brown. They were the color of mature acorns fallen from sessile oaks.

"I have a green ribbon that is the precise color of the stem of a tulip in the spring. I've never seen the like of it in the wild. I've never seen the like of it on a *ribbon* in the wild, I mean. I have, of course, seen it in nature—that's the whole point."

Acorns and tulip stems—what was she on about?

"Is your tulip-stem-green ribbon on a hat?"

"No, it is in a drawer!"

"I beg your pardon?"

"I have quite the collection of ribbons, but I haven't the collection of hats and dresses and such in need of adornment."

"Ah."

She wondered whether to say more. There was no reason to, particularly, but she didn't want him to think her a frivolous girl with a meaningless collection of fripperies. "Ribbons are also inexpensive, relatively speaking."

"Ah," he said again, and he did manage to infuse those single syllables, those *Ah*s with a great deal of understanding.

"There is not much else in the world a lady can buy that is beautiful yet inexpensive. My sister and I used to occasionally buy ribbons together, and we frequently gazed at them in shop windows. She was quite the seamstress, and she used to spin elaborate tales about the equally elaborate—and utterly impractical—imaginary garments to which she might affix them."

He looked at her for a long time. She had said too much and, at the same time, nothing of import.

"Miss Brown," he finally said, "are you sure you cannot stay and enjoy the evening with us?"

"Oh, no," she said, realizing that she was still standing awkwardly before him. "Lord Harcourt is upstairs sitting with his mother so I could come down and retrieve that."

She reached for the book. He made to hand it to her, to meet her halfway, but as he did so, he rotated his hand so that instead of her hand making contact with the book, it made contact with the top of his wrist.

She wasn't wearing gloves. She hadn't thought to redon them for her quick errand.

This was the second time today she had found herself skin-to-skin with Lord Marsden because she wasn't wearing gloves when she ought to have been.

Diantha was not a swooner. She couldn't afford to be. Swooning, she'd always thought, was the prerogative of the privileged, of women who could make themselves unconscious for a time and trust not only that nothing menacing would happen to them in that state but also that any responsibilities they held would simply wait for their reanimation.

This, though. This was as close as she had ever come. And it was only her palm on his wrist. It was a much less decisive touch than earlier, when he'd helped her out of the coach.

It was just that it seemed . . . intentional. Assisting a lady as she alit from a conveyance was a utilitarian, polite sort of gesture. Holding her book hostage, as he seemed to be doing, was . . . less polite. She would have said it almost seemed tinged with peril. Except it was just a book. And she could reach for it easily, should she choose.

She did not reach for it. She merely stayed where she was, frozen like the divine lemon ice that had been served between courses at dinner, looking down at Lord Marsden's left hand. It was veiny, like his forearms had been that night at his house. His fingers were long. Her own fingers ran perpendicular to his as her hand stayed where it had landed—where he had landed it?—across his wrist. She imagined him as a boy, being beaten so as not to favor this hand.

She was seized with the most absurd urge to slide her hand around until it was properly covering his, and to interlace her fingers and his.

With great effort, she pulled away. Lifted her gaze from his hand to his face. He was looking at her.

She had begun to perspire. Her breath was coming faster, and it was difficult to get a full breath in.

She was *not* a swooner.

She turned and fled.

It was only once she was back upstairs that she realized she'd forgotten her book—again.

The next morning, Diantha and Lady Harcourt went down to breakfast early and found Lord Marsden seated in front of a plate and a book.

Diantha sighed, too loudly, apparently, for she drew his attention from where she was standing in the doorway. But at this hour, she had expected to have the breakfast room to themselves. Now she and Lord Marsden would have to talk. She would have to look at his hands.

He took off his glasses. He really did look handsome with them on. Well, he looked handsome with them off, too, but there was something about the juxtaposition of the circular wire frames and the square lines of his jaw that was . . . unexpectedly pleasing.

"Lord Marsden," she said, dipping into an abbreviated curtsy. "Good morning."

He got to his feet. "Lady Harcourt. Miss Brown. You ladies are up early."

"As are you," she said, guiding the dowager to the table.

"I don't like to waste the best part of the day," Lady Harcourt said. "I find that whatever one's pursuit, it is generally more enjoyable—and productive—in the mornings. My main pursuit these days is . . ." She trailed off, as she tended to do when she lost her train of thought.

"You do enjoy spending time in your garden, among your flowers," Diantha supplied. "And morning is certainly a lovely time for that." She turned to Lord Marsden. "If we are up early enough, the gardens at Mollybrook echo with birdsong. It is quite extraordinary."

She experienced a sudden pang. She would miss those birds.

She had been thinking about how much she would miss the family, but she would miss their homes, too.

"I share your outlook, my lady," Simon said to Lady Harcourt. "I am at my sharpest in the mornings."

"What pursuit to you undertake in the mornings?" Lady Harcourt asked.

"Reading, generally, though not usually novels." He placed a marker in his book and closed it. It was hers. He was reading *her* book, the one she'd left behind last night. She wasn't sure if she was affronted or flattered.

"I will fix you a plate, my lady," she said to cover her discomposure as she crossed over to the sideboard.

"What pursuit do *you* undertake in the mornings?" Lady Harcourt called, directing the question to Diantha.

"Your morning pursuits are my morning pursuits," she called back, grateful for the meaningless conversation.

Back at the table, she set a plate in front of the dowager. "I must confess that although I understand with my intellect the logic of your preference for mornings, I am a natural night owl."

"Are you indeed?" Lady Harcourt asked.

"I am." She returned to the sideboard and helped herself to a slice of toast. She wasn't one for a large morning meal. She wasn't one for mornings, period. "Left to my own devices, I would be prowling about the house until the wee hours, and in the mornings, I would be late to rise."

The confession amused Lady Harcourt. "We are on holiday, are we not?"

"We are!"

"Then you ought to go back to bed. Isn't that part of the joy of a holiday, shirking one's responsibilities?"

"I suppose it is, but I am already up and content to stay where I am." To punctuate her statement, she sat next to Lady Harcourt. She left unsaid that she hadn't any choice about being content where she was—this morning in particular, but also in a more generalized sense. Lady Harcourt was an early riser; therefore Diantha was, too.

Lady Harcourt turned toward Lord Marsden. "I used to holiday on the shore, near Lydd-on-Sea. Have you ever been, sir?"

Oh no. Lady Harcourt often had flashes of true memories, but of all the occasions for her to suddenly remember! Diantha turned to Lord Marsden and, attempting to imitate the jolly tone Miss Morgan sometimes deployed, said, "I see you have helped yourself to my book, my lord!"

If the observation was awkward, or overloud, Lord Marsden did not remark on it. He merely grinned and said, "Yes, and it contains the most remarkable story about a Dutchman in America who slept for twenty years and awakened to find he had missed the revolution, among other things."

Diantha had to smile. "Rip Van Winkle" was a departure from

the parlor politics of the Austen novels he had been reading. "Yes, and if I recall, his initial character flaw was that he was always trying to avoid work—and his wife."

"You say 'initial' as if he is cured of his laziness by his extraordinary experience. But at the end, he is as idle as ever."

It was Diantha's turn to smile. "You are quite right. And his wife is dead, and he doesn't miss her at all."

"That sounds like a daft story," the dowager declared.

Diantha and Lord Marsden shared an amused look as he slid the book across the table to her. "I am sorry I kept it. I ought to have asked one of the servants to deliver it to you yesterday evening, but I made a selfish decision. When you departed, I was a mere few pages from the end of *Frankenstein*. I thought to merely read a few pages of your book, but . . ." He shrugged sheepishly. "I found myself irrevocably engrossed."

"I can hardly scold you, my lord. I know this feeling."

"I shall return both volumes to you now." He produced *Frankenstein* from the chair next to him.

"What is the verdict on that one?"

"I found it extraordinary."

"How so?"

"To begin with, I could not put it down. You see this? He pointed to a mostly healed abrasion on the bridge of his nose. "This is a reading injury."

"A reading injury!"

"Yes. I started this book the night before we departed. I was tired. It was a struggle to keep my eyes open. Eventually, I lost the battle with exhaustion and the book fell out of my hands toward my head. I started to awaken, and in my attempt to catch it before it struck me on the head, I pivoted just right—just wrong—such that I was rewarded with a nasty paper cut."

"I heard Lord Stonely telling Miss Morgan that you cut yourself shaving." Diantha had been seated near the pair yesterday at tea and had been a mite surprised by how intimate they seemed.

"That's what I told the others," Lord Marsden said. "A reading injury sounded so . . . unmanly."

She laughed. To think, moments ago she had been nervous about the prospect of being near Lord Marsden, and now they were laughing over a shared secret.

"My lord," Diantha said with a smile, "your argument is circular. You say you found the book extraordinary because you couldn't put it down. Why couldn't you put it down?"

"You are of course correct." He gazed at the ceiling as if trying to find the words to summon. "Well, to begin with, it's interesting from a religious perspective, isn't it?"

"Many people might say it is blasphemous."

"Well, that's rather the point, is it not? Victor fancies himself God, and how does that work out for him?"

"Hmm." Diantha couldn't argue with anything Lord Marsden was saying, but for her, the novel's religious themes weren't primary.

"But I suppose my chief interest," he went on, "is to do with what made the creature who he was. Was he born bad, or was he made bad? He started out an innocent, did he not? Was he not forced into baseness by neglect and rejection? By cruelty?"

"Hmm," she said again.

"You keep saying 'hmm.' What does it mean?"

"Nothing. Of course you are correct; that is a major theme of the book. I simply hadn't considered it."

"I beg your pardon? How can one read *Frankenstein* and not consider questions of nature versus nurture?"

"I suppose because I was fixated on what I view as the novel's main theme: revenge."

"Hmm."

"Now you are 'hmm-ing' me."

He chuckled. "For the same reason you were hmm-ing me. I hadn't given the question of revenge much consideration, but, of course, the monster does get his revenge."

"Yes, and at what cost? That is what I find interesting. He could have stayed away. He could have had a decent life."

"How?" Simon asked. "He was alone, newborn and alone."

"Perhaps we can agree that the central theme of the book is loneliness. Fear of it, in particular. The lengths to which people—or monsters—will go to avoid it."

"Miss Brown, I wasn't going to say anything, but . . ." The book had been resting on the table between them, and he took it back and flipped through it until he found what he was looking for.

"I stumbled on one of your markers." He redonned his spectacles and read aloud. "'Let me see that I excite the sympathy of some living thing.'"

He looked at her expectantly.

"It is a plea," she said. "The monster is asking Dr. Frankenstein to make him a companion."

She could tell by the furrowing of his brow that her answer had not sufficed. He didn't need the passage explained; he wanted to know why she had chosen it.

She found herself wanting to tell him, though she did so in the form of a question. "Do you ever think that love and rage are the same?"

"What do you mean?"

"A few lines later, the monster says to the doctor, 'I will revenge my injuries; if I cannot inspire love, I will cause fear.'" That line had seemed rather too savage to commit to paper, but she had committed it to memory.

"How could love and rage be the same?"

"If not the same, precisely, then underlain by the same animating force. See how easily the creature changes tack?"

Lord Marsden looked startled. Fair. It was a bold assertion. But then his face underwent a change, startlement giving way to something more like wonder. "I think . . . I think you may be right, and I think I shall have to reevaluate some . . . assumptions I have made in my own affairs."

Well, how often did that happen to a lady? How often did a

gentlemen tell her she was right? Even more, that her ideas had challenged his way of thinking?

She decided to reward him with a little more truth. "Like the monster, I have rage in my heart." She eyed him. His expression remained implacable. "I have not shocked you."

"No. I have wondered if there are . . . storms beneath the surface of you."

Diantha wasn't certain if she was taken aback or thrilled by that observation. She tried to be glib: "I have betrayed my true nature!"

"No, no. Perhaps it is only that I have been watching you too closely."

Goodness. She was getting the lightheaded sensation again, the swoony feeling. She pushed it away.

"Regardless," he went on, "I do not think your true nature is rage."

She ought to be affronted. What did he know? Who was he to opine on her true nature?

She was not affronted.

"I think I ought to have a look at this book the two of you are so enamored of," Lady Harcourt said, startling Diantha. She had, for several minutes, forgotten about Lady Harcourt. She was chagrined.

She wondered if Lord Marsden was experiencing the same sentiment, for his eyes widened as he slid the book to the lady. "It is all yours." He glanced at Diantha as if belatedly seeking permission to lend her volume. She nodded vigorously, as if the loan could somehow supersede the neglect that had preceded it.

"It sounds terribly exciting," Lady Harcourt said, "but I am not one for reading of late."

"Perhaps I could read it to you," Lord Marsden said.

"Oh, would you?"

"I will read it to you, my lady," Diantha said, and to Lord Marsden she explained, "I used to read to her quite often, but we have fallen out of the habit."

"I prefer the young man to read to me."

"I should like nothing more, my lady."

"Remind me your name?"

"Simon. I am your son Archie's friend." He glanced at Diantha. "And Miss Brown's friend."

For some reason, Diantha's mind landed on the image of his forearms. It wasn't a very . . . friendly image.

"Shall we begin?" Lord Harcourt asked, opening the book. Yet again, he glanced over at Diantha. "Miss Brown, we shall be occupied here for a good while, so you may as well leave us."

What was he saying? "I beg your pardon?"

"Go." He made a shooing motion with one hand. "The night owl can go back to bed, if she likes, or otherwise attend to her own pursuits."

Could she . . . do that? What would she do with this unexpected gift of time? While she recognized that here at Gurglewood there were limited possibilities, they felt endless. "How will I know when . . ."

Lord Marsden produced a timepiece from a pocket. "Let us meet back here in, say, two hours?"

Two hours! A frisson of excitement rose in her chest. "But what if—"

"If we run into any trouble, we shall find you. Or, no, we shall find Archie. That way you needn't remain nearby if you don't care to."

She opened her mouth, closed it. He raised his eyebrows and shot her a look of impatience, but she rather thought it was feigned. At the very least it was a friendly sort of impatience.

"Lady Harcourt and I are meant to attempt to take the waters this afternoon at one o'clock," she said.

"Excellent," Lord Marsden said, and when she didn't respond—she was still pinned in place by a curious mixture of excitement and indecision—he added, "One o'clock is six hours from now, and we shall see you in two."

She was carrying her volume of stories by Washington Irving.

She handed it back to him. It felt like the least she could do in exchange for a few hours of freedom.

"No," he said, holding his hands up. "I cannot hold your possessions hostage any longer."

"You're not holding anything hostage! You're keeping *Frankenstein* to read to Lady Harcourt. And you're borrowing the other volume. Like we always do."

Like we always do.

She'd spoken as if they were long-standing friends.

The thing was, after that conversation just now, about rage, both hers and Dr. Frankenstein's monster's, it rather felt as if they were.

But also, and again, she wasn't sure if *friends* or *friendly* were precisely the right words.

The forearm image returned.

He still seemed hesitant, so she said, "I have packed other books. Besides, I shan't be reading the next while. At least keep it for now." He nodded, and she added, "I haven't gotten to it yet, but the reason I purchased that volume was a story entitled 'The Legend of Sleepy Hollow.'"

"All right, then. I thank you."

She had made it fully out the door when he called after her. "Miss Brown!"

He held on to the doorframe with one hand and wrapped his head and torso around it to speak to her in the corridor. "Miss Brown, for what it's worth, you do excite the sympathy of at least one existing thing—or person, in this case: me." He paused. "If that was something you were concerned about."

10

A Holiday from One's Holiday

Simon enjoyed the morning he spent with Lady Harcourt, but not as much as he enjoyed giving Miss Brown a few hours to herself. After that, he took tea with the whole group—they served scones he had helped make—he and Christine had added some lemon zest to them—and everyone had exclaimed over them. And then a ramble in the woods, some time with "The Legend of Sleepy Hollow," and the evening meal.

It had all been very pleasant.

Less pleasant was when, as they were preparing to move to the drawing room, Miss Brown excused herself and withdrew with Lady Harcourt. It was the second night she'd done that. A pattern was forming, one he did not care for.

"Do you think," he asked everyone and no one when there was a lull in the conversation after her departure, "that Miss Brown ought to have a holiday, too?"

"She is, isn't she?" Archie asked.

"Not precisely," Simon said.

"She is absolutely not," Miss Morgan said.

Simon shouldn't have been surprised. Olive Morgan noticed things.

"She may, I grant, be enjoying a change of scenery. She may—or may not—be enjoying a wider cast of characters. But she most decidedly is not having a holiday. If she were, she'd be down here with us now."

Archie looked aghast. "I should have thought. I will go sit with Mother so she can come down."

"I can sit with your mother tomorrow," Olive said. "We can divide the time."

"A fine idea," Archie said. "I shall go up right now and relieve Miss Brown."

"Does anyone know what happened with Miss Brown's family?" Simon asked. He hadn't thought he would solve the Miss Brown problem so immediately and so thoroughly, and he wanted to tap into the collective knowledge of the group before the lady herself reappeared.

Everyone swung around to look at him, including Archie, who had risen from his seat but not yet left.

Simon added, "She mentioned in passing that she'd been living with her sister before she came to serve as companion to your mother."

"You know, I'm not entirely certain," Archie said. "My mother and Miss Brown's mother were childhood friends. The Clarks—Clark was Miss Brown's mother's maiden name—lived in a town not far from Mollybrook, and I gather they used to see each other quite a lot in the summers, at dances and the like. I am afraid I lose track of the story at that point. Mother did used to tut about the circumstances the Brown sisters had found themselves in, but I am ashamed to admit that I never took care to find out the details."

"Your father had recently died," Effie said placatingly. "You were juggling a great deal, both in terms of the estate and of his more personal . . . legacy. I would imagine your mother asked you to engage Miss Brown's services and you didn't feel the need to delve into the particulars."

"But oughtn't I to have at some point subsequently?" Archie asked. "As my mother deteriorated, oughtn't I to have learned more about the woman taking care of her so loyally?"

"I can assist." Everyone swung their attention to Olive. "Why are you all looking at me like that?" She affected a wide-eyed expression of innocence. "Can I help it if people tell me things?"

Simon suppressed a smile. He had warmed to Olive over the past year or so. She conveyed a kind of blithe world-weariness he used to think shallow, but he was increasingly convinced he had been mistaken. He must have been—witness how close Olive and Effie were, and Effie was an excellent judge of character.

"After all that buildup," Olive said, "I don't think it's that dramatic a tale—or a particularly unusual one, alas. Father gambles away the family fortune. Tries to hide it. Is discovered, and by that time owes a terrible sum to some terrible men. Tale as old as time."

"We are talking of Jedidiah Brown, are we not?" Effie asked. "Did he not die under mysterious circumstances? I seem to remember hearing about it and thinking it terribly dramatic."

"Yes," Olive said. "It was never clear if he died by his own hand or fell victim to the aforementioned terrible men. Miss Brown's sister married an older man, and Miss Brown went to live with them." She shrugged. "And from there, I suppose, she came here. Miss Brown's sister died, too, at some point, though under what circumstances, I don't know."

"Scarlet fever," Simon supplied, though he regretted it when everyone turned to him. "She mentioned it in passing." That was the second time he'd claimed Miss Brown had mentioned something to him in passing. He needed to be careful; he was making it seem as if he and Miss Brown were doing an awful lot of . . . passing.

He considered the downfall of the Brown family. Such a tragedy, the way the careless actions of one man could ripple through generations. Simon stewarded his estate with great vigilance. He wouldn't call himself cheap so much as careful. He avoided extravagance, out of a generalized sense of the importance of conservation, but he took care of what—and who—needed looking after. He couldn't imagine having a child and then gambling that child's future away. Of course, he couldn't imagine having a child and ignoring it utterly, either.

He couldn't imagine having a child at all.

Although . . . what was he doing now with all his *couldn't imagines* but a sort of imagining?

It took a while for Miss Brown to appear after Archie left. Simon had begun to think she wasn't coming. By the time she arrived, the group had, as with the previous night, split into smaller conclaves. Simon was, again, reading by himself in a corner.

Everyone greeted Miss Brown. She was invited to play cards with Olive and Clementine, but she protested that she didn't know how.

Effie said, "Miss Brown, perhaps you could settle a disagreement my wife and I are having regarding whether publishing a recurring feature entitled 'Secrets of a Dressmaker' in our magazine is tawdry and beneath us or thrilling and sure to be lucrative."

Poor Miss Brown.

Simon stood. "Or, Miss Brown, you could join me in a discussion of literature." He held up her book.

"I think I shall allow myself to be rescued by Lord Marsden," she said with a laugh, and just like that, she was crossing to his corner of the room and settling herself on one end of a small settee that was placed perpendicular to his chair.

"What kind of pen is that?" she asked, nodding at the writing instrument he'd left on the side table between them.

"The nib is punched out of a thin sheet of steel. It doesn't require sharpening as does a quill. This one is made by hand by a blacksmith near Galecroft, my country estate." He handed it to her.

She turned it over in her palm. "How extraordinary."

"I have heard tell of a factory in Birmingham beginning to produce them on an industrial scale," he said.

"Are we on the verge of a revolution in writing instruments?" She smiled as she handed it back.

He chuckled. "I think so. And look, I can switch out the nibs if I like." He produced a pouch from his pocket and extracted from it a broader nib than the one he had been using.

He waited for her to ask what he was writing, and he was prepared to show her, but she did not.

"I must confess," she said, "that I am feeling rather guilty for displacing Lord Harcourt for the evening. I told him I'd had a lovely break this morning, while you read to his mother, but he insisted."

"What did you do with your time this morning?" Simon asked, though he thought to add, "If you would like to answer."

"I am rather embarrassed to admit that I did nothing of import. I walked into town, and I looked into shop windows."

"Did you see any ribbons?"

"Yes, but none of particular note. So I'm afraid my outing proved unfruitful."

"Perhaps the outing itself was the point, rather than any fruits it might have yielded."

"Yes, I think you're right. It was a holiday." She smiled. "A holiday from my holiday."

"I am not sure two hours can properly be considered a holiday. And I am not sure you are even on holiday at all."

"What do you mean? What do you call this?" She gestured vaguely around the room.

He tried to think how Olive had explained it. "I call this, this exact moment, a brief respite from your duties, which—and mind you, I am not suggesting you bear any resentment toward Lady Harcourt—have followed you here. If you are on a holiday, it is a mere shadow of a holiday."

She didn't speak for a moment, just looked at him and blinked. If he thought for a moment that she might be fighting tears, he must have been mistaken, for she said, "I did take a proper holiday, once. Two summers ago."

"I remember."

She furrowed her brow; he had confused her.

"I remember because Archie was feeling particularly guilty about leaving his mother for our Earls Trip that year, and in the course of discussing it, he mentioned that you'd taken a holiday and he'd covered for you, so he supposed you could do the same for him." He paused for a moment, as if considering whether to say more. Curiosity won out, for he asked, "Where did you go?"

"For the first part of the holiday, I went to Barbury, a town not too far from Mollybrook. It's where I grew up and lived my whole life until I came to be with Lady Harcourt."

"Visiting old friends? It can't have been a trip to see family, for you told me you had none."

"No. Well, I visited my sister's grave, which I suppose in a way amounts to visiting family. I went to see her every day. Beyond that, I took a room at an inn and read novels and embroidered and did all the things I generally do in Lord Harcourt's household, but I did them by myself." Her eyes danced. "And I stayed up terribly late at night and laid in terribly late in the morning."

"Was it refreshing?"

"It was."

"And what did you do for the second part?"

Something shuttered in her face, but she recovered quickly. "I went to another town nearby and . . . did much the same thing. Which is to say, a whole lot of nothing."

She had spoken cheerily enough, but he hadn't missed that slip in her facade, the brief dimming of her brightness. He was very much afraid he had been the cause of it, with his questioning.

"It was very kind of Lord Harcourt to allow me to join you this evening," she said with a gaiety he clearly heard as false, "but I should—"

"You won't dislodge him," Simon said. "He will have settled in for the evening and won't countenance your reappearance this soon." He searched her face. "You needn't stay here with me, though, if that was your attempt to extricate yourself. But if you have been worried that I will speak to anyone about . . . the night we both lost our minds, you needn't be." He made an attempt at humor. "I know I am not meant to reference it at all. We need a code word."

"We most certainly do not," she said, but warmth had returned to her eyes. "If you're not talking about something, you don't need a code word."

"As long as you promise me you do indeed have the . . . matter in question sorted out."

"I promise." She tilted her head and regarded him. "You want to ask me *how* I have it sorted out."

He dipped his head in acknowledgment.

"And *I* want to ask *you* to trust me."

He did not care for that answer. He wanted to hear it explicitly stated that she had rebuffed the gentleman in question and that all was well. But what could he say? That he *didn't* trust her and therefore needed to meddle in her affairs? "All right."

A slight awkwardness settled, until she quite overtly changed the subject. "I know you and Lord Harcourt were school friends, but tell me about how you met. What was your first impression of him? You are correct in your assertion that if I were to try to dislodge him upstairs, he would resist. Was he always so upstanding?"

It took Simon a moment to adjust to the new topic, but he let himself be carried along, casting his mind back to his first year at school.

"I tried to avoid him, initially."

"You did?"

He smiled. "He reminded me of my brothers."

"How so?"

"He shared their interests in outdoor pursuits: riding, hunting, sailing."

"But why avoid him? Your brothers were kind enough to you, to hear it told, even if the age gap made true closeness impossible."

"To hear it told? Miss Brown, I am not sure how you can know that given that the conversation you are referencing never happened." He smiled to show he was in jest. "I thought I had nothing in common with my brothers. To the extent that they took notice of me, or that I spent time with them, I was always being exhorted to run somewhere or shoot something or move out of the way of a mast before I got brained. It's not that I don't appreciate the appeal of the out of doors. In the correct doses. Which for me are much smaller doses than for my brothers—or Archie. That was why he reminded me of them. And unlike me, Archie had no interest in the school part of school. He was not a scholar. So I formed an impression of him that while superficially correct, was nevertheless in error."

"How was it in error?"

"I was only seeing the outside of him. What he looked like—a Corinthian. What he did—ride horses and shoot things. I came to learn, thanks to his cheerfully relentless insistence on sitting by me at meals, that on the inside, we had a great deal in common."

He thought she might ask what those things were, and he was prepared to answer. An interest in justice and fairness. Similar challenges with their families.

Instead, she nodded as if she agreed with him and asked, "And how did you come to be friends with Lord Stonely?"

Was Simon . . . disappointed that she wasn't going to press him to talk more about his family?

He forced himself to answer the question at hand. "Effie came a little bit later that first year. Some of the other boys started picking on him, so Archie adopted him, too, appointed himself his protector."

"That sounds like Lord Harcourt."

Suddenly, Olive appeared in Simon's peripheral vision. "Finally. We've been trying to get your attention."

He swiveled to find everyone looking at him—at them. Olive lowered herself to sit next to Miss Brown on the other side of the settee and said, "Miss Brown, Lady Stonely and I have yet to take the waters. We were asking Lord Stonely to comment on the experience, but I am not sure we can trust him to be a reliable reporter. He does tend to overdramatize."

"Is it possible to be overdramatic about freezing to death?" Effie called from across the room.

"Miss Brown, I understand that you and Lady Harcourt immersed yourselves this afternoon," Miss Morgan said.

"Yes. Well, I did. Lady Harcourt only went in a little way."

"And was it unbearably, soul-shatteringly cold?" Effie asked cheerily.

"It was certainly cold, and Lady Harcourt did not care for it. But for my part, I felt that once one has grown accustomed to it, it's not so bad. I would go so far as to say it's rather invigorating."

"Well, it must have been," Olive said, "for you are positively glowing." Was it Simon's imagination or did Olive glance at him suspiciously?

"That's exactly—practically word for word—what Marsden said," Effie said. "I think water that cold requires a certain sturdiness of character that most of us lack."

"Speak for yourself, my dear," Julianna said.

"I wasn't referring to you, my love," Effie said, and Simon barely refrained from rolling his eyes. "You have the sturdiest character I know."

"And to think," Julianna said, failing to suppress a fond grin, "he fancies himself a poet."

"We are game to try it tomorrow," Olive said. "Will you accompany us, Miss Brown? Be our guide?"

Miss Brown began to demur, but Clementine intervened. "I shan't be going in, and the dowager and I are overdue for a catch-up. So that leaves the rest of you ladies to meet your icy fates together."

Miss Brown didn't agree, but she didn't disagree, which was enough for Olive to pronounce the matter settled. "Shall we say three o'clock?"

The other ladies concurred, and after some pleasant conversation, Miss Brown announced that she meant to retire for the evening. Simon checked his timepiece. It wasn't terribly late, even by his standards, but he felt the urge to do the same.

He was, suddenly, yearning for the solitude of the gentlemen's cave. Or perhaps it was more properly called the gentle*man*'s cave, singular, for despite Archie and Effie's plan to leave the house to the ladies, in practice, neither could bear to be departed from his wife once she was present. This meant Simon had been alone in the outbuilding yesterday night, as he assumed he would be for the rest of the holiday.

He took it as a sign that he had been correct in his assessment that Earls Trip had to evolve with the times. That marriage and responsibilities must necessarily change the shape of the tradition.

"I shall also take my leave," he said, waving off the good-natured jeers from his friends over his early-to-bed habit. "Allow me to escort you out, Miss Brown. Or perhaps it is you who will escort me, as I clearly need rescuing from this lot."

He had only to escort her, or she him, out the door and to the base of the staircase. It took all of ten seconds.

He wanted to say so much more. He wanted to know more about her experience of the pool. He wanted to know what novels she had read on her holidays two summers ago. He wanted to know what was etched on her sister's gravestone.

He wanted to know everything.

Knowing he could have none of what he wanted, at least not now, he settled for bowing and saying, "Good night, Miss Brown."

"Good night, my lord."

A kind of melancholy settled as he crossed the garden to the gentlemen's cave. Mere minutes ago, he had been looking forward to being alone, but as he made himself ready for bed, he found his solitude had somehow become a burden. He was missing company.

And he had to admit that it wasn't Archie and Effie's company he was missing.

11

A Slow Turning

September 17, 1823
Earls Trip, day 10

Diantha began the next day as she had the previous, in the breakfast room with Lady Harcourt and Lord Marsden.

She was glad to see Lord Marsden, and she wasted no time, once she had settled the dowager with her plate, in opening the book he'd returned to her last night and slipping out a piece of paper.

A piece of paper he'd written on—that must have been what that unusual pen had been for. She hadn't been able to miss it, as it had been protruding almost an inch from the book.

"My lord, are you mocking me?"

He looked as if he were trying not to laugh as he removed his spectacles and set down his book. "I'm sure I don't know what you're talking about."

"You seem to have adopted my habit of copying down bits of prose." She waved the scrap of paper and read aloud from it. "'Ducks and geese are foolish things, and must be looked after, but girls can take care of themselves.'"

His smile broke through his feigned seriousness. "It's from 'The Legend of Sleepy Hollow.' Did you read it yet? I meant it to amuse you! I thought you would take it as a compliment!"

"Girls *can* take care of themselves, I find," Lady Harcourt interjected.

"Indeed," Diantha agreed, her heart light.

There was no reason for it to be. She had, as she'd assured Lord Harcourt, solved her matrimonial problem, but a solution was not the same thing as a happy outcome. Lord Marsden had suggested, yesterday, that Diantha wasn't truly on holiday. His criterion seemed to be that she wasn't able to set aside her responsibilities, namely, Lady Harcourt. But what she had set aside since she arrived at Gurglewood were thoughts of Mr. Baldwin and what lay ahead. She was surprised sometimes to find that hours had passed without her having thought about it whatsoever.

"Should we say grace?" Lady Harcourt asked.

"Oh," Diantha, startled, said. "We don't generally at breakfast, but certainly we shall, if you like."

The dowager seemed, via a somewhat impatient hand gesture, to indicate that she did like. Diantha looked at Lord Harcourt.

"You want me to do it?"

She wasn't sure why he found that remarkable.

"I don't generally pray," he added.

That *was* remarkable. "But you are a man of faith."

"I don't know about that."

"You don't? You were bound for the Church. You refused my . . . When we spoke about a certain matter recently, you—"

"The matter for which we don't require a code word?" he said blithely.

She ignored the teasing. "You said your God would disapprove."

"Well, he's not *my* God." He paused. "If he exists."

"*If* he exists? I *beg* your pardon!"

Lord Marsden sighed, seeming to signal a capitulation to actually talking, rather than merely teasing. "If I am a man of faith, it is because I spend a great deal of time thinking about faith, primarily the contradictions inherent in living a faithful life."

"What do you mean?"

"Consider last year's Earls Trip, which was to Brighton."

"All right."

"I wanted to see the Royal Pavilion. I have an interest in architecture."

"You do?"

"Is that so unusual?"

"It's just that I thought I knew everything about you."

"Why would you think that?"

It was a good question, and not one she had an answer for. She made a gesture to indicate that he should continue speaking.

"We met Julianna there—Stonely's wife, though of course she was not yet Lady Stonely. She secured for us a tour of the Pavilion's interior. She commissioned me to write a story about it for her magazine, and, not to be overdramatic, but the whole affair caused a minor crisis of faith."

"The Royal Pavilion caused a crisis of faith?" Goodness, what a mystery Lord Marsden was. He contained so many layers.

"Not the Pavilion per se, but what it represented. Why is it moral for one man, one family, to live in such splendor, when so many want for so much? Why is it moral for me to? And back to the king: Is he truly chosen by God? Is God playing chess? If so, are we the pawns? Or did he call checkmate at some point—perhaps when he realized the endless wars with France were in fact endless?—and abandon us to our fate?"

She was astonished. "You would have made a very interesting vicar."

"I think I would have made a fine vicar. My personal questions aside, it would have allowed me a simpler, more direct way to do good."

"But arguably, what you do now in Lords has a much greater impact, affects far more people."

"Perhaps. And you, Miss Brown? Are you a woman of faith?"

"I am somewhat embarrassed to admit that I give God very little thought. I did rail at him in my younger years, at various crisis points in my life. But at some point, I suppose I decided that I could argue with God, or I could get on with my life."

"What an astonishingly forthright conversation we are having," Lady Harcourt said, and again Diantha was startled at how easily she could forget herself when she was speaking with Lord Marsden.

"I consider myself a lady of faith," the dowager said. "Though I don't go to church much these days on account of my condition."

Simon met Diantha's gaze. She could tell he was surprised. It *was* surprising, to outsiders, when Lady Harcourt had her flashes of lucidity. They wouldn't necessarily lead to memories of her biography, or her family; they were snippets of the past.

"But back when I did go to church, or when I was meant to," Lady Harcourt continued, "I often found myself struck with a megrim."

"I remember, my lady. They always seemed to arrive on Sunday mornings."

"Yes, so unfortunate."

"I think," Lord Marsden said, not even bothering to try to temper a grin, "that we can make a distinction between being faithful and being observant."

"Yes," Lady Harcourt said. She turned to Diantha. "I like him."

I like him, too.

"What are we meant to wear?" Miss Morgan asked that afternoon by the edge of the pool.

"I'm sure I don't know," said Lady Stonely, "but my husband has assured me that the gentlemen have gone for a long ride, by which I believe he meant they are giving us our privacy."

"Hmm." Miss Morgan turned to Diantha. "What did you and the elder Lady Harcourt wear yesterday?"

"Our dresses," Diantha said. "Mine is still quite damp. And I only brought two." She looked down at herself. "Perhaps I ought to go change into the still-wet one in order to preserve this one."

"I think we should go in in our shifts," Miss Morgan said.

Diantha found herself agreeing. "Being weighed down by the amount of wet fabric that comprises a dress was neither pleasant nor practical. A shift is lighter and will dry faster."

"It's decided, then. Will you unbutton me?" Miss Morgan turned and presented Diantha with a line of buttons down her back.

Diantha made quick work of them, and it wasn't until she was disrobed herself that the reality of the circumstance sank in: She was standing in her shift with a countess—albeit an unconventional one—and the sister to a countess.

Well, there was nothing for it. "If you would like my advice?"

The ladies both answered in the affirmative.

"I suggest immersing yourselves quickly, and fully. It is very cold, and in my estimation, it is better to submit to that fact than to resist it."

She took her own advice, but she was the only one. The other two ladies got partway in and began shrieking.

Shrieking became laughing—Diantha joined in on that part—and after a minute, she was alone in the pool.

"I am sorry, Miss Brown!" Miss Morgan cried. "I cannot do it!"

"Nor I, but I shall attempt to immerse my legs." Lady Stonely sat on the stone edge of the pool and winced as she extended her legs into the water. "My goodness. While I am sure there is some benefit to taking these waters, I am less certain it outweighs the suffering induced along the way."

"How do you do it, Miss Brown?" Miss Morgan came to sit by Lady Stonely, but she left her limbs on land.

"Once you get used to it, it's not so bad," Diantha said. "Which if you think about it, is true about many aspects of life."

"Yes," Miss Morgan said with a sudden urgency that surprised Diantha. "I certainly know that to be true."

"I would even go so far as to say that if you sit in the discomfort for a while, if you pay close enough attention to the subtle undercurrents—no pun intended—of what you are feeling, you begin to notice a kind of slow turning."

"A slow turning?" Lady Stonely asked, leaning toward Diantha with what appeared to be genuine interest.

"Pain is replaced by a kind of exhilaration." She closed her eyes, trying to think how to articulate it. "It's almost as if I can feel the blood traveling through my veins." She tilted her head back, let the warm sun on her face exist in juxtaposition to the cold otherwise enveloping her.

"It can only last so long, though," she said with a smile as she heaved herself out of the pool. "But I will say, this is the best part." Standing by the edge, she held her arms out to her sides and took a deep breath. "The aftermath of immersion . . . It makes me feel . . . Well, it's difficult to put into words."

"Try," Lady Stonely said. "The aftermath of immersion makes you feel—what?"

The answer was out before she could overthink it. "Invincible."

Later, by the fire, Lady Stonely asked Diantha to write an account of the pool for her magazine.

"What do you mean? The bit about how it's best to get in all at once?"

"Yes, but not only that. The feeling of invincibility it confers. The overall experience, empirically and subjectively. A report and a review simultaneously, if you will."

"I . . ." Diantha had been poised to decline, as if by rote. But why? Why could she not write an account for a lady's magazine? She had told Lord Marsden, all those weeks ago, that even though she wasn't using her education, she did have it. Another thought landed.

"How much would you—"

She cut herself off. One wasn't supposed to talk about money in polite company.

But perhaps the rules were relaxed when polite company included a woman of business wearing a wet shift?

"How much would I pay?" Lady Stonely posed the question for Diantha, her tone suggesting it was not an unwelcome one.

"Generally not a great deal for first-time writers, but I am open to negotiation."

"I . . ." Diantha didn't know how to negotiate.

"Name your price, Miss Brown."

"Ten shillings?" she tried, having no idea if she was under- or overselling herself, though it did seem rather a lot of money for what would amount to a few hours of work.

"Done."

"Truly?"

"Yes." The countess extended her hand, and Diantha gathered she was meant to shake it, in the fashion that gentlemen did.

It was a bit of a thrill.

"Well, don't you drive a hard bargain, Miss Brown?" Miss Morgan said.

"I have need of funds," Diantha said, seeing no need to dissemble, given that no one was finding the frank discussion or the striking of a business arrangement untoward.

"Do you now?" Miss Morgan said, her eyes narrowing, not unkindly but in a way that made Diantha think she *ought* to have dissembled.

She could only take this truth-telling so far. What would she even say? *Yes, I am paying an odious man called Anthony Baldwin half my life savings to appear to ruin me, after which time I shall retire to a life of deprivation, so please send all the blunt my way*?

"Don't you think it would be lovely to immerse oneself in the pool at night?" she asked as a means of changing the subject.

It worked. Miss Morgan shuddered. "I do not think. Imagine how bone-chilling that water would be without the tempering impact of the sun."

"But imagine what an experience it would be to sit in the water and tip one's head back and see the sky awash in stars. It would add a layer of sensory stimulation. Perhaps two layers, for have you noticed that if you pay attention, you can hear the gurgling of the brook over there?"

Both the ladies made expressions that seemed to indicate that they were listening to the water.

"Oh!" Miss Morgan exclaimed. "I've just got the name! Gurglewood! 'Gurgle' plus 'wood'!" She tilted her head. "I don't know if that makes it better or worse."

"You must try it, Miss Brown," Lady Stonely said. "Take the waters at night and incorporate your observations into your report."

Diantha laughed, as she believed the lady to be in jest.

"In fact, as your editor, I insist."

Oh, dear. "While I would be happy to indulge you, I can't see how it can work, operationally."

"I will stay with Lady Harcourt this evening," Miss Morgan said. "I was already planning to anyway."

"I beg your pardon?" Diantha asked.

"Yes, Archie and I are conspiring to spell you off in the evenings, so you may have a true holiday."

"That is kind of you, but not—"

"So, tonight, I will stay beyond the time you would normally return. Well, you can return, and prepare yourself for your investigative mission, but I will remain."

"But . . ."

"You needn't worry about the gentlemen. The only one of the gentlemen who can countenance the cold is Simon, and he goes to bed frightfully early."

That would explain why Diantha and Lady Harcourt always met him in the breakfast room.

"And I can personally attest to the fact that my husband spends the night with me," Lady Stonely said.

"As does Archie with my sister," Miss Morgan said. "The gentlemen were meant to stay together in the outbuilding, but Archie and Effie are apparently unable to be parted from their ladies for even a night." She rolled her eyes to communicate her opinion on the matter of such overly uxorious gentlemen. "Poor Simon, left alone in the outbuilding all night. Do you know that they have been calling it the gentleman's cave?"

"Well," said Diantha, happily defeated by their logic, "apparently I am to take the waters under the stars this evening while listening to the brook." She was unaccountably excited. "But what if it is not a clear evening?"

"It will be," Miss Morgan said, and Diantha had no idea how she could possibly know that.

12

Absurdly Named Comets

Simon enjoyed another evening with his friends, and with Miss Brown. Although he wasn't sure why he had thought of it like that, as if there were two groups of people in the drawing room: friends, and Miss Brown. As if she occupied her own category.

Was she not his friend?

He thought back to that extraordinary night in August, the one they weren't supposed to talk about. Suddenly overwarm, he got up and went to stand by a window, opening it a crack.

He observed the room. Whereas the prior evening had seen Simon and Miss Brown conversing away from the others, today she was firmly ensconced in the wider circle, having been shepherded there after they dined by Lady Stonely, who was talking animatedly about the magazine business. He had only partially followed the conversation, but it was clear that Miss Brown was engaging in it in a way she hadn't previously.

So in addition to being his friend, it appeared Miss Brown was making headway with the others.

Did that . . . annoy him?

No, no. He thought back to her wrenching observations about *Frankenstein*, made both in conversation and via one of her slips of paper. He ought to be made happy by observing her talking and laughing with everyone. Simon well knew the comfort of friendship generally, and the balm provided by these particular people.

He was struck with another notion: He was spending an awful lot of time observing and thinking about Miss Brown.

He ought to stop doing that. He had turned down her outrageous proposal. They had their unspoken agreement not to speak of that night. Miss Brown was intelligent and competent. She had assured him on two occasions now that she had resolved the issue of the unwanted proposal.

So everything was fine. Everything was—

"Simon, I trust you will be taking in tonight's celestial display?"

Olive, intruding on his thoughts.

Which was also fine. It was *welcome.*

"Is that why you've opened this window?" she asked. "Are you trying to get a peek already? Isn't it too early?"

"I'm afraid I don't know what you're talking about."

"I'm talking about the comet!"

"The comet? Which comet?"

"I'm surprised you didn't read about it in the papers. This week is meant to provide for peak viewing."

He had been spending too much time reading novels. It was the only explanation for his having missed the news of a comet, something he was quite interested in.

"Will you be venturing out to see it?" he asked Olive.

"Oh, no. Comets are not a particular interest of mine."

"What is the name of this comet?"

"It is called . . . Comet Ozymandias."

Ozymandias? Simon was aware that comets were often named after people, their discoverers, primarily, but that seemed an odd name. Odd, but also . . . was there something familiar about it?

Ah. He had it.

"Wasn't Ozymandias the Christian name of that duke you . . ."

Were being flirtatious with. He couldn't say that. But he did distinctly remember that after the upheaval following Earls Trip two years ago, Olive and Clementine's father had confined them to the house until Olive announced that she had her sights set on a visiting Scottish duke with an absurd name.

Yes, Simon remembered it *because* the name had been so absurd, and Olive so smitten. "Ozymandias Macduff. Wasn't that his name?"

"Oh, yes, I'd forgotten all about him," Olive said blithely. "What an amusing coincidence." She tilted her head as if suddenly struck with an outlandish thought. "Do you think the comet is *named after him*?"

"I suppose it's possible." He paused. "Likely even, with that name." Perhaps her onetime mark had an astronomical bent.

"Well, then I *certainly* shan't be losing any sleep to see it."

And with that, she flounced off.

Simon tried to get the boys interested in a comet-viewing party, but he had no luck. One would think they could have wrenched themselves from the company, and the beds, of their wives to witness such a rare celestial occurrence. He paused to wonder how rare. Simon had not read sciences at school, but he was aware that comets returned on a cycle, and that each had its own particular period. This might be their one and only chance to see Comet Ozymandias.

He was sitting by the fire. It had been an unseasonably warm autumn, but it was cold at night, and since he was likely to be out for several hours, he had rationalized making a small fire, despite the fact that it would cast unwanted light. Even if he didn't get to see the comet, he was glad he'd come out. Since he spent most of his time these days in London, he rarely got to marvel at the night sky.

Again he had the sensation of missing Galecroft. Something about this trip was calling to mind the more enjoyable experiences he'd had there, which he supposed had been buried under the higher volume of unpleasant memories. He regretted that Mother seemed to have claimed Galecroft for herself.

Perhaps it was time to do something about that.

A splashing sound drew his attention. Someone was in the pool. Huzzah. He was in the mood for company and therefore glad that one—or, ideally, both—of the boys had reconsidered their plans for the evening.

He heaved himself up. "I do wish Olive had given us more details for—"

He was interrupted by a shriek. A distinctly feminine shriek.

Miss Brown. He froze, unsure what ought to be his next move. Flee? Apologize?

Join her?

Good God, no! Where had that thought come from?

He got hold of himself and turned his back to the pool. Not that he had or could see anything, not beyond the pale skin of her face. It was dark, and she had been submersed up to her chin. "Miss Brown, my sincerest apologies. I thought you were someone else."

"Someone you were meeting under cover of night?"

Was she . . . teasing him?

No, she can't have been. He answered her question earnestly. "I thought you were Archie and Effie."

"Alas, no. I am only me."

Only me. "You speak as if you believe your presence to be a disappointment."

"Well, I am not who you were expecting."

That was true. In more ways than one. "Miss Brown, I honestly can't think of anyone I'd rather have stumbled upon out here." He wasn't sure why he had said that, except that he felt oddly compelled to honesty. "However, now that I have, I shall leave you." He would hate to miss the comet, but it couldn't be helped. "I've a fire lit that I must put out, but I shall do so as efficiently as possible and be on my way."

"Wait!" she called, as if he had already begun his retreat. He had not. "If Lords Harcourt and Marsden are on their way out, it is I who should withdraw."

"They are not. They told me as much. I just assumed, when I heard someone in the pool, that they'd changed their minds."

"Changed their minds about what? May I inquire as to what you were doing out here to begin with?"

He smiled at the absurdity of conversing like this, he on land and Miss Brown . . . not on land. He suddenly wondered, with not a little alarm, what she was wearing beneath the surface of the water.

"Of course, it is none of my affair," she said. "Disregard the question."

"I don't mind answering. I was merely . . . momentarily distracted. I'm out here watching for the comet."

"Comet! Is there meant to be a comet tonight?"

"Yes. Did Miss Morgan not tell you about it? I saw you talking to her earlier."

"She did not, and I marvel at such, for the whole point of my being out here is so I can behold the night sky while taking the waters."

"I hadn't thought to try that, but it sounds lovely. A feast for two senses."

"I told the ladies exactly that. And if you listen for the brook, it's three senses. Lady Stonely has engaged me to write an account of taking the waters. When I mentioned I thought the experience would be even more enjoyable by starlight, she exhorted me to include an account of such. But Miss Morgan never mentioned anything about a comet."

"Well, I am on the lookout for it. Or I was. I shall leave you to your privacy."

"Oh, no, please don't miss your chance on my account. I . . ."

"Yes?"

"Lord Marsden, I think it is safe to say that in our recent acquaintance, we have dispensed with formalities. Would you agree?"

"I believe we have done more than dispense with them. We

have expunged them entirely. Annihilated them, one might even say."

She laughed, and he was pleased to have amused her. He was sorry he could not see the crinkles at the sides of her eyes that laughter always conjured. "Indeed, and I'm afraid that is my doing."

"I believe we shall need a code word after all if you are going to be any more specific in your reference to our annihilation of formalities."

She laughed again. He was pleased again. He missed the crinkles again.

"I am done referring to it," she said. "I would, however, like to point out that you are standing with your back to me now. I would like to further propose that you return to your fire but keep yourself angled thusly. I may be hearty, but my endurance has its limits and I must remove myself from this pool soon. This way, you may remain on comet watch, and I will take myself back to my room."

"I will of course do as you say—I don't even find it that scandalous; you did rather inflate my expectations with that buildup—but here is a counterproposal. I will remove to the fire and keep my back to it. Then perhaps you would care to join me. Warm yourself before you retire. I shan't look at you at all."

He expected her to decline, but she said, "It would be wonderful to see the comet."

"Well, here is your chance."

"Which I shall seize so long as I don't displace you."

"We are agreed."

As Simon returned to the fire and set up a chair for her near it and a chair for him on the other side facing away from it, he marveled at how confident, how at ease, he had sounded just then. As if he wasn't about to conduct a conversation with Miss Brown while she was wearing a soaking wet dress.

She would be wearing a dress, would she not?

He and Archie and Effie had gone in naked.

But that was before anyone else arrived.

Perhaps she would be wearing a shift. That would be—

"Any luck?"

He cleared his throat. "Not yet."

"Oh, the heat from the fire feels divine."

"Doesn't it, though?"

"I already enjoy the sensation that unfolds on one's skin—under one's skin—when one gets out of the pool. It is magnified, I think, by proximity to a heat source."

"I agree. How would you characterize that sensation?"

"It's a good question, and one I shall have to answer for the article I'm meant to write." She huffed a little sigh, and Simon wanted more than anything to peek over his shoulder. Not for any untoward reason. Merely to see what she was wearing.

Or not wearing.

But in a not untoward way.

"I think," she said, mercifully pulling him from the morass of his own mind, "that there must be a scientific explanation to do with temperature differentials. I can't comment on that, but I can comment on how it feels."

"And how does it feel?"

She was silent a moment, and he could see her in his mind's eye. She would be affecting her thinking pose, tilting her head slightly to the left.

"When you first get into the water, it is a shock, an utter shock. One can think of nothing else. I pause to add that my account is dependent on adherence to my methodology, which dictates that one must get in smoothly, all at once, and submerse oneself entirely."

"This is also my methodology."

"Well, then you know this feeling. One is overwhelmed, but in a welcome way."

Overwhelmed in a welcome way. "Yes. There is no room for anything except the sensations immediately at hand."

"Exactly. And then one begins to acclimatize."

"Which can be rather difficult to do when one's companions are shrieking."

She laughed—that was the third time. "Did your companions shriek, too?" she asked.

"They most certainly did."

"I think I must concede a point that Lady Stonely made earlier, that while everyone always accuses ladies of being prone to hysteria, and excesses of sentiment generally, gentlemen are equally afflicted."

It was Simon's turn to laugh. "Do go on with your account."

"All right. One is in the water. One is *not* shrieking. But eventually, even those with the strongest will are defeated by the cold."

"And then one must exit."

"And that is the best part."

"I quite agree."

"How would *you* characterize the sensation that follows?" she asked.

"Something . . . rises within one." That was a poor description but the best Simon could do.

"Yes," she agreed. "One grows warm from the inside out, which ought to be illogical given that one is, objectively, quite cold."

"Yes. A sensation swirls beneath the surface of one's skin. It amasses. Grows."

"Indeed. It is akin to . . . falling off a cliff."

She had the measure of things. "Miss Brown, I look forward to reading your article."

"I confess to being rather nervous about it. I have no qualifications whatsoever."

"I know this feeling. I think I mentioned that I once wrote an article for Lady Stonely's magazine—well, for its predecessor. I felt that I was out of my depth."

"This was the account of the Royal Pavilion. How did you manage, in the end?"

"I suppose I just forged ahead and did it. I acted like a person who could write a magazine article, and lo, I became one."

"You pretended so convincingly you persuaded even your greatest skeptic—yourself."

He smiled. "Exactly. And, of course, it did spark a crisis of faith."

It was a curious thing, to be conversing with Miss Brown but not looking at her. They were speaking quite intimately, and though he could not see her, he could picture the scene they made. Her skin would be lit by the flames, and her dark hair would disappear into the inky night. It would be too dark to distinguish between the gray bits of her irises and the blue bits, but in his mind's eye he could do so.

Silence settled for a few minutes. It was exceedingly companionable. How could it not be, given that they'd just shared a great deal of fellow feeling, agreeing on everything from pool-entering methodology to article-writing fakery?

He decided to bank on all that fellow feeling, to take a risk. "Miss Brown, I know you said the matter was settled, and I am glad to hear it, but will you tell me who was attempting to force you to marry him? I am aware that it is none of my affair, but I am asking all the same."

"Well, I made it your business, at least a little bit, did I not?" She paused. "Perhaps we *do* need a code word, so that we may talk about the thing we're not supposed to."

He chuckled. "All right. How about . . . obelisk?"

"Obelisk!" she exclaimed. "As in the Egyptian monuments?"

"Yes. I was trying to think of a word that is pleasing to say yet suitably weighty, and it popped to mind."

"All right. Obelisk." She went silent again for several moments. "My sister's late husband was the man in question. He wanted me to marry him."

"And you have no interest."

"I would rather be impaled on an obelisk."

He couldn't help but chuckle again. Miss Brown truly did say the wittiest things sometimes. "Understood. And you conveyed that to him, if not in precisely those terms?"

"I did. He was not prepared to take no for an answer."

Simon was about to suggest that she confide in Archie. Archie would tell this blackguard where to go. In addition to being a natural protector, Archie was aware—or ought to be—that he owed a great debt to Miss Brown.

She kept talking, though, and he wasn't inclined to interrupt her.

"In some ways, it feels as if I've only just gotten away from him, though of course I've been with Lady Harcourt for years."

"What is he like, apart from his suitability, or lack thereof, as a prospective husband?"

"Quite simply, he is a brute."

"Why did your sister marry him, then?"

"Because he was a brute with money—enough money, anyway. Nothing like . . ."

He could imagine her looking around the property.

"Here. He had some kind of inheritance from his father, and he made a fine case to my sister, wooing her with small gifts, which for her, I imagine must not have seemed small." She paused. "I have referenced my family's fall from fortune."

"Yes." He did not tell her he had asked the others about it.

"My father was overfond of gambling." She paused again. "That is understating the matter."

"I understand."

"Do you? I don't. I don't understand how a man could spend the money needed to sustain his family on a high-stakes card game common sense tells him he is almost certain to lose."

He wanted to tell her how sorry he was, but he suspected she would not respond well to such an overture; it would be interpreted as pity. Part of him wondered if she was only speaking so openly because he wasn't looking at her. He settled for saying something less than he wanted to. "I suppose logic is not at work in the minds of gamblers."

"Yes, but that implies I ought to feel sympathy for him. I do not."

"This is the rage you spoke of."

"I suppose this is its origin, yes. But lest you think me overdramatic, allow me to tell you one story about my father's . . . Well, I was going to say 'follies,' but the correct word is 'crimes.'"

"I am ready to hear it, if you are ready to tell it."

"He gambled my sister away."

"Good God!"

"Yes. He was very deep into a game of cards, a game that included a visiting American industrialist who was trouncing the lot of them. As a last-ditch effort, my father wagered my sister's hand. My sister was just out, and very pretty. He carried miniatures of both of us. I imagine he showed the gentleman.

"Mr. Hill—the man who became my sister's husband—had been making overtures. My sister had rebuffed him. But when my father came home with the news—he was quite distraught, I will give him that—she changed her mind. She ran away with Mr. Hill." She sniffed. "She should have gone with the American industrialist."

"Miss Brown, I am endeavoring to remain calm in my listening, but it is difficult to imagine a father wagering away his child." Simon was continuing his strategy of saying less than he would've preferred.

"I can't pretend to understand it. I know only that he could never walk away from the table."

"Do you think he started out like that?"

"I know he started out like that. His father covered his debts, so it wasn't an issue for a while. At worst, he had a 'habit' people would gossip about when he sustained major losses. But then his father died, and his fortune went to his son by his second wife—my father's mother died in childbirth. I do not know the mechanisms behind the inheritance. I do know that my father appealed to his stepmother for funds, and she turned him down. For the record, I do not blame her for that.

"We economized. My mother took in piecework." She paused again. Every time she did so, Simon wanted to jump in, whether to encourage her to continue or to tell her that he understood and she needn't say more, he wasn't sure. But he kept himself silent. He would wait until *she* felt she was done.

It brought to mind a few instances from his childhood where he'd tried, at some family dinner or other, to recount something that had happened at school. His brothers had always been talking. They'd been so *boisterous*. He'd hadn't minded, inherently, but it had made it hard to get a word in. And on the rare occasion he had made a toehold, if he paused at all to gather his thoughts, that was the end of that.

He endeavored never to do that to others, and doing it to Miss Brown was unimaginable.

"My lord, I am glossing over a great deal of suffering here. I should prefer not to recount it all, but suffice it to say that things became quite unpleasant. And then, about a year later, my father disappeared. His body was found in a river. We never knew the circumstances of his death. Perhaps the American industrialist—we never knew how my father settled things with him after my sister married Mr. Hill—came to collect. Perhaps he could no longer face the consequences of all that he had done—after the business with my sister, my mother had gone into an almost catatonic state. She didn't talk to anyone. She barely ate. She just slept and, when up, either worked obsessively on the piecework she had taken in to attempt to sustain us, or sat in a chair by the window stared listlessly. We had lost our house by this time and were living in a small cottage, so it was impossible to avoid her melancholy. Then, a few months after my father died, she did, too. Consumption, they said, but I believe she simply willed herself to die."

Simon had never felt such a mix of sentiment before. He wanted to resurrect Mr. Brown from the dead so he could murder him. He wanted to find this nameless American industrialist and interrogate him—and possibly murder him, too. But mostly, he wanted to take young Miss Brown and her sister in his arms and spirit them away from all that had befallen them.

He expressed none of this, merely said, "So you went to live with your sister and Mr. Hill."

"Yes. And things were improved materially in that household, though only marginally. Mr. Hill did have some money, but once he'd wooed my sister with it, he closed the taps. She never had enough for the meals he expected, forget clothing and the necessities of life."

"Or for ribbons."

"Or for ribbons," she agreed. "Poverty would have been one thing, had he been kind to her, or even indifferent. She never shared the worst of it, but I often heard him shouting at her. She was never able to give him a child, and the more time passed, the angrier he became. He would insist they . . . try all the time, whether she wanted to or no."

Simon winced.

"She did conceive once, and his demeanor changed. But it didn't last—the pregnancy, or the warmth from Mr. Hill."

The next pause was long enough that it couldn't rightly be considered a pause. Simon broke his rule about interjecting. "At some point, you came to Mollybrook."

"Yes. Lady Harcourt swooped in, like an angel from above. She always maintained she didn't remember where she heard about my situation. 'I can't remember, my girl.'" Miss Brown said, lowering her voice and putting on quite a credible impression of the dowager. "'I suppose I heard about it at some party or other. I am sorry your mother and I lost touch.' I believe that my sister wrote to her, though she always denied it, as did Lady Harcourt."

"Does it matter, the mechanism by which you came to be with the dowager?"

"I felt that it did, initially. I still had the idea, back then, that I didn't want to be anyone's charity case."

The way she said that implied that she had shed that concern.

He wondered—he wondered desperately—if time had ground her pride out of her. He hoped not. He thought back to that marker.

A person may be proud without being vain.

"You have been indispensable as a companion and caretaker for Lady Harcourt," he said carefully.

"Yes," she said quietly.

He ventured a little further. "You ought to be proud of your work."

"I am," she said, and he was happy to hear it. "But it *is* work."

"I never doubted it. Harcourt has confided in Stonely and me about the toll extracted by the caretaking effort. I imagine that toll is much higher for you."

"Perhaps, perhaps not. He is her son, and she rarely recognizes him as such. He pays a different cost."

"Yes." He was struggling to connect the pieces of her story. Did she not want to continue in her position as companion to the dowager? "So your late sister's husband proposed marriage, you said no, but he was, as you said, not inclined to accept that answer."

"I thought I needed a credible reason to decline. Something to make him not want me."

"Hence your visit to my home last month."

"I thought we were using the code word to talk about that unfortunate evening."

He smiled, though she couldn't see it. "Hence . . . obelisk."

"Yes, and I am sorry for it. It was the wrong approach. But as I've said a number of times, you needn't worry about the situation. I have devised another plan."

What did that mean? *I have devised another plan* was not the same as having delivered a refusal and it having been accepted.

"My lord, may I ask you a question?"

"Of course."

"You may turn around if you like. I brought a blanket to warm myself post-bathing, and I am thoroughly covered by it. And while I appreciate your aim to adhere to proprieties, I would venture to suggest that being out here at all is as improper as your seeing me covered in a blanket would be."

He wanted so badly to turn. He wanted to see her.

"And," she added, "I seem to recall someone claiming to be, what was it? Profoundly uninterested in adhering to social mores he considers nonsensical?"

He laughed and turned, and it was as if they were bosom friends reunited after a long separation. Her smile was fond, he flattered himself, and everything about her was familiar. The shape of her mouth as it smiled. The shape of *her*, despite the fact that she was indeed covered from ankle to chin with a blanket.

But everything was also different. She was wearing a blanket instead of a dress. And her hair *wasn't* disappearing into the night as he had thought it might be. The light cast by the fire was greater than in his invented version of this scenario, and her hair was clearly visible. It was down, though, which he had neither imagined nor seen before. It curled damply around her ears, gradually becoming less wavy closer to her shoulders.

"Did you put your whole head under the water?" he asked, since they were dispensing with the veneer of politeness.

"I did. I decided to try total immersion this time, since I was alone—or so I thought."

She was fascinating. Fearless, and fascinating. "What was your question?" He couldn't wait to hear it.

"It's about work."

Oh. That was . . . a bit disappointing? "What about it?"

"I said I was proud of my work. Are you proud of yours? I imagine you must be."

"I am."

"But do you *enjoy* it? That is what I truly want to know."

"Not particularly," he said, choosing not to overthink his answer. "Much of it is deadly dull."

"But you seem so terribly devoted to it," she said, laughingly, and there were those crinkles he had wanted so badly to see. They were worth the wait.

"I am devoted to my work, but that doesn't mean it's not dull." He smiled. There was something delightful about being so forthright.

"Then why do it so earnestly? You could be a more typical peer, showing up for votes, swanning off the rest of the time."

"I consider it my duty. And I'm not saying that just because something is dull, it's not worth doing. In fact, sometimes the dullness feels like the whole point."

"I'm not sure I follow," she said.

"There's a devotional aspect to tedious work."

"Devotional?"

"Oh, don't listen to me," he said. "I don't know what I'm talking about. It's not as if I am doing the Lord's work."

"I think I understand what you mean. It's not unlike tending to Lady Harcourt. The days are all the same. Even when they're different, they're the same, which I realize makes no sense."

"It makes sense. A committee discussion of the Warehousing Bill is, technically, different from a committee discussion of the Silk Manufacture Bill, and yet . . . it is not."

"Precisely. Singing 'Sally in the Valley,' which, as you know, her ladyship is currently fixated on, a dozen times is different from singing 'Over the Hills and Far Away,' which was the prior preoccupation, a dozen times, and yet it is not. I think that must be the nature of devotional endeavors—repetition can feel weighty, perhaps even holy, when it is in service of something important."

"Yes, precisely." He was pleased by how aptly she was summarizing a position he had struggled to articulate. "May I ask what has brought on this line of questioning?"

"Oh, I don't know. I suppose I have been pondering the question of why I do what I do. I know why I did it to begin with—you heard that sad story. But why do I *keep* doing it?" She waved a hand as if dismissing an answer he was about to make, but he did not have one at the ready.

He'd been trying to puzzle through if there was a deeper meaning to all her questions.

"Of course," she said, "I do it because I have nowhere else to go. I have no one to keep me."

I have no one to keep me.

Simon felt the sentence echoing in his chest, pinging around and hitting tender, hidden flesh.

"Oh, don't listen to me," she said. "I am talking nonsense. Let us speak of happier things. I always knew you and Lords Harcourt and Stonely were bosom friends, but I must say it is a delight to see you in action. How lucky you all are to have each other."

"Yes," he said, for it was true, though he wondered how she had come to that conclusion. He hadn't spent much time with the boys since the ladies got here. The arrival of their wives had distracted them.

"What do you think is the most important trait in a friend?" she asked.

"I suppose it must be compassion. Understanding." Those were the traits Effie and Archie had in spades that Simon most benefited from.

"Hmm."

She sounded skeptical. "You do not agree?"

"I don't disagree, but for me the answer would be loyalty."

"Loyalty." He turned the word over in his mouth.

"A quality you have in spades, my lord, or you wouldn't have kept secret my appalling lack of manners in the matter of the . . . obelisk." When he didn't say anything, she added, "Or about what I told you this evening about my father."

"Well," he couldn't resist pointing out, though he smiled to show he was in jest, "you only just told me that. My loyalty on that matter has yet to be tested."

But that was essentially what she was doing, wasn't it, with her question about the qualities of friendship? She was testing him. He wanted to pass.

"I think the quality you are after, Miss Brown, isn't loyalty so much as it is trustworthiness. I am a person whose friends can trust him."

"Does that mean you are not loyal to your friends?"

"No, of course not, but loyalty to me seems a larger concept. I am loyal to institutions. Not blindly so, mind you. Institutions can and should change."

"Is that why we ladies are here?"

"I don't follow."

"The institution of Earls Trip. Lord Harcourt told me it was your idea that the wives and his mother and the hangers-on—the hangers-on being Miss Morgan and me—should join you. I believe you suggested that the tradition needed to accommodate the reality of the fact that you aren't bachelors anymore."

"Well, I am. But yes, I suppose your assessment is correct. Earls Trip is a kind of institution, though I hadn't been thinking of it that way. A true institution, I believe, is a force for good, or a potential force for good, in the life of all."

"Parliament, for example."

"Yes. Or the Church. Both of which give us structure, and meaning."

"Can family be an institution?"

"I suppose, but in my case more traditional institutions have stepped in where family fell short."

"Marriage is an institution."

"Indeed."

"And one that you respect."

"I suppose I do, though I'm not sure how you can know that."

"You said as much, in a speech in July of 1820."

"I did?" He was astonished, and not a little flattered, she could cite something he'd said so specifically.

"Yes, it was during the Queen Caroline affair. You said something along the lines of your respect for the bonds of holy matrimony being such that you did not offer your support for the queen's defense lightly."

He chuckled. "I may have been speaking out of political expediency."

"Really?"

"No," he said quietly. "Not really."

"I thought not."

He cast himself back to the summer in question and tried to imagine Miss Brown reading his words. "My support for the queen had little to do with my feelings on the institution of marriage, though. It was more a question of fairness."

"Why was the king able to cavort around taking lovers quite publicly, but when the queen took one with the utmost discretion, even after that letter of separation, it was a matter to be taken up by the House of Lords?"

"Yes." She should have been the one giving the speech. "Though I must point out that neither monarch seemed to have much respect for the institution of marriage."

She laughed. "Indeed."

"My point," he said, "is that institutions keep society together. To that end, we owe them our loyalty."

"Is that why you wouldn't ruin me? Because you respect the institution of marriage?"

"I told you, I respect myself too much." He paused. He ought not to bring this up yet again, but he couldn't help himself. "What are you going to do?"

"I have a plan."

"You keep saying that, but I would like to know what that plan is."

"You'll forgive me, my lord, but I don't owe you an accounting of my plan."

He wanted to protest, to say that she *did* owe him an accounting, but on what grounds could he make that argument?

Abruptly, tersely, she sat forward on her chair, as if she were about to rise from it, and said, "I should go. Miss Morgan is sitting with Lady Harcourt for me. She won't have expected me to be gone this long."

He wanted to object. He wanted to entreat her to stay, to talk with him around the fire until the sun rose. A startling thought landed. "We quite forgot about the comet."

"Oh! Yes!" She tipped her head back, and he did too.

The sky was very beautiful, but he saw nothing out of the ordinary.

"I always wanted to learn about the constellations," she said. "My sister and I used to stargaze, but the only one I know is the hunter. He's not here, though, is he?"

"Orion," Simon said. "He will become visible toward morning. It isn't until winter you can see him this time of night. But there are several here now." He pointed out Andromeda and Pegasus.

"Pegasus, born of the blood of Medusa when Perseus beheaded her," Miss Brown said.

"Yes." He chuckled. "And wasn't Andromeda chained to a rock at some point, in sacrifice to some angry god or other?"

"Yes, but I think Perseus rescued her." She paused. "Perseus was rather busy, it would seem."

They shared a laugh. She was so *witty.*

"I should go," she said again, but this time the phrase wasn't fraught, as it had been after she'd informed him she didn't owe him an accounting of her plans. Now, she was merely taking her leave. She stood and performed an abbreviated curtsy, which was rather comical given the blanket that was still shrouding her. "I hope I haven't made you miss the comet."

"I am sure you haven't," he said, when what he meant was *It was worth it.* "Regardless, my understanding of comets is that when they visit us, they are around for a time." He stood and angled his head so he could look right in her eyes. He would freely admit that he was attempting to send her a message. "I shall try again tomorrow."

13

The Patroness of Journalism

September 18, 1823
Earls Trip, day 11

Diantha spent most of the next day wondering if what had transpired the night before had in fact transpired. Had she developed delusions? An imagination the likes of which the world had never seen? Perhaps she ought to start writing novels rather than merely reading them.

The worst part—the best part?—was that she had almost told Lord Marsden the whole story. Meaning, about the blackmail. Meaning, about what damage she might have inflicted upon Lady Harcourt—and the entire family.

She was glad she hadn't, of course. She was keeping it secret for a reason. But it had felt so natural to confide in him. For a moment there, she had been teetering on the edge of confessing everything. It would have been so easy. It would have been such a relief.

Lady Harcourt had slept uncharacteristically late, which suited Diantha, because she had gotten very little sleep. She'd been out late, of course, but she'd had a terrible time settling once she'd spelled off Miss Morgan and gotten into bed.

The dowager's tardy awakening meant they had missed Lord Marsden in the breakfast room. That afternoon, they spent some time with the ladies, dipping their feet in the pool. Everyone, including the younger Lady Harcourt, joined.

"Oh, it is as cold as you all say!" she exclaimed, retracting her legs as soon as her toes hit the water.

Everyone else, including the dowager, sat on the pool's edge with their dresses hiked up and their lower legs submerged. It wasn't the all-consuming sensation that full-body immersion incited, but it was refreshing.

Lady Stonely said, "I do love to swim. Having recently learned, I have the zeal of a convert. I had been looking forward to this pool, but I find I cannot last very long." She pulled her legs out.

"You are all weaklings!" Miss Morgan said teasingly. "And so am I!" She removed her legs, too, leaving only the elder Lady Harcourt and Diantha in the water.

"I did not enjoy our attempt at bathing the other day," the dowager said, "but I quite like having just my legs in. It is pleasantly bracing."

"I agree," Diantha said, and the other ladies exclaimed over the strength of her constitution.

Eventually, the dowager pulled her legs out, and Diantha followed.

They stayed where they were, wet legs stretched out in the sun.

"I wanted to tell you all something," the younger Lady Harcourt said, and her sister, Miss Morgan, squealed and clapped her hands.

"It is perhaps early to be sharing this news, but I wanted to explain why I have been so absent from the group these recent days." She flashed a smile that seemed a mite nervous. "I am expecting a child."

Miss Morgan, who clearly already knew the happy news, increased the speed of her clapping. "I am going to be an aunt!" With a final clap, she interlaced her fingers under her chin and said, adopting a theatrically menacing tone, "I am going to be *such* a bad influence."

Diantha found herself a bit overcome as she listened to Lady

Stonely voice her congratulations. She was so happy for Lady Harcourt—and Lord Harcourt. She had watched them marry and start a life together, and now they were making a family. She found herself inexplicably sad that she would not be around when the baby came. "Congratulations, my lady. You are going to be a wonderful mother."

Lady Harcourt, who was seated next to Diantha, turned. "Oh, Miss Brown, do you really think so?"

"Indeed, I do."

The young countess had a big heart and a grand spirit of adventure. Her children would be lucky.

"I *know* so."

"My own mother was wonderful, but I was so young when she died, I fear I can't remember precisely what made her so."

"There isn't a formula to emulate, Clementine," Miss Morgan said. "You need only be yourself, for your self is wonderful, and all will be well."

"You are going to have a child," the elder Lady Harcourt, who was on the other side of the younger countess, said.

"Yes. And it will be your grandchild."

Tears sprang to the dowager's eyes.

The younger Lady Harcourt embraced the elder. "It will be very fortunate to have you for a grandmother."

"I always wanted a grandchild. Do you think it's going to be a boy or a girl?"

"I don't know," young Lady Harcourt said. "I have heard tell of expectant mothers who have an inkling, but I have none. Perhaps it is too early for that."

"I hope it's a girl," the dowager said firmly.

"I say, my lady, you may be the only matriarch of a noble family hoping for a girl instead of an heir!" Miss Morgan said.

"Girls are stronger, and better equipped to weather the trials of the world," the dowager said. "They are also more fun."

"I couldn't agree more," Miss Morgan declared as everyone laughed.

"I have been feeling unwell," the young Lady Harcourt said, "which is why I haven't been at breakfast, or around much generally. I have been attempting to be present in the evenings, but that seems to be all I can manage."

"My sister was the same," Diantha said. "May I show you a remedy she swore by?"

Everyone's attention swung to her, and she realized they were trying to square what she'd said with her claim that she had no family. "My sister was with child once. She got rather far along, but she lost it."

The ladies murmured their condolences, and Diantha was struck by how . . . not alone she felt, despite the fact that she had just confirmed that she was without family. The elder Lady Harcourt reached over the younger and clasped Diantha's hand, giving it a quick squeeze.

Tears threatened. How could she leave them?

But what other choice did she have? It was leave them, or publicly humiliate them.

"I would be quite happy to hear your sister's remedy," young Lady Harcourt said, drawing Diantha from her thoughts.

"It would be something I'd show you, rather than tell you. May I take your arm?"

"Please do."

"It is something my sister's midwife showed her." She turned Lady Harcourt's arm over in her lap and searched for the spot on her wrist. "She said when nausea threatened, to apply pressure here. It did used to provide relief. You can do it yourself, of course, one side at a time, but she found it more effective if I did it for her, both sides at once."

"Thank you, Miss Brown. I am feeling well at the moment—it must be the sparkling company—but I shall try it at the earliest opportunity."

"You may find," the dowager said, "that you will feel better soon. For many ladies, the illness does go away after the first few months."

"So I have heard, and so I hope," young Lady Harcourt said. She turned to Diantha with a knowing, borderline censorious expression. "Now, I would like to discuss a very important topic."

Dread flooded Diantha's gut. *Did she know?*

No. How could she? That would only be possible had Lord Marsden told Lord Harcourt Diantha's secret. And he didn't even know the most incriminating part. More to the point, he wouldn't have betrayed her confidence. He was an obelisk, upright and infallible.

"I understand that you are in possession of a copy of *Frankenstein*," the countess said. "I understand that it is quite the thrilling story."

"Oh!" Diantha laughed, thankful the ladies would not know it was mostly out of relief. She had entertained the notion that young Lady Harcourt was onto her about Lord Marsden, but she was only onto her about *Frankenstein*. "Yes! And yes, it is quite thrilling. But also heartbreaking. And wise. And cautionary."

"I wholeheartedly agree," Lady Stonely said. "And did you know that Mrs. Shelley reportedly wrote it on a dare? She and Percy, who I hasten to add was not yet her husband, were holidaying with Lord Byron, and Byron reportedly suggested they attempt to pen ghost stories. I don't know that it was framed as a competition, but if it was, I think we can agree who came out of it the victor."

"Miss Brown," the younger Lady Harcourt said, "you know how fond I am of Gothic novels. I fail to see why you haven't lent this book to me!" She spoke with mock admonishment. "I trust you will do so now."

"I cannot. I have lent it to . . . someone else." Before anyone could ask who—though she reminded herself that she often lent novels to Lord Marsden in company, when he called on the family, and no one had said a word about it—she added, "But of course I shall give it to you as soon as I have it back."

"What is the book about?" the elder Lady Harcourt asked, and Diantha didn't point out that Lord Marsden had read at least some of it to her the other morning. Since he hadn't given it back, she had been assuming he planned to continue the exercise.

"It is rather gruesome." She hesitated to recount its plot. A few sentences would make it sound more sensational, and scandalous, than it was.

"It is about a doctor who brings to life a creature made of cadaver parts," Lady Stonely, apparently not possessed of any of Diantha's circumspection, said mildly. "And then the monster ruins the doctor's life. In a nutshell."

"That sounds familiar," Lady Harcourt said. "And a lady wrote this book, you say? On what sounds like a dare?"

"Yes," Lady Stonely said. "It was written by Mary Shelley, wife of the poet Percy Bysshe Shelley."

"Though perhaps we ought to refer to him as Percy Bysshe, husband of the novelist Mary Shelley," Miss Morgan said, and everyone laughed.

"You see?" the dowager said. "Ladies are a great deal more fun than gentlemen."

Dinner passed uneventfully but pleasantly, and as the group rose to move to the drawing room where evenings were spent, Miss Morgan took Diantha's arm. "Miss Brown, I want to hear all about your immersion under the stars last night. I didn't get a chance to ask you about it this afternoon."

And indeed, they hadn't spoken, beyond brief whispers, when Diantha arrived in her room last night, damp and invigorated, to relieve Miss Morgan from her post watching over Lady Harcourt.

"All these happy couples," Miss Morgan whispered as they watched everyone sit—they were trailing a bit behind the crowd. "I find it exceedingly disagreeable."

Diantha *giggled.*

When was the last time *that* had happened? She was slightly taken aback.

"I am pleased to have found a friend in you on this trip," Miss

Morgan said. "I had thought I would be lonely, what with everyone paired off."

"Well, there is Lord Marsden." Diantha observed him taking his seat apart from the larger group. He had, as per usual, brought a book with him. Diantha herself had sat there more than once, carrying on a semiprivate conversation with him. But it was not to be this evening, for Miss Morgan was steering her toward a settee on the other side of the room.

Miss Morgan flapped a hand dismissively. "Yes, but Lord Marsden isn't going to marry."

"He isn't?" Diantha thought back to what he'd said on the topic the night she'd visited him. *I am disinclined to marriage at this point in my life.* She'd assumed that meant he was taking his time but that he'd get there eventually.

"Apparently not." Miss Morgan performed an exaggerated shrug.

"Isn't that unusual for a gentleman in his position?" Diantha asked. "Who will inherit the title?"

"I had the very same question, and I turned to *Debrett's.* The answer is his cousin Ambrose Courteney, son to his father's younger brother. To hear it told, he is, let's just say, not a great intellect. Not that anyone is compared to Simon. But this Ambrose fellow apparently also lacks any kind of charm that might make up for it."

"I wonder why Lord Marsden has closed his mind—and his heart, I suppose—to the possibility of marrying," Diantha mused.

"All I can get out of my sister is that he has his reasons."

"Hmm."

"Hmm indeed. I am sure that Lord Marsden is delightful once you get to know him. I, however, do not know him, despite having spent considerable time in his company."

"He is somewhat inscrutable," Diantha allowed, though she was rather pleased to think she *did* know Lord Marsden.

"I suppose that's the generous interpretation. I was going to say boring."

"Boring!" Diantha regretted the vehemence of her exclamation, but Miss Morgan did not seem to notice. In fact, she appeared quite cheery as she surveyed the room, an attitude Diantha found incompatible with insulting someone.

"Perhaps he isn't boring so much as he simply isn't overly talkative," Diantha said, attempting to strike a diplomatic, and not defensive, tone. "People like that are often good listeners, I find."

Miss Morgan swung around to regard her. "Do you?"

"Well, generally speaking, yes."

Miss Morgan leaned closer in. "Miss Brown, did you get enough time nearly freezing to death under the stars last night? For your article, I mean? I would be more than happy to sit with Lady Harcourt again tonight. Archie is up there now. You could spell him off and then I could spell you off."

Lord Marsden's parting words from last night echoed in Diantha's mind. *I will try again tomorrow.*

She cleared her throat. "Miss Morgan, I would be most grateful for another night free to conduct my research. I believe the article will be much improved for it. Are you certain you do not mind?"

"Am I certain? Am I not known as a patroness of journalism?"

If Miss Morgan was a patroness of journalism, Diantha wasn't aware of it, but she held her tongue.

Diantha found him by the fire. Fully clothed.

Well, of course he was fully clothed. As was she. It was just that she might have thought he would be taking the waters. She had brought the same blanket from last night, she supposed because she was pretending she was here to conduct further experiential research for her article.

She crept toward him—his back was to her, as it had been last night, but this time only because he was sitting staring at the flames.

Everything happened at once: She covered the last few steps toward the ring of light cast by the fire. He turned in his seat. She said, "Have you seen it?" He said, "I haven't seen it."

And then she realized that while he was, technically, fully clothed, he wasn't wearing a coat or waistcoat. And his sleeves were rolled up, exposing those forearms she found so . . . provoking.

Diantha was not a swooner, she reminded herself.

He stood, belatedly, and gestured to the chair he'd been occupying. The act put him closer to the flames, which illuminated the cords of muscles running down his arm in a way that made her feel she was looking at a living, breathing statue, which turned out to be so much more compelling than the cold marble kind.

"Please, sit." He took note of her blanket. "Unless you were planning to take the waters again?"

"No, no. I was just—" What? She had no idea what she was doing. The blanket was a prop.

She sat. Took a moment to catch her breath and decided, perhaps ill-advisedly, to risk the truth. Well, not *the* truth, *a* truth. A little one, not the big one. "I was hoping to find you out here."

His smile was her reward. "I was hoping to find you out here, too."

If she relaxed a mite then, it was a mistake, for he said, "I have reflected since we parted yesternight, and I have several questions."

The prospect of an interrogation made her wary. Questions were different from the patient listening he had provided last night. But what could she do but submit? Well, she could leave. But she wouldn't. "All right. I may not have several answers for you, but go ahead."

"One: Why was ruination your first plan when you were in search of a means of rebuffing Mr. Hill?"

Goodness, he was getting right into it.

"And, two, a related question: If you truly believed that the man was not going to take no for an answer, that you needed to make yourself ineligible by deeds and not mere words, would the obvious solution not to have been to marry someone else? Someone less . . . distasteful?"

"Allow me to answer both questions with one of my own:

Where, pray tell, would I have found someone else to marry?" Diantha didn't wait for a response, for it was a rhetorical question. "But even if I could have, I wouldn't have. My sister chose marriage as an escape from a dire situation, and I observed, in close quarters, the consequences of that choice."

He simply said, "Yes."

So even though he was interrogating her this evening, he was still deploying his brand of intent, patient listening. Making room for her to speak. Conveying that he was genuinely interested in what she had to say.

She cast her mind back to those early years in Mr. Hill's house. "I will add that even if things had been different, if my sister had been happily married, I still would have accepted the offer from Lady Harcourt. I wouldn't have wanted to feel like a third wheel." She huffed a mirthless laugh. "If I am going to be an outsider, I prefer to be paid for such.

"Mind you, my sister would not have seen the situation the same way I did. She would not have wanted me to leave, had the circumstances been less fraught. As it stood, she encouraged me to."

"You speak as if you and your sister are close. *Were* close. My apologies."

"No apology is needed. I like thinking of my sister in the present tense. I used to talk to her. After she was gone, I mean."

"But you don't anymore?"

"No. I did talk to her grave that time I went on holiday to Barbury. But talking to her in the course of daily life started to seem rather too foolish. But I do sometimes feel as though she is with me. Which is also foolish."

"Not foolish, I think. Human."

She paused before asking the question she wanted to ask. But why? They were sitting in the dark, sharing secrets, for the second night in a row—at least she was properly clothed this time. "Do you feel that way about your brothers?" She did not have a grasp on the nature of his relationship with his brothers. His mother clearly favored them, but did he hold them responsible for that?

It did occur to her that there was no reason she *ought* to have a grasp on his relationship with his brothers. It occurred to her to wonder why she cared.

He didn't answer for a long time, and she would have thought she'd overstepped, but again, if whispering outside by a fire with no one else nearby wasn't already overstepping, what was?

"The truth of it, Miss Brown," he finally said, "is that I wish my brothers were alive not because I miss them, though I do, in an abstract sort of way, but because if they were, I wouldn't be earl."

"You don't want to be earl." It was a surprising notion, yet not.

"I don't want to be earl." Then, like a comet through the dark—not that there were any comets here—a peal of laughter. True mirthful laughter, not the bitter huff one might expect to be associated with such an assertion.

"I've never said that aloud, Miss Brown. I've hardly even allowed myself to think it. But yes, all things considered, I'd rather not be the earl of anything, much less my father's estate."

"Is there any consolation in the notion that were you not earl, you wouldn't have a seat in Lords? You are very devoted to that work."

"I am. But a sense of devotion to one's work need not arise from enjoyment, as I think we established last night."

"Indeed."

"Although I don't know that the alternative, a life in the Church, would have been terribly different. You have been questioning me, these recent days, and on the evening of . . . the obelisk, about my arrested career path. Whatever I do or do not think, or believe, about God, that life would also have been built on a foundation of duty."

"The idea doesn't appeal?"

"To be honest, and this is another thing I've never said aloud, no, a life in the Church did not particularly appeal, in and of itself."

"Then why were you going to do it?"

"We were a typical family. James was the heir, Michael was the spare—by two minutes, a fact he found affrontingly arbitrary and liked to complain about. He went to the army. I was the third. The spare spare. What else was I to do but prepare for the Church? I had a scholarly bent, too, which helped. And though the life I would have had did not inherently appeal, it felt important, as I said last night." He shrugged. "I suppose it worked out for the best. As you said yourself, my work in Lords has done, or has the potential to do, more good than looking after a parish."

"What about all those souls you would have saved?"

He whipped his gaze to hers, and it took a beat for him to realize she was jesting.

He laughed for the second time that evening. She was growing attached to the sound of his laughter.

"I'm going to tell you a scandalous secret, Miss Brown."

"Oh, good. I can't think when someone last did that."

She hadn't been so free with jesting since before Thea died.

He grew serious. "I do not think most people's souls need saving."

"Well, you would have made a very radical vicar, indeed." She wasn't jesting anymore, not exactly, but she was endeavoring to sustain the conversation, to keep the mood as it was so he would keep talking.

"There's a book on the topic I found illuminating. Life-changing, even. I could lend it to you if you're interested." He paused. "You probably aren't. It isn't nearly as exciting as any novel I've read—though of course I have not read many."

"I am interested," she said quietly, dropping the teasing.

Something was passing between them. Understanding, to be sure, but it felt like more than that.

He cleared his throat. "All things considered, and speaking purely selfishly, I would rather have stayed the course in seminary, my doubts aside. Despite its lack of inherent appeal, life as a country vicar would have had its consolations, chief among them that it would have been mine. My own life, out from under the . . ."

"Shadow of your brothers?"

"Something like that."

Hmm. She had the impression that he'd been going to say something else.

"Something like what?" she pressed, as if she knew him well enough to do so.

He answered her as if he knew her well enough to allow himself to be pressed. Perhaps he did. "If my brothers cast a shadow, it was not their doing. It was my mother's."

"You were in earnest when you called yourself the spare spare."

"I was."

"I am sorry."

"She is not an easy woman."

"But you have an obligation to her."

"Perhaps," he said, which she thought an odd response. "Regardless, although I know we aren't meant to speak of it, I should like to apologize sincerely for shouting at you the night . . . of the obelisk. It was her behavior I was upset by, and there was no call to punish you for it."

"Thank you for that, but I do think we are even in terms of appalling behavior, so please let this be the final time we speak of it."

"Not even in code?" he teased.

"I'm sure I haven't talked about obelisks so much in my entire life as I have these recent days."

He chuckled. "Do you remember, in *Pride and Prejudice*, when, after Elizabeth rebuffs Mr. Collins's suit, everyone is surprised when Charlotte Lucas turns up engaged to him?"

It took Diantha a moment to shift to the apparent change in topic, but after a beat, she said, "I do."

"Charlotte explains herself to her friend by saying she isn't a romantic."

"Yes," she said, casting her mind back to the story. "She explains that she is settling for Mr. Collins."

"I do not agree with that characterization—'settling.' She says, 'I ask only a comfortable home; and considering Mr. Collins's character, connections, and situation in life, I am convinced that my chance of happiness with him is as fair as most people can boast on entering the marriage state.'"

"You've learned it by heart."

"Miss Brown, that scene is etched onto the very muscle you speak of." He paused. "I had no idea novels could do that. I had no idea novels could be *true*."

How curious. Diantha agreed with the sentiment, which he articulated so beautifully, but she found the passage in question an odd inspiration for it.

"Of course," he went on, "I know novels are *not* true, strictly speaking. They are fancies, products of the mind. One might even call them lies."

"If they are lies, they are true lies."

"You understand."

"Yes. But I am not sure I understand the truth of the particular passage you are quoting. You will forgive me, but how can one not interpret it as being about Charlotte settling for less than she deserves?"

"Because I am not interpreting it to be strictly about marriage. I wasn't, perhaps, a natural for the life in the Church I was pursuing, but Harcourt was going to give me a living."

"Ah, I see. You would have lived on the grounds of Mollybrook."

"Yes."

"You would have been proximate to your friends."

"Friends I consider family."

She supposed what he was leaving unsaid was that such a plan would also mean an escape from his difficult mother.

"So," he continued, "like Charlotte Lucas, I would not have considered it settling. It was a kind of happiness, a not-insignificant happiness, that was within my grasp."

"How strange to think that had life unfolded as you'd planned, we would have met each other frequently at Mollybrook." Not that the dowager had ever attended church with any frequency, but they did meet the vicar from time to time.

"Meeting you at Mollybrook would have been another reward for following that path," he said, as if paying her such a compliment were nothing. She didn't know what to say and feared she was blushing. She gave thanks for the darkness.

"I see what you're doing," he said.

What was she doing? "I beg your pardon?"

"I am meant to be questioning you, and we've gotten quite distracted."

"All right," she said, no longer so wary of his inquiries.

He examined her for a long moment before he spoke. "You were determined that Mr. Hill could be rebuffed by virtue of your becoming ineligible to be a wife. But you would've preferred ruination than marriage to someone else, someone suitable, is what you're saying?"

"I suppose I am."

"You are a remarkable woman, Miss Brown."

"But it wouldn't have been ruination in the sense you mean, would it? I am no longer of society the way you are, or, more properly, the way the women you know are. If my reputation had been ruined, it wouldn't have mattered, not really. So what I was calling ruination would merely have been escape."

"But you are no longer in search of such ruination? Or such escape?"

She didn't say no, because of course that wasn't true. She tried to redirect the conversation. "We have been forgetting to look for the comet."

"Miss Brown, may I ask, had Mr. Hill not entered the picture, what had you been planning to do once . . . You will forgive my indelicacy, but once Lady Harcourt no longer requires your services?"

So much for the comet. It seemed the questioning was to continue. "I had been saving diligently."

"I wonder at your use of the past perfect tense. You *had been* saving. For what had you been saving? What did you want? What *do* you want?"

"Oh, Lord Marsden, I want so very many things, but I can't have any of them."

"Tell me about them anyway." The way he spoke, matter-of-factly and as if he were entitled to that information, made something in her stomach buzz. It was as if there were a swarm of insects inside her.

She wanted to squirm under his continued scrutiny. Instead she looked at him and told him the truth. "I want a small cottage with ample bookshelves and space for a vegetable garden. Perhaps some fruit trees. I should like to learn to grow my own food and preserve it. I will feed the birds, and make observations of their habits."

He waited a beat. "That's it?"

"Should there be more?"

"You are describing a life of quiet poverty."

She smiled. They had different definitions of poverty. "Perhaps, but the cottage would be mine, as would the books inside it. I could go outside any time of night if I wanted to see the constellation Orion. I would be beholden to no one."

"Wouldn't you get lonely, though? Is that not the flip side of being beholden to no one?"

"I am already lonely." She could scarcely believe she was admitting that so openly. "I wonder if being alone, truly alone, might be a more consoling sort of loneliness than being alone in company."

He nodded, didn't speak for a while. But then he said, "I understand this logic, Miss Brown."

He did understand. That was the remarkable thing about Lord Marsden. He understood so many things.

"Ideally, though," she continued, for now that the taps had been opened, she could not stop the flow of truth, "my cottage would be near to a village that could be reached on foot. So I would have opportunity for sociability."

"Well, it sounds lovely. What is stopping you? Assuming you have dispatched with the threat posed by Mr. Hill."

"I cannot afford it. Even this quiet life of so-called poverty is too dear. It is years away, at best."

"I see."

Hence her use of the past perfect tense. She had calculated that if she continued her economizing, she ought to be able to afford such a life in the space of half a dozen years. But that was before Mr. Hill. Before Mr. Baldwin. Before her father put her in this circumstance to begin with.

Before all the men who were intent on keeping her down.

Lord Marsden looked at her for a long time, long enough that she grew uneasy and fell back on diversionary tactics. She tipped her head back. "I should very much like to see the comet."

"There may be too much light being cast by these flames," he said, standing abruptly. "If you want to look for the comet, we ought to walk a way off."

Did he *not* want to look for the comet? A bit bewildered, she followed him into the darkness. He led her to where the manicured turf of the garden met the woods. The rushing of the brook was louder out here.

It was darker out here, too. They both gazed at the sky, and as a minutes ticked by, Diantha relaxed. She considered the blanket she was still carrying. "My lord, would you think me terribly forward if I suggested we spread this blanket on the ground and sit on it? It might make the task of comet-waiting more comfortable."

By way of answer, he took the blanket from her; shook it out over the turf. "It certainly isn't any more forward than being out here to begin with."

She made to lower herself to the ground, but he shot out a hand and stopped her. "Miss Brown, will you tell me your name? Your Christian name? I wonder that I have never heard it."

"Why should a companion have a Christian name?"

"Doesn't everyone have a Christian name?"

"I suppose so, but there are certain vocations, or perhaps I should say stations in life, in which one might as well not."

He laughed, but unlike earlier, there was no mirth in it.

"Have I offended, my lord?"

"No. You have empathized."

"I beg your pardon?"

"It is perhaps ill-done of me to compare our positions, but if it weren't for Archie and Effie, no one would ever call me by my Christian name, either."

"It is not the same."

"I know, but I would like to hear you elucidate how it is not the same."

"Your Christian name has given way to your title. You have become so important that you are synonymous with the estate you own, with the land itself. It's a glorious thing."

"Is it?"

"Most people would think so."

"But you are not most people."

What a curious thing to say.

"Never mind," he said. "Do go on."

"I, by contrast, have not had my name replaced by something grander; I have merely had it taken away. As my fortunes have fallen, so has my name. And now it is gone entirely."

"There are different ways to measure fortunes."

"Are you going to suggest you'd rather be penniless and alone than wealthy and respected?"

"Not precisely, but I would like to be respected for something other than my wealth."

"And you are."

"Am I?"

She decided to tell him more truth. "You are respected by me. Not that that amounts to much."

"It amounts to a great deal. And if I may alter the terms of your question: Respect aside, I think I would rather be penniless but flush with friends than wealthy and alone."

"How fortunate for you that you are neither. You have wealth *and* good friends you have said you consider family."

"Are you not part of Harcourt's family? Does the dowager not consider you family?"

"She sometimes thinks I am her mother. You have seen her refer to me as such. It doesn't happen much anymore, but there were times we would carry on entire conversations with me in the role, relitigating the past in such a way that she found the outcome more favorable."

"That was a service rendered."

"Yes, a *service*." She emphasized the word, not because she regarded herself as a servant, not exactly, but . . . "I would go so far as to say that playing at being in a family when one hasn't one only serves to throw into sharper relief how alone one is, elementally."

"I hadn't thought of it that way, but I see the sense in that stance."

"For what it's worth, I do not believe that Lady Harcourt, when she was of sounder mind, ever considered me family. I was the daughter of a friend, someone she pitied, and that pity lined up with her need for help. Mind you, I think she found me acceptable. Perhaps she even grew to like me. But at the beginning, our coming together was transactional."

"Be that as it may, has the nature of your relationship not evolved? And what about Archie and Clementine? And Olive. Do you not consider them friends?"

"I suppose so, but we don't speak like . . ."

"Like what?"

"We don't speak like this." It was out before she could think better of it: more dribbles of truth.

"Yes." He cleared his throat. "Which brings me round to my original question: Will you tell me your Christian name? Mine is Simon, by the way, but you've probably heard Archie and Effie call me that."

"I have."

Why was she hesitating? She had told him so much already. She trusted him. She supposed her reluctance was attached to a fear of being disappointed. As she had endeavored to articulate to him a few minutes ago, to be alone in the world was one thing. To be, for a time, *not* alone, and to then have that taken away, to be forced to revert to one's elemental solitude . . . well, that might be unendurable.

But how could she refuse to answer this simple question from a man who had been so kind to her? "My name is Diantha," she said quietly.

"It is lovely to meet you, Diantha. As you know, I'm Simon." His hand found hers in the dark, and to her absolute astonishment, he bowed over it and placed his lips on the back of it, right at the base, close to her wrist. If she had ever been greeted thusly by a gentleman, a long time ago in her previous life, it had been a formality, a quick buss of the lips against the fabric of her gloves.

This was not that.

To begin with, Lord Marsden—Simon—left his lips on her skin for what felt like ages. The contact was causing fine hairs to stand on end all the way up her arm. And just before he withdrew, he opened his mouth wider, brushing the inner parts of his lips—and *Oh! Was that his tongue?*—against her skin.

If Diantha had been startled, before, by the feeling of his wrist against her hand when he'd returned her book the other night, it was nothing against the shocking, galvanizing sensation of the wetness of his mouth against *her* wrist.

When he dropped her hand, she let loose a shaky exhale, realizing she'd been unwittingly holding her breath.

They were still standing, having been distracted from their intention to sit by their discussion of names and subsequent "introduction." Lord Marsden knelt on the blanket and reached his hand up to help her down. It reminded her of the other times their hands had touched—not only that night in the drawing room, but the day the ladies arrived at Gurglewood and he helped her down from the coach.

This time, to her utter shock, he didn't release her hand. He lay on his back and tugged her down with him, under the twinkling stars. "Lying is better than sitting. You can see the whole sky this way—since we don't know from which direction to expect the comet."

Surely, he would release her hand once they were settled. But, no, he kept it.

She was lying on her back next to Lord Marsden, holding his hand, waiting for a comet.

Her heart was zinging around in her rib cage, in contrast to the quiet dark that surrounded them. She listened for the brook, wandering if she would be able to hear it over the machinations of her body. She did, but only just.

"Are you named after the flower?" he asked suddenly. "You should see the dianthus that cover the forest floor at Galecroft in the spring. It's a carpet of pink." He paused. "I should spend more time at Galecroft. I have been thinking lately that I miss it, but I am just realizing that it's been *years* since I have seen the dianthus there in the spring. And yet the sight of such is etched into my memory."

Diantha took a few moments to steady her breath before she answered. He waited, as she had come to understand he would do. "I suppose I'm indirectly named after the flower. My mother was fond of Greek mythology. Diantha was Zeus's flower, or Demeter's. Someone's flower. Apparently it translates as 'divine flower.'"

"It suits you."

She wanted to ask him *Which part?* The *divine* part or the *flower* part? She had trouble seeing either, but to want him to elaborate was the height of foolishness. Instead, she said, "My sister was called Amalthea."

"Zeus's nurse."

"I have to say, I'd rather be a flower than a nurse, but I suppose I have in effect become a nurse."

"And now you place flowers by your sister's grave," he said quietly.

"Yes." A memory surfaced. "My sister used to love flowers. She had a grand flower garden in our childhood home—the first one. And then a more modest one during her time with Mr. Hill. We used to write letters. We probably exchanged hundreds of them, and . . ."

She trailed off because thinking of letters made her think about how close she had come to telling Lord Marsden everything. How much she *wanted* to tell him everything.

She regrouped. "She used to press flowers and send them to me along with her letters. I wish I had saved them. I used to, initially, but they always grew so dry and brittle." Suddenly, she was choking back tears. "I always thought there would be more. An endless supply of dead, flat flowers."

"You must miss her letters. Well, of course you must miss her, too, but there is a particular joy in receiving a letter from someone close to your heart, don't you find?"

"Yes," she croaked, and goodness, this man was going to be the end of her. "Our letters were unremarkable." Well, most of them were. If only Diantha had hewn to the principle of unremarkability, she wouldn't be in the mess she was today.

But then, she wouldn't be here, now, either, comet hunting and secret spilling with Lord Marsden. *Simon.* For certainly her rash visit to his home in August was a precondition to their current . . . relationship.

"Our letters were full of the news of the day," she continued, aiming to cover her discomfiture. "Well, neither of us ever had much news, so it was more the minutia of the day. And my sister's minutia were often about the dreaded Mr. Hill. I don't miss hearing about him. But it is an odd feeling, having no one to write to, even if, on the whole, our letters didn't amount to much."

Except for the one that did.

"I think," he said, "that perhaps the total of hundreds of letters full of minutia is more than the sum of their parts."

"How do you mean?"

"There's something exceedingly intimate about the exchange of hundreds of letters. I would imagine. I haven't much experience with letter writing. But the exchange of, as you call it, minutia, implies a degree of familiarity, of acceptance, that is really rather fortunate. I suspect that even if the minutia aren't missed, the act of recording them, and reading about them, is."

The tears from before were back, and they were winning the battle. She told herself it was all right. It was too dark for him to see.

"*Diantha*," he said urgently, "are you quite all right?"

How did he *do* that?

The sound of her Christian name on his lips made the volume of tears increase. A small sob escaped. She was *mortified.*

"Are you crying?" He sat up.

She did, too. "I don't mean to." She wasn't a crier. Or at least she'd never thought she was. She hadn't cried at her sister's funeral, for Heaven's sake. She hadn't cried when Mr. Hill blackmailed her.

She wasn't a crier. She wasn't a swooner.

Except when she was.

He took her in his arms, and if she'd thought that kiss on her hand was shocking, it had nothing on this. He was warm and solid. Her head rested against his chest. If she listened, could she hear his heartbeat? Likely not, for her own was thundering in her ears, and—

He dropped his arms and pulled back.

She was sharply disappointed. But she wasn't crying anymore, so his intervention had worked—assuming the cessation of her tears had been his aim.

She scrambled to her feet. "I must go."

He was silent a moment. She waited, though she wasn't sure why. She didn't require his permission to leave.

Eventually, he got to his feet. "We can try again tomorrow."

We.

She did not correct him, just said, "Good night, my lord."

She had taken a few steps away, when, suddenly, he was by her side.

"Don't call me my lord."

She was about to apologize, but he kept talking.

"You may always write to me."

"I beg your pardon?"

"You said it was an odd feeling, having no one to write to. I surmised from the context that 'odd' meant 'not good.' If that is the case, I offer myself as a correspondent. I don't know that I would be any good at it, given my aforementioned inexperience, but if you should care to send me letters, I should be happy to receive them, and to answer them."

"But what would I say?"

"We seem to have managed to fill the hours just fine in the flesh. Can letters really be that different?"

Something inside Diantha lunged toward the idea of continuing her dialogue with Lord Marsden. Perhaps it would be some consolation after her "ruination."

Or perhaps he would be angry enough at her for lying to him that he wouldn't want to write to her.

She told herself that she hadn't lied. She hadn't said anything that was untrue. She'd told him she had another plan. And she did.

She was so tired, suddenly. "I must bid you good night . . . Simon." She hesitated. "I know you don't want me to call you 'my lord,' but I can hardly call you by your Christian name in company."

"I would be quite happy to have you call me Simon in any circumstance, but I suppose you are correct. Perhaps we ought to leave the Christian names to when we are alone. Will you join me tomorrow in my comet vigil?"

"I wish I could, but Miss Morgan has been sitting with her ladyship these past two nights. She believes I am conducting research for the article I'm meant to be writing for Lady Stonely's magazine. I do not think I can ask her to do so for a third night."

"Hmm," Simon said. "That is unfortunate."

Diantha was a little surprised, and in truth, a little hurt by his easy agreement. "Well. Good night."

"Good night," he echoed, and there were the tears again, as Diantha walked back to the house. Only this time, they weren't in response to the sudden frisson of being understood, of being seen. They were far simpler; they were tears of sadness that her time communing with Simon under the stars had come to an end.

14

Reading Injuries

September 19, 1823
Earls Trip, day 12

Simon was alone in the breakfast room the next morning when he had a revelation.

It was relatively late, and he had long since finished eating. He was nursing his tea and reading one of Effie and Julianna's magazines—or trying to. Every time he heard someone approach, he nearly jumped out of his skin.

The dowager must be sleeping late again.

He ought to ask Archie how she was doing. She had seemed in good spirits, but perhaps the change in routine was catching up to her. The ladies had decided against an attempt to add hot water to the pool, deeming it too much trouble and unlikely to make much of a difference. He hoped the dowager had not taken a serious chill. It would be—

He checked himself. Why was he spending so much time thinking about Lady Harcourt? He cared about her, certainly, but she had other, closer people to look after her, Archie and Clementine, and of course Miss Brown. Diantha, he supposed, even though she hadn't expressly . . .

Oh. *Oh no.*

He clattered his teacup into his saucer by hands suddenly made clumsy.

Simon liked to think he possessed a reasonable degree of self-awareness. Therefore, he had to entertain the possibility that he wasn't thinking about the dowager so much as he was thinking about Diantha. Or perhaps he was thinking about the dowager as a proxy for thinking about Diantha.

Was it possible that he had . . . developed an infatuation with Diantha?

Simon had always been a natural scholar. Despite the fact that he had read philosophy, despite his tenure in seminary, he had always been partial to science—hence his interest in the elusive comet, he supposed. He prided himself on looking at the facts of the world and drawing logical conclusions.

He forced himself to list the relevant facts:

He thought about Diantha more than he suspected was usual.

He called to mind the image of her wet hair more than was seemly.

When he read a book, he searched for passages he thought she would like.

And, oh, dear God, he had purchased two dozen lemons and charmed—and he was not, as a rule, charming—the cook into transforming them into lemon treats for her because she had once told him she had a fondness for lemon.

He felt ill. Truly ill, as if his breakfast might make an encore appearance. In truth, his stomach had been unsettled since Diantha's late-night visit to his home last month, but this was an order of magnitude worse.

Archie ambled in at that exact, unfortunate moment, and said, "Simon. Good morning. How are you faring? I feel as though I've hardly seen you these recent days."

Right. If Archie had barely seen Simon, Simon would have liked to think it was Archie's fault. That he was spending all his time with his wife.

But was that the case? He had to add another item to his list:

He spent an inordinate amount of time huddled with Diantha, in the drawing room, or outside under the stars, baring his soul and demanding that she do likewise. Perhaps to the exclusion of his friends.

And, oh, good Lord, he had all but begged her to write him letters.

"Are you quite all right?" Archie asked.

"Yes, yes. Something about my breakfast did not agree with me, but I am fine."

He took a brisk inhalation. Here he had thought the second part of their trip, the earls-plus-girls week, would feature him as the odd man out. He'd expected the other two gents to be swanning off with their respective brides, but if they were, he hadn't been around to notice.

"What if the three of us gents set off on an adventure?" he suggested, for he needed to break free, to be away from this place for a while.

Archie agreed.

"You rouse Effie," Simon said, "and I shall appeal to Cook for a basket of victuals, and we can ride off and see where the winds take us."

The winds took them to a pub two towns over.

"Just ale, I should think," Archie said when they sat at a rickety oak table. "I must've eaten two dozen of those biscuits you procured, Simon."

"The cook here is very good, Archie," Effie said.

"Indeed, and her talents extend to the vegetable dishes Clementine favors."

"Perhaps you ought to lure her back to Mollybrook with you," Effie said.

"She won't go," Simon said. "She has a grandniece here she is raising."

"Well, the grandniece can come, too, can she not?" Effie asked.

"The grandniece is thriving after a difficult few years with unreliable parents—the cook's nephew being her father. Would you really uproot a child in such circumstances for your own convenience, Archie?"

"I would not," Archie said, regarding Simon quizzically, "now that I know the backstory. Anyway, the cook has had a terrible time distinguishing between the two Lady Harcourts. It has made for some amusing mishaps."

Amusing mishaps? Simon had no knowledge of amusing mishaps. How had he missed them?

Well, he knew how. And wasn't that what Archie had meant this morning when he'd said he hadn't seen much of Simon?

"Can it be any more confusing than my situation?" Simon asked. "If I were to marry, there would be three Countesses of Marsden."

Effie laughed. "Yes, Simon is rather more awash in dowagers actual and potential than you are, Archie."

"But only if he were to marry," Archie said.

"That's why I said 'potential,'" Effie said.

"But is he ever going to marry?" Archie asked.

"I don't know, is he?" Effie countered.

"I'm right here, you know," Simon said. "I can hear you."

They all laughed, but Archie sobered and said, "But what is the answer? Is Simon ever going to marry and add another Countess of Marsden to his collection?"

Simon said, "Not anytime soon, no. Or so I always thought."

"But now you think yes?" Archie asked.

"Or perhaps merely not no?" Effie suggested, and when Archie shot him a bewildered look, he shrugged and said, "Baby steps?"

Simon said, "My resolve was never not to marry, it was not to marry while Mother was alive."

"But now?" Effie prompted.

"If anything, my visit to Frances should have confirmed the wisdom of that stance. But now Mother herself is suddenly making noises about my marrying. What am I to do? Let her choose a bride for me whom she will proceed to terrorize?"

"Simon," said Archie, "I am not sure you have a bride problem so much as you have a mother problem."

"Indeed. I have avoided thinking about her while on holiday, and it has been a reprieve. But in truth, I cannot allow what Frances told me to pass with no consequences. I think I need a way to . . . remove my mother from my life."

Yes. That felt right, questions of marrying, or not, aside. He turned to the boys. He hadn't been avoiding them on purpose, but he had missed them. "How do I do that?"

"Well, I should think to start, you could insist she move into the dower house at Galecroft," Effie said.

"Or if that's not enough, give her the London house and rent another for your own purposes," Archie said.

"It sounds so simple when you say it like that," Simon said.

"It is not simple," Archie said. "It is not simple at all. But I will tell you that I never faced down my father, and I regret it." He turned to Effie. "Ef is the bravest of us all in that regard, and could perhaps provide some counsel."

"I don't know if it was bravery, so much as survival," Effie said.

"What do you mean?" Simon asked.

"I didn't believe I could live without Jules, and once something is a matter of survival, one becomes . . . well, I was going to say braver, but that isn't the word. One becomes single-minded. One does what needs to be done."

The conversation was becoming unsettling. Simon wanted to return to the reprieve, where he was on holiday and therefore didn't have to think about Mother. He cleared his throat. "Well, happily, I have only two Countesses of Marsden in my life at the moment, and they never cross paths, so I think you win, Archie, for a household full of title confusion."

"It's really only Miss Brown who's the problem," Archie said.

"How do you mean?" Simon asked, alarmed. Had they been observed together?

Clementine and Mother use each other's Christian names, and of course, I call them 'Clementine' and 'Mother.'"

"Or 'Darling' and 'Mother,'" Effie said. Archie waved a hand dismissively, which only caused Effie to double down. "Or 'Dearest Sweet Soul of my Soul' and 'Mother.'"

Simon relaxed. Well, he relaxed as much as he ever did, which he would admit was not a great deal.

Archie rolled his eyes at Effie. "Yes, yes, the point is, the only member of my household who addresses both of them as 'Lady Harcourt' is Miss Brown. I did tell her she ought to use their Christian names."

"But she refused," Simon said.

"Yes. How did you know?"

"It just seems like something she wouldn't want to do. After all, you are still calling her 'Miss Brown' and not 'Diantha.'"

"How did you know she's named 'Diantha'?"

Simon had erred. He shrugged, trying to affect an air of nonchalance. "I must have heard it somewhere."

The ale arrived, providing a handy exit from a conversation that had the potential to become dangerous, and they made a toast. "To River's Embrace," Effie said.

"Oh, no, we're not reviving River's Embrace," Archie said, and after a few minutes of good-natured bickering, he turned to Simon. "Why don't you name the place?"

"*I* certainly don't have any ideas."

"Are you sure?"

"What do you mean?" Why was he being so odd?

"Simon," Archie said, "are you keeping something from us?"

"You *are* being rather peculiar lately," Effie said.

"Peculiar?" Simon echoed, his mind swirling.

"Never mind," Archie said, taking a long draught of his ale.

Were they onto him? Perhaps they hadn't been as wrapped up in their wives as he'd thought.

He was starting to panic.

"I must come clean about something!" he blurted. He needed a decoy. He wasn't in the habit of lying to the boys, but this wasn't lying, exactly. How could he lie when he didn't understand what was in his own heart? No, he was merely throwing them off the scent, buying the time he needed for self-reflection. And, he consoled himself, he was doing so by telling them the truth. *A* truth.

Effie and Archie put down their mugs and gave him their attention.

"I can no longer carry around this burden," he said, playing his role with a degree of theatricality he wouldn't have thought himself capable of.

"Well, my goodness, Simon," Effie said. "Out with it, then."

"This injury to my nose"—he touched the scabbed-over scrape—"was not the result of a shaving mishap. It was, in fact, a reading injury."

"What in Heaven's name is a reading injury?" Archie asked.

He explained, and when he was done, a momentary silence settled.

Then they burst out laughing.

"This was exactly why I didn't tell you," Simon harumphed, but he was pleased that his diversionary tactic seemed to have worked.

"What book were you reading?" Archie asked.

"Does it matter?"

"Humor me."

"I believe it was *Frankenstein* that so injured me."

"Where did you get a copy of *Frankenstein*? I don't think you mentioned its providence when we were talking about it the other day."

"Miss Brown lent it to me," Simon said. He had been avoiding saying so the other day, but, he reasoned again, everyone knew Miss Brown was in the habit of lending him books.

"My Miss Brown?"

By God, if Archie didn't stop calling her that, Simon was going to have an apoplexy.

"Yes," he said, congratulating himself on what he hoped was a mild demeanor.

"What's the matter, Simon?" Effie asked.

"Not a thing."

"I remember last time you called on us at the London house, Miss Brown lent you a copy of *Pride and Prejudice.* I did not notice *Frankenstein* pass between you."

Simon's face was burning now along with his ears. Excuses, lies—more lies—were bubbling up inside him, but he forced himself to remain silent.

Archie, apparently unfussed by receiving no answer to his query, went on to say, "Since Clementine came to live with us, I have learned that Miss Brown is quite the reader of novels. The two of them are always talking about them."

"How could you not know that someone who had been a member of your household for so many years was a reader of novels?" Simon asked.

"I . . . don't know." Archie's brow furrowed. Perhaps the question had dislodged him from the question of the origin of Simon's copy of *Frankenstein.*

How could anyone not notice everything about Diantha? That she read books and collected ribbons and was fiercely proud—but not vain, as Miss Austen had said.

That she *did* have a kind of rage roiling beneath the seemingly placid surface of her.

That was the answer: Most people didn't see beneath the surface of Diantha.

Simon did. And he very much feared life would never be the same again.

He decided to voice a question he was aware would seem to Archie as if it had come from out of nowhere. "When was the last time you raised Miss Brown's wages?"

"I . . ." Archie looked bewildered, then stricken. "You know, I don't believe that I ever have."

"Over, what has it been? Nine, almost ten, years?"

"I shall remedy the situation at once."

"I should think so."

Simon considered going further down this unexpected path he found himself on, but was it wise? Probably not.

He did it anyway.

"Have you considered what will happen to Miss Brown"—it felt strange to call her that, for she had transformed fully into Diantha in his mind—"after your mother, you will forgive the indelicacy, but after your mother no longer has need of her?"

"What do you mean, what will happen?"

Good God, Archie could be a dolt sometimes. "Where will she go? Where will she live?"

"She will stay on with us, won't she?"

"I don't know. Will she?"

"She is practically a member of the family, is she not?"

"Are you asking me?"

"No." The furrow was back. "No." Archie picked up his mug and took a long drink.

Simon did likewise. He had no idea what he was doing. Why he had said all that. Except that it stood to reason that more money could only help Diantha in her quest to save for her life of quiet poverty.

Several hours later, Simon still had no idea what he was doing, but he was doing it anyway.

They were gathered, all of them, in the drawing room after dinner. He was brooding, sitting apart from the card-playing crowd in his usual chair. Well, he wasn't brooding so much as he was willing Diantha to come and sit by him, as she had before.

It wasn't working.

She was laughing at something Olive was saying, and rather boisterously.

He scanned the room. Archie was watching her, too.

Archie suddenly shifted his gaze to Simon. Simon looked away quickly.

He opened his book. Endeavored to read it.

And was utterly taken aback when she appeared, towering over him like . . . well, he didn't know what. But he was sitting, and she was standing, and she was backlit in such a way that she almost looked like she was a divine creature passing judgment on him.

Perhaps she was.

"Di— Miss Brown."

"May I join you?"

"Yes, of course."

He closed his book, but beyond that, he was frozen. He didn't know what to do, what to say.

He was being ridiculous. He had, moments ago—speaking of ridiculous—been trying to lure her here with the power of his mind. What had been his aim then?

He opened the book, extracted a ribbon, and held it out to her. "Archie and Effie and I went on an excursion today. We visited a town some ten miles off. We were walking down the street and I saw this on the ground. It is a mere scrap, of course. But I thought of you."

What was he saying? *I saw a dirty bit of ribbon on the ground and it make me think of you?*

"I tried to clean it as well as I could. And I didn't know if you'd want to cut off the frayed edge, so I left it alone. It's too small for any useful purpose, but since you mentioned your collection is largely ornamental, I thought you might like it."

He should stop talking.

It was difficult, but he managed it.

Which left him sitting before Miss Brown, holding a frayed bit of ribbon.

She didn't take it. She didn't speak. She didn't do anything.

He had made a mistake.

But, no, it appeared that she had been frozen, too. For once she came to life, she took the ribbon with her eyes shining.

"It is beautiful, my lord."

"Will you please stop my-lord–ing me!" he whisper-yelled.

She looked up from the ribbon, and he knew what she was thinking. She could hardly call him Simon in this setting, even though they were apart from the others.

"Don't call me anything," he amended.

"What if I call you kind?" She turned the ribbon over in her hands. "This is a beauty."

"I know it is green, and you already have at least one green ribbon." He closed his mouth. He had attempted to do something kind, to make a gift. He shouldn't apologize for it.

"I have nothing this color," she said. "This is a green so dark, it is almost black. I have never seen the likes of this hue."

"That is what I thought. It is so dark, it would be suitable for mourning, yet it is also so *striking* that it doesn't seem somber whatsoever."

"Thank you," she said, and, turning her head so she was fully faced away from the larger group, she mouthed, "Simon."

It was a complete and utter thrill.

"Tell me about how your ribbon collection started." He wanted to know everything about her. He supposed that wasn't new, but he was newly *aware* of this wanting. It had become a surface-level desire.

"I was quite young. I'd always liked ribbons. What girl doesn't, I suppose. But I like to think I always had a practical streak, even when my family was enjoying happy, prosperous times. A ribbon could embellish an otherwise plain garment, or update it for a new Season. I found it almost like a game, to remake an old dress.

"But it *was* just a game. There *were* new dresses, and hats. We weren't rich, but we were comfortable. But then we started to fall from fortune, and my habit became less about clever thrift and more about survival. We learned how to darn and, as I told you, my sister was quite an accomplished seamstress. She became one out of necessity."

He murmured a vague affirmation. He wanted her to keep going. He was thrilled that she was speaking so easily, and at such length.

"I kept buying ribbons, though, when I found myself with a coin or two, which for many years was exceedingly infrequently. And then when I came to stay with Lady Harcourt, I took my first wages and went right out and bought a ribbon. The tulip-stem-green one I previously told you about, in fact." She rubbed two fingers together as if she were feeling the ribbon in question. "I don't know why. At that point, I had many more pressing needs than a ribbon."

"But were ribbons not pressing, in their own way?"

"I can't see how. They were illogical purchases. What sense does it make to buy ribbons when one is in dire financial circumstances?" She smiled. "Perhaps it was an act of rebellion."

"I think it was an act of self-preservation."

She tilted her head, struck her thinking pose. "What do you mean?"

"You were buying something for yourself, and not just any old thing, but a small treasure, something you used to love. Perhaps it was the only through line to your old life."

For a moment, he feared he had overstepped, but she said, her voice a mite shaky, "I hadn't thought about it that way, but that feels true."

Encouraged, he dared to say more. "Perhaps it *was* an act of rebellion, too, but not of the childish, petulant sort. It was an assertion of agency. An insistence on the import of beauty in and among suffering."

She held a hand to her heart, searched his face. "My goodness."

He shrugged, feeling that while he may not have overstepped, had exposed too much of himself. "Stonely tells me that beauty is important, that it feeds the soul."

"You say that as if you are a skeptic."

"I am not a skeptic; I am just not as good at seeing beauty, and finding it, as Stonely is." He nodded at the ribbon she still held. "Or as you are, given your secret collection." He cleared his throat. "So not skeptical, Diantha, so much as inexpert."

She smiled, and if he had thought, before, when she'd been

towering over him, that she was passing judgment, he must have been mistaken, for he had the sudden, absurd thought that if she was dispensing anything, it was absolution.

Oh no. She was crying. Well, she was attempting *not* to cry, but he could see her efforts, because he could see beneath the surface of her. "I am sorry, I—"

"Do not be sorry," she interrupted, "for saying such kind, wise things." She swallowed.

He tamped down the impulse to exhort her to continue. He was always having to do that around her, but he did not want to be the sort of man people spoke to because he commanded it, especially people who were saying important, fragile things.

It took her a few moments to gather herself. "I have wondered, over the years," she started slowly, "if my fondness for ribbons is a folly I ought to rid myself of. Am I being like my father, spending money he doesn't have in ways he ought not to? I tell myself no, since I spend pennies and I've still managed to save. Still, what is the point of a drawerful of ribbons?"

"Perhaps the point is solace."

"Yes," she said quietly.

"Would you show me your collection sometime? When we all find ourselves back in Town?"

She flashed him a small smile. "If you like."

Though he didn't know when such a demonstration might occur. It was one thing for them to converse when he called on Lady Harcourt, for her to leave to collect a book to lend him, quite another for her to run and fetch her ribbon collection. Especially if Archie was present. As he always was. That last visit had been an aberration.

An alarming, unwelcome thought landed in Simon's head: After this holiday, he would never again have occasion to speak to Diantha alone.

"Miss Brown!"

Simon and Diantha looked toward the voice. It was Olive, beckoning.

"We are going to play Pass the Slipper! Come join us! Both of you! You've done enough huddling and talking of novels. Come!"

Diantha stood immediately. Simon was more circumspect, reluctant to leave their têtê-à-têtê.

But Diantha was already gone.

Polly, the housemaid, was making a circuit of the room as the others arranged the furniture so everyone could sit in a circle. She passed by him, her hands full of discarded glasses. He wondered what time Polly finished her evening duties. An idea formed.

"Polly," he said, rising, wondering what had come over him, "allow me to assist."

15

The Opposite of Fright

Diantha was beside herself with nerves when Lord Harcourt asked her to remain back as the others retired for the evening.

It took what felt like ages for everyone to make their good nights, and Diantha spent the time fretting over what he could possibly want.

"Miss Brown," he said after they were finally alone, "I should prefer to have this conversation in my office at Mollybrook, but I felt it could not wait."

Her heart sank. He was going to sack her. Why else could they not wait until after the holiday? Either Mr. Hill had told him everything, or Simon had told him . . . something.

It must have been Mr. Hill. She trusted Simon. Which was, itself, a surprising and buoying thought, but one she would have to examine later, for she was currently occupied being sacked.

But on the other hand, how would Mr. Hill have reached Lord Harcourt here? If he had visited the London house, he would have found no one home. If he'd sent a letter, it would be waiting there.

"You have been my mother's companion for nearly a decade now," Lord Harcourt said.

She wasn't sure if that had been a question or a declarative statement, but she thought it best to err on the side of the former and said, "Yes, my lord."

"You have always addressed me as 'my lord.'"

Again, she wasn't sure if he was asking or telling. "I . . . yes." She paused. "My lord."

He narrowed his eyes. "Miss Brown, I should like to discuss the terms of your employment."

She steeled her spine. But, mortifyingly, tears sprang to her eyes. What good was a stiff spine when one was crying? She squeezed her eyes shut for a long second and willed the tears away. She reminded herself that it wasn't as if she'd be out on the street tomorrow. She had enough money to go somewhere else. Figure out a way forward. "You needn't make a big speech, or any speech. I shall gather my things and go."

He recoiled. "Go? Where would you go?"

"I am not sure." She kept her gaze on the floor. "If I could stop off briefly at Mollybrook to—"

"Good Heavens! I'm not going to sack you! Did you think I'd called you here to sack you?"

"I . . ."

"You did! I don't know whether to be incredulous or affronted. Why on earth would I *sack* you?" He shifted in his chair, maneuvering himself so he was directly in her line of sight. "Miss Brown, I can think of no prospect more inconvenient than the notion of your leaving our household. How would we manage without you?"

Diantha was flooded with relief. Did anything feel so good as a reprieve?

But also, she *was* going to have to leave his household. They *were* going to have to manage without her.

"I asked you to stay back," Lord Harcourt said, "in order to discuss whether we can still properly call you a companion."

She was confused. "What else would you call me?"

"Can you be a companion to someone who doesn't know who she is anymore?"

What a curious question. "My lord, I fear that question is too philosophical for me."

"What I mean is, isn't what you're doing these days more akin to nursing?"

"I don't think so. It is akin to . . ."

"What?"

She'd been going to say it was what a daughter would do, but she didn't want to be presumptuous. "It's not that different from what you do."

"Except you do more. You handle the . . . delicate matters."

"Well, the maids do, really," she said. "I merely assist."

Lord Harcourt cocked his head, regarded her as if she were a bit of a mystery. "Do you remember when my mother went wandering last May, at Mollybrook?"

"Yes." That had been a terrible day. They'd had to enlist the help of the tenants to look for her. She was found unharmed in one of the cottage gardens. It had given Diantha the fright of her life. "I am sorry again about that." She still felt the shame of it. She had no idea how the dowager had slipped away.

He waved away her apology. "I heard you with her afterward. I followed you upstairs to make sure all was well. You helped her change, and wash. You brushed and braided her hair."

Diantha bowed her head. "It's nothing you wouldn't do, were you a lady."

"That is precisely my point. You have become more like a member of the family than an employee. And that's true not merely in terms of your relationship to my mother. It's true in terms of your relationship to me. Do you remember two years back, when I was about to leave for Earls Trip? I was, I am slightly embarrassed to say, in a bit of a tizzy. I'd convinced myself I couldn't leave. You forced me to go."

"I didn't *force* you." Goodness, would the mortifications never cease?

"You made a grand speech about the importance of respite in relation to the task of caregiving."

Diantha was sure she'd never made a grand speech in her life, but she did recall having to shoo his lordship out the door that year. She and Simon had recently spoken of it.

"You didn't speak to me like a companion would. You haven't for many years."

Oh, dear. He was correct. She had overstepped. "Please accept my apologies, my lord. I shall endeavor to—"

"What? Act more like a companion? Perhaps you could start by letting me speak my piece?"

No, apparently the mortifications were not going to end. She nodded.

"My point, Miss Brown, and I admit I didn't anticipate taking so long to get round to it, is that I want to acknowledge that you are doing a great deal more than the job description of a typical companion. And while you are like family, we both know that you are *not* family. It is important to me that you know what a critical role you play in my household, and we must face the fact that my mother will not be with us forever. Therefore, I shall be raising your wages."

All she could do was gape at him.

"You may speak now."

The tears that had been threatening earlier returned. Partly because of the content of what he'd said, but mostly because he was being so kind, and kindness was, paradoxically, the very thing that might do her in. She was accustomed to hardening herself in the face of adversity. She was less sure what to do in the face of kindness. Logic would dictate that she soften herself, but she wasn't sure if she knew how to do that.

She did, she reminded herself. She'd been practicing these past two evenings with Lord Marsden. It had been so easy to tell him things, in the dark. It was less easy here, but she reminded herself that Lord Harcourt was Lord Marsden's closest friend.

One thing she had come to understand about Lord Harcourt was that he had an excess supply of empathy. He had his own brand of intelligence that was built on it. So she decided to take a risk.

"Do you remember, my lord, the summer before that Earls Trip you referenced just now? I asked for and you granted an extended holiday."

"Yes. You used that as an example of why I should leave on my own trip without guilt. 'I had my holiday,' you said. 'And now it is time for yours.'"

"Did I? Well, I am sure I meant it. But I want to tell you why I needed that holiday."

"You may if you like, but by your own logic, one needn't have a reason for a holiday beyond the respite it provides."

"Perhaps, but in that case, I went to visit my sister's grave, but then I went to a village called Greychurch."

"I know the name. It is between here and Mollybrook, is it not?"

"Yes, and not far from Barbury, where I grew up. A friend of my mother's was from there, and when I was a girl, she used to paint such a lovely picture of the place." She paused. "I had begun to consider my future. What I might do with myself once your mother is . . ."

"I understand. Please continue."

"I went to see Greychurch. To see if I could imagine myself retiring there. To see if I could afford to retire there."

"And could you? Can you?"

"Imagine myself there, yes. I found the sweetest cottage about a mile south of town, situated on the banks of a brook and surrounded by willows as tall and majestic as the cottage was small and cozy. Other trees on the property were home to many bird feeders, and the whole place was awash in birdsong.

"The cottage was, of course, occupied, but it has stood in my imagination since as a kind of ideal vision of my future."

He gazed at her. She'd purposely answered only one of his questions—could she imagine herself in the cottage? She did not speak on the other question—could she afford the cottage?

"Thank you for telling me that."

"I'm not sure why I did. It isn't relevant." It was just that he had spoken in such a heartfelt manner, and she had wanted to respond in kind. She wanted him to know that her raised wages would be spent in service of something good.

Or they *would* have been.

"Well," he said, "I shall be raising your wages, effective immediately. I was thinking something along these lines."

He handed Diantha a piece of paper on which was written a sum double the amount of her current wages. She had to swallow a gasp. With that kind of money coming in, her cottage, or something like it, would be within reach in half the time she'd planned.

But again, it didn't matter, because she didn't *have* time. She had only six months. Less. It would be five months when they returned home.

Still, Lord Harcourt didn't know that—thank Heavens. And she appreciated the gesture, more than he knew.

So she smiled and said, quite sincerely, "Thank you."

She also wondered if Simon had put him up to this.

"You are most welcome." He stood. "I bid you good night, Miss Brown."

An odd sort of embarrassment overtook Diantha as they made their way out of the sitting room. It wasn't shame. When it came down to it, she agreed with his assessment of the value of her labor. Just that she felt . . . unsettled. By what, she wasn't precisely sure. Her newfound riches? Having had a rather vulnerable conversation with Lord Harcourt?

Perhaps it was the fact that if he knew about Mr. Hill, about her letter, he wouldn't be saying such kind things. He wouldn't be doubling her wages.

"Oh, Miss Brown," he said before he mounted the stairs. "One more question."

"Yes?"

His eyes were dancing. "Your village of Greychurch. Does it in fact have a gray church?"

"It does. A handsome one that seems rather too large and grand for such a modest place, situated on one end of the village green."

"I thought so. I would be remiss if I didn't point out the hypocrisy of your disparagement of the Gurglewood moniker as too literal when you yourself are considering retiring to a village called Greychurch."

"My lord, I have never said anything against Gurglewood as a name."

He grinned. "Perhaps not, but you've thought it."

Diantha found Simon outside. As expected. She'd known it had been he who'd sent Polly to her room after everyone had gone to bed, insisting that she sit with her ladyship. "His lordship specifically asked me to," she'd said when Diantha tried to demur. Diantha hadn't asked which lordship.

"Simon," she said, approaching the fire. "Polly sent me."

"Diantha. I didn't want you to miss the comet." He winked and gestured for her to sit.

He had sent Polly. She wondered, as she settled herself in the chair next to his, what other manipulations he had undertaken on her behalf. "I had a very interesting discussion with Lord Harcourt earlier this evening. Did you have anything to do with it?"

"I can't think that I did, but perhaps you should tell me what you discussed before I proclaim my innocence."

"He has raised my wages. Quite significantly."

"I'm sure he feels the services you render are worth it."

"I wonder if he had an ulterior motive."

"One thing to know about Archie is that he isn't particularly cunning. He *is* particularly generous."

"Are you saying I'm overthinking all this?"

He grinned. "I would never say that."

She decided to let it be. "Well, have you seen any evidence of our comet?"

"None whatsoever."

"There is no comet, is there?"

"I am beginning to think not. All I have to go on is what Miss Morgan told me."

"I mean no disrespect to Miss Morgan, but it does seem odd that she would know of the approach of a comet and you, who read the papers and know the stories of the constellations, would not."

"Mm." He leaned back in his chair. He was more dressed than last night. Although he was in his shirtsleeves, they weren't rolled up, and he wore a loosely tied cravat around his neck.

That was . . . disappointing.

Still, there was something about his attitude, his posture, that was different. He was fully relaxed, limbs sprawled, gazing at her with a knowing look. If she didn't know better, she would have said he was the very picture of a rake. And that wink earlier.

She recalled that trip through his family portraits. She'd been feigning interest, and later, she'd been the one protesting the impropriety of being escorted into his mother's bedchamber. She remembered exactly what he'd said.

I am, at my core, profoundly uninterested in adhering to social mores I consider nonsensical, and so many of them are. I recognize the obligation to do so in company, but I don't see the need to in my own home.

Everyone thought Lord Marsden so respectable and proper. Straitlaced, even, possibly bordering on humorless.

Everyone was wrong.

"I have more questions," he said.

"All right." Somewhat to her surprise, she didn't mind the prospect of a renewed interrogation. Perhaps she even relished it. She had always been so careful, so circumspect, and she would have to continue to guard her big secret, but beyond that, she found she *wanted* to submit to his questioning. It was a bit like going in the pool: initially painful yet ultimately invigorating.

And the end of the holiday was looming. They had tonight, and tomorrow night, and then they would depart. Diantha would return to her life. Her problems. Her loneliness.

She sat in the chair next to him.

"I want you to tell me about this rage you have spoken of a few times."

Oh. That was not what she had expected. But had she thought he would inquire about the weather? Simon didn't do meaningless chatter. He was more *What is the lesson of* Frankenstein*?* and *What are your thoughts on marriage?*

When she didn't answer right away, he said, "You said two evenings ago that it probably started when your father gambled your sister away. How does it manifest now, all these years later?"

"Well, I am not about to go stalking across the Arctic with murder in my heart if that is your concern."

"It is not."

"I suppose . . ." She had never thought about it. It wasn't as if she walked through life seething with anger. Just that sometimes it . . . flared. She tried to think what those instances had in common. "I think it manifests when it feels like I can't get anything I want. And I don't mean my silly retirement fantasy. I mean little things. Daily things."

"Such as?"

He was relentless. She didn't mind. And it was easy to talk to him, relatively speaking, when they were both looking at the fire instead of each other.

"All right. Here is an example. Sometimes I just want to go out."

"Out. What does that mean?"

"In the beginning, when I first entered the employ of Lady Harcourt, we used to go out rather a lot. To visit her friends, to parties, to the shops, or merely to promenade in the park. Sometimes, she used to say, 'Diantha, my girl, my legs need to move.' That was her way of saying we needed to manufacture an errand to get us out of the house.

"I didn't realize it as it was happening, but our world shrank. In fact, at first, I think I enjoyed the respite of fewer social obligations. I am someone who grows somewhat agitated when I don't have sufficient doses of solitude. It is difficult to explain."

"I understand. Being with people is depleting. One needs to prepare oneself for it, and arrange time to recover from it."

"Yes! That is well said. But even for me, the world can only recede so far and for so long before I begin to miss its charms. What I wouldn't give to go out for an ice, when we are in London, or to attend a dance in the local assembly rooms when we are at Mollybrook."

"You could ask Archie. I am certain he would accommodate you."

"He would let me out of my cage."

"I . . . yes."

"I am sorry. I am being glib and ungrateful at the same time, which is rather a feat, isn't it? It's just that this is my life. My world is small. By its very nature, the role of companion means subsuming one's agency to that of one's employer. But I take an odd sort of solace in reminding myself that I am not unique, that it is always this way for women."

"What do you mean?"

"A wife is subservient to her husband. A mistress is subservient to her keeper."

He made a vague noise that from anyone else she would have interpreted as disagreement. From him, she thought it might signal dismay.

"I admit I had never thought of it like that," he said.

"Think of the words themselves. We say a man 'takes' a wife, as if she were a flower he may pluck at will. A gentleman 'keeps' a mistress, as if she were an animal in a cage.

"And before that, we do what our fathers want. They give us to another man to marry, transferring the title as surely as if we were a piece of land.

"And before you start pointing out the rare instances of employed ladies, those occupations have as their foundation service to others. Governesses. Teachers. Nuns. The only woman I know who has an interesting job is Lord Stonely's wife. And she's rather the exception, don't you think?"

He was silent. She had said too much. He wanted to know about what inspired her to anger, and she had delivered a treatise on the role of ladies in society.

"Some women find genuine love," he said quietly. "Clementine and Julianna did."

She could make no argument there. "I suppose it's different then. But your examples are not typical. That kind of love is rare. And it doesn't change the nature of the arrangement, not elementally. A good husband might be a benevolent keeper, but he's a keeper all the same."

They were getting too off topic. She didn't mind answering his questions, but she didn't want to talk about love and marriage with him. "Back to the discussion at hand: I want things for myself, and not having them makes me so angry sometimes that I wonder if I am . . . defective somehow."

"Don't we all get angry at times?"

"I don't know that we do. I'm talking about a terrible lot of anger. It's very unseemly."

"Is it, though? I am having trouble imagining it, picturing you so angry that you offend polite company."

"You are correct, I suppose. It is more of an internal anger."

"I am no expert, but I wonder if it isn't better to let it out in some fashion."

"I have been known to scream into my pillow in the dead of night."

"Have you!"

"Don't sound so delighted! I told you it was unseemly."

"Perhaps you could hurl things at other things, in secret."

"Things at other things? What do you mean?"

"Oh, I don't know, plates at walls, perhaps. Would it not be satisfying to see them shatter?"

"I am sure it would be, but it is, of course, impossible." Strangely appealing but impossible.

"Why impossible?"

"Where am I going to get plates I have leave to destroy?"

"Yes, I see the problem."

"And even if I did have a stack of expendable plates, isn't it wrong to destroy a perfectly good plate?"

"A fair question."

"I suppose part of the reason I enjoy taking the waters," she said, "is that it imparts some of the same wild, transgressive feeling I imagine would arise from your plate-smashing scenario."

"Yes, I hadn't thought to use the word 'transgression,' but we spoke about how taking the waters feels like falling off a cliff." He stood. "Let us do it."

"Fall off a cliff?" she teased, though she knew what he meant, and she knew she was going to agree.

"No. Go in the pool." He held out his hand. "I won't look at you. It shall all be very proper."

"Proper!" That was a stretch.

"Well, as proper as any of this"—he waved a hand back and forth between them—"has been."

"I take the point." She stood. "I shall have to take my dress off and go in in my shift. I have two of each on this trip, and experience has taught me that while a dress takes days to dry, tonight's wet shift will be dry enough to wear two days from now."

Part of her couldn't believe she was talking about her shift in front of him. Another part of her felt completely at ease doing so.

He cleared his throat. "All right. I shall turn my back. You go in, call to me when you are settled, and I shall join you. Unless you'd prefer I go first."

"I should prefer that we go together," she said, before she could think better of it. But really, getting into the pool *was* like jumping off a cliff, and she suspected it would be a great deal more satisfying with a . . . friend. "We can . . . not look at each other while we do it."

"All right," he said again. "I shall step away to make myself ready and meet you at the edge of the pool in a bit. I will keep my eyes on the sky. After all, we can't forget that we're meant to be watching for our comet." He winked again.

Who was this version of Simon, so playful and knowing?

"I shall hold my hand out. When you are ready, take it and we shall immerse ourselves together."

It occurred to Diantha that his plan would preserve her modesty but not his. His eyes would be on the sky, but in order to find and take his hand, she would have to look at him.

She said nothing to that end, merely agreed and stepped away from the fire to remove her dress and stays.

When she turned back around, her breath caught. He was wearing breeches and nothing else. The pool was close enough to the fire that he was limned in golden light, and he was standing, as he had said he would be, with his face tilted toward the sky and his arm out, waiting for her.

He looked like a living statue, a man beautiful enough to be in a museum but clever enough to have escaped its confines.

It occurred to her that this was not the first time she had likened Simon to a statue, to a work of art in the form of a man.

As she drew closer, she could see the planes of his body—the curve of his shoulders, the long, lean muscles in the arm held at attention at a right angle to his torso. He almost looked like da Vinci's *Vitruvian Man*.

She took the hand waiting for her, and the statue came to life. He was still looking at the sky, but he smiled. He lowered their joined hands and swung them back and forth as if they were great friends about to set off on an adventure.

A laugh escaped. She hadn't known it was there until it was *there*—out in the world, echoing in the dark.

He laughed, too, and she loved to hear it.

"I am going to shift my gaze from the sky to the ground, else I shan't be able to see my way into the water. But I won't look at you."

Look at me, she wanted to say.

It felt suddenly as if he were the only one who ever had. He had looked at her, and he had *seen* her. The person she was underneath her position as companion to Lady Harcourt.

He had seen her with her armor off, and now she wanted him to see her with everything off. Well, nearly everything. She glanced down at her shift, which was fluttering around her legs, as it was a breezy night.

"*I* am looking at *you*," she said.

He only smiled, and she watched him shift his gaze to the ground as he said he would. He tightened his grip on her hand. "Are you ready?"

"I am ready."

They entered the water in perfect unison, down to the bench, down to the pool's floor. Wordlessly, they sat.

He kept her hand.

She blew out a breath.

"I am now going to transfer my gaze back to the sky," he said, and she was flooded with fondness for this kind, careful man who was, in concert with her, being a bit transgressive.

Could a person be "a bit" transgressive, though? Were there not merely two states, *transgressive* and *not transgressive*?

With that in mind, she maneuvered herself so she was right in front of him and said what she'd wanted to so badly before. "Look at me."

He remained frozen in place, his eyes on the horizon—she must have arrested him mid gaze-transfer.

She took his other hand. "I am beneath the water. There is nothing to see."

That did it. His gaze found hers, and he said, incredulously, "Nothing to see? There is *you* to see."

"Yes," she said, and they looked at each other, fingers of both hands interlaced. They looked at each other and breathed. They looked at each other and let the cold water do its work.

They had done so much talking. So many words had passed between them these last days and nights. They had talked of monsters and ribbons, grief and rage, duty and God.

Now, it was time to set words aside. He must have known it as well as she, for he gazed evenly at her. He was looking at her now, and looking *inside* her. She wanted him to see everything.

She wanted to stay here forever.

He must have shared the sentiment, for they remained like that for quite a long time, longer than she'd ever stayed immersed.

"Diantha," he finally said, "we have to get out."

"I don't want to," she whispered raggedly.

"Your teeth are chattering. Come. It will turn dangerous if we remain any longer."

He scrambled out ahead of her, and as with the coach, helped her out, though it was up onto land this time rather than down. There was no more polite averting of gazes or pretending not to look. As she came out of the pool, water raining from her drenched shift, she felt the weight of his attention.

She looked at him, too, shamelessly. His breeches were plastered to his body, and she could make out the shape of him beneath.

She blew out a breath, and with it a puff of steam. It jolted him into motion. He led her to the fire, which was very low now, and took up the blanket she had brought with her. She, like a silly girl, had hoped they might lie back on it again this evening and gaze at the stars. She had hoped he might hold her hand again. She could not have imagined what had transpired instead.

"You are freezing," he said urgently, wrapping the blanket around her.

"I am," she conceded, newly aware of the violent shivering of her limbs.

"Come," he said, and, retaking her hand, he led her to the new, small structure Lord Harcourt had built in the garden.

"I am alone in here," he said as he pushed open the door and gently prodded her in ahead of him.

"We stayed in the water too long," he said urgently, lighting a branch of candles, leading her to a narrow bed and proceeding to lie her on it and pile its covers on her. Then he plucked covers from the room's other two beds and added them atop. "Warm yourself, and I will start a fire. I need to run around back to fetch some wood. We're all out in here."

"No! Don't leave me!" she said, and though she ought to have been sheepish about the vehemence of that outburst, she wasn't.

"Please," she added in a more measured tone. She wasn't sure what had prompted the request, except that, as earlier, she was exquisitely aware of the impending end of the holiday, of her essential aloneness lurking around the edges of the scene, threatening.

"Of course I won't if you don't want me to," he said, perching on the edge of her bed.

"You're freezing, too," she said, for the candles he'd set on the nightstand were enough to illuminate the gooseflesh covering the arms she had so often admired. She held back the covers, and he hesitated only a moment before he slid in next to her.

Whatever trepidation he'd felt before, he must have dispensed with, for once under the covers, he rolled over and took her in his arms, pressing their bodies together. They were both shivering.

"We stayed in too long," he said again.

"I think we stayed in the exact right amount," she said, and it didn't feel like a bold declaration, so much as the truth.

"Yes," he said, tightening his hold on her and tucking her head against his chest. "Try to relax. Try not to resist."

He was talking about the cold, she knew, but she pretended he wasn't.

What if the thing she didn't resist was . . . him? Them. This.

She squirmed in his tight embrace, slithering up his body. It caused him to issue a terse, cautionary "Diantha."

She was not in the mood to receive any warning, or admonishment. She was cold and hot at the same time, and she was *so* tired of never getting to have what she wanted.

She kissed him. She would have assumed she didn't know how to do it, but it turned out she did.

"Diantha."

She would have assumed his second utterance of her name, this time with a kind of tortured resignation, would have been a signal that she should stop, but it turned out it wasn't.

She wondered how much of her life she'd spent assuming things that weren't true.

After a few more moments of hesitation on his part, he began kissing her back. His lips were so soft. But also hard, or perhaps more accurately, insistent. They were working hers with an intensity that made her dizzy. And then, oh dear, he opened his mouth. She got the sense that she was meant to do the same, so she did.

She heard her own gasp as his tongue slid into her mouth.

She'd had no idea. Thea had told her that the coming together of a lady and a gentleman could have many moods. That the lady could enjoy herself.

Enjoy had not been a strong enough word.

She followed the cues of her body, and she took what she wanted. She wanted to touch his chest, so she did. And when he made a noise that seemed to indicate that he enjoyed it, she did it some more. When they broke their kiss, panting, she wanted to tip her head back, because she wanted him to kiss her neck. So she did, and he did. It was so easy, here, with him, to take what she wanted. To *receive* what she wanted, for he was giving as much as she was taking. He had one hand on the back of her neck and one hand on her arse, both kneading, and she thought back with delight to their evening meal the first night, when she had discovered his ambidexterity. He had informed her that he was equally adept or equally incompetent with both hands.

He was very good at this.

As he lavished attention on her neck, it was as if he were opening a new frontier. She had been so focused on his mouth on hers, and then on the idea of his mouth on her neck. But now she wanted it lower. Her breasts felt heavy; her nipples ached. She reached up and untied the string at the top of her shift and pushed the wet fabric off one shoulder.

"*Oh*," he groaned, and though she was almost certain it was a groan of pleasure, it seemed the sight of a bare breast had had the opposite effect of what she'd been aiming for. He removed himself from her. Not from the bed, but from her person. He put a good six inches between them. She started to protest, but he pressed his fingers against her lips. "Shh."

"But—"

"You must go."

"I don't—"

"Think of poor Polly." He got out of bed.

An unwelcome thought arose. She had been so sure of herself just then, confident that she could be guided by the sensations arising in her body, that it was permissible—nay, *right*—to take what she wanted. But now it felt as if he were trying to shuffle her off. Perhaps it hadn't been as enjoyable for him as it had for her.

She sat up, covering herself with the bed linens. "Lord Marsden, I am sorry. I didn't mean . . . Was that. . . ?"

"*Simon*," he corrected vehemently. And then, more gently: "That was the most exciting thing that has ever happened to me."

Relief flooded in, and she tried to speak, but he talked over her, which was notable as it was the first time he'd ever done that. "But now I am going to go outside and find your dress and stays. And you are going to dress and go to the main house and go to bed."

She put herself together as best she could while he was gone, and when he returned, he helped her with her dress.

When he was done, he spun her around, picked up the candle so he could better regard her, and said, "Well, at least Polly knows you have a fondness for taking the waters at night."

"Do I look a fright?"

"No." She rather thought his expression had turned fond. "You look whatever is the opposite of fright."

"What is the opposite of fright?" she asked.

"I don't know. You have years of novel reading experience on me. You tell me."

"I suppose the opposite of fright, if you take it to be mean 'horrid' or 'terrible' or 'alarming,' is pleasing or delightful or soothing."

"Yes," he said. "Also: beautiful."

She was warm now, from her head to her toes, from her heart to her soul.

"We didn't see the comet," he said, picking up the line she had used several times the last few nights.

"We can try again," she said, picking up his.

The next morning, Diantha did a little manipulating of the dowager before breakfast. "Wouldn't it be nice if Lord Marsden read to you some more this morning?" And, later, at breakfast, to Simon, she said, "Lady Harcourt was just saying she wished you would read to her some more today, but I think she is shy to ask you."

He fell over himself to accommodate them.

And so Diantha was freed to undertake her larger mission.

She took the liberty of knocking on Miss Morgan's door. It was bold, but she needed privacy, and barging in on the lady was less bold than what was to follow. She had learned that Miss Morgan was not fond of breakfast, preferring instead to take a tea tray in her bedchamber.

Diantha didn't get the impression that Miss Morgan was surprised by much, but Diantha's appearance at her door had apparently done the job. "Miss Brown!"

"Miss Morgan, would you . . . help me? I find myself in need of . . . advice."

Why did she keep trailing off her sentences? It signified a kind of wishy-washiness she abhorred. She had spent all her time this morning plotting how to get here, and not enough, apparently, on what to actually say.

"Miss Brown, I assure you I am quite prepared to dispense advice. It is one of my favorite ways to pass the time." She stepped back and gestured Diantha inside. "Please excuse the mess."

The bedchamber was strewn with more clothing than Diantha owned. Miss Morgan picked up a hat that had been resting on the room's lone chair and said, "Sit." She herself perched on the bed.

Something in Diantha's chest twinged. She was transported to the days when she and Thea used to hole up in her bedroom, chatting about everything and nothing.

"My dear lady," Miss Morgan said, "please tell me what is troubling you."

Diantha was giving herself away. It was Simon's fault. He had chipped away at her defenses such that she was having trouble concealing her feelings in the usual way. "I must be assured that you'll keep what I am about to tell you in the strictest confidence." She paused. "We don't know each other well, but I feel I can trust you."

"Oh, you can. You have no idea the secrets I've kept. *No idea.*"

Diantha couldn't help but smile. "I suppose that's why they're secrets."

"You might even call me a secret mistress."

"I don't know that you are the correct person to advise me in this matter, but I also don't know who else to ask."

"I am at your service."

"I feel that perhaps you are less . . . shockable than your average young lady."

"Oh, will you just come out with it, Miss Brown!"

Diantha was a bit startled by Miss Morgan's exacerbated outburst.

"Dissembling does not suit you."

"I know. I know. It is a most unattractive trait." Diantha straightened her spine and reminded herself that she was accomplished at bursting in on people and saying unexpected, scandalous things. "I am considering whether to give away my maidenhood."

"Oh, my."

"I have shocked you." How dismaying. She shouldn't have come.

"You've shocked me, yes, but you haven't scandalized me."

"I . . . well, all right, then. So, should I do it?"

"My dear, you are going to have to provide me with some context! You are going to have to sit down right here and talk for ages!"

The way she patted the space next to her on the bed also reminded Diantha of Thea, so much so that it gave her pause.

"Are you quite all right?" Miss Morgan asked. "Apart from the question at hand, which I concede might be quite discomposing."

"Yes. You merely reminded me of my sister there for a moment, and I . . . I miss her so very much."

"Oh, *Miss Brown*. I'm so sorry."

People said things like that all the time, tossed off condolences as if they were weather reports. The words themselves had become devalued, Diantha often thought. But not with Miss Morgan.

Miss Morgan managed to imbue them with an urgency that felt genuine. And then she added: "I don't know how I would go on if my sister died."

"You just do."

"I suppose you do, but I imagine the world is never the same."

All Diantha could do was nod, for her throat was suddenly clogged with tears.

Miss Morgan regarded Diantha for a long time, as if she knew she needed a moment, before saying, "Will you come sit beside me and tell me what is on your mind?"

Yes. She had never wanted anything more, suddenly.

She moved to the bed, only for Miss Morgan to get up.

"I shall be right back!" she said, and after a quick trip to a half-unpacked trunk in the corner, she returned with a bottle of brandy.

Diantha was startled. It wasn't even noon, and brandy was not a very ladylike libation.

Miss Morgan proceeded to slosh some brandy into a teacup. "Oh, don't look so scandalized, Miss Brown. It doesn't suit you." She added a splash of tea, took a sip, and said, "A little brandy in one's tea is sometimes just the thing. But I only have the one cup, so we shall have to share." She held out the cup.

"I think those proportions would suggest a little tea in your brandy is just the thing. But why not?" Diantha took the cup and sipped.

"I knew I liked you, Miss Brown."

"Would you call me Diantha?" The request was probably improper, but so was drinking brandy at half eleven. She and Miss Morgan were both the daughters of gentlemen. While the household generally deferred to formal address, there was no reason Diantha shouldn't call friends by their given names. She just didn't have any friends.

Well, except Simon, of course. Her cheeks heated, thinking of him saying her name last night, first as if he were issuing a warning, and then as if he were flying the white flag of surrender.

Olive smiled. "Diantha. Your name is much prettier than mine. You are a goddess. I am a fruit. An ugly fruit. My sister gets Clementine, and I get Olive. The injustice!"

Miss Morgan's—Olive's—mock pouting was putting Diantha at ease. Or perhaps credit for that ought to go to brandy-with-a-splash-of-tea.

"Yes," Olive went on, "we shall use each other's Christian names, but the degree of informality implied by such also dictates that you must tell me why you were blushing a moment ago."

"If I was blushing, it was because I was recalling a conversation I recently had."

"You were recalling a *conversation*? Is that what we're calling it?"

Diantha laughed along with Olive. "It *was* a conversation I was recalling, but . . . there are other activities I could recall if I so chose."

"Once again, I implore you to speak plainly."

All right. This was what she'd come here for. It was going better than she'd expected. She forced herself to maintain an outwardly calm tone as she said, "I have kissed the gentleman in question on the mouth. I have been in a state of undress with him."

"I see. And you want me to tell you if those activities should escalate. If you should surrender your maidenhood."

"Well, not tell me, exactly, but . . . advise me." She was making a mull of this. "Not that I am implying that you have personal experience in these matters, of course. I merely regard you as a lady wise to the ways of society, a lady who might help me think through the . . . consequences."

"Oh, I have personal experience in these matters." Olive studied Diantha. "You are scandalized."

"Not scandalized, just . . ."

"You are right to consider the consequences, for there will be some. Ideally none that arrive nine months later. But there are ways to prevent that. The other potential consequence is, of course, being found out. Ruination." She paused. "I am assuming we are speaking about the possibility of your giving away your maidenhood outside the context of marriage, yes?"

"Yes." It was almost comical that while Diantha had initially proposed the appearance of ruination without actual ruination, she was now seeking advice about actual ruination without the appearance of such. "I am certain, however, that the gentleman in question would be discreet. No one will know. It's more . . ."

"That *you* will know. You want to know how you will feel."

"Yes," Diantha said quietly.

"I understand. I have done things I ought to be ashamed of."

"But are you?" That was what she was truly asking, wasn't it?

"Not . . . precisely."

"Yes, I thought the word 'ought' was doing a lot of work in that sentence."

Olive chuckled. "I was not ashamed. I *am* not ashamed. It's more that from this vantage point—the actions in question occurred many years ago now—I worry that my past might . . . catch up with me."

"Meaning it might disqualify you from marriage? A family?"

"Yes. I didn't used to be worried about such things. You see, the reason I am not ashamed of my actions is that they weren't undertaken with any old gentleman." She took a large slurp of her "tea." "I was wildly in love with my gentleman. But he died."

"Oh, I am sorry." Diantha tried to imbue the statement of condolence with the same sincerity that had characterized Olive's earlier.

"He was my secret lover, though we did plan to marry. But then he went to *Upper Canada*, of all places, and he *died.* I shall tell you everything after extracting a vow of secrecy—we will be bound in an agreement of mutually assured destruction—but let us consider your circumstances first. If you're worried anything you do today might disqualify you from marrying in the future, I believe that's a reasonable fear. I used to think I didn't care if my past disqualified me, as you say, because I was determined I should never find another love like the one I had. And I shan't." She took another sip. "But time has done its work, dulling the edges of my grief such that I sometimes imagine that perhaps I *could* have a family, find a companion." She smirked. "If not for the disqualifying part."

"My apologies if this sounds indelicate, but if you were to find such a companion, a prospect, so to speak, would you have to tell him about your past? You are from a good family. You are liked and admired. Why would he ever need to know?"

"Because I shouldn't want to start a partnership on a lie. Because the kind of man I would want to spend my life with wouldn't be the kind of man to whom I could countenance lying."

Goodness. Olive Morgan had hidden depths.

"Well, I don't need to worry about that," Diantha said. "I don't plan to marry."

Olive smirked. "I have heard that a fair few times of late, but all right. That's one thing you needn't worry about, then."

It amazed Diantha that there was going to be no further discussion on the matter, that Olive was going to take Diantha's statement that she didn't plan to marry at face value.

"Who is the gentleman in question?" Olive asked.

"I can't say."

"Is it Simon?"

All Diantha could do was blink—and panic.

"Do not look so shocked, my dear. It's perfectly obvious."

"It *is*?" Diantha was dismayed. Truly dismayed.

"Well, it is now that you've told me you've been kissing and in a state of undress with a man. Who else is it going to be?"

"I didn't say that all those things had happened here, or recently."

"When else would they have happened? Are you not with Lady Harcourt—the elder Lady Harcourt—all of the time?"

"Oh, dear."

Olive waved a hand dismissively. "Don't worry, no one else knows. As I said, it's only in retrospect that I guessed the identity of your paramour."

"He's not my paramour!"

"And the gentlemen themselves are not that smart when it comes to these things," Olive said, apparently having decided to ignore Diantha's protest.

"What things?"

"Sentimental matters. Romantic matters. What I am saying, Diantha, is that your secret is safe with me, and, I should think, safe in general. And by the by, don't let questions of timing affect your plans. I can sleep in Lady Harcourt's room anytime you like."

"You would do that?" Diantha had been assuming that she would have to try to enlist Polly again.

"Of course!" Olive brushed her hands together as if dispensing with a pesky logistical matter. "All right, so you want to undertake intimate relations with Simon. Do you know how it works?"

"Yes, I know how it works!" Diantha laughed, and Olive did, too.

"So your hesitation is not of a technical variety."

"No, it's more that . . ."

"What does Simon have to say about all this?"

"He says nothing. In fact, he was the one who halted our last encounter. This is the source of my discomfiture. If more is to happen, I shall have to be the instigator."

"Ah. So you are asking me if you ought to proposition Simon?"

"I suppose I am."

"I think you should."

"Truly?"

"If everything you have told me is true, I don't see a downside. You want to do it. You're not concerned about any future you might be compromising. We know he would be discreet."

"Do we?" She thought so. He had kept her confidence until now, but that was a matter of him holding his tongue when it came to Diantha's affairs. If they were to lie together, it would be his affair, too, no? Diantha was talking to Olive about it. Did Simon not have the right to talk to his friends about it if he so chose?

"Of course we do!" Olive exclaimed. "Simon is the most upstanding of gentlemen. In fact, I think the only potential obstacle to your plan is that he'll be so upstanding, he'll refuse to do it."

"That is a distinct possibility."

If Olive only knew what else Simon was too upstanding to do.

"I imagine he was caught off guard last time," Olive mused.

"I think we both were."

"Right. So he'll be prepared this time. He'll be ready to defend the castle."

"Defend the castle!" Diantha laughed. Just a little at first, and she tried to smother it, but the notion of Lord Marsden fortifying a castle against an invading horde—and the invading horde was her? Well, it was too amusing.

Olive joined, and soon the two of them were shaking with laughter. Olive laughed so hard, she tipped over.

Diantha recovered herself first. And, again, the thought that had been haunting her rose: *How am I going to leave this?*

This, meaning them, the Harcourt family, but also this newfound closeness. This friend.

16

Smash Therapy

After Simon was done reading to the dowager and had given her into Archie's care—he wondered where Diantha was, for he hadn't seen her since breakfast—he made his way into the kitchen.

"Christine, I have an odd question for you."

"I shall endeavor to have an odd answer for you, my lord," she said as she passed him a blob of dough to knead.

"Do you know a place I could purchase some plates?"

"Dining plates?"

"Yes."

"We've several dozen here, various kinds. You may help yourself." She opened a hutch. "These are the everyday ones we use to eat here in the kitchen." She opened a different cupboard. "And these are the ones we serve you and your friends on."

"Yes." How was he going to explain this? "While I thank you for your generosity, I can't use the household plates. I wouldn't want them to break."

"What are you going to be doing with these plates, if you don't mind my asking."

"I don't mind you asking, but I can't answer."

"You are a curious one." She shook her head at him, but her

eyes were bright. "There is a potter in town. On a little lane off the high street. There's a house with a blue door at the corner."

"Thank you," he said, and he set off to purchase some plates.

"I beg your pardon? You want me to what?"

"Break these plates," said Simon, who had made a successful shopping expedition to town.

"Have you lost your wits?"

Simon might very well have lost his wits. It was early evening, and he and Diantha were standing behind the gentlemen's cave, the back of which, because Archie had had it built quickly, was a solid wall of brick.

He gestured at the stack of crockery he had placed a half dozen yards from the wall. "They aren't the household plates. I bought them specially."

Diantha swung around from looking at the plates. "I repeat: Have you lost your wits?"

Yes. I have entirely lost my wits. It is not enough to give you a ribbon; I must give you plates to smash. Love and rage are the same thing, remember?

"Not at all," he said. "You said you sometimes grew angry enough to scream into your pillow. You may recall that I suggested hurling things at other things." He gestured, serially, to the stack of plates, and to the wall.

"You want me to throw those plates. At that wall."

"Yes. Well, only if *you* want to. I got some teacups, too. The potter gave them to me for free because they're failed teacups."

"Failed teacups?"

"Yes, they have mistakes." He held one up. "This one is much thicker on one side than the other." He held up another. "And the handle on this one is attached only on one end. He apparently usually sells them at a steep discount, but since I bought so many plates, he gave them to me."

"You are . . . extraordinary."

"Well, so are you."

She laughed. She picked up a plate. She retracted her arm. She lowered her arm. "I cannot summon the necessary anger."

"Yes, you can. When was the last time you went out?"

"A few days ago when I walked to town when you shooed me out of the breakfast room so you could read to Lady Harcourt."

"When was the last time you went out before that?"

She didn't answer, which he hoped meant he was making headway. "Have you been to a party lately?"

She retracted her arm again.

"Or to shop for ribbons?"

She threw, but the plate fell well short of the wall. It didn't even break.

He regrouped. "Do you not think it ought to be against the law to wager the fate of human beings in card games?"

She went dead still, and he feared he had gone too far. But after a moment that felt as if it lasted an eternity, she stooped, picked up another plate, and retracted her arm again.

Smash!

The plate broke, but only into three pieces. The potter in town was quite talented. He made hearty crockery.

"Huzzah!" Still, Simon felt she could do better. "Why, when a couple is discovered in a compromising scenario, is the lady's reputation ruined for all time, while the gentleman will shake off the stink?" He had used her phrase—*shake off the stink*—intentionally.

She picked up another plate and hurled it at the wall. It broke into many more pieces.

"Yes!" They were getting somewhere.

She picked up another plate and turned to him, as if she were waiting for another prompt.

All right. He kept thinking he was going too far, but it seemed he was not. Or perhaps "too far" was what was indicated. "Why do we live in a world in which a gentleman can force a lady to marry him?"

That did it. The next plate she threw shattered into dozens—nay, hundreds—of pieces.

She picked up another plate and hurtled it at the wall.

And another.

And then, to his absolute shock, she answered his question. "Because he knows something that will hurt people the lady loves if he tells."

"*Pardon?*"

She wasn't listening to him anymore, though; she was hurling plates against the wall.

He was frozen. He didn't want to stop her. She was doing what he'd brought her here to do, but he needed to know more about what she was describing, which to his ears sounded like blackmail.

"What in Heaven's name is happening here?"

Diantha joined Simon in his frozen state, but the plate she had last released hit the wall a second later, shattering dramatically.

"It is time to dine." The voice was Olive's.

Simon turned.

"Cook has prepared quite a feast for our final night together, and I volunteered to come find you two."

Explaining his way out of this scenario was not possible, so Simon merely said, "Thank you. We shall be right along."

"I shall come with you right now," Diantha, unfrozen, said to Olive.

Since Simon had already, in Olive's eyes, anyway, shattered all polite norms, he took Diantha's arm to interrupt her progress, leaned over, and spoke in her ear. "This isn't over. I will see you tonight."

He was somewhat surprised that she appeared that evening. It would have been easy for her not to. She could have gone to bed, and tomorrow, there would be a flurry of activity as the household made ready to leave, the ladies first, in the coach, and the gentlemen later, on horseback. She could have slipped from his grasp.

He was waiting for her in the usual spot, but he hadn't lit a fire, so he felt her approach more than saw it.

And then there she was, standing directly before him, the outline of her distinguishable from the blackness of the night more by memory than by sight.

The last time. The last night. The last comet-hunting outing.

But there was no comet, and there were truths to uncover, so he stood and said, "Come with me."

She made no protest as he took her to the gentlemen's cave. He had left the fire going, and he led her to sit by it, depositing her on one end of the settee that faced it and sitting himself at the other. He would have wished for separate armchairs, for he needed to be as free from distraction as possible in order to have this conversation, but the space was small and its furnishings limited.

They spoke in unison. He said, "Tell me what you meant before," and she said, "I cannot tell you any more."

They did it again, him saying, "*Tell* me," and her saying, "*No.*"

He wanted to shout. If someone was blackmailing her, it needed to *stop.*

"You said you would keep my confidence," she said.

"I have. I am. I will. But—"

She held up a hand. "You said trustworthiness was the most important quality in a friend."

"I didn't say that; you did."

"Well, either I can trust you, or I can't. Which is it?"

He was taken aback. She'd spoken with a tone that fell somewhere between exasperation and anger. Angering Diantha was not something he had ever wanted to do, and faced with a choice such as that—*either I can trust you, or I can't*—there was no question. He turned so he was facing her, one leg on the ground, the other tucked up on the settee. It was an awkward position, but he wanted her to see him head-on when he said, "You can trust me."

"And either *you* can trust *me*, or you can't. You don't. Which is it?"

Again, she had his back against a wall. He gave the only answer there was: "I trust you."

"Then know that I have the situation in hand."

Simon, the parliamentarian, was defeated.

"What are you going to do when you get home?" she asked, and he recognized the question for what it was: an unsubtle attempt to change the subject.

He answered it, though he understood that in so doing he was allowing his goals to recede further. "I am going to have a very unpleasant conversation with my mother." He laughed, and he heard the bitterness in it. "We can't all have mothers as lovely as Lady Harcourt."

"Did Lord Harcourt and his mother always have a good relationship? Back to when he was young?"

He did not speak initially. He wasn't sure how she had turned him so neatly from his mission. He didn't like to be the kind of man who was so easily swayed.

He took some consolation in the idea that perhaps he wasn't the kind of man who was easily swayed, generally speaking. Perhaps he was only easily swayed by her. It was a strangely mollifying notion.

"Yes," he said, surrendering. "It was evident that she loved him very much. They were quite close."

"They still are. I don't mean to issue a rebuke, but I don't think you ought to have used the past tense there."

"You are, of course, correct. I stand chastened."

"I know how much it hurts Lord Harcourt when she doesn't know him. And I know she so rarely does. But when she is calm, he sits with her, and she holds his hand. She doesn't hold my hand, or that of the younger Lady Harcourt. Lord Harcourt calms his mother, even when she doesn't know who he is."

"Perhaps she does know who he is, in some way that is beyond conventional knowing," Simon speculated.

"That is exactly it, and I knew you would understand, even though you wouldn't seem to be the sort of person who would."

He knew what she meant. Simon the parliamentarian might have met his match in Diantha, but he was still Simon the parliamentarian. He was still guided by logic. No one—well almost no one—would expect him to be prattling on about knowledge acquired by mystical means.

"Perhaps you know me in a deeper way." It was an arresting thought. He'd always thought Effie and Archie were the only people who truly knew him, but that wasn't true anymore, was it? "There's that word again—'knowing.' There are different kinds of knowing. I believe that. And I believe you are correct in your assessment that Lady Harcourt knows Archie in some essential way, even if she doesn't recognize him visually, or isn't able to summon the proper language to communicate with him, or the memories to place him temporally."

"Some part of her can place him sentimentally, if not temporally."

"Yes."

"How lucky he is to have that," she said. "I would never say that to him, for I understand that even as he is what I would consider fortunate, he has felt his mother's decline as a terrible burden. It has been, objectively, a terrible burden."

"Both things can be true."

"Yes."

Silence fell, but it wasn't heavy. Her change of subject had done its work, subsuming Simon into the familiar, treasured rhythms of conversation with Diantha. She had shifted the mood by asking him what he was going to do when he got home. He was tempted to ask her the same, but he couldn't. For one thing, the question was too close to asking her to tell him what Mr. Hill had on her. But it was also a fraught question in a deeper sense. He thought back to her saying that she missed going out. He had suggested she ask Archie for leave to go out for an ice or to a dance and she had agreed that he would certainly give it. *He would let me out of my cage*, she'd said.

What would returning home from Earls Trip be but going back in?

Even if this had been a working holiday for her, what he had once called a shadow holiday, it *had* represented a kind of freedom. Look at them now, seated by the fire in the gentlemen's cave while someone else sat with Lady Harcourt.

"Simon," she said, and something about the way she turned her head toward him, the light from the fire catching the planes of her face, made his breath catch. He had seen her these past few nights in varying degrees of dishevelment, but tonight she was fully dressed, wearing the same pale yellow gown she'd worn to dinner, and her hair was coiled into a tidy chignon.

He wanted to tangle his fingers in her hair and muss it up. He wanted to peel the dress from her and see her again. He wanted to touch her, the way she had clearly offered last night.

He wanted. Oh, he wanted so badly he thought he might die of it.

"I have come with a proposal," she said, sliding across the settee and turning so she was right in front of him.

His mind flashed back to the last time she had come to him with a proposal.

"I would like for us to lie together tonight."

Just like the last time, pandemonium broke out in Simon's body, his mind—his whole self.

"Hear me out," she said, but he didn't want to do that, so he closed the distance between them and kissed her.

He was going to trust her. About everything, but also about this. If she wanted this, he did, too. He would silence the analytical voice in his head. She had called him upstanding, that night from a lifetime ago. This night, he was going to be something else.

He was going to do what he wanted because it was, apparently—astonishingly, miraculously—also what she wanted. He was going to do all the things he had just been thinking. He started with her hair, sliding his hands to the back of her head and searching for pins, or hardware of some kind, while keeping his mouth on hers. She was kissing him as ardently as he was her, sighing into his mouth in a way that made his prick come to attention.

He wasn't having any luck with her hair. He broke their kiss and muttered, "God damn it," even as she made a mew of protest. She reached up to help him, but he batted her hands away. He wanted to take her hair down himself.

"It's one big pin," she said against his mouth. "Find the rounded edge and pull straight out." She turned in place on the settee, presenting her back to him, nestling close enough that her bottom was nudging his prick.

He fumbled with her hair, and once it was down, he realized what he really wanted was to see it falling over her bare shoulders, down her bare back. He was faced with a row of buttons down the back of her dress, so, happily, it was easy enough to make his desires reality.

His hands shook as he slipped the buttons through their holes. He made himself go slowly, to be more considered than he had been with her hair. He wouldn't get to do this again, and damned if he wasn't going to commit every moment of it to memory. He wanted to etch the experience of it—the experience of *her*—into his mind, so he could take it out and revisit it in the lonely days to come.

He couldn't see her face, but he could tell by the way she was holding herself stiffly that she was not at ease. He brushed a hand down the side of her neck as he pulled the dress down one shoulder. Both neck and shoulder felt coiled with tension.

"Has the water helped the pain in your shoulders?" He should have asked earlier.

"Not particularly."

He pulled the dress off the other shoulder, unlaced and set aside the half stays she wore, and untied her shift. Her dress and shift pooled around her waist, and he got what he'd been aiming for: a view of her hair tumbling down her bare back. Her spine curved slightly as it emerged from the dark curtain of hair, suggesting both strength and vulnerability.

He brushed the hair to one side and placed his hands over her shoulders, one on each side at the junction with her neck, and massaged.

She let loose a low moan that sounded almost pained. He froze, his pulse beating its way through his whole body, down his arms, into his prick, down his legs.

"Don't stop," she said, and the next stroke elicited another moan, which, now that he knew it signaled pleasure and not distress, almost did him in right then and there.

He applied himself to the taut muscles, aiming for a pressure that might loosen them but not cause pain. She continued to make the most astonishing, bordering on lewd, noises, and he had never heard anything better.

"I should have done this sooner," he murmured. What a wasted opportunity.

She fell back against his chest, sighing and letting her head loll against him. From here, he had a view of the front of her—her long, elegant neck, her small, pink-tipped breasts that looked like they would fit perfectly into his hands.

Sighing, she angled her head back farther. He deduced that she wanted him to kiss her neck, as she had last night. It was his pleasure to oblige. He lowered his head and put his mouth where his hands had been a moment ago. And, his hands now free, he indulged his wish to see how her breasts fit in them.

They groaned in unison when he made contact. "Perfect." He whispered his verdict across the taut skin of her neck as he kneaded the soft flesh he was holding, circling his thumbs around periodically to tweak nipples made hard by the attention.

He tried to pull his hips back, away from her enough to sever the contact between her bottom and his prick. He wanted this to last. He *needed* this to last. It would have to last him the rest of his life.

He only made it a few inches before she noticed—and objected. Attempting to turn in place, she became tangled in her dress and shift, both of which were still bunched around her waist. He moved to help her emancipate herself, but it didn't quell her frustration. She let loose a vaguely irked noise, batted away his hands, stood, and swiped at her clothing until it fell to the floor.

"Dear God," he mumbled, for there she was, standing before him in all her glory. He had thought, that night they were in the pools together, that he could see beneath the surface of her. And perhaps he could. Perhaps he had. But now he was seeing the literal surface of her, the container for all the wisdom and suffering and joy and pain that made her who she was. He had the feeling that most men preferred the order of events to be reversed: One saw the naked lady and then later—perhaps—one got to know her well enough to see beneath the surface.

She cleared her throat, and he realized that at some point in the last few moments while he'd been waxing poetic over her body and soul and the relationship between them, she had placed her hands on her hips and acquired an expression he could not parse.

"What is the matter?" he asked urgently.

"I have completely disrobed and you remain fully attired, that is what is the matter," she said, and he realized that expression had been wryness.

He laughed, and she did, too, and they started jointly on his clothing, smiling like idiots as they did so. She set to work on his cravat while he shrugged out of his coat and waistcoat. He untucked his shirt from his breeches, and she pulled it over his head. He sat back down and struggled with his boots, and she, playing valet, helped him tug them off.

"Finally," she huffed as they divested him of his breeches and small clothes.

He stood to join her. If he were Effie, he would have been able to make an observation about feeling like he was the first man and she the first woman and this, this very moment, the beginning of the world. But he wasn't, so he told himself not to bother with words and just drank her in, from her mussed dark hair to the tips of her toes, which he was sure were the loveliest toes ever to walk the earth.

He never would have expected Diantha to be missish, and she wasn't, but there was something about the way she pressed her lips together and clasped her hands behind her back that suggested bashfulness. But on the other hand, there was something about the way she was openly staring at his member—which was throbbing and at attention, and there wasn't a thing he could do about it—that suggested the opposite of bashfulness.

"May I touch it?" she asked, and the question made him laugh. Not at her. There was no mockery in it. It was the unlikely, astonishing fact of being here, with Miss Diantha Brown, to begin with. And possibly also the fact that while he was trying and failing to find the proper poetical terms to describe her soul, the first thing out of her mouth was to ask whether she could touch his prick.

"By all means," he said.

And then she did, and that stopped him laughing quick as anything.

"I knew it was meant to be hard, but I didn't think it would be that hard," she said, and he groaned. "Am I hurting you?"

"No. Yes. But please continue doing so."

She stroked him, and he thought better of his invitation. This needed to not be over before it could truly begin, so he put his own hand on hers, and drew her to him. "You are making it that hard."

He kissed her again, deeper this time, shamelessly sweeping his tongue into her mouth and gathering her body against his. He stroked down her back, cupped her arse in his hands. She lifted a leg, trying to wrap it around his body.

"Oh, no, you don't." He picked her up and carried her to one of the beds, sparing a moment to chuckle over how two weeks ago, he had thought this space very like his school sleeping quarters.

He had never done this at school.

He arranged her gently against the headboard and proceeded to kiss her everywhere. He started with her ankles and worked his way up, stopping when a brush of his lips against an inner thigh summoned a breathy moan.

His progress was interrupted when she grabbed his head and pulled on it. Chuckling, he came up so they were eye to eye, and they kissed again. It felt simultaneously like it could go on forever and that it would be over too soon. Pleasure was building at the base of his spine. He willed it to recede.

He thought back to her describing the experience of immersion in the pool. She had likened it to being overwhelmed in a good way. To being heated from within.

He had agreed.

He'd had no idea.

"Simon," she whispered.

He let a hand slide down her torso, stopping briefly to make a lap around a breast. "Yes?"

"I don't know!" She writhed. "Just . . . Simon."

She knocked the breath right out of him. He didn't know what to say, so he endeavored to ease the tension for her, sending his hand to its destination between her legs, seeking out the nub of flesh he found there.

"Oh!"

He stopped. "Is all well?"

"Yes!"

He resumed his ministrations.

"No!"

He stopped.

She laughed. "I am sorry! It's just that while I was familiar with how this was meant to go theoretically, this is . . . not turning out the way I expected."

This was not turning out the way Simon expected, either. It was . . . so much more. He tried not to think about it. "Would you care to register a complaint?"

"No!"

He appreciated that this experience had, at times, retained the kind of lightheartedness that sometimes characterized his interactions with Diantha. But he felt now that the time for lightheartedness was done.

She must have, too, for she looked up at him and just about cracked his heart in two when she said, "Will you come inside me now?"

He made to do as she asked.

"But will you . . . pull out at the right time? Is that how it works?"

He nodded again, and judging by the pang in his chest, his heart *did* break then. He supposed he was thinking of all the children who hadn't been born: her sister's, Frances and James's.

He slid in, and dear God, he had never been this . . . what? Overwhelmed? Joyous? Devastated?

Yes. All of those things.

His breath hitched. To his mortification, he was swallowing a sob. Because he was thinking of *his* children, too, the ones who wouldn't be born, at least not for a long time, because he couldn't marry.

And even if he could, *she* couldn't. Or wouldn't.

She was moving beneath him, sighing, and he was thrusting his hips, the pleasure-pain growing.

He was overtaken by a kind of predetermined grief, a mourning for the life he would not get to have. He thought back to Diantha saying *I want so very many things, but I can't have any of them.*

He began to understand why she characterized herself as rageful. He wasn't angry at her but at . . . the world. The world that gave her so few choices and gave him dismal ones.

"Tell me what Mr. Hill has over you." He thought to return his hand to the source of her pleasure.

She gasped as he pressed against it, but said, "I can't."

"Tell me."

She moaned. He kept going. Of course he kept going. Was he meant to stop, because she wouldn't tell him what he wanted to know? Impossible.

"Oh!" she cried, and then, again, lower, "*Oh.*" And then, to his utter astonishment, she said, "I wrote a letter. Years ago. To my sister. He read it."

And then she shattered around him and underneath him, and if he had tried to stop himself from following her, he would not have succeeded, but he didn't try. Why, when he was powerless against her?

A few minutes later, they were still breathing heavily. They lay side by side, staring at the ceiling.

"What did the letter say?" he pressed.

She remained silent, and as he came back to earth, a kind of shame rolled in. Why had he been so belligerent? Why couldn't he trust her when she said she had the matter in hand?

It wasn't as if he thought her incapable of handling her own affairs. Look at how far she had come in life, even with her father, and Mr. Hill, impeding her.

Perhaps another approach was indicated. Perhaps Diantha had had her fill of men meddling in her life.

He rolled over. Held himself up on his elbows and regarded her.

Oh, he *adored* her.

He flopped back over, unable to hold himself up at the same time he was contemplating the depths of his adoration. It was too much.

To his complete and utter shock, she started talking. It all came out in a single stream, her words nearly tumbling over one another. He stayed as still as possible, fearful if he moved even an inch, she might stop. "Lady Harcourt told me about a time years ago when she went on holiday and met a man she fancied and they had relations and not only did she not feel bad about it, she said the experience buoyed her and provided solace and gave her the strength to endure her unhappy marriage to the late earl, and even though I never said her name in the letter, Mr. Hill knew who I was talking about and said he was coming back in six months' time, which is now five months' time, and that if I didn't agree to marry him upon his return, he would make the contents of the letter public."

That was . . . unlike anything Simon had imagined. But it *was* the missing piece of the puzzle to why she was so intent on ruination, or, as she said, rendering herself ineligible for marriage.

He remained on his back, staring at the ceiling, partly because he still feared that too quick or too decisive a movement might startle her, make her bolt, but partly because he had no earthly idea what to say.

"Say something!" she cried, and the idea of her commanding his speech when he had just decided to withhold it would have made him laugh, had he not been so distressed.

He rolled back over. He wanted to touch her, to stroke her face and assure her that all would be well. But Simon didn't make promises he couldn't keep.

"You ought to talk to Archie."

It was the wrong thing to say; he knew it the moment it was out.

"And tell him what? That I betrayed his family and put their reputations at risk, so therefore he should . . . what?" Her voice was rising as she spoke. "Raise my wages even more than he already has? Call out Mr. Hill? No. I have it in hand."

He wanted to demand she explain *how* she had it in hand, but he knew it would be futile. He settled for saying what was in his heart. Well, part of what was in his heart. "Why won't you let me help you?"

It was still the wrong thing to say. She gazed at him for a long moment, and he heard what she wasn't saying, that she *had* asked him for help. She had come to him first.

Oh, his heart.

"I should go."

"Not yet!"

If she left, they would never get back here, to this place where they were naked together, bodily and metaphorically.

"It is later than it has ever been," she said.

She was covering herself up—in both senses. She was redressing and running her fingers through her hair. And though it was happening invisibly, he didn't need eyes to see that she was shuttering something inside her, too.

Was this how it was going to end, with such utter lack of fanfare?

"Diantha," he called as she made to leave, and she must have taken pity on him—his voice had sounded eminently pitiable—for she paused by the door.

He didn't know what to say to make her stay.

Nothing. The answer was nothing. He couldn't make her do anything—and even if he could, he wouldn't. He swallowed the lump rising in his throat and said, "It is late enough—early enough—that you ought to be able to see Orion. Look for his belt. Look to the east to see the Pleiades, the seven sisters he hunts."

"The ladies of the night sky have calamitous luck, don't they?" she asked bitterly. "Pursued by hunters, chained to rocks, beheaded."

And before he could think what to say, she was gone.

17

Retirement Planning

September 21, 1823
Earls Trip, day 14

They left in reverse order the next morning, settling the ladies into Archie's coach after breakfast—after a breakfast everyone ate together, so Simon could not get Diantha alone. Not that he knew what he'd have said if he had. He had stayed up most of the night trying to think how he might help without betraying her confidence, or, barring that, trying to puzzle out what her supposed solution could be. Perhaps whatever her plan was, it would work. She was intelligent. If he knew it would work, he could rest his mind.

As it was, his mind was exceedingly *un*rested when the three gentlemen said their goodbyes to the staff—he was going to miss Christine and told her so sincerely—and rode off.

So much for the restorative effects of a holiday. So much for respite and fellowship and a balm to the soul and all that rot.

At least he didn't have to talk.

He had hoped the ride would soothe him with its repetition, or, barring that, exhaust him.

It was not to be. They hadn't been underway more than an hour before Archie, who was leading the way, suddenly pulled up his reins. "May we take a detour here? Stop for refreshment?" He nodded at a directional sign that read *Greychurch*.

Such a request, given that they'd decided to break the back of the ride before stopping for a midday repast, was odd, and Simon wanted to get home, but before he could voice an objection, Effie was agreeing and Archie was turning off the main road.

They rode into town, and Archie stopped in front of a church where a woman was watering some autumn flowers. He slid off his horse, tipped his hat, and said, "Good afternoon. I understand there is a brook in or near your lovely village?"

"No, sir."

"Ah, well, I must have been mistaken."

"Perhaps you mean the river? Little Boar River?"

"Oh, perhaps I do. Is it . . . quite little?"

The woman looked at him like he was daft. "It is indeed, sir, especially when it turns south of town."

"Would you be so kind as to point us toward it?"

"Turn back the way you came, make a left at the first road, and that will take you directly to its banks."

"What on earth was that about, Archie?" Effie said.

"Just following a hunch."

Effie shot Simon a bemused look and shrugged as they turned around.

The river was unremarkable, as rivers went. It was indeed small. It had muddy banks and a few scraggly willows were growing at odd angles at its edge.

Archie pulled out a compass, and after a moment, said, "Let us follow the river a way."

"Are you going to tell us what this is about?" Simon asked, for clearly they were not stopping for refreshments.

"Not yet," Archie said cheerily.

"Well, I do love a mystery," Effie said, and they set off at a trot parallel to the water. There wasn't much to see, the vegetation being rather pathetic.

As the river veered, Archie pointed at a large oak that looked to be in better shape than the trees they'd seen so far. "Look. Someone has mounted rather a lot of bird feeders on this tree."

"What are we doing?" Simon asked. Oh, how he wished for home.

"We're almost there." Archie nudged his horse into a canter.

"Almost where?" Simon called after him even as he and Effie moved to follow.

They found Archie around another bend in the river, dismounting in front of a cottage. He gazed at it, which caused Simon to follow suit. The small house was a bit shabby, its thatched roof in particular having seen better days, and the willows that flanked the garden were overgrown. It was nevertheless quite charming, its stone exterior covered with climbing vines and its window boxes filled with lavender.

It had a great deal of potential.

"This must be Miss Brown's cottage," Archie said.

Simon was almost startled off his mount.

"What do you mean?" Effie, actually getting off his, asked.

Simon collected himself and dismounted as if he were a regular sort of person, not the sort of person who had nearly fallen from his horse due to startlement.

"Miss Brown went on holiday two summers ago," Archie said. "She told me recently that she came here."

Oh. This was the "other town" Diantha had visited after Barbury. Simon looked around with renewed interest.

"Apparently her mother had a friend who lived in Greychurch and used to sing its praises," Archie said. "Miss Brown wondered if this was a place she could see herself retiring. She told me about a cottage that struck her fancy. This must be it. She described its location as being on a brook a mile south of town and mentioned majestic willows standing in juxtaposition to a small, cozy cottage. She must not have known the brook was in fact a river."

"I can see where she erred there," Effie said. "It is rather unimpressive as rivers go. If I had to name this cottage, it certainly wouldn't be River's Embrace."

Simon examined the cottage with more care. There was a quality of quiet elegance about it. It was indeed small and cozy, but at the same time, it wasn't cute or coy.

"Miss Brown grew up in Barbury, which isn't far." Archie went on. "So it is not surprising that Greychurch, the hometown of a friend of her mother's, should be nearby. I hadn't given it any thought, but when we passed the sign, I felt compelled to investigate."

"I can see Miss Brown here," Effie said.

"Can't you, though?" Archie said, and Simon was unaccountably affronted. Not that he disagreed with them. He could easily—alarmingly easily—see Diantha here. She would read by the river. She would tend to the lavender. There was space for her vegetable patch. Someone had already hung bird feeders.

Was this her plan? Her means of escape from Mr. Hill's treachery?

It couldn't be. She had described to him her ideal retirement. She hadn't done so in terms as specific as Archie had apparently pulled from her, but this place certainly matched the daydream she had sketched of a small cottage with room for a vegetable garden, walkable to a village. But she had quite clearly told him that future was going to take her years of saving to attain.

"Oh." Effie pointed as a hen strolled toward them. "Does Miss Brown have an interest in animal husbandry?"

Simon didn't know her to be inclined toward animals, but Diantha took care of that which was in her charge.

"Not that I know of," Archie said, "but can't you picture her collecting eggs in the morning for her breakfast?"

"Indeed, I can," Effie said.

Simon was . . . put out. The sense of affront from earlier had grown. It wasn't that he couldn't imagine Diantha collecting eggs for her breakfast here; he certainly could. He just would have thought this insight would be rarer. That he knew her more intimately than the boys did, and that therefore this vision—this ability to picture her here contentedly living out her days—would be uniquely his.

"Simon, are you quite all right?"

The question had come from Effie, who was suddenly at Simon's side.

"Yes," he said, because he was. He was getting carried away. The boys had just spent a sennight with Diantha. Archie lived in the same house with her. Of course they knew her.

But they didn't know everything.

"Would you mind terribly if we turned back to the village?" he asked. "I saw a shop there I'd like to visit."

If the boys thought the request odd, they said nothing, and soon Simon was pushing open the door to Miss Dewey's Dresses, the boys on his heels. He had tried to persuade them to wait outside, but they weren't having it.

Why was he here? It was hard to say. It wasn't as if he had plans to see Diantha again anytime soon.

But they would all be in London for at least a little while—Archie's coach was taking the ladies there. So Simon could call. As he always did. As if everything was the same as it always was.

He almost laughed out loud. Everything was so absurd.

Everything was so fraught.

A bell on the door summoned a shopkeeper, a plump, flaxen-haired woman in a very pretty dress that suggested she was the titular Miss Dewey. If she was surprised to see three unfamiliar gentlemen in her modest shop, she didn't show it, merely offered a welcoming smile. "May I help you, sirs?"

"I would like to buy some ribbon," Simon said, relieved when the boys said nothing. "I see you have a sign in your window advertising such."

"Of course, sir. What kind of ribbon?"

Hmm. "What . . . kinds do you have?"

"Oh, all kinds. Velvet, satin, grosgrain, silk."

They should not have come. Here he had thought a ribbon was a ribbon, but of course it made sense they came in different fabrics, as clothing did. Plucking a scrap of ribbon off the ground was entirely different from making a purchase.

"Perhaps you can tell me what you intend to do with the ribbon you want to buy?" Miss Dewey asked.

He couldn't tell her that.

When he didn't answer, she compounded his regret over having come by asking, "Is it to become a watch fob? A mourning band?" Miss Dewey narrowed her eyes, searching Simon's face. "Or perhaps it is a gift for a lady? Will it become trim for a hat? A sash for a dress?"

She was getting warmer, but he could hardly say, *It is indeed a gift for a lady, but it is for her to put into a drawer.*

"Why don't I show you some of my favorites?" Miss Dewey suggested when he still didn't speak.

He nodded his agreement, again thankful for the boys' silence, though wary of it, too.

"Here are a few." Miss Dewey reappeared from the back room with an armful of spools she set on the counter. "I've more in back if you'll allow me—"

"That one." Simon pointed.

"You don't want to see any more?"

"No. That one is . . ." *Perfect.* "Sufficient."

"One-inch, satin," Miss Dewey observed. "Lemon yellow."

"Yes," Simon said. The color was exactly why he'd chosen it: a clear, cheery yellow the exact color of lemons.

"An excellent choice, sir." Miss Dewey produced a pair of shears. "How much would you like?"

He had no idea. Was he not meant to purchase the whole spool?

"How about two yards?" Miss Dewey suggested. Ah. Of course, he was meant to buy a certain length.

Miss Dewey, who seemed to have grasped that the only way this transaction was going to conclude was for her to steer it through to the end, said, "Two yards should be more than enough for a sash, say."

More than enough for a sash, and way too much for a lady to add to a collection she kept in a drawer, but it was easier to simply agree.

Soon, they were remounting their horses, Simon in possession of two yards of lemon-yellow ribbon that the boys were still not saying anything about. Their silence made him nervous.

He had to get over himself. Act like he normally did.

How, though? What the hell was he going to do when he got back to Town? When he next saw Diantha?

As the miles slipped by, a question began to take shape. What if he *didn't* go back to Town?

He had no earthly idea what to do about Diantha, but there was another problem he *did* know how to tackle. He didn't *want* to, but he knew how. And he'd been ignoring it long enough.

18

Best-Laid Plans

There was a letter from Mr. Baldwin waiting for Diantha when she and both Countesses of Harcourt arrived back at the London house. It was a shock, yet not a shock. She had been waiting for it, after all. He had said, after they discussed the terms of her ruination, that he would be in touch with details.

She held off on opening it while their return operation unfolded. Their trunks were unloaded. Mrs. Saunders had tea and an easel and paints waiting in the garden. Diantha and the dowager refreshed themselves while the younger Lady Harcourt, who had been looking quite green on the jostling journey, went to rest. After their tea, Lady Harcourt decided to attempt to paint the pool at Gurglewood from memory, and Diantha opened her book.

She had the letter tucked into the book. It would have been a logical moment to open it. No one was paying her any mind.

She did not open it.

Instead, she remarked on the quality of the stone Lady Harcourt was painting, and that set the two of them off on a discussion of what time of day it ought to be in the painting, and how the light should subsequently look shining on the stone at the edge of the pool.

When it was time for the evening meal, which the younger Lady

Harcourt joined them for, they shared memories of the cold water and wondered aloud when Lord Harcourt would arrive.

Diantha wondered silently if Simon was returning to his London house. She assumed so, but she hadn't asked him.

Would he call, as he sometimes did?

How was she to be in his company now, after all that had unfolded between them? And she didn't just mean their lying together. How could she sit in the garden with him and other members of the household and pretend that everything was the same as it had always been?

But was the alternative preferable? That he *didn't* call?

What would happen when they traveled to Mollybrook, which she assumed would happen in the coming days—each year, after Parliament closed and Earls Trip ended, they decamped to the family's country estate for the autumn and stayed through the holidays.

Lord Harcourt didn't generally see his friends over that stretch.

And then . . . at some point . . . she would be gone.

A kind of dread took hold in her gut.

"Miss Brown, are you all right?" the younger Lady Harcourt asked. "You'll forgive me for saying, but you look distressed. Is the food not to your liking?"

"Oh, no, no. I am quite all right." She picked up her fork. "Just woolgathering."

After some evening reading—Diantha had taken over for Simon in reading aloud from *Frankenstein*—the dowager pronounced herself ready for bed.

Diantha got her settled.

This was the time to read the letter.

She did not read the letter.

She took her gut full of dread and went to bed.

Lord Harcourt was in the breakfast room the next morning, having arrived very late the previous night.

"How was your ride, my lord?" she asked.

"Fine, thank you. It is good to be home."

"Did the other gentlemen enjoy the ride?"

Goodness, what was she doing*? Did the other gentlemen enjoy the ride?*!

"We had a fine journey, though poor Simon is off again this morning. He's riding on to Galecroft."

"Oh!" She hadn't expected that, having all but talked herself into the notion that he would be returning to his London house.

So he wouldn't be calling. He would be far away.

Which was fine. But it also meant she wouldn't know *why* he wasn't calling. Would he be absent simply because he was at Galecroft, or was he at Galecroft because he was avoiding her?

"He had some business to attend to with his mother," Lord Harcourt said.

Of course. He had intimated as much. And he had told her his mother spent most of her time at their country estate—the place where she had the shrine to his brothers.

It made sense. Diantha just . . . hadn't been ready for him to be so far away.

Even if he hadn't been going to call regardless. It was better knowing he was nearby.

"I wonder if he will stay on with his mother or return to Town," she mused.

Lord Harcourt set down his teacup and eyed her.

She was doing it again, trying to fish for information about Simon. She was acting like a lovestruck girl.

She was—

Oh. Oh no.

She wasn't *acting* like a lovestruck girl. She *was* one.

She was in love with Simon.

She started coughing. It was as if her body was rejecting the very notion.

If only it could.

"Miss Brown, are you all right?"

She got hold of herself. “Yes, thank you. A sip of tea gone wrong.”

Though Lord Harcourt had been watching her closely enough before the coughing fit that he had to have noticed she hadn’t drunk any tea. “But if you will excuse me for a moment?”

“Of course.”

She fled to her room.

Whereupon the dread that had taken up residence yesternight began blooming, a dark flower watered by the realization that she was in love with Simon Courteney, the Earl of Marsden.

Dread was becoming panic.

She sat on her bed with a thud and told herself to breathe. To pretend she was in the icy water at Gurglewood and to bear up under the onslaught of sensations.

She relaxed her shoulders and blew out a long, slow breath, as she would have done were she immersed.

After a few moments, she was composed enough to rise, walk to her nightstand, and extract the letter from Mr. Baldwin.

Inside she found a mere handful of sentences.

3 December. My mother will host a ball. She will call in the coming weeks and invite Lady Harcourt personally. Please send the bank draft to the below address.

December was too soon.

She would write back and tell him as much. Mr. Hill had said six months, and only six weeks of those six months had elapsed. She didn’t want to leave the dowager, or the countess, or the earl, any sooner than she had to. Or Olive Morgan, who called every few days.

Oh, who was she fooling? That was all true, but the person she most didn’t want to leave was Simon.

She took another deep breath, hoping to stop her thoughts from racing any further out of her command.

She had told Simon she had a plan. And she did. If it was happening sooner than she would have preferred, what of it? She was lucky it was happening at all. She would send the bank draft and make sure that when the invitation was issued, it was accepted by Lady Harcourt. In fact, the timing was *good*: A successful week-long holiday had just been had. Next to that, a few hours at a local party was nothing, or so she would point out. At said party, Mr. Baldwin would perform the "ruination" as planned, and fail to come up to scratch, also as planned.

What Diantha *didn't* have a plan for was what came next. She told herself, as she had so many times in recent weeks, that even after paying Mr. Baldwin, she wasn't going to be out on the street. She had enough money to keep herself sheltered and fed while she determined her next move. She took Simon's point that no one was going to hire a fallen woman as a governess, but perhaps if she left London, she could find a school, or an orphanage, or . . .

Her thoughts were gathering speed again, threatening to get away from her. She performed some more breathing.

December was too soon.

No. December was fine. Everything was unfolding exactly as she had planned. Her manipulations had been successful.

19

The Too Many Countesses Problem

September 28, 1823
Seven days since Earls Trip

A week later, Simon sent a note to Archie and Effie asking them to come to his house that evening.

"It looks smashing in here, Simon," said Effie, who had not seen his refurbished library. "Much less stuffy."

"Brandy?" Archie asked, who was pouring himself a glass.

"No," said Simon, whose stomach was in an uproar. Honestly, his stomach had been in an uproar since the night Diantha made her unexpected appearance in this very library. Sometimes a minor uproar, sometimes major, but the unsettlement had become a familiar state.

"Though I *was* fond of that purple paper," Effie said from a corner where he was examining the wall. "But this is much more you. Very subtle, very refined."

"I have something to tell you," Simon said, and he'd used his Parliament voice, though he hadn't meant to. The Parliament voice was deeper, and more commanding, than the way he usually spoke.

Effie, who was stroking the new wallpaper, looked over his shoulder with startlement.

Archie, across from Simon, raised his eyebrows.

"Well," said Effie, coming over and joining them by the fire and nodding at the brandy decanter on a side table. "You'd better pour me one of those."

Once Effie was settled with his drink, Simon opened his mouth to speak.

What came out was: "I met my mother last week at Galecroft."

That wasn't what he'd called them here to tell them. Well, he would of course have told them about it eventually, but it wasn't why he'd summoned them.

"Oh, right," Effie said. "How did you fare?"

"She is moving here." He paused, thinking back on his "conversation" with her. "After the holidays. She is not pleased."

"Well, good for you," Archie said.

"I decided to take your advice and rent a place in Town. If left to my own devices, I'd rather be at Galecroft when Parliamentary duties don't require my presence here. It's ridiculous that I've been letting my mother keep me away. So we shall essentially swap places, but I'll also rent another place here."

"And will you tear down that overwrought shrine to your brothers at Galecroft?" Archie asked.

"I don't think I will. Perhaps I will do some planting around it to soften it. I regret that I didn't know them better, that we didn't have more time as adults to . . . be brothers. But I plan to invite Frances to occupy the dower house, and with Mother absent, I think she may accept. For her sake, and mine, I think it will be nice to honor my brothers." He quirked a smile. "And, really, the more ridiculous shrine is the entryway here."

"*That's* true," Effie said. "Though I do somewhat admire it for just *how* ridiculous it is."

"Well," Simon said, "my mother can do whatever she likes with the place now."

"Simon," Effie said, "was it awful? I didn't have to talk to my father. Just when I would have had to, he died. It was quite a bit more convenient than your situation."

"It wasn't as bad as I thought it would be. It wasn't pleasant, of course. I did what you two are always telling me and used my Parliament voice. I told her it wasn't a discussion or a negotiation, then I left. It took all of five minutes."

"Well, cheers to you." Archie lifted a glass, and they toasted.

He could have left it there. It was big enough news. But the truth was, he was imagining life at Galecroft with Frances in the dower house and . . . well, he was imagining having his own version of the "too many countesses" problem.

He wanted it so badly he thought he might expire before he could attempt to attain it.

That was why they were here, he reminded himself. So he could attempt to attain too many Countesses of Marsden.

He blew out a breath. "There is more."

"What's the matter?" Archie set down his drink.

Effie did the same. "Whatever it is, we can help."

Simon had alarmed them. He had indeed sounded rather pained. He would have laughed at himself, but he could summon no laughter on account of . . . all the pain.

The thing to do was to approach his confession the same way he had approached the pool at Gurglewood—just make the plunge.

"I am in love!"

There was a beat of silence in which Simon was sure he would indeed finally expire, but then Effie exclaimed, "Simon! That's wonderful!"

"Yes, huzzah!" Archie said.

"You must be so happy," Effie gushed. "You must tell us everything."

"Happy? I am miserable."

Archie laughed.

"Don't laugh at him," Effie scolded.

"I am in earnest," Simon said. "Being in love feels . . . like having eaten rotten meat."

"Oh, Simon," Effie said, "please tell me you have not said those words to her. Please tell me you have not said them to another living soul whatsoever."

"I have not, but you're being rather dramatic."

"'Loving you feels like eating rotten meat'?" Archie said. "Do you hear yourself?"

"I do hear myself, and I am only telling the truth. I've spent weeks now feeling unwell, as if a marauder has taken up residence in my belly. It's very like the feeling one has after one has eaten spoiled food and is about to—"

"I understand," Archie said. "You need say no more."

"Have you considered," Effie said, "that there is a way to convey your meaning more poetically? To soften the blow, so to speak? For example, instead of 'rotten meat,' may I suggest 'feculent flesh'? Or 'contaminated comestible'? Or—"

Simon silenced Effie with a look.

"Who is it?" Archie asked.

Simon had searched his soul before summoning the boys. He had vowed not to betray any of Diantha's confidences, and he had asked himself if this was one. He had decided it was not. This was about his love for her, his wild, gut-churning love for her. In a sense, it didn't even concern her.

He took a deep breath, and said, "It is Miss Brown."

"My Miss Brown?" Archie said.

"For God's sake, will you *stop* calling her that!"

He had struck them dumb, which would have been amusing if it weren't for the ever-present gut-churning.

Effie recovered first. "Several aspects of our trip are suddenly making a great deal more sense."

"Such as?" Simon asked.

"That yellow ribbon you purchased," Effie said.

"Don't forget the dark green one he found on the road," Archie said.

"Yes!" Effie laughed. "'Loving you is like eating rotten meat, and as a token of my affection, please accept this dirty scrap I plucked out of the mud.' Oh, and Archie, wasn't he so concerned that Miss Brown ought to be able to join us in the evenings?"

"Yes, but he was right to be concerned about that. As he was right to urge me to raise Miss Brown's wages."

"You knew!" Effie exclaimed.

"I wouldn't say that I *knew*. But I did observe that in addition to his concern over Miss Brown's employment situation, he suddenly seemed to know a great deal about her personal history. There were other tells, too."

"The novels!" Effie shouted. "The lady novelist fixation! And—"

"Are you going to help me, or are you going to mock me?" Simon interjected. Honestly.

"Well, I should think both," Effie said, raising his eyebrows at Archie.

"Definitely both," Archie said, but he schooled his expression and added, "Miss Brown is a fine lady, Simon."

"She is," Effie agreed. He swung around to look at Simon. "How may we assist?"

"You may tell me what to do!" Simon said, aware that he had delivered that plea in the opposite of his Parliament voice. He sounded utterly pathetic.

"Well," Archie said, resting his chin on his fist in a thoughtful posture that made Simon think they might actually be getting somewhere, "perhaps you could start by telling her how you feel."

Simon scoffed. "I can't do *that*. Are you daft?"

"He's not daft," Effie said. "He's right." He paused. "Definitely leave off the bit about rotten meat, though."

"Let us be serious for a moment," Archie said. "Why can't you tell her? What is your aim?" He looked, suddenly, displeased. "Are your intentions honorable?"

Effie, not leaving space for Simon to speak, said, "This is why you had it out with your mother." He turned to Archie. "You remember he said he could not take a wife while his mother was around?" He looked back to Simon. "I admit I took that to mean you couldn't take a wife until your mother was dead, but perhaps that was only my own tendency toward the Gothic talking."

"I did mean that." Simon turned to Archie, and added, quietly, "And, yes, my intentions are honorable. I want her to marry me. *I* want to marry *her*."

That was the first time he had said those words aloud, and he was irrationally afraid that now that they were out in the world, he wouldn't be satisfied with anything less.

"Well, then, what's the problem?" Archie asked. "If you're concerned about my mother, you needn't be. We shall work something out. Miss Brown has been a godsend, but we can't hold her hostage forever."

"The problem is, *she* doesn't want to marry—me, or anyone." Simon thought back to one of their first conversations, when he'd suggested marriage to someone suitable as a way out of Mr. Hill's trap. He had not been thinking, then, of putting himself forward as a candidate, a fact he found remarkable from this vantage point. "She is adamantly opposed, in fact. She observed her sister's disastrous marriage up close, and she has quite a lot to say about how men are always 'keeping' women—fathers, husbands, and so on."

Archie and Effie exchanged amused looks.

"What?"

"I seem to recall we have heard something similar once or twice recently," Effie said.

"Yes, yes," Simon said, knowing that Effie was referring to the reluctance both his and Archie's now-wives initially had to the idea of marriage. "It's not the same."

"How is it not the same?" Archie asked.

Well, for one thing, neither of your wives were being blackmailed when you met them.

Still, Simon had decided there were no circumstances under which he would expose Diantha's secret. And it wasn't relevant, not really. He was here because he needed the boys to help him figure out how to get Diantha to marry him. That it would solve her blackmail problem was a convenient benefit, but it wasn't his chief motivation.

His chief motivation was love. The assurance of his future happiness.

He continued to feel terribly ill.

Perhaps his chief motivation ought to be to get his stomach to settle.

"I wonder if I ought to raise Miss Brown's wages again," Archie said. "How much do you think a lady would require to retire to a charming cottage in an overly literally named town?"

"I beg your pardon?" What was he talking about?

"I can't imagine how *you* are complaining about overly literal names," Effie said, sniffing, but he threw out a number.

Archie countered it, and soon the two of them were engaged in a discussion over the cost of Diantha's dream cottage.

"Given that it isn't for sale at the moment, you will no doubt have to offer more than it might otherwise be worth," Effie said.

"This isn't helping," Simon said.

"Oh, but it is," Archie said.

"You're getting off topic," Simon said.

"Are we?" Effie asked.

"Yes! You're supposed to be helping me think of ways to convince Miss Brown, who is opposed to the institution of marriage, to marry me anyway."

"That is precisely what we're doing," Archie said. "If she has her cottage, then and only then will she be truly free to marry you, should she choose to."

"I beg your pardon?"

"Once again, I remind you that I have some experience with women who profess not to want to marry. Effie does, too."

"Oh yes, indeed," Effie said.

"The trick, with this sort of woman, is to make it so she doesn't *have* to marry," Archie said.

Oh. *Oh.*

"Think of it as the opposite of blackmail," Archie said.

Blackmail. The very thing Diantha was trying to escape. They had a point. Was marriage to Simon any better if Diantha was only choosing it as the least bad of various fates?

"Would you call that whitemail?" Effie wondered.

"But what if, under these hypothetical circumstances in which she is entirely free to choose her own fate, she doesn't want to marry me?" Simon asked. "What if she doesn't . . . choose me?"

"Then she doesn't choose you," Effie said gently. "Then you shall be heartbroken. We'll help."

"What he's saying," Archie said, "is do you want to marry Miss Brown if *she* doesn't want to marry *you*? Do you want to marry *anyone* who doesn't want to marry you?"

"No, of course not."

Archie turned up his palms. "Well, then."

Simon was getting it now. "You are saying I pay for Miss Brown to retire, and only then will she be free to choose me."

"No, I'm saying *I* pay for Miss Brown to retire, and only then will she be free to choose you."

"Yes, you can't do it, Simon," Effie said. "Have you been listening to anything we've been saying? If you do it, it's not a free choice, is it?"

Simon was at once touched and bewildered.

Touched: "You would do that for me?"

"Yes, of course," Archie said.

Bewildered: "What's the difference if I give her a lot of money or you give her a lot of money? Won't you just be a proxy for me?"

"No. I have come to understand, recently, how much I have taken Miss Brown for granted. I have endeavored to begin making up for that. This will provide the opportunity to complete that mission."

"Thank you" was all Simon could manage. So he said it again: "Thank you."

"It is nothing," Archie said, but it wasn't nothing. It was the reason Simon had called the boys here. He had known, in some hidden part of himself, that they would help.

He also needed them to help with something else, namely the

problem of the blackmailing brother-in-law. Diantha seemed to believe all that was necessary to put him off his scheme of ruining Lady Harcourt's reputation was to ruin her own, thereby rendering herself unmarriageable. He feared she gave him too much credit. What's to say the man wouldn't reveal the contents of her letter purely out of spite? But one thing at a time. She'd said he was coming back in five months. And Simon had promised Diantha he would keep her secret. If his plan to win Diantha's heart—and hand—worked, they would tackle the wretched man together.

"I am pouring you a drink now, sour stomach or no," Effie said. He handed Simon a glass and lifted his own. "She will be free to choose you, now, Simon, and I for one cannot fathom why she wouldn't."

20

The Glow-Up

September 29
Eight days since Earls Trip

The next morning, Simon summoned Mrs. Tavish and told her he wanted to have a party.

Or, at least, he thought he told her. The way she stood regarding him as if he were a statue in a museum made him question whether something had gone awry, communication wise.

"A party, my lord?" she finally said.

"Yes. I shall furnish you with a list of attendees."

"And you would . . . like me to write out invitations."

"That is how it is generally done, is it not?"

"The countess may prefer to write them herself."

Right. "The countess won't be attending." He nodded at a chair. "Mrs. Tavish, will you sit for a moment? I need to inform you of some impending changes to the structure of the household." He considered how best to explain. As far as he had observed, Mother wasn't close with any of the servants, but one never knew where the staff's loyalties lay. He decided that short and to the point was best. "The countess will be moving here, to this house, permanently."

Was he mistaken, or did Mrs. Tavish furrow her brow ever so slightly?

He forged onward. "I will be renting a house in Town for myself and will split my time between it and Galecroft."

"And the countess will . . . not be splitting her time between the two properties as she has historically done?"

"No. She will be here full-time." He paused. "And I will not be here." He hoped he had made his point. Though, why was he dissembling? Why not make himself crystal clear? "I have decided that my mother and I should not spend any more time together."

"And when is this . . . shuffle meant to occur?"

"After the holidays."

She nodded. That brow furrow from before must not have signaled confusion, for it was deepening.

"I will spend the holidays here, and Mother will remain at Galecroft," he added, for they usually spent Christmas together at Galecroft, though from this vantage point, he couldn't think why he'd subjected himself to that for so many years. "So there will be time for everyone to grow accustomed to the idea."

He studied the housekeeper, whom he suddenly realized he didn't know very much about. She had always been the London housekeeper. He associated her with his childhood. With the lonely years. He had been close to the cook at Galecroft, who had long since retired, but other than her, he didn't have a particularly close relationship with any of his staff.

He decided to take a risk. After all, he was, apparently, a risk-taker now. "Mrs. Tavish, I will be in need of a housekeeper at my new home. In fact, I will need someone to advise me on the procurement of the right type of home. I have been assuming you would prefer to stay on here with my mother, but if that isn't the case, you are welcome to come with me."

"Oh, I should like that very much, thank you, sir." The furrow disappeared.

Extraordinary.

"Excellent. We shall discuss details later. But first, the party."

She smiled, and he realized he had never seen her smile. "What kind of party to you want to have?"

He *didn't* want to have a party, but it could not be avoided. "What . . . are my choices?"

"A card party, perhaps? I imagine you are wanting to keep it intimate?"

"What do you do at a card party?"

Simon could not blame her for looking at him like he was daft. "Play cards," he said. "Yes, I know. But how would that go? Sketch the scene for me."

"We would set up tables. Have a refreshment room."

"Not *that* intimate," he said, reasoning that a card party wasn't the right context for his plan.

"Well, we could polish up the ballroom."

"Oh, goodness, no, not a ball. Something more intimate than a ball but less intimate than a card party."

"A musicale?"

He considered it. "Does everyone watch the players, or do people . . . roam around?"

"A bit of both, I should think. People can mingle before the music, and we can serve refreshments after."

"Perfect."

"Shall I arrange the musicians or would you like to? Do you have a preference as to style?"

"I shall arrange." He would ask Olive.

"Very good. I will handle the rest. You merely need tell me when you would like this to occur."

"As soon as possible." No, wait. He considered the other matter he had on his mind. "Let's say a fortnight."

That ought to be enough time, no?

Well, no time like the present to find out. He made for the stairs but stopped a few steps from the bottom and gazed at the ceiling. "Mrs. Tavish, do you think we ought to try to cover this monstrosity for the party?"

"I could have it repainted."

He considered it. "Better not. We'll leave it for Mother." He laughed. There was something darkly poetic about the party—and the outcome he hoped it would yield—unfolding beneath his angelic, rifle-wielding brothers.

Simon found his long-suffering valet pressing a pair of breeches.

"Janes, I am having a party in two weeks' time, and I should like some new attire."

"Very good, sir," Janes said.

On the surface of things, Janes appeared calm. But his nostrils were flaring ever so slightly, and Simon understood that to mean that he was not, in fact, calm.

"I am sorry I've been such a disappointment, Janes."

"My pardon, sir, you haven't been anything of the sort."

"I have, and you know it. My brother was fond of clothes. One might even have called him a dandy."

"Oh, good gracious, no." Janes cleared his throat. "I beg your pardon. I meant to say, I wouldn't go so far as to characterize the late earl thusly. I made sure he stayed on the right side of the line between well-turned-out and dandy."

Ah, pride of profession. Simon respected it. "You can no doubt appreciate that I am more conservative than my brothers were. Not politically, but . . . constitutionally, and therefore sartorially."

"Yes."

"I should like to . . . look better but . . . remain within my sphere." He paused. "I am not making sense."

"You are making perfect sense. I consider it a welcome challenge."

"It's not that I don't appreciate that attire may be a mode of artistic expression," Simon said. "You are familiar with my friend Edward Astley, the Earl of Stonely."

"Indeed."

Simon wasn't sure if that *indeed* had contained within it a hint of scandal or a hint of admiration. It had contained a hint of something. He pressed onward.

"I have always taken his attire as an expression of his artistic temperament. But if that's the case, what does my attire express about me?"

The valet remained silent. They both knew the answer.

"That I am a church mouse."

"I wouldn't say that, sir."

"You don't have to; I did. Mind you, I don't want to look like Stonely."

"No, of course not. We shall find a happy medium. A query, if I may: Is it merely the party with which you are concerned? Or would you permit a broader remaking of your lordship's wardrobe and countenance?"

"Countenance? I thought we were talking about attire."

"Yes, yes," Janes soothed. "Of course we are."

"Well, in answer to your question, while it was the party that prompted this line of thinking, I suppose the logic of it ought to extend to the rest of life, too."

"Very good. May I make one further inquiry?"

"Certainly."

"What has prompted this sudden interest in your outward aspect?"

"I . . ." He didn't know how to answer.

"Allow me to ask the question another way. Were you perchance hoping to catch the eye of a young lady?" He coughed. "Or anyone else?"

"No, no." Simon felt himself redden. "Well, perhaps." He didn't know how to explain himself. It wasn't as if he thought a new coat and a well-tied cravat were truly going to influence things, but . . . He put on his Parliament voice. "There is a lady, yes, and I should like to put my best foot forward."

"I understand," Janes said with an attempt at solemnity, but the occasion proved too joyful for even his legendary stoicism.

One corner of his mouth quirked up and he said, "We shall have you all shined up in no time, sir."

* * *

What followed was a fortnight in which Simon found himself at the center of a flurry of fittings and fabric, poking and prodding. He had seen a play once, years ago, in which the main character was a girl being raised by poor but goodhearted laborers. Through some twist of fate he'd forgotten, it was discovered she was secretly the sister of a duke. A clever bit of stagecraft showed the process of transforming her from peasant to peeress. She stood on a contraption of some sort that rotated slowly while an army of servants fussed and flapped and exclaimed even as the orchestra spun up a frenzied crescendo.

Simon felt, these recent days, as if he were that unfortunate girl. He hadn't realized that the process of, to use Janes's phrase, getting him all shined up, was going to be so arduous. It was an odd mixture of excruciatingly awkward and deadly boring.

But then, suddenly, it was done. The orchestra faded out, the world stopped spinning around him, and Janes stepped back, beaming, and said, "Voilà."

But then he stepped forward again. "Allow me to make one final adjustment." He took Simon's spectacles off—he had been summoned from his library, where he'd been reading, and he hadn't thought to take them off himself. "You have very striking brown eyes, if you don't mind my saying, sir."

"I don't, and I thank you."

It was the night of the party, and Simon was standing in his chambers on a small platform in front of a series of mirrors Janes had installed. He had tried on many iterations of new costumes, Janes having had more than one tailor coming and going from the house in recent weeks. But this was the first time Simon was wearing all his new clothing at once. He had had shining new Hessians, too. And he'd submitted to a haircut and a shave—that must have been what Janes had meant when he'd suggested making over Simon's countenance in addition to his wardrobe.

A rap on the door heralded the arrival of a footman. "A letter from your mother, my lord."

"I'll take that, thank you," Janes said, smoothly, plucking the letter from the silver tray on which it rested. He raised his eyebrows at Simon as he tucked the letter into his pocket. He was seeking permission to destroy it.

Simon granted it with a small nod.

His mother had begun writing, making a case that they ought to set aside their differences. Since he'd been spending so much time with Janes, what with the flurry of fittings, Janes had noticed Simon's distress as he'd read the first of her letters.

"The interesting thing about correspondence," he'd remarked to Simon, "is that it is a two-way activity. One person posts a letter. But for the act of correspondence to be complete, the recipient must elect to read it."

Astonished, both at the content of Janes's speech and the equanimity with which it was delivered, Simon had asked him to get rid of the letter, and now the valet did so as a matter of course. Simon didn't even open them, an act—or, more properly, an abstention—he found entirely liberating.

"In fact," Janes called after the retreating footman, "in the future, will you please deliver letters to his lordship from her ladyship to me, and I shall see them properly routed."

The footman, after looking at Simon for confirmation and receiving it, retreated, and Janes went to the fire, threw the letter into the flames, and said, "Now that that's been properly routed, let us return to the matter at hand."

The matter at hand being Simon's attire. In truth, Simon was a little overcome. A fortnight ago, as they embarked on their mission, he would have said that he and Janes did not entirely trust each other. Now, the man was an ally. In fact, Simon suspected—hoped—he was on his way to becoming a true friend. But Janes would not want to hear such a sentiment, so Simon said something else, in a language Janes would appreciate. "These boots are awfully comfortable."

"I broke them in myself, my lord."

"Goodness. That was above and beyond the call of duty."

"Was it, though? Or is concerning myself with the state of your boots exactly my duty?"

Simon chuckled. Now that he and Janes were friendly, their relationship could withstand a certain amount of good-humored ribbing. Janes never smiled—Simon hadn't seen another of those half smiles he'd been graced with the day he'd tasked Janes with remaking him—but there was a wryness about him that he allowed to come through in flashes.

Simon regarded his reflection. The mirrors were arranged so that if he angled his body sideways, he could see both his front and his back. Janes had put him in cream breeches, a black waistcoat, and coat of deep blue superfine. The coat was too bright to be called navy but fell short of being royal.

"I never would have chosen this blue, yet it suits me, I think."

"I noticed that when the tailor came with swatches that it flattered your complexion."

Janes had embraced his charge: smartening Simon up without making him into a popinjay.

"I must say, if you'll forgive me the vanity, I look rather well."

"You look *extremely* well, my lord."

"Janes, do you remember the time my brother Michael got foxed at a party—I think it was given by one of the neighbors at Galecroft, but I can't be certain. I was very young and only know the story second hand, as a kind of family lore. To hear it told, he came home with a gash through his coat that looked like it had been inflicted by an exotic animal of some sort, one not native to our shores."

"Oh, I remember that occasion. And I remember that coat." Janes placed a hand to his heart. "I remember it fondly."

"Well, I hope to return to you with my new clothing intact, but I thought I ought to warn you that it is possible that this party might yield some . . . drama."

Aha! There was a half smile!

"I am all anticipation, my lord."

"In fact, I wonder if I might ask you to assist." Simon paused, but he wasn't sure why, for if Janes agreed to help, Simon was going to have to tell him everything. "Do you remember when I said I wanted to put my best foot forward for a certain lady? It turns out that doing so is going to require a bit of logistical assistance."

The half smile became a full one. "I should like nothing more, my lord."

21

Good Deeds

Simon Courteney, the Earl of Marsden
requests the honor of your company for
an afternoon of music and merriment
to be held on the twelfth day of October 1823,
at four o'clock in the afternoon at Number Seven Park Lane

October 12
Twenty-one days since Earls Trip

Diantha had entertained the notion that Simon was having a party solely to get her out of the house. He had, after all, written a personalized note on the back of the invitation.

Archie, please bring everyone.

It was amusing, really, how easily the household had embraced the idea that the dowager should attend the party. Diantha had been waiting on bated breath for Mrs. Baldwin to call and had been fretting about how to convince Lord Harcourt that his mother should accept the invitation she would be issuing.

But then Simon wrote and summoned them, and Lord Harcourt thought it was a fine idea. When Diantha suggested that if he was going, they didn't need her tagging along, he disagreed, informing her that yes, they most certainly did need her tagging along.

So she might have thought it was all for her. Simon made gestures of that sort. He brought her ribbons the color of the forest and procured stacks of plates for her to throw at walls.

Or he used to.

Which is why she *would* have thought the party was a means to get her out of the house. But she hadn't seen him in three weeks—he hadn't been to see the dowager, or the earl. There had been no sign of or word from him since Gurglewood. So she had to conclude that their . . . affair had ended.

Well, *of course* it had ended. It had never been going to extend beyond the confines of the holiday. She was forced to conclude that Simon's regard for her had ended. She told herself it was for the best. She didn't *want* his ongoing scrutiny. It would only make it harder to do what needed to be done.

"Well, don't you ladies look stunning?" Lord Harcourt said when Diantha and the dowager descended the stairs. Diantha didn't know about stunning. She was wearing an evening dress that, while pretty enough, was quite old. She hadn't occasion to wear an evening dress for ages. But she wasn't alone; the dowager's dress was at least half a dozen Seasons out of date. Diantha consoled herself that her simple white satin gown had aged well enough.

The younger countess, though, *did* look stunning. She seemed to have, in the past week, passed out of the period of illness and was looking extremely well. Her skin glowed against a simple yet elegant dress of pink sarcenet with an embroidered overlay.

"Miss Brown," Lord Harcourt said, "might I have a word before we depart?"

"And I shall tell you, Emma," said the younger countess to the older, "about the absurd hat my sister is going to be wearing this evening. We shall have to watch for it."

Diantha followed Lord Harcourt into his office, a familiar wariness rising within her.

"This won't take long, but please take a seat."

She knew enough not to preemptively offer to leave the premises with her belongings, but she couldn't help fearing he had somehow found out about her plan with Mr. Baldwin. Had he intercepted her correspondence? He wasn't the type to disrespect someone's privacy like that, but perhaps a servant had—

"How do you think the party will go?" he asked as he opened a desk drawer.

Oh. He was merely worried about his mother. "I don't know," she answered honestly. "I can be prepared to depart early with her ladyship if need be. But she will be familiar with several of the attendees."

"Yes, it will be a regular Gurglewood reunion."

"I find it curious that Lord Marsden is hosting a party. I have never known him to do so."

"Nor have I," Lord Harcourt said cheerily.

"Have you any insight as to the reason for the apparent change of heart?"

He pulled a piece of paper out of his desk and regarded her with an odd intensity. "I can honestly say I have no idea." After a moment, he grinned. "Let me amend that statement. I can honestly say that he hasn't told me anything about his motivations for hosting this party. I do have my suspicions, though."

What did that mean? She was trying to figure a way to press him without making it seem that she was overly fixated on Simon and his party, when he passed her the paper.

"This is for you."

This indenture was written in the top left corner, in large letters. The rest of the vellum was covered with writing done in a tight, small hand.

She scanned it, trying to make sense of it. "Is this a deed of some sort?"

"It is, and you will notice your name there."

"*My* name?"

"Yes, it's for your cottage in Greychurch." He paused. "At least I *hope* it's your cottage in Greychurch. It looked the part. Let us just say it is the deed for *a* cottage in Greychurch."

"I beg your pardon?" She was thoroughly bewildered. "Why would my name be on a deed for a cottage in Greychurch?"

"Because you own it."

"Impossible."

"Not impossible. I bought it, and now I'm transferring it to you."

She burst into tears.

He shot to his feet. "Miss Brown!"

She waved him off—but she did accept the handkerchief he produced—and croaked, "Why would you do that?"

"I continued to reflect, after our previous discussion, on your remuneration. I concluded that I have been underpaying you for years. I also considered how I would retire tenants at Mollybrook. Why should I not do the same for you? When you are ready, of course. This is not meant whatsoever to suggest I want you to leave. I merely want you to know that your future is secure."

Diantha had two reactions at the same time. One was a groundswell of relief so powerful it made her feel almost faint.

The second was a sinking feeling that he must know. Why else would he have said that—*Your future is secure*?

But if he knew, would he not have addressed the matter with her? If he knew, would he not be angry, or upset, or . . . something?

She decided to allow herself, for one night at least, to sink into the feeling of relief. To let it win out over suspicion. After all, the only way Lord Harcourt could know what she'd done was if Simon had told him. She didn't think he had. She still, after all that had unfolded between them—or perhaps because of it—trusted him.

"And," said Lord Harcourt, rising from his desk, "should you at any point decide you *aren't* interested in a cottage in Greychurch, it is easily sold."

22

Party Central

Simon had asked Olive Morgan to arrive early, and here she was, looking like a popinjay herself. "Will you join me in my library for a moment?" he asked.

"Of course. And you'd better get your fill of looking at my hat while we're here, for it won't do to have the host of the party gawking at me the whole time."

"It is a most . . . striking piece of headwear."

It contained several small birds of unknown provenance nesting in a mass of what appeared to be seagrass.

"Please, sit."

"I have become known for my fanciful hats, and who am I to disappoint my admirers?" she said breezily. Olive was a mysterious sort. On the surface, she was blithe and, he'd always thought, a bit shallow. But he had come to suspect that she had hidden depths.

That didn't mean she wasn't manipulative.

Which he hoped to harness to his advantage this evening.

He went around and sat at his desk. "Olive, there was no comet, was there?"

"It turns out I was mistaken about that." She made a face of exaggerated concern. "And you're such an early-to-bed sort. I hope your sleep patterns were not too much disturbed."

He refrained from rolling his eyes but only just. “I have a rather unusual favor to ask of you.”

“Oh, good. I adore granting unusual favors.”

He told her the plan. She was delighted, but, as he predicted, unsurprised, and she agreed readily to assist. “I am all aflutter. But I’m curious, why me? Why not one of your earl friends?”

“Three reasons. One: There is a high probability they would muck things up. They would mean well, but in their heartfelt desire to see me happy, I can imagine them being entirely too heavy-handed. I require a lighter touch. Two, and please don’t allow this to offend: you are more believable as someone who might be sticking her nose—literally, in this case—into someone else’s business.”

“That’s true,” she said, unfussed at being deemed a busybody. “What’s the third reason?”

“I believe that you are, at heart, a romantic.”

That *had* surprised her. She looked at him for a long moment before saying, “Don’t tell anyone.”

He smiled. “Your secret is safe with me.”

“I understand my mission, but what am I to do if I find you alone?”

“I suppose you close the door and go back to the party as if nothing happened. Nothing *will* have happened.” He allowed himself, for a moment, to contemplate that outcome. “Except that I shall be dead inside. I shall appear animated, alive, but inside, I shall be dead. I shall be Frankenstein’s monster in reverse, a live man made dead.”

“My Heavens. Who is the one with the secret heart of a romantic?”

“I am beginning to think, Miss Morgan, that romance gets us all sooner or later, even the seemingly impervious among us.”

Simon greeted his guests wearing his party face and his party clothes. The latter made quite an impression. Most people didn’t remark directly on it, but he clocked brows raising and, later, observed people whispering amongst themselves.

Of course, some people did comment.

"Simon!" Effie did not bother hiding how agog he was. "What has *happened* to you?"

"I have undergone somewhat of a makeover."

"Somewhat!" Effie exclaimed.

Simon shrugged. "I am endeavoring to look a bit less . . . church-mousey."

Effie continued to exclaim, and Simon turned to greet Julianna, who said, "What my husband has failed to say is he thinks you look very smart, as do I."

That stopped Effie. "Well, of course. I ought to have led with that." His eyes narrowed. "Is something afoot?"

"No," Simon said, and he heard how unconvincing he was.

Effie murmured something Simon couldn't hear and started looking around. Most of the guests had arrived and were standing in the ballroom that had been set up for the concert, conversing in small groups. "Where is Archie?"

"Archie's household is running a little late."

Because he'd written on their invitation a start time thirty minutes later than he had on everyone else's.

He slipped away just as the music started.

Simon took a chair by the fireplace. Just over two months ago, he had been sitting in this library waiting for Miss Brown, only he hadn't known it. She had appeared on the scene like an unexpected comet, crashing into his house and his life.

Today, he was again waiting for her in his library.

The difference between the two instances was knowledge. He knew what—and whom—he was waiting for this time. He was Eve, having eaten of the fruit of the tree of knowledge of good and evil, except it was more like the tree of the knowledge of love and acceptance.

He knew what the stakes were this time.

23

What You Thought You Wanted

"Are we late?" Lord Harcourt asked as he followed Diantha and both Ladies Harcourt into Simon's house.

"We must be," the young Lady Harcourt said, "for I can hear the music playing already."

They were met by an exceedingly well-turned-out gentleman Lord Harcourt greeted as Mr. Janes. When he apologized for their apparent tardiness, Mr. Janes said, "Not at all, my lord. We are saving seats for you."

Diantha couldn't help but look up as they passed through the entryway. She wasn't sure what she expected to see. Perhaps nothing, for her visit here two months ago had begun to feel like a fever dream. But no, there they were: angelic, rifle-wielding James and Michael. She hoped Simon's talk with his mother had been successful. She wondered what success in that endeavor would look like. She regretted not having asked him what his aims were.

She regretted so many things.

Mostly that today was very likely to be the last time she would ever see him.

Her heart was pounding as they entered the ballroom, which was furnished with rows of chairs. Four musicians at the front were playing a perfectly unremarkable rendition of Schubert's

String Quartet No. 14—apparently, Simon's tastes did not run to the avant-garde as Olive's did.

Diantha was glad they were late. It meant they hadn't had to greet Simon personally. Of course, that would have to happen after the music, but she could use the time to settle in, to adjust to being here, in Simon's house, in Simon's presence.

It was not to be, though. Just as she was about to take her seat, which was on an aisle, Mr. Janes tapped her on the shoulder and whispered, "Miss Brown, could you come with me for a moment?"

"Of course."

It was only as they were descending the stairs that she wondered how he knew her name. Due to their tardiness, he had quickly passed coats off to a maid and hustled them up to the ballroom. No introductions had been made. She only knew his name because Lord Harcourt had invoked it.

"Is everything all right?" she asked.

"Yes, yes, but your assistance is required."

Oh, oh no. He was slowing at a door she knew. This was Simon's library.

He rapped on the door and opened it, and when she hesitated at the threshold, he gently pushed her over it and closed the door behind her.

She felt as if she were plunging into the pool at Gurglewood.

She opened her mouth. Simon rose from a chair by the fire. She closed her mouth.

He took her breath away. Part of it was that he was wearing the most extraordinary blue coat. And, come to think of it, a cravat tied in a knot more elaborate than she'd ever seen him sport. He was undeniably handsome.

But most of her breathlessness was that he looked so very much like himself.

"I wanted you to see my new coat," he said.

She blinked. That was not how she had expected to be greeted.

"But now I am going to take it off."

He did, and his waistcoat, too, then proceeded to untie his cravat and roll up his sleeves, and, oh, those *forearms.*

She found her voice. "What are you *doing*?"

"I would say that I'm here to ruin you, but since I was already here and you have arrived secondarily, perhaps it is more accurate to say that you're here to ruin me."

"I don't—"

"But that isn't right, either, for you have *already* ruined me." He placed a hand over his heart.

She found herself doing the same, whether she was mirroring the gesture, or because her own heart felt as if it might beat out of her chest, she couldn't say.

"We are going to be discovered here in—he pulled out a timepiece—five minutes' time."

"What is *happening*?"

"You are, of course, free to leave before that happens."

"Simon!"

"I understand that you have recently come into some property," he said mildly.

She gasped. "You put Lord Harcourt up to that!"

"I did no such thing. It was his idea. Whatever he said to you—and I have no idea what that was—was his own doing, and, I'm sure, genuinely meant. My point is merely that you don't need to be here. You have your cottage. You have your future."

"And if I stay?"

"We must place ourselves in a compromising position so that we may be discovered." He looked at his timepiece again. "Which will happen in four minutes."

She had the most ridiculous urge to laugh. Or perhaps to cry. "You've decided to ruin me after all."

"I have arranged for us to be discovered here. If ruination is still your aim, I shall oblige."

"You would do that? What about your own reputation?"

"It turns out I care about your getting what you want more

than I care about my reputation. So if ruination, or the appearance thereof, is still your desired outcome, it is within your grasp."

"I don't—"

He held up a hand. "But. Let us get our terminology right. It is indeed you who have ruined me. For so many things: for a life of the mind, for a life of duty, for life as a bachelor. You've ruined all my plans, Miss Brown. I've gone and fallen in love with you."

She didn't know what to say. Surely Miss Austen had some words of advice for a lady in a situation like this, or at least a witty rejoinder.

No, no, it turned out that Miss Austen was letting her down.

"So, to recap"—Simon made another glance at the watch—"you now find yourself presented with three choices. One: Leave out that door." He pointed to a small door behind him. "It opens onto a servants' staircase that will take you back upstairs. Two: We are discovered here, I cry off, and you finally get what you thought you wanted. Three: We are discovered here, I come up to scratch, and we marry."

Three! She shouted. But only inside, for her mouth was still not cooperating. Or perhaps it was her lungs that were letting her down, for she had the notion that speech required breath, and she was having a terrible time catching hers.

"And by the way," Simon went on, "I've dispensed with my mother. Well, that makes it sound like I've murdered her. I'm giving her this house—good riddance; goodbye to the ghosts of Number Seven Park Lane—and getting another. In case that makes a difference—should you be inclined to select option three but like to remain close to Lady Harcourt.

"But I should also point out that I have a number of cottages at Galecroft. I am currently in the process of trying to convince James's widow to move into the dower house there, and I believe I am making good progress on that front, but there is another that might be suitable as a . . . retreat. Should, say, the lady of the estate want a space that is all hers. It is not on a river, but there is a pond nearby."

Diantha had heard what Simon said, but she was having trouble absorbing it. Her mind kept catching on one phrase he had used: *what you thought you wanted.*

With great effort, she found her voice. "You didn't tell Lord Harcourt what I did?"

"I did not." She thought he might take offense at the implication that he was less than trustworthy—she would have understood if he hadn't, ultimately, been able to keep her secret—but he only smiled fondly. "I haven't, and I won't. But I must tell you that regardless of how tonight unfolds, I think you ought to assume your sister's late husband will make public what he knows about the dowager."

"But if I can't marry him . . ."

"Is that enough?"

"I . . ." Of course it wasn't enough. Why had she ever thought it would be? She had been so singularly focused on the immense task of rendering herself ineligible in Mr. Hill's eyes that she hadn't thought through the potential consequences of "success."

"You needn't worry. Archie and Effie and I encountered a strikingly similar situation to do with Clementine and Olive, and I promise you, we can make sure your brother-in-law holds his tongue. But for that, you are going to have to speak to Archie, or allow me to do so on your behalf."

She heard footsteps outside the main door. It almost sounded as if someone were stomping.

"If you're going to go, Diantha, you'd best do so."

The footsteps came to a stop outside the door.

She catapulted herself into Simon's arms.

He kissed her, so well and thoroughly that she was only vaguely aware of the door opening.

A shriek loud enough to break glass had her pulling back from the kiss, but Simon kept her wrapped in his arms.

"Good Heavens!"

It was Olive Morgan, wearing a look of astonishment Diantha would have thought genuine if she didn't know better.

"Lord Marsden! What are you *doing*? Unhand the lady this *instant*! Oh, my nerves! I think I'm going to *faint*!"

It wasn't long before a small crowd assembled. Someone produced smelling salts for Olive, who appeared magically refreshed but sniffed them anyway.

Lord Stonely pushed himself to the front of the crowd. "Marsden!" There was, Diantha thought, a hint of amusement in his tone.

"Marsden!" Lord Harcourt appeared, and there was no amusement in his. "Have you lost your mind?"

This was it. Time to make her choice. But of course, it wasn't a choice. Or perhaps it was the only choice. Perhaps Simon had always been Diantha's only choice. Something in her must have known it all along, for why would she have made that reckless appearance in this same place two months ago?

She untangled herself from Simon and said, "It is all right, my lord. We are engaged to be married."

Epilogue

The Groom was Resplendent in Yellow

Simon Courteney, Earl of Marsden, and Miss Diantha Brown
request the honor of your presence at their wedding,
to be held on the fifteenth day of November, 1823,
at ten o'clock in the morning at Galecroft.

It was a rather unconventional wedding invitation, as these things went. There was no mention of the parents of either party.

It was a rather unconventional wedding, too. It was attended by only seven people. The bride was escorted by the groom's best friend, who had easily forgiven her for almost accidentally ruining his family, and the groom walked off his nerves before the ceremony with the widow of his late brother.

The bride wore a new dress trimmed with lemon-yellow ribbon, and the groom wore a waistcoat to match. It was, he thought, a truly preposterous garment, but it made both his betrothed and his valet happy, and he was content to make himself ridiculous in service of such a cause.

In front of their friends and the vicar in the chapel at Galecroft where Simon used to hide away and read when he was a boy, they pledged themselves to each other. They signed the papers, and everyone cheered.

Then Simon spirited his bride away before they joined the wedding breakfast. He took her to the graves of his brothers.

"I would like to make this into a happier, softer tableau." As it was, the stones stood alone, unadorned in the center of the garden. "I intend to plant some flowers in the spring." He planned to pick some of the flowers and press them between the pages of books he would go on to lend to her. Not that they would replace those that her sister had sent, but perhaps she, like he, would feel the beauty of a fresh start. "I should like this to be a place I want to come. A place *we* want to come."

"I can see it," Diantha said. "Perhaps we can take a picnic lunch here from time to time."

"Yes. And perhaps sometimes Frances can join us."

"I intend to press your case with her at breakfast."

"Yes, do try to make friends with her. I fear I am not enough to lure her to the dower house, but I wager you are."

"Do you know," Diantha said, "I think Frances was the only one who wasn't weepy at the ceremony?"

"Yes, one expects an excess of sentiment from Effie, but wasn't Archie surprisingly overcome?"

"It's hard to imagine he is the same gentleman who threatened my brother-in-law at knifepoint."

"Indeed." Simon and the boys had made a quick, ruthless trip to Barbury and extracted the damning letter. Probably Simon shouldn't have dictated all the details to Diantha, but he wanted her to understand that she had nothing to worry about. That he—and his friends—would always protect her. That she was no longer alone.

He pulled her into his arms. He was so overcome with love and gratitude and relief that he went so far as to pick her up and spin her around. He was sure he had never done something so silly, so carefree, in his life.

She started kissing him while they were still spinning, but her aim was off, and her lips landed on his temple. Soon, they were laughing. But then they were kissing again.

"My lord," she said, affecting a tone of scandal as she broke the kiss. "Our guests are waiting for us!"

"Yes, yes. They can wait a while longer." He set her down. "I wanted to give you this."

He produced the small statue.

"An obelisk!" she exclaimed.

"It is a reproduction of the Obelisk of Montecitorio I had commissioned."

She rotated it, examining all its sides.

"I am not certain the artisan properly copied the hieroglyphs," Simon said. "Short of traveling to Rome and doing a comparison, I would have no way of knowing if I've been swindled. Perhaps it's his wife's recipe for eel pies." He ought to have thought this through better. "I suppose it's not very romantic. I meant it to signify that your secrets are safe with me. As is your heart. As are you, all of you." He paused. "Perhaps I should have plucked something from among the family jewels. We can still do that."

"No, no. This is the most romantic thing I can imagine receiving." She smiled, a little shyly. "I have something for you, too. Will you come inside with me so I may give it to you?"

"Of course." He would go anywhere with her.

They approached the house, where she had been staying in a guest room. "I shouldn't like to encounter anyone yet, though," she whispered.

"We shan't." He took her on an elaborate route through the lesser-known nooks and crannies of the house, which set them both to laughing again. Eventually, they made it to her bedchamber. Everything was packed up, as tonight they would both be occupying a new room. Not his mother's old one, merely a pretty, south-facing one she had helped him select.

She rummaged through a satchel and produced a book. *Sense and Sensibility.* "Do you remember when I lent you this book? It was before your 1822 Earls Trip, I believe."

"Yes." He had read it in Brighton and thought of Diantha—

whose name he hadn't yet known was Diantha. How much had changed.

"I thought you might like to reread it."

"Am I meant to reread the book or am I meant to note this overlarge piece of paper inside it?"

She shrugged. "Whatever you like, my lord."

"Will you *stop* my-lord–ing me!"

"Whatever you like, *Simon*."

He shivered. That did something to him, every time. He wondered if the sound of his Christian name on her lips would ever cease to thrill. He rather hoped not.

He slid the paper from the pages. It was a painting, that of an amateur, judging by the way two hues in the watercolor borders had run together in a way that did not look intentional.

Oh, no, it was a note. There was lettering in the center of the page. It was a fancier version of one of Diantha's markers.

My heart is, and always will be, yours.

They kissed for a long time. They kissed so long that eventually someone knocked on the door.

Laughing, they pulled apart and made themselves as presentable as possible before answering.

It was Olive Morgan.

"For Heaven's sake, you two. Everyone is waiting." She rolled her eyes and turned, apparently trusting they would follow.

They did.

Their friends broke out into cheering when they appeared. Someone handed Simon a glass.

"A toast to the couple!" Frances said warmly, and everyone raised their glasses.

"You gentlemen are all married now," Olive observed. "Three holidays have yielded three wives. Perhaps we ought to toast Earls Trip."

They toasted Earls Trip.

"No, no," Archie said. "What we ought to toast is Gurglewood. None of this would have happened had I not had the smashing idea to refurbish Gurglewood."

"You simply cannot let that name stand another moment, Archie," Effie said. "I beseech you to turn to the vastly superior River's Embrace."

"I have it," Simon said, for he did. He had the perfect name. "Pleiades House."

"After the constellation?" Archie asked. "The Seven Sisters?"

"Yes. There are seven of us, are there not? Lady Harcourt, of course you are our northern star. And then there's you and Clementine." He turned to Effie. "And you and Julianna. And my wife and me. And—"

"Poor Olive," Olive interrupted, but she was laughing. "Ever alone. The seventh wheel." She winked. "It's a lovely name, Simon."

"It is *perfect*," Effie said. "You are always proclaiming us a found family, Simon. We three have always been like brothers." He gestured around the table. "And now we have sisters."

"It *is* rather perfect," Archie said, affecting a tone of annoyance. "It is so perfect I suppose I shall have to give up Gurglewood."

And with that, they all lifted their glasses and toasted Pleiades House.

Acknowledgments

My thanks to everyone at Kensington: Elizabeth May, for her love of this series in general and for Simon and Miss Brown in particular; Jane Nutter, for her work promoting my books; Erica Ferguson, for her eagle eye; and Carly Sommerstein, for taking such good care of the book. Dawn Cooper made another amazing cover, under the direction of the art folks at Kensington.

Courtney Miller-Callihan and Sandra Owens remain my steadfast friends and cheerleaders.

Once again, I found myself writing this book through family tragedy. Once again, I wouldn't have made it through without my sister.